COLLECTION FOLIO

George Sand

Pauline

ÉDITION ÉTABLIE ET PRÉSENTÉE
PAR MARTINE REID

Gallimard

Femmes de lettres

PRÉSENTATION

Dans les années 1820, une jeune femme du nom de Laurence S… se retrouve un soir, à sa grande surprise, dans la petite ville de Saint-Front. Elle pensait avoir pris la route de Lyon où elle était attendue, elle est en réalité revenue sur les lieux qu'elle a habités pendant quatre ans avant de partir pour Paris et d'y devenir comédienne. Attribuée à la surdité d'un vieux cocher, la méprise tient en réalité du lapsus. Belle, riche et talentueuse, Laurence est désormais une actrice de renom et non cette sous-maîtresse modeste, soutien de famille, qu'elle était lorsqu'elle a quitté Saint-Front. Revenir dans cette « petite ville fort laide », c'est défier les préjugés de la province qui voit dans toute comédienne une fille perdue, retrouver son milieu d'origine et lui montrer l'artiste qu'il a reniée, renouer aussi avec Pauline D…, amie d'enfance. Malgré ses craintes, tout se passe au mieux : comme à la scène, Laurence quitte Saint-Front sur un triomphe.

Quinze mois plus tard, apprenant le décès de la mère de Pauline et la ruine de cette dernière, la généreuse Laurence offre l'hospitalité à son amie. Celle-ci se retrouve bientôt à Paris dans un confortable hôtel particulier que fréquentent hommes de lettres et gens de théâtre, artistes et politiciens. Par calcul, un familier de la maison, Montgenays, feint de s'éprendre d'elle alors qu'il est en réalité amoureux de Laurence. Aveuglée par la jalousie, Pauline se dresse alors avec énergie contre celle qui l'a recueillie et quitte son amie à jamais brouillée avec elle. Le roman se termine par quelques considérations sur le danger de changer « les vertus domestiques » de leur lieu naturel d'exercice.

George Sand a construit *Pauline* sur un jeu de symétries et d'échos : deux jeunes filles, deux vieilles femmes, deux hommes, deux lieux, deux temps constituent la trame de ce bref roman. Aux quatre années passées à Saint-Front, pendant lesquelles les deux jeunes filles ont travaillé à s'unir d'une amitié profonde, répondent les quatre années à Paris au cours desquelles, à l'inverse, la méfiance et la jalousie vont peu à peu les séparer. Face au personnage de Pauline, que les contraintes de la vie provinciale ont meurtrie, Sand a placé celui de Laurence, âme noble et artiste véritable. Les mères des deux jeunes filles répondent elles aussi à une construction en pendant : madame D... a le cœur sec et la vanité toujours en éveil ; madame S..., en revanche, sait apprécier une fille dont le talent lui permet désormais de vivre dans l'aisance. De même, les vilenies de Montgenays, homme sans principes, appellent la prudence et le dévouement de l'acteur Lavallée, ami véritable.

Le caractère duel du récit est encore accentué par la singulière histoire de sa rédaction. En effet, de l'aveu même de Sand, *Pauline* fut commencé au printemps 1832 avant d'être égaré puis oublié. Quelques années plus tard, en 1839, alors que le directeur de *La Revue des Deux Mondes*, François Buloz, lui réclamait des textes à publier, l'auteur, « en ouvrant un *in-quarto* à la campagne », y trouva « la moitié d'un volume manuscrit intitulé *Pauline* » ; « la mémoire de la première donnée me revint aussitôt, explique-t-elle dans la notice au roman datant de 1852, et j'écrivis le reste sans incertitude ». La reprise et la poursuite du texte semblent avoir occupé Sand quelques jours du mois de décembre 1839. À François Buloz, elle écrit le 12 décembre : « […] voici la moitié de ma nouvelle. Je ne puis vous en faire davantage. Il est huit heures du matin et je n'ai pu commencer qu'à deux heures. Si vous croyez que j'aie encore le temps de vous en fournir la continuation je travaillerai la nuit prochaine. Mais si cela vous suffit pour ce numéro j'aimerais mieux achever au numéro prochain ». Elle ajoute : « Tâchez aussi de me trouver de l'argent ces jours-ci. Il faudra que je donne des étrennes au jour de l'an. En attendant, je vous donne cette nouvelle pour les vôtres. » Aux deux moments de rédaction correspondent sans doute les deux parties du texte, la première consacrée à la peinture de la vie provinciale, roman réaliste en miniature, la seconde à Paris, roman sentimental cette fois, où la justesse de l'observation le cède davantage au « romanesque ».

Quand, en mai 1832, la publication d'*Indiana* la rend célèbre du jour au lendemain, celle qui signe d'abord « G. Sand » a déjà écrit quelques romans en collaboration avec Jules Sandeau, dont *Rose et Blanche ou La comédienne et la religieuse* (1831). À la fin de l'année, elle aura ajouté à son palmarès un deuxième roman, *Valentine*, et plusieurs autres textes dont une nouvelle, *La Marquise*, qui raconte la passion d'une aristocrate pour un acteur de la Comédie-Française. Comme Laurence, il interprète les grands rôles du répertoire classique. Ainsi l'imaginaire sandien est-il hanté très tôt par le théâtre et la figure de l'artiste : malgré les préjugés d'une société continuant de lui prêter des mœurs scandaleuses, ce dernier jouit d'une heureuse liberté de parole et de conduite ; sans autre personnalité que celle des personnages qu'il interprète au fil de sa carrière et de ses curiosités, l'artiste ne possède pas une identité, un caractère, mais mille. Heureux Protée dans une société qui travaille inlassablement à identifier et à fixer (socialement et sexuellement), celui ou celle qui « joue la comédie » semble avoir fait singulièrement rêver une jeune femme instable, à l'identité et au passé familial complexes, à la mélancolie résolument romantique. À la fin de l'année 1832, Sand s'éprendra d'ailleurs un moment de la comédienne Marie Dorval, l'une des meilleures interprètes du théâtre romantique — Laurence peut lui devoir quelques traits.

Dans *Pauline*, George Sand dresse un constat ironique et grinçant de ce qu'elle appelle, forgeant pour l'occasion un néologisme, la *provincialité*. Elle y peint avec minutie l'ennui de la province, ses mœurs figées en pesantes habitudes, ses mesquineries, ses menus événements. Bien avant Balzac, dont *Eugénie Grandet* date de 1834, et l'accablant portrait de la femme de province, dans *Les Français peints par eux-mêmes*, de 1841, elle fait de son héroïne un être à la condition pitoyable, tant dans son dévouement forcé pour une mère à laquelle elle a sacrifié sa jeunesse que dans sa passion aveugle pour un homme qui la méprisera une fois qu'elle se sera donnée à lui. Mais, à la différence de l'auteur de *La Comédie humaine*, Sand condamne son personnage à un malheur irrémédiable, et à une jalousie sans fin, que n'atténuent ni les secours de la religion ni les joies de la bienfaisance.

Comme elle l'avait déjà risqué dans *Indiana*, *Valentine*, *La Marquise* et quelques nouvelles, Sand interroge par ailleurs les conventions du genre romanesque, et, sous l'aspect lisse d'une prose sans grands effets, déjoue les attentes du lecteur. Pauline est bien l'héroïne du roman qui porte son nom, mais une héroïne *négative*, si l'on entend par là qu'elle ne peut servir de modèle à personne ni susciter une quelconque sympathie. Le roman ne se clôt pas sur l'assurance de sa punition ou de sa rédemption, sur la réconciliation avec son amie d'autrefois moins encore. Si Sand termine son récit par une « morale », il s'agit ici d'une morale *à l'envers*. La vertueuse Pauline n'a rien gagné (l'envie l'a égarée), la bonne Laurence a fait fausse route (le souci de se racheter par la générosité l'a perdue), un curieux principe de réalité l'a emporté. Le dénouement est plat, la leçon qui l'accompagne insiste sur ces « vertus domestiques » qui n'ont décidément de sens que dans le milieu très étroit qui les a érigées en règle (pour le malheur de ceux qui se trouvent forcés de s'y soumettre). La noblesse de sentiment n'est pas du côté de ceux qui croient en être les détenteurs, aristocrates et bourgeois de province, vains hypocrites que la vue de la comédienne fait pâlir d'amour et de jalousie ; la dignité de conduite se trouve dans le monde tant décrié des comédiens et des bohèmes, la véritable générosité aussi.

Retrouvé et achevé en 1839, *Pauline* doit sans doute beaucoup au fait d'avoir été conçu en 1832, dans l'effervescence d'une naissance littéraire hors du commun, celle de « George Sand ». La méchante petite ville de province ne figurant sur aucune carte n'est pas sans évoquer La Châtre dont, dans *Histoire de ma vie*, Sand rappellera la physionomie peu amène ainsi que le caractère étroit et cancanier de ses habitants. Quelques détails sont également directement inspirés de la vie de l'auteur et il n'est jusqu'aux initiales des patronymes des héroïnes, Laurence S... et Pauline D..., qui ne fonctionnent sur le mode du clin d'œil autobiographique : aux noms de Dupin et Dudevant, l'auteur vient en effet de préférer celui de Sand, troquant ses « noms de famille » pour un patronyme de pure fantaisie. Peut-être Pauline re-

présente-t-elle ce que Sand aurait pu être et demeurer (elle qui a longuement veillé sa propre
grand-mère malade), comme Laurence celle
qu'elle aurait voulu devenir. Entre la défroque de
l'une et le fantôme de l'autre, la toute neuve
« George Sand » rêva peut-être un instant, comme
la comédienne de sa fiction, de faire retour au
pays natal et d'y dissiper par son talent autant que
par ses charmes les innombrables médisances dont
elle avait été l'objet. Dans la réalité, elle ne s'y
prêta pas et eut même soin, comme elle le rappelle
dans *Histoire de ma vie* toujours, de rompre à jamais
avec celles qui avaient été ses amies au couvent
des Anglaises et dont la vie désormais n'avait plus
rien en commun avec la sienne. George Sand était
née, et du passé faisait résolument table rase.

MARTINE REID

NOTE SUR LE TEXTE

Pauline a d'abord paru dans *La Revue des Deux Mondes* en deux livraisons, les 15 décembre 1839 et 1ᵉʳ janvier 1840. Le texte a ensuite été publié chez Magen et Cormon en mars 1841 dans un volume qui contenait également *Les Mississippiens*, « tableau dialogué ». Seul ou avec d'autres textes, le roman a ensuite été régulièrement réédité jusqu'à la fin du XIXᵉ siècle. Le manuscrit est conservé dans le fonds Lovenjoul de la Bibliothèque de l'Institut.

Nous reproduisons le texte de l'édition originale de 1841 qui comprend de légères différences d'avec les suivantes. Seule la ponctuation a été modernisée en quelques endroits.

PAULINE

I

Il y a trois ans, il arriva à Saint-Front, petite ville fort laide qui est située dans nos environs et que je ne vous engage pas à chercher sur la carte, même sur celle de Cassini[1], une aventure qui fit beaucoup jaser, quoiqu'elle n'eût rien de bien intéressant par elle-même, mais dont les suites furent fort graves, quoiqu'on n'en ait rien su.

C'était par une nuit sombre et par une pluie froide. Une chaise de poste entra dans la cour de l'auberge du *Lion Couronné*. Une voix de femme demanda des chevaux, *vite, vite !...* Le postillon vint lui répondre fort lentement que cela était facile à dire ; qu'il n'y avait pas de chevaux, vu que l'épidémie (cette même épidémie qui est en permanence dans certains relais sur les routes peu fréquentées) en avait enlevé trente-sept la semaine dernière ; qu'enfin on pourrait partir dans la nuit, mais qu'il fallait attendre que l'attelage

1. César-François Cassini de Thury (1714-1784) était célèbre pour avoir établi la première carte géométrique et planimétrique de la France.

qui venait de conduire la malle-poste fût un peu rafraîchi.

« Cela sera-t-il bien long ? demanda le laquais empaqueté de fourrures qui était installé sur le siège.

— C'est l'affaire d'une heure, répondit le postillon à demi débotté ; nous allons nous mettre tout de suite à manger l'avoine. »

Le domestique jura ; une jeune et jolie femme de chambre, qui avançait à la portière sa tête entourée de foulards en désordre, murmura je ne sais quelle plainte touchante sur l'ennui et la fatigue des voyages. Quant à la personne qu'escortaient ces deux laquais, elle descendit lentement sur le pavé humide et froid, secoua sa pelisse doublée de martre, et prit le chemin de la cuisine sans proférer une seule parole.

C'était une jeune femme d'une beauté vive et saisissante, mais pâlie par la fatigue. Elle refusa l'offre d'une chambre, et, tandis que ses valets préféraient s'enfermer et dormir dans la berline, elle s'assit devant le foyer, sur la chaise classique, ingrat et revêche asile du voyageur résigné. La servante, chargée de veiller son quart de nuit, se remit à ronfler, le corps plié sur un banc et la face appuyée sur la table. Le chat, qui s'était dérangé avec humeur pour faire place à la voyageuse, se blottit de nouveau sur les cendres tièdes. Pendant quelques instants, il fixa sur elle des yeux verts et luisants pleins de dépit et de méfiance ; mais peu à peu sa prunelle se resserra et s'amoindrit jusqu'à n'être plus qu'une mince raie noire sur un fond d'émeraude. Il retomba dans le bien-être égoïste de sa condition, fit le gros dos, ronfla sourdement en signe de béatitude, et finit par s'endormir entre les pattes d'un gros chien qui avait trouvé moyen de vivre en paix avec lui, grâce à ces perpétuelles concessions que, pour le bonheur des sociétés, le plus faible impose toujours au plus fort.

La voyageuse essaya vainement de s'assoupir. Mille images confuses passaient dans ses rêves et la réveillaient en sursaut. Tous ces souvenirs puérils qui obsèdent parfois les imaginations actives se pressèrent dans son cerveau et s'évertuèrent à le fatiguer sans but et sans fruit, jusqu'à ce qu'enfin une pensée dominante s'établît à leur place.

« Oui, c'était une triste ville[1], pensa la voyageuse, une ville aux rues anguleuses et sombres, au pavé raboteux ; une ville laide et pauvre, comme celle-ci m'est apparue à travers la vapeur qui couvrait les glaces de ma voiture. Seulement, il y a dans celle-ci un ou deux, peut-être trois réverbères, et, là-bas, il n'y en avait pas un seul. Chaque piéton marchait avec son falot après l'heure du couvre-feu. C'était affreux, cette pauvre ville, et pourtant j'y ai passé des années de jeunesse et de force ! J'étais bien autre alors… J'étais pauvre de condition, mais j'étais riche d'énergie et d'espoir. Je souffrais bien ! ma vie se consumait dans

1. La description n'est pas sans rappeler celle que Sand fit à maintes reprises de La Châtre, proche de Nohant. Dans *Histoire de ma vie* (Ire partie, chap. 7), elle se plaint de la malpropreté et de la laideur de la petite ville, tout en reconnaissant qu'elle y est attachée.

l'ombre et dans l'inaction ; mais qui me rendra ces souffrances d'une âme agitée par sa propre puissance ? Ô jeunesse du cœur ! qu'êtes-vous devenue ?... »

Puis, après ces apostrophes un peu emphatiques que les têtes exaltées prodiguent parfois à la destinée, sans trop de sujet peut-être, mais par suite d'un besoin inné qu'elles éprouvent de dramatiser leur existence à leurs propres yeux, la jeune femme sourit involontairement, comme si une voix intérieure lui eût répondu qu'elle était heureuse encore, et elle essaya de s'endormir, en attendant que l'heure fût écoulée.

La cuisine de l'auberge n'était éclairée que par une lanterne de fer suspendue au plafond. Le squelette de ce luminaire dessinait une large étoile d'ombre tremblotante sur tout l'intérieur de la pièce, et rejetait sa pâle clarté vers les solives enfumées du plafond.

L'étrangère était donc entrée sans rien distinguer autour d'elle, et l'état de demi-sommeil où elle était l'avait, d'ailleurs, empêchée de faire aucune remarque sur le lieu où elle se trouvait.

Tout à coup l'éboulement d'une petite avalanche de cendre dégagea deux tisons mélancoliquement embrassés ; un peu de flamme frissonna, jaillit, pâlit, se ranima, et grandit enfin jusqu'à illuminer tout l'intérieur de l'âtre. Les yeux distraits de la voyageuse, suivant machinalement ces ondulations de lumière, s'arrêtèrent tout à coup sur une inscription qui ressortait en blanc sur un des chambranles noircis de la cheminée. Elle tressaillit

alors, passa la main sur ses yeux appesantis, ra-
massa un bout de branche embrasée pour exami-
ner les caractères, et le laissa retomber en s'écriant
d'une voix émue : « Ah ! Dieu ! où suis-je ? est-ce
un rêve que je fais ? »

À cette exclamation, la servante s'éveilla brusquement, et, se tournant vers elle, lui demanda si
elle l'avait appelée.

« Oui, oui, s'écria l'étrangère ; venez ici. Dites-
moi, qui a écrit ces deux noms sur le mur ?

— Deux noms ? dit la servante ébahie ; quels
noms ?

— Oh ! dit l'étrangère en se parlant avec une
sorte d'exaltation, son nom et le mien, Pauline,
Laurence ! Et cette date ! 10 *février* 182... ! Oh !
dites-moi, dites-moi pourquoi ces noms et cette
date sont ici.

— Madame, répondit la servante, je n'y avais
jamais fait attention, et, d'ailleurs, je ne sais pas
lire.

— Mais où suis-je donc ? comment nommez-
vous cette ville ? N'est-ce pas Villiers, la première
poste après L... ?

— Mais non pas, madame ; vous êtes à Saint-
Front, route de Paris, hôtel du *Lion Couronné*.

— Ah ! ciel ! » s'écria la voyageuse avec force
en se levant tout à coup.

La servante épouvantée la crut folle et voulut
s'enfuir ; mais la jeune femme, l'arrêtant :

« Oh ! par grâce, restez, dit-elle, et parlez-moi !
Comment se fait-il que je sois ici ? Dites-moi si je
rêve ? Si je rêve, éveillez-moi !

— Mais, madame, vous ne rêvez pas, ni moi non plus, je pense, répondit la servante. Vous vouliez donc aller à Lyon ? Eh bien ! mon Dieu, vous aurez oublié de l'expliquer au postillon, et, tout naturellement, il aura cru que vous alliez à Paris. Dans ce temps-ci, toutes les voitures de poste vont à Paris.

— Mais je lui ai dit moi-même que j'allais à Lyon.

— Oh dame ! c'est que Baptiste est sourd à ne pas entendre le canon, et avec cela qu'il dort sur son cheval la moitié du temps, et que ses bêtes sont accoutumées à la route de Paris dans ce temps-ci…

— À Saint-Front ! répétait l'étrangère. Oh ! singulière destinée qui me ramène aux lieux que je voulais fuir ! J'ai fait un détour pour ne point passer ici, et, parce que je me suis endormie deux heures, le hasard m'y conduit à mon insu ! Eh bien ! c'est Dieu peut-être qui le veut. Sachons ce que je dois retrouver ici de joie ou de douleur. Dites-moi, ma chère, ajouta-t-elle en s'adressant à la fille d'auberge, connaissez-vous dans cette ville mademoiselle Pauline D… ?

— Je n'y connais personne, madame, répondit la fille ; je ne suis dans ce pays que depuis huit jours.

— Mais allez me chercher une autre servante, quelqu'un, je veux le savoir. Puisque je suis ici, je veux tout savoir. Est-elle mariée, est-elle morte ? Allez, allez, informez-vous de cela ; courez donc ! »

La servante objecta que toutes les servantes étaient couchées, que le garçon d'écurie et les postillons ne connaissaient au monde que leurs chevaux. Une prompte libéralité de la jeune dame la décida à aller réveiller *le chef*, et, après un quart d'heure d'attente, qui parut mortellement long à notre voyageuse, on vint enfin lui apprendre que mademoiselle Pauline D... n'était point mariée, et qu'elle habitait toujours la ville. Aussitôt l'étrangère ordonna qu'on mît sa voiture sous la remise et qu'on lui préparât une chambre.

Elle se mit au lit en attendant le jour, mais elle ne put dormir. Ses souvenirs, assoupis ou combattus longtemps, reprenaient alors toute leur puissance ; elle reconnaissait toutes les choses qui frappaient sa vue dans l'auberge du *Lion Couronné*. Quoique l'antique hôtellerie eût subi de notables améliorations depuis dix ans, le mobilier était resté à peu près le même ; les murs étaient encore revêtus de tapisseries qui représentaient les plus belles scènes de *L'Astrée*[1] ; les bergères avaient des reprises de fil blanc sur le visage, et les bergers en lambeaux flottaient suspendus à des clous qui leur perçaient la poitrine. Il y avait une monstrueuse tête de guerrier romain dessinée à l'estompe par la fille de l'aubergiste, et encadrée dans quatre baguettes de bois peint en noir ; sur la cheminée, un groupe de cire, repré-

---

1. Paru entre 1607 et 1619, le volumineux roman d'Honoré d'Urfé (1567-1625) avait rencontré un succès considérable. Ses personnages avaient inspiré la production de tapisseries, de papiers peints et d'objets décoratifs.

sentant Jésus à la crèche, jaunissait sous un dais de verre filé.

« Hélas ! se disait la voyageuse, j'ai habité plusieurs jours cette même chambre, il y a douze ans, lorsque je suis arrivée ici avec ma bonne mère ! C'est dans cette triste ville que je l'ai vue dépérir de misère et que j'ai failli la perdre. J'ai couché dans ce même lit la nuit de mon départ ! Quelle nuit de douleur et d'espoir, de regret et d'attente ! Comme elle pleurait, ma pauvre amie, ma douce Pauline, en m'embrassant sous cette cheminée où je sommeillais tout à l'heure sans savoir où j'étais ! Comme je pleurais, moi aussi, en écrivant sur le mur son nom au-dessous du mien, avec la date de notre séparation ! Pauvre Pauline ! quelle existence a été la sienne depuis ce temps-là ? L'existence d'une vieille fille de province ! Cela doit être affreux ! Elle si aimante, si supérieure à tout ce qui l'entourait ! Et pourtant je voulais la fuir, je m'étais promis de ne la revoir jamais ! — Je vais peut-être lui apporter un peu de consolation, mettre un jour de bonheur dans sa triste vie ! — Si elle me repoussait pourtant ! Si elle était tombée sous l'empire des préjugés !… Ah ! cela est évident, ajouta tristement la voyageuse ; comment puis-je en douter ? N'a-t-elle pas cessé tout à coup de m'écrire, en apprenant le parti que j'avais pris ? Elle aura craint de se corrompre ou de se dégrader dans le contact d'une vie comme la mienne ! Ah ! Pauline ! elle m'aimait tant, et elle aurait rougi de moi !… je ne sais plus que penser… À présent que je me sens si près d'elle, à présent que je suis sûre de la retrouver dans la situation où je l'ai connue, je ne peux plus résister au désir de la voir. Oh ! je la verrai, dût-elle me repousser ! Si elle le fait, que la honte en retombe sur elle ! J'aurai vaincu les justes défiances de mon orgueil, j'aurai été fidèle à la religion du passé ; c'est elle qui se sera parjurée ! »

Au milieu de ces agitations, elle vit monter le matin gris et froid derrière les toits inégaux des maisons déjetées qui s'accoudaient disgracieusement les unes aux autres. Elle reconnut le clocher qui sonnait jadis ses heures de repos ou de rêverie ; elle vit s'éveiller les bourgeois en classique bonnet de coton ; et de vieilles figures, dont elle avait un confus souvenir, apparurent toutes refrognées aux fenêtres de la rue. Elle entendit l'enclume du forgeron retentir sous les murs d'une maison décrépite ; elle vit arriver au marché les fermiers en manteau bleu et en coiffe de toile cirée ; tout reprenait sa place et conservait son allure comme aux jours du passé. Chacune de ces circonstances insignifiantes faisait battre le cœur de la voyageuse, quoique tout lui semblât horriblement laid et pauvre.

« Eh quoi ! disait-elle, j'ai pu vivre ici quatre ans entiers sans mourir ! j'ai respiré cet air, j'ai parlé à ces gens-là, j'ai dormi sous ces toits couverts de mousse, j'ai marché dans ces rues impraticables ! et Pauline, ma pauvre Pauline vit encore au milieu de tout cela, elle qui était si belle, si aimable, si instruite, elle qui aurait régné et brillé comme moi sur un monde de luxe et d'éclat ! »

Aussitôt que l'horloge de la ville eut sonné sept heures, elle acheva sa toilette à la hâte ; et, laissant ses domestiques maudire l'auberge et souffrir les incommodités du déplacement avec cette impatience et cette hauteur qui caractérisent les laquais de bonne maison, elle s'enfonça dans une des rues tortueuses qui s'ouvraient devant elle, marchant sur la pointe du pied avec l'adresse d'une Parisienne, et faisant ouvrir de gros yeux à tous les bourgeois de la ville, pour qui une figure nouvelle était un grave événement.

La maison de Pauline n'avait rien de pittoresque, quoiqu'elle fût fort ancienne. Elle n'avait conservé, de l'époque où elle fut bâtie, que le froid et l'incommodité de la distribution ; du reste, pas une tradition romanesque, pas un ornement de sculpture élégante ou bizarre, pas le moindre aspect de féodalité romantique. Tout y avait l'air sombre et chagrin, depuis la figure de cuivre ciselée sur le marteau de la porte, jusqu'à celle de la vieille servante non moins laide et rechignée qui vint ouvrir, toisa l'étrangère avec dédain, et lui tourna le dos après lui avoir répondu sèchement : « Elle y est. »

La voyageuse éprouva une émotion à la fois douce et déchirante en montant l'escalier en vis auquel une corde luisante servait de rampe. Cette maison lui rappelait les plus fraîches années de sa vie, les plus pures scènes de sa jeunesse ; mais, en comparant ces témoins de son passé au luxe de son existence présente, elle ne pouvait s'empêcher de plaindre Pauline, condamnée à végéter là comme la mousse verdâtre qui se traînait sur les murs humides.

Elle monta sans bruit et poussa la porte qui roula sur ses gonds en silence. Rien n'était changé dans la grande pièce, décorée par les hôtes du titre de salon. Le carreau de briques rougeâtres bien lavées, les boiseries brunes soigneusement dégagées de poussière, la glace dont le cadre en chêne sculpté avait été doré jadis, les meubles massifs brodés au petit point par quelque aïeule de la famille, et deux ou trois tableaux de dévotion légués par l'oncle, curé de la ville, tout était précisément resté à la même place et dans le même état de vétusté robuste depuis dix ans, dix ans pendant lesquels l'étrangère avait vécu des siècles ! Aussi tout ce qu'elle voyait la frappait comme un rêve.

La salle, vaste et basse, offrait à l'œil une profondeur terne qui n'était pourtant pas sans charme. Il y avait dans le vague de la perspective de l'austérité et de la méditation, comme dans ces tableaux de Rembrandt où l'on ne distingue, sur le *clair-obscur*, qu'une vieille figure de philosophe ou d'alchimiste brune et terreuse comme les murs, terne et maladive comme le rayon habilement ménagé où elle nage. Une fenêtre à carreaux étroits et montés en plomb, ornée de pots de basilic et de géranium, éclairait seule cette vaste pièce ; mais une suave figure se dessinait dans la lumière de l'embrasure, et semblait placée là, comme à dessein, pour ressortir seule et par sa propre beauté dans le tableau : c'était Pauline.

Elle était bien changée, et, comme la voyageuse ne pouvait voir son visage, elle douta longtemps que ce fût elle. Elle avait laissé Pauline plus petite de toute la tête, et maintenant Pauline était grande et d'une ténuité si excessive, qu'on eût dit qu'elle allait se briser en changeant d'attitude ; elle était vêtue de brun avec une petite collerette d'un blanc scrupuleux et d'une égalité de plis vraiment monastique. Ses beaux cheveux châtains étaient lissés sur ses tempes avec un soin affecté ; elle se livrait à un ouvrage classique, ennuyeux, odieux à toute organisation pensante : elle faisait de très petits points réguliers avec une aiguille imperceptible sur un morceau de batiste dont elle comptait la trame fil par fil. La vie de la grande moitié des femmes se consume, en France, à cette solennelle occupation.

Quand la voyageuse eut fait quelques pas, elle distingua, dans la clarté de la fenêtre, les lignes brillantes du beau profil de Pauline : ses traits réguliers et calmes, ses grands yeux voilés et nonchalants, son front pur et uni plutôt découvert qu'élevé, sa bouche délicate, qui semblait incapable de sourire. Elle était toujours admirablement belle et jolie, mais elle était maigre et d'une pâleur uniforme qu'on pouvait regarder comme passée à l'état chronique. Dans le premier instant, son ancienne amie fut tentée de la plaindre ; mais, en admirant la sérénité profonde de ce front mélancolique doucement penché sur son ouvrage, elle se sentit pénétrée de respect bien plus que de pitié.

Elle resta donc immobile et muette à la regarder ; mais, comme si sa présence se fût révélée à Pauline par un mouvement instinctif du cœur, celle-ci se tourna tout à coup vers elle et la regarda fixement sans dire un mot et sans changer de visage.

« Pauline ! ne me reconnais-tu pas ? s'écria l'étrangère ; as-tu oublié la figure de Laurence ? »

Alors Pauline jeta un cri, se leva, et retomba sans force sur un siège. Laurence était déjà dans ses bras, et toutes deux pleuraient.

« Tu ne me reconnaissais pas ? dit enfin Laurence.

— Oh ! que dis-tu là ? répondit Pauline. Je te reconnaissais bien, mais je n'étais pas étonnée. Tu ne sais pas une chose, Laurence ? C'est que les personnes qui vivent dans la solitude ont parfois d'étranges idées. Comment le dirai-je ? Ce sont des souvenirs, des images qui se logent dans leur esprit, et qui semblent passer devant leurs yeux. Ma mère appelle cela des visions. Moi, je sais bien que je ne suis pas folle ; mais je pense que Dieu permet souvent, pour me consoler dans mon isolement, que les personnes que j'aime m'apparaissent tout à coup au milieu de mes rêveries. Va, bien souvent je t'ai vue là devant cette porte, debout comme tu étais tout à l'heure, et me regardant d'un air indécis. J'avais coutume de ne rien dire et de ne pas bouger, pour que l'apparition ne s'envolât pas. Je n'ai été surprise que quand je t'ai entendue parler. Oh ! alors ta voix m'a réveillée ! elle est venue me frapper jusqu'au cœur ! Chère

Laurence ! c'est donc toi vraiment ! dis-moi bien que c'est toi ! »

Quand Laurence eut timidement exprimé à son amie la crainte qui l'avait empêchée depuis plusieurs années de lui donner des marques de son souvenir, Pauline l'embrassa en pleurant.

« Oh ! mon Dieu ! dit-elle, tu as cru que je te méprisais, que je rougissais de toi ? moi qui t'ai conservé toujours une si haute estime, moi qui savais si bien que dans aucune situation de la vie il n'était possible à une âme comme la tienne de se dégrader ! »

Laurence rougit et pâlit en écoutant ces paroles ; elle renferma un soupir, et baisa la main de Pauline avec un sentiment de vénération.

« Il est bien vrai, reprit Pauline, que ta condition présente révolte les opinions étroites et intolérantes de toutes les personnes que je vois. Une seule porte dans sa sévérité un reste d'affection et de regret : c'est ma mère. Elle te blâme, il faut bien t'attendre à cela ; mais elle cherche à t'excuser, et l'on voit qu'elle lance sur toi l'anathème avec douleur. Son esprit n'est pas éclairé, tu le sais ; mais son cœur est bon, pauvre femme !

— Comment ferai-je donc pour me faire accueillir ? demanda Laurence.

— Hélas ! répondit Pauline, il serait bien facile de la tromper ; elle est aveugle.

— Aveugle ? Ah ! mon Dieu ! »

Laurence resta accablée à cette nouvelle, et, songeant à l'affreuse existence de Pauline, elle la regardait fixement avec l'expression d'une compassion profonde et pourtant comprimée par le respect. Pauline la comprit, et, lui pressant la main avec tendresse, elle lui dit avec une naïveté touchante : « Il y a du bien dans tous les maux que Dieu nous envoie. J'ai failli me marier il y a cinq ans ; un an après, ma mère a perdu la vue. Vois comme il est heureux que je sois restée fille pour la soigner ! Si j'avais été mariée, qui sait si je l'aurais pu ? »

Laurence, pénétrée d'admiration, sentit ses yeux se remplir de larmes.

« Il est évident, dit-elle en souriant à son amie à travers ses pleurs, que tu aurais été distraite par mille autres soins également sacrés, et qu'elle eût été plus à plaindre qu'elle ne l'est.

— Je l'entends remuer », dit Pauline ; et elle passa vivement, mais avec assez d'adresse pour ne pas faire le moindre bruit, dans la chambre voisine.

Laurence la suivit sur la pointe du pied, et vit la vieille femme aveugle étendue sur son lit en forme de corbillard. Elle était jaune et luisante. Ses yeux hagards et sans vie lui donnaient absolument l'aspect d'un cadavre. Laurence recula, saisie d'une terreur involontaire. Pauline s'approcha de sa mère, pencha doucement son visage vers ce visage affreux, et lui demanda bien bas si elle dormait. L'aveugle ne répondit rien, et se tourna vers la ruelle du lit. Pauline arrangea ses couvertures avec soin sur ses membres étiques, referma doucement le rideau, et reconduisit son amie dans le salon.

« Causons, lui dit-elle ; ma mère se lève tard ordinairement. Nous avons quelques heures pour nous reconnaître ; nous trouverons bien un moyen de réveiller son ancienne amitié pour toi. Peut-être suffira-t-il de lui dire que tu es là ! Mais, dis-moi, Laurence, tu as pu croire que je te… Oh ! je ne dirai pas ce mot ! Te mépriser ! Quelle insulte tu m'as faite là ! Mais c'est ma faute après tout. J'aurais dû prévoir que tu concevrais des doutes sur mon affection, j'aurais dû t'expliquer mes motifs… Hélas ! c'était bien difficile à te faire comprendre ! Tu m'aurais accusée de faiblesse, quand, au contraire, il me fallait tant de force pour renoncer à t'écrire, à te suivre dans ce monde inconnu où, malgré moi, mon cœur a été si souvent te chercher ! Et puis je n'osais pas accuser ma mère ; je ne pouvais pas me décider à t'avouer les petitesses de son caractère et les préjugés de son esprit. J'en étais victime ; mais je rougissais de les raconter. Quand on est si loin de toute amitié, si seule, si triste, toute démarche difficile devient impossible. On s'observe, on se craint soi-même, et on se suicide dans la peur qu'on a de se laisser mourir. À présent que te voilà près de moi, je retrouve toute ma confiance, tout mon abandon. Je te dirai tout. Mais d'abord parlons de toi, car mon existence est si monotone, si nulle, si pâle à côté de la tienne ! Que de choses tu dois avoir à me raconter ! »

Le lecteur doit présumer que Laurence ne raconta pas tout. Son récit fut même beaucoup moins long que Pauline ne s'y attendait. Nous le transcrirons en trois lignes, qui suffiront à l'intelligence de la situation.

Et d'abord, il faut dire que Laurence était née à Paris dans une position médiocre. Elle avait reçu une éducation simple, mais solide. Elle avait quinze ans lorsque, sa famille étant tombée dans la misère, il lui fallut quitter Paris et se retirer en province avec sa mère. Elle vint habiter Saint-Front, où elle réussit à vivre quatre ans en qualité de sous-maîtresse dans un pensionnat de jeunes filles, et où elle contracta une étroite amitié avec l'aînée de ses élèves, Pauline, âgée de quinze ans comme elle.

Et puis il arriva que Laurence dut à la protection de je ne sais quelle douairière d'être rappelée à Paris, pour y faire l'éducation des filles d'un banquier.

Si vous voulez savoir comment une jeune fille pressent et découvre sa vocation, comment elle l'accomplit en dépit de toutes les remontrances et de tous les obstacles, relisez les charmants *Mémoires* de mademoiselle Hippolyte Clairon[1], célèbre comédienne du siècle dernier.

Laurence fit comme tous ces artistes prédestinés, elle passa par toutes les misères, par toutes les souffrances du talent ignoré ou méconnu ; enfin, après avoir traversé les vicissitudes de la vie pénible que l'artiste est forcé de créer lui-même, elle

---

1. Claire-Josèphe-Hippolyte Léris de La Trude, dite Mlle Clairon (1723-1803), l'une des plus célèbres actrices du XVIIIᵉ siècle, adepte de la diction naturelle et amie des philosophes. Elle publia ses *Mémoires* en 1799.

devint une belle et intelligente actrice. Succès, richesse, hommages, renommée, tout lui vint ensemble et tout à coup. Désormais elle jouissait d'une position brillante et d'une considération justifiée aux yeux des gens d'esprit par un noble talent et un caractère élevé. Ses erreurs, ses passions, ses douleurs de femme, ses déceptions et ses repentirs, elle ne les raconta point à Pauline. Il était encore trop tôt ; Pauline n'eût pas compris.

II

Cependant, lorsqu'au coup de midi l'aveugle s'éveilla, Pauline savait toute la vie de Laurence, même ce qui ne lui avait pas été raconté, et cela plus que tout le reste peut-être, car les personnes qui ont vécu dans le calme et la retraite ont un merveilleux instinct pour se représenter la vie d'autrui pleine d'orages et de désastres qu'elles s'applaudissent en secret d'avoir évités. C'est une consolation intérieure qu'il leur faut laisser, car l'amour-propre y trouve bien un peu son compte, et la vertu seule ne suffit pas toujours à dédommager des longs ennuis de la solitude.

« Eh bien ! dit la mère aveugle en s'asseyant sur le bord de son lit, appuyée sur sa fille, qui est donc là près de nous ? Je sens le parfum d'une belle dame. Je parie que c'est madame Ducornay, qui est revenue de Paris avec toutes sortes de belles toilettes que je ne pourrai pas voir, et de bonnes senteurs qui nous donnent la migraine.

— Non, maman, répondit Pauline, ce n'est pas madame Ducornay.

— Qui donc ? reprit l'aveugle en étendant le bras.

— Devinez, dit Pauline en faisant signe à Laurence de toucher la main de sa mère.

— Que cette main est douce et petite ! s'écria l'aveugle en passant ses doigts noueux sur ceux de l'actrice. Oh ! ce n'est pas madame Ducornay certainement. Ce n'est aucune de *nos dames*, car, quoi qu'elles fassent, à la patte on reconnaît toujours le lièvre. Pourtant je connais cette main-là. Mais c'est quelqu'un que je n'ai pas vu depuis longtemps. Ne saurait-elle parler ?

— Ma voix a changé comme ma main, répondit Laurence, dont l'organe clair et frais avait pris, dans les études théâtrales, un timbre plus grave et plus sonore.

— Je connais aussi cette voix, dit l'aveugle, et pourtant je ne la reconnais pas. »

Elle garda quelques instants le silence sans quitter la main de Laurence, en levant sur elle ses yeux ternes et vitreux, dont la fixité était effrayante.

« Me voit-elle ? demanda Laurence bas à Pauline.

— Nullement, répondit celle-ci ; mais elle a toute sa mémoire, et d'ailleurs notre vie compte si peu d'événements, qu'il est impossible qu'elle ne te reconnaisse pas tout à l'heure. »

À peine Pauline eut-elle prononcé ces mots, que l'aveugle, repoussant la main de Laurence avec un sentiment de dégoût qui allait jusqu'à l'horreur, dit de sa voix sèche et cassée : « Ah ! c'est cette malheureuse *qui joue la comédie* ! Que vient-elle chercher ici ? Vous ne deviez pas la recevoir, Pauline.

— Oh ma mère ? » s'écria Pauline en rougissant de honte et de chagrin, et en pressant sa mère dans ses bras pour lui faire comprendre ce qu'elle éprouvait.

Laurence pâlit, puis, se remettant aussitôt : « Je m'attendais à cela, dit-elle à Pauline avec un sourire dont la douceur et la dignité l'étonnèrent et la troublèrent un peu.

— Allons, reprit l'aveugle, qui craignait instinctivement de déplaire à sa fille, en raison du besoin qu'elle avait de son dévouement, laissez-moi le temps de me remettre un peu ; je suis si surprise ! et comme cela, au réveil, on ne sait trop ce qu'on dit... Je ne voudrais pas vous faire de chagrin, mademoiselle... ou madame... Comment vous appelle-t-on maintenant ?

— Toujours Laurence, répondit l'actrice avec calme.

— Et elle est toujours Laurence, dit avec chaleur la bonne Pauline en l'embrassant, toujours la même âme généreuse, le même noble cœur...

— Allons, arrange-moi, ma fille, dit l'aveugle qui voulait changer de propos, ne pouvant se résoudre ni à contredire sa fille ni à réparer sa dureté envers Laurence ; coiffe-moi donc, Pauline ; j'oublie, moi, que les autres ne sont point aveugles et qu'ils voient en moi quelque chose d'affreux. Donne-moi mon voile, mon mantelet... C'est bien, et maintenant apporte-moi mon chocolat de santé, et offres-en aussi à... cette dame. »

la relation entre
la mère + Pauline

Pauline jeta à son amie un regard suppliant auquel celle-ci répondit par un baiser. Quand la vieille dame, enveloppée dans sa mante d'indienne brune à grandes fleurs rouges, et coiffée de son bonnet blanc surmonté d'un voile de crêpe noir qui lui cachait la moitié du visage, se fut assise vis-à-vis de son frugal déjeuner, elle s'adoucit peu à peu. L'âge, l'ennui et les infirmités l'avaient amenée à ce degré d'égoïsme qui fait tout sacrifier, même les préjugés les plus enracinés, aux besoins du bien-être. L'aveugle vivait dans une telle dépendance de sa fille, qu'une contrariété, une distraction de celle-ci pouvait apporter le trouble dans cette suite d'innombrables petites attentions dont la moindre était nécessaire pour lui rendre la vie tolérable. Quand l'aveugle était commodément couchée, et qu'elle ne craignait plus aucun danger, aucune privation pour quelques heures, elle se donnait le cruel soulagement de blesser par des paroles aigres et des murmures injustes les gens dont elle n'avait plus besoin ; mais, aux heures de sa dépendance, elle savait fort bien se contenir, et enchaîner leur zèle par des manières plus affables. Laurence eut le loisir de faire cette remarque dans le courant de la journée. Elle en fit encore une autre qui l'attrista davantage : c'est que la mère avait une peur réelle de sa fille. On eût dit qu'à travers cet admirable sacrifice de tous les instants, Pauline laissait percer malgré elle un muet, mais éternel reproche, que sa mère comprenait fort bien et redoutait affreusement. Il semblait que ces deux femmes craignissent de s'éclairer mutuellement

40   pouvoir à Pauline ?

sur la lassitude qu'elles éprouvaient d'être ainsi attachées l'une à l'autre, un être moribond et un être vivant : l'un effrayé des mouvements de celui qui pouvait à chaque instant lui enlever son dernier souffle, et l'autre épouvanté de cette tombe où il craignait d'être entraîné à la suite d'un cadavre.

Laurence, qui était douée d'un esprit judicieux et d'un cœur noble, se dit qu'il n'en pouvait pas être autrement ; que d'ailleurs cette souffrance invincible chez Pauline n'ôtait rien à sa patience et ne faisait qu'ajouter à ses mérites. Mais, malgré cela, Laurence sentit que l'effroi et l'ennui la gagnaient entre ces deux victimes. Un nuage passa sur ses yeux et un frisson dans ses veines. Vers le soir, elle était accablée de fatigue, quoiqu'elle n'eût pas fait un pas de la journée. Déjà l'horreur de la vie réelle se montrait derrière cette poésie dont au premier moment elle avait, de ses yeux d'artiste, enveloppé la sainte existence de Pauline. Elle eût voulu pouvoir persister dans son illusion, la croire heureuse et rayonnante dans son martyre comme une vierge catholique des anciens jours, voir la mère heureuse aussi, oubliant sa misère pour ne songer qu'à la joie d'être aimée et assistée ainsi ; enfin elle eût voulu, puisque ce sombre tableau d'intérieur était sous ses yeux, y voir passer des anges de lumière, et non de tristes figures chagrines et froides comme la réalité. Le plus léger pli sur le front angélique de Pauline faisait ombre à ce tableau ; un mot prononcé sèchement par cette bouche si pure détruisait la mansuétude mysté-

Laurence commence à comprendre 41
qu'elle n'a compris la situation
de Pauline

rieuse que Laurence, au premier abord, y avait vue régner. Et pourtant ce pli au front était une prière, ce mot errant sur les lèvres une parole de sollicitude ou de consolation ; mais tout cela était glacé comme l'égoïsme chrétien, qui nous fait tout supporter en vue de la récompense, et désolé comme le renoncement monastique, qui nous défend de trop adoucir la vie humaine à autrui aussi bien qu'à nous-mêmes.

Tandis que le premier enthousiasme de l'admiration naïve s'affaiblissait chez l'actrice, tout aussi naïvement et en dépit d'elles-mêmes, une modification d'idées s'opérait en sens inverse chez les deux bourgeoises. La fille, tout en frémissant à l'idée des pompes mondaines où son amie s'était jetée, avait souvent ressenti, peut-être à son insu, des élans de curiosité pour ce monde inconnu, plein de terreurs et de prestiges, où ses principes lui défendaient de porter un seul regard. En voyant Laurence, en admirant sa beauté, sa grâce, ses manières tantôt nobles comme celles d'une reine de théâtre, tantôt libres et enjouées comme celles d'un enfant (car l'artiste aimée du public est comme un enfant à qui l'univers sert de famille), elle sentait éclore en elle un sentiment à la fois enivrant et douloureux, quelque chose qui tenait le milieu entre l'admiration et la crainte, entre la tendresse et l'envie. Quant à l'aveugle, elle était instinctivement captivée et comme vivifiée par le beau son de cette voix, par la pureté de ce langage, par l'animation de cette causerie intelligente, colorée et profondément naturelle, qui caractérise

les vrais artistes, et ceux du théâtre particulièrement. La mère de Pauline, quoique remplie d'en-
têtement dévot et de morgue provinciale, était une
femme assez distinguée et assez instruite pour le
monde où elle avait vécu. Elle l'était du moins
assez pour se sentir frappée et charmée, malgré
elle, d'entendre quelque chose de si différent de
son entourage habituel et de si supérieur à tout ce
qu'elle avait jamais rencontré. Peut-être ne s'en
rendait-elle pas bien compte à elle-même, mais il
est certain que les efforts de Laurence pour la faire
revenir de ses préventions réussissaient au-delà de
ses espérances. La vieille femme commençait à
s'amuser si réellement de la causerie de l'actrice,
qu'elle l'entendit avec regret, presque avec effroi,
demander des chevaux de poste. Elle fit alors un
grand effort sur elle-même, et la pria de rester
jusqu'au lendemain. Laurence se fit un peu prier.
Sa mère, retenue à Paris par une indisposition de
sa seconde fille, n'avait pu partir avec elle. Les en-
gagements de Laurence avec le théâtre d'Orléans
l'avaient forcée de les y devancer, mais elle leur
avait donné rendez-vous à Lyon, et Laurence voulait y arriver en même temps qu'elles, sachant bien
que sa mère et sa sœur, après quinze jours de séparation (la première de leur vie), l'attendraient
impatiemment. Cependant l'aveugle insista tellement, et Pauline, à l'idée de se séparer de nouveau, et pour jamais sans doute, de son amie,
versa des larmes si sincères, que Laurence céda,
écrivit à sa mère de ne pas être inquiète si elle re-
tardait d'un jour son arrivée à Lyon, et ne com-

manda ses chevaux que pour le lendemain soir. L'aveugle, entraînée de plus en plus, poussa la gracieuseté jusqu'à vouloir dicter une phrase amicale pour son ancienne connaissance, la mère de Laurence.

« Cette pauvre madame S…, ajouta-t-elle lorsqu'elle eut entendu plier la lettre et pétiller la cire à cacheter, c'était une bien excellente personne, spirituelle, gaie, confiante… et bien étourdie ! car enfin, ma pauvre enfant, c'est elle qui répondra devant Dieu du malheur que tu as eu de monter sur les planches. Elle pouvait s'y opposer, et elle ne l'a pas fait ! Je lui ai écrit trois lettres à cette occasion, et Dieu sait si elle les a lues ! Ah ! si elle m'eût écoutée, tu n'en serais pas là !…

— Nous serions dans la plus profonde misère, répondit Laurence avec une douce vivacité, et nous souffririons de ne pouvoir rien faire l'une pour l'autre, tandis qu'aujourd'hui j'ai la joie de voir ma bonne mère rajeunir au sein d'une honnête aisance ; et elle est plus heureuse que moi, s'il est possible, de devoir son bien-être à mon travail et à ma persévérance. Oh ! c'est une excellente mère, ma bonne madame D…, et, quoique je sois actrice, je vous assure que je l'aime autant que Pauline vous aime.

— Tu as toujours été une bonne fille, je le sais, dit l'aveugle. Mais enfin comment cela finira-t-il ? Vous voilà riches, et je comprends que ta mère s'en trouve fort bien, car c'est une femme qui a toujours aimé ses aises et ses plaisirs ; mais l'autre vie, mon enfant, vous n'y songez ni l'une ni l'autre !… Enfin, je me réfugie dans la pensée que tu ne seras pas toujours au théâtre, et qu'un jour viendra où tu feras pénitence. »

Cependant le bruit de l'aventure qui avait amené à Saint-Front, route de Paris, une dame en chaise de poste qui croyait aller à Villiers, route de Lyon, s'était répandue dans la petite ville et y donnait lieu, depuis quelques heures, à d'étranges commentaires. Par quel hasard, par quel prodige, cette dame de la chaise de poste, après être arrivée là sans le vouloir, se décidait-elle à y rester toute la journée ? Et que faisait-elle, bon Dieu ! chez les dames D… ? Comment pouvait-elle les connaître ? Et que pouvaient-elles avoir à se dire depuis si longtemps qu'elles étaient enfermées ensemble ? Le secrétaire de la mairie, qui faisait sa partie de billard au café situé justement en face de la maison des dames D…, vit ou crut voir passer et repasser derrière les vitres de cette maison la dame étrangère, vêtue singulièrement, disait-il, et même magnifiquement. La toilette de voyage de Laurence était pourtant d'une simplicité de bon goût ; mais la femme de Paris, et la femme artiste surtout, donne aux moindres atours un prestige éblouissant pour la province. Toutes les dames des maisons voisines se collèrent à leurs croisées, les entrouvrirent même, et s'enrhumèrent toutes plus ou moins, dans l'espérance de découvrir ce qui se passait chez la voisine. On appela la servante comme elle allait au marché, on l'interrogea. Elle ne savait rien, elle n'avait rien entendu, rien compris ; mais la personne en question était fort étrange, selon elle. Elle faisait de grands pas, parlait avec une grosse voix, et portait une pelisse fourrée qui la faisait ressembler aux animaux des ménageries ambulantes, soit à une lionne, soit à une tigresse : la servante ne savait pas bien à laquelle des deux. Le secrétaire de la mairie décida qu'elle était vêtue d'une peau de panthère, et l'adjoint du maire trouva fort probable que ce fût la duchesse de Berry[1]. Il avait toujours soupçonné la vieille D... d'être légitimiste au fond du cœur, car elle était dévote. Le maire, assassiné de questions par les dames de sa famille, trouva un expédient merveilleux pour satisfaire leur curiosité et la sienne propre. Il ordonna au maître de poste de ne délivrer de chevaux à l'étrangère que sur le *vu* de son passeport. L'étrangère, se ravisant et remettant son départ au lendemain, fit répondre par son domestique qu'elle montrerait son passeport au moment où elle redemanderait des chevaux. Le domestique, fin matois, véritable Frontin de comédie, s'amusa de la curiosité des citadins de Saint-Front, et leur fit à chacun un conte différent. Mille versions circulèrent et se croisèrent dans la ville. Les esprits furent très agités, le maire craignit une émeute ; le procureur du roi intima à la gen-

---

1. Marie-Caroline de Bourbon-Sicile (1798-1870), duchesse de Berry en 1816, suivit Charles X et sa famille en exil en 1830. Rentrée en France en 1832, elle tenta de soulever le Midi puis la Vendée contre Louis-Philippe. Tout le monde, un temps, crut l'avoir aperçue courant les routes. Sand semble commettre un léger anachronisme, puisque le roman se déroule sous la Restauration.

et de son intimité, lui nommant avec une merveilleuse mémoire jusqu'au plus petit de ses enfants, l'intrigua pendant un quart d'heure, et finit par s'en faire reconnaître. Elle fut si aimable et si jolie dans ce badinage, que le bon maire en tomba amoureux comme un fou ; voulut lui baiser la main, et ne se retira que lorsque madame D... et Pauline lui eurent promis de le faire dîner chez elles ce même jour avec la belle actrice de *la capitale*. Le dîner fut fort gai. Laurence essaya de se débarrasser des impressions tristes qu'elle avait reçues, et voulut récompenser l'aveugle du sacrifice qu'elle lui faisait de ses préjugés en lui donnant quelques heures d'enjouement. Elle raconta mille historiettes plaisantes sur ses voyages en province, et même, au dessert, elle consentit à réciter à monsieur le maire des tirades de vers classiques qui le jetèrent dans un délire d'enthousiasme dont madame la mairesse eût été sans doute fort effrayée. Jamais l'aveugle ne s'était autant amusée ; Pauline était singulièrement agitée ; elle s'étonnait de se sentir triste au milieu de sa joie. Laurence, tout en voulant divertir les autres, avait fini par se divertir elle-même. Elle se croyait rajeunie de dix ans en se retrouvant dans ce monde de ses souvenirs, où elle croyait parfois être encore en rêve.

On était passé de la salle à manger au salon, et on achevait de prendre le café, lorsqu'un bruit de socques dans l'escalier annonça l'approche d'une visite. C'était la femme du maire, qui, ne pouvant résister plus longtemps à sa curiosité, venait *adroitement* et comme par hasard voir madame D... Elle se fût bien gardée d'amener ses filles, elle eût craint de faire tort à leur mariage si elle leur eût laissé entrevoir la comédienne. Ces demoiselles n'en dormirent pas de la nuit, et jamais l'autorité maternelle ne leur sembla plus inique. La plus jeune en pleura de dépit.

Madame la mairesse, quoique assez embarrassée de l'accueil qu'elle ferait à Laurence (celle-ci avait autrefois donné des leçons à ses filles), se garda bien d'être impolie. Elle fut même gracieuse en voyant la dignité calme qui régnait dans ses manières. Mais, quelques minutes après, une seconde visite étant arrivée, *par hasard* aussi, la mairesse recula sa chaise et parla un peu moins à l'actrice. Elle était observée par une de ses amies intimes, qui n'eût pas manqué de critiquer beaucoup son *intimité* avec une comédienne. Cette seconde visiteuse s'était promis de satisfaire aussi sa curiosité en faisant causer Laurence. Mais, outre que Laurence devint de plus en plus grave et réservée, la présence de la mairesse contraignit et gêna les curiosités subséquentes. La troisième visite gêna beaucoup les deux premières, et fut à son tour encore plus gênée par l'arrivée de la quatrième. Enfin, en moins d'une heure, le vieux salon de Pauline fut rempli comme si elle eût invité toute la ville à une grande soirée. Personne n'y pouvait résister ; on voulait, au risque de faire une chose étrange, impolie même, voir cette petite sous-maîtresse dont personne n'avait soupçonné l'intelligence, et qui maintenant était connue et applaudie dans toute la France. Pour légitimer la curiosité présente, et pour excuser le peu de quelle n'arrivera jamais l'élégante de petite ville, même lorsqu'elle copie exactement l'élégante des grandes villes ; enfin toutes ces recherches de la chaussure, de la manchette et de la coiffure, que les femmes sans goût exagèrent jusqu'à l'absurde, ou suppriment jusqu'à la malpropreté. Ce qui frappait et intimidait plus que tout le reste, c'était l'aisance parfaite de Laurence, ce ton de la meilleure compagnie qu'on ne s'attend guère, en province, à trouver chez une comédienne, et que, certes, on ne trouvait chez aucune femme à Saint-Front. Laurence était imposante et prévenante à son gré. Elle souriait en elle-même du trouble où elle jetait tous ces petits esprits qui étaient venus à l'insu les uns des autres, chacun croyant être le seul assez hardi pour s'amuser des inconvenances d'une bohémienne, et qui se trouvaient là honteux et embarrassés chacun de la présence des autres, et plus encore du désappointement d'avoir à envier ce qu'il était venu persifler, humilier peut-être ! Toutes ces femmes se tenaient d'un côté du salon comme un régiment en déroute, et de l'autre côté, entourée de Pauline, de sa mère et de quelques hommes de bon sens qui ne craignaient pas de causer respectueusement avec elle, Laurence siégeait comme une reine affable qui sourit à son peuple et le tient à distance. Les rôles étaient bien changés, et le malaise croissait d'un côté, tandis que la véritable dignité triomphait de l'autre. On n'osait plus chuchoter, on n'osait même plus regarder, si ce n'est à la dérobée. Enfin, quand le départ des plus désappointées eut éclairci les rangs, on osa s'approcher, mendier une parole, un regard, toucher, demander l'adresse de la lingère, le prix des bijoux, le nom des pièces de théâtre le plus à la mode à Paris, et des billets de spectacle pour le premier voyage qu'on ferait à la capitale.

À l'arrivée des premières visites, l'aveugle avait été confuse, puis contrariée, puis blessée. Quand elle entendit tout ce monde remplir son salon froid et abandonné depuis si longtemps, elle prit son parti, et, cessant de rougir de l'amitié qu'elle avait témoignée à Laurence, elle en affecta plus encore, et accueillit par des paroles aigres et moqueuses tous ceux qui vinrent la saluer.

« Oui-da, mesdames, répondait-elle, je me porte mieux que je ne pensais, puisque mes infirmités ne font plus peur à personne. Il y a deux ans que l'on n'est venu me tenir compagnie le soir, et c'est un merveilleux hasard qui m'amène toute la ville à la fois. Est-ce qu'on aurait dérangé le calendrier, et ma fête, que je croyais passée il y a six mois, tomberait-elle aujourd'hui ? » Puis, s'adressant à d'autres qui n'étaient presque jamais venues chez elle, elle poussait la malice jusqu'à leur dire en face et tout haut : « Ah ! vous faites comme moi, vous faites taire vos scrupules de conscience, et vous venez, malgré vous, rendre hommage au talent ? C'est toujours ainsi, voyez-vous ; l'esprit triomphe toujours, et de tout. Vous avez bien blâmé mademoiselle S... de s'être mise au théâtre, vous avez fait comme moi, vous avez trouvé cela révoltant, affreux ! Eh bien ! vous voilà toutes à ses pieds ! Vous ne direz pas le contraire, car enfin je ne crois pas être devenue tout à coup assez aimable et assez jolie pour que l'on vienne en foule jouir de ma société. »

Quant à Pauline, elle fut du commencement à la fin admirable pour son amie. Elle ne rougit point d'elle un seul instant, et bravant, avec un courage héroïque en province, le blâme qu'on s'apprêtait à déverser sur elle, elle prit franchement le parti d'être en public à l'égard de Laurence ce qu'elle était en particulier. Elle l'accabla de soins, de prévenances, de respects même ; elle plaça elle-même un tabouret sous ses pieds, elle lui présenta elle-même le plateau de rafraîchissements, puis elle répondit par un baiser plein d'effusion à son baiser de remerciement, et, quand elle se rassit auprès d'elle, elle tint sa main enlacée à la sienne toute la soirée sur le bras du fauteuil.

Ce rôle était beau sans doute, et la présence de Laurence opérait des miracles, car un tel courage eût épouvanté Pauline si on lui en eût annoncé la nécessité la veille ; et maintenant il lui coûtait si peu, qu'elle s'en étonnait elle-même. Si elle eût pu descendre au fond de sa conscience, peut-être eût-elle découvert que ce rôle généreux était le seul qui l'élevât au niveau de Laurence à ses propres yeux. Il est certain que, jusque-là, la grâce, la noblesse et l'intelligence de l'actrice l'avaient déconcertée un peu ; mais, depuis qu'elle l'avait posée auprès d'elle en protégée, Pauline ne s'apercevait plus de cette supériorité, difficile à accepter de femme à femme aussi bien que d'homme à homme.

Il est certain que, lorsque les deux amies et la mère aveugle se retrouvèrent seules ensemble au coin du feu, Pauline fut surprise et même un peu blessée de voir que Laurence reportait toute sa reconnaissance sur la vieille femme. Ce fut avec une noble franchise que l'actrice, baisant la main de madame D… et l'aidant à reprendre le chemin de sa chambre, lui dit qu'elle sentait tout le prix de ce qu'elle avait fait et de ce qu'elle avait été pour elle durant cette petite épreuve.

« Quant à toi, ma Pauline, dit-elle à son amie lorsqu'elles furent tête à tête, je te fâcherais si je te faisais le même remerciement. Tu n'as point de préjugés assez obstinés pour que ton mépris de la sottise provinciale me semble un grand effort. Je te connais, tu ne serais plus toi-même si tu n'avais pas trouvé un vrai plaisir à t'élever de toute la hauteur au-dessus de ces bégueules.

— C'est à cause de toi que cela m'est devenu un plaisir, répondit Pauline un peu déconcertée.

— Allons donc, rusée ! reprit Laurence en l'embrassant, c'est à cause de vous-même ! »

Était-ce un instinct d'ingratitude qui faisait parler ainsi l'amie de Pauline ? Non. Laurence était la femme la plus droite avec les autres et la plus sincère vis-à-vis d'elle-même. Si l'effort de son amie lui eût paru sublime, elle ne se serait pas crue humiliée de lui montrer de la reconnaissance ; mais elle avait un sentiment si ferme et si légitime de sa propre dignité, qu'elle croyait le courage de Pauline aussi naturel, aussi facile que le sien. Elle ne se doutait nullement de l'angoisse secrète qu'elle

l'extrême subjectivité de notre expérience

excitait dans cette âme troublée. Elle ne pouvait la
deviner ; elle ne l'eût pas comprise.

Pauline, ne voulant pas la quitter d'un instant,
exigea qu'elle dormît dans son propre lit. Elle
s'était fait arranger un grand canapé où elle se
coucha non loin d'elle, afin de pouvoir causer le
plus longtemps possible. Chaque moment aug-
mentait l'inquiétude de la jeune recluse, et son
désir de comprendre la vie, les jouissances de l'art
et celles de la gloire, celles de l'activité et celles de
l'indépendance. Laurence éludait ses questions. Il
lui semblait imprudent de la part de Pauline de
vouloir connaître les avantages d'une position si
différente de la sienne ; il lui eût semblé peu délicat à elle-même de lui en faire un tableau sédui-
sant. Elle s'efforça de répondre à ses questions par
d'autres questions ; elle voulut lui faire dire les
joies intimes de sa vie évangélique, et tourner
toute l'exaltation de leur entretien vers cette poésie du devoir qui lui semblait devoir être le par-
tage d'une âme pieuse et résignée. Mais Pauline ne
répondit que par des réticences. Dans leur premier
entretien de la matinée, elle avait épuisé tout ce
que sa vertu avait d'orgueil et de finesse pour dis-
simuler sa souffrance. Le soir, elle ne songeait déjà
plus à son rôle. La soif qu'elle éprouvait de vivre
et de s'épanouir, comme une fleur longtemps privée d'air et de soleil, devenait de plus en plus
ardente. Elle l'emporta, et força Laurence à
s'abandonner au plaisir le plus grand qu'elle con-
nût, celui d'épancher son âme avec confiance et
naïveté. Laurence aimait son art, non seulement

55

pour lui-même, mais aussi en raison de la liberté et de l'élévation d'esprit et d'habitudes qu'il lui avait procurées. Elle s'honorait de nobles amitiés ; elle avait connu aussi des affections passionnées, et, quoiqu'elle eût la délicatesse de n'en point parler à Pauline, la présence de ces souvenirs encore palpitants donnait à son éloquence naturelle une énergie pleine de charme et d'entraînement.

Pauline dévorait ses paroles. Elles tombaient dans son cœur et dans son cerveau comme une pluie de feu ; pâle, les cheveux épars, l'œil embrasé, le coude appuyé sur son chevet virginal, elle était belle comme une nymphe antique, à la lueur pâle de la lampe qui brûlait entre les deux lits. Laurence la vit et fut frappée de l'expression de ses traits. Elle craignit d'en avoir trop dit, et se le reprocha, quoique pourtant toutes ses paroles eussent été pures comme celles d'une mère à sa fille. Puis, involontairement, revenant à ses idées théâtrales, et oubliant tout ce qu'elles venaient de se dire, elle s'écria, frappée de plus en plus : « Mon Dieu, que tu es belle, ma chère enfant ! Les classiques qui m'ont voulu enseigner le rôle de Phèdre ne t'avaient pas vue ainsi. Voici une pose qui est toute l'école moderne ; mais c'est Phèdre tout entière… non pas la Phèdre de Racine peut-être, mais celle d'Euripide, disant :

Dieux ! que ne suis-je assise à l'ombre des forêts[1] *!…*

---

1. Sand cite bien la *Phèdre* de Racine (1677) ; le vers est prononcé lors de l'entrée en scène de Phèdre dans l'acte I, scène 3.

Pauline n'a pas choisi cette vie, mais Laurence n'est pas consciente de ça

Si je ne te dis pas cela en grec, ajouta Laurence en étouffant un léger bâillement, c'est que je ne sais pas le grec... Je parie que tu le sais, toi !...

— Le grec ? quelle folie ! répondit Pauline en s'efforçant de sourire. Que ferais-je de cela !

— Oh ! moi, si j'avais, comme toi, le temps d'étudier tout, s'écria Laurence, je voudrais tout savoir ! » *↑ ambigüe !*

Il se fit quelques instants de silence. Pauline fit un douloureux retour sur elle-même ; elle se demanda à quoi, en effet, servaient tous ces merveilleux ouvrages de broderie qui remplissaient ses longues heures de silence et de solitude, et qui n'occupaient ni sa pensée, ni son cœur. Elle fut effrayée de tant de belles années perdues, et il lui sembla qu'elle avait fait de ses plus nobles facultés, comme de son temps le plus précieux, un usage stupide, presque impie. Elle se releva encore sur son coude, et dit à Laurence : « Pourquoi donc me comparais-tu à Phèdre ? Sais-tu que c'est là un type affreux ? Peux-tu poétiser le vice et le crime ?... »

Laurence ne répondit pas. Fatiguée de l'insomnie de la nuit précédente, calme d'ailleurs au fond de l'âme, comme on l'est malgré tous les orages passagers, lorsqu'on a trouvé au fond de soi le vrai but et le vrai moyen de son existence, elle s'était endormie presque en parlant. Ce prompt et paisible sommeil augmenta l'angoisse et l'amertume de Pauline. « Elle est heureuse, pensa-t-elle... heureuse et contente d'elle-même, sans effort, sans combats, sans incertitude... Et moi !... Ô mon Dieu ! cela est injuste ! »

Pauline ne dormit pas de toute la nuit. Le lendemain, Laurence s'éveilla aussi paisiblement qu'elle s'était endormie, et se montra au jour fraîche et reposée. Sa femme de chambre arriva avec une jolie robe blanche qui lui servait de peignoir pendant sa toilette. Tandis que la soubrette lissait et tressait les magnifiques cheveux noirs de Laurence, celle-ci repassait le rôle qu'elle devait jouer à Lyon, à trois jours de là. C'était à son tour d'être belle avec ses cheveux épars et l'expression tragique. De temps en temps, elle échappait brusquement aux mains de la femme de chambre, et marchait dans l'appartement en s'écriant : « Ce n'est pas cela !... je veux le dire comme je le sens ! » Et elle laissait échapper des exclamations, des phrases de drame ; elle cherchait des poses devant le vieux miroir de Pauline. Le sang-froid de la femme de chambre, habituée à toutes ces choses, et l'oubli complet où Laurence semblait être de tous les objets extérieurs, étonnaient au dernier point la jeune provinciale. Elle ne savait pas si elle devait rire ou s'effrayer de ces airs de pythonisse ; puis elle était frappée de la beauté tragique de Laurence, comme Laurence l'avait été de la sienne quelques heures auparavant. Mais elle se disait : « Elle fait toutes ces choses de sang-froid, avec une impétuosité préparée, avec une douleur étudiée ; au fond, elle est fort tranquille, fort heureuse ; et moi, qui devrais avoir le calme de Dieu sur le front, il se trouve que je ressemble à Phèdre ! »

Comme elle pensait cela, Laurence lui dit brusquement : « Je fais tout ce que je peux pour trouver ta pose d'hier au soir quand tu étais là sur ton coude… je ne peux pas en venir à bout ! C'était magnifique. Allons ! c'était trop récent. Je trouverai cela plus tard, par inspiration ! Toute inspiration est une réminiscence, n'est-ce pas, Pauline ? Tu ne te coiffes pas bien, mon enfant ; tresse donc tes cheveux au lieu de les lisser ainsi en bandeau. Tiens, Suzette va te montrer. »

Et, tandis que la femme de chambre faisait une tresse, Laurence fit l'autre, et en un instant Pauline se trouva si bien coiffée et si embellie, qu'elle fit un cri de surprise. « Ah ! mon Dieu, quelle adresse ? s'écria-t-elle ; je ne me coiffais pas ainsi de peur d'y perdre trop de temps, et j'en mettais le double.

— Oh ! c'est que, nous autres, répondit Laurence, nous sommes forcées de nous faire belles le plus possible et le plus vite possible.

— Et à quoi cela me servirait-il, à moi ? dit Pauline en laissant tomber ses coudes sur la toilette, et en se regardant au miroir d'un air sombre et désolé.

— Tiens, s'écria Laurence, te voilà encore Phèdre ! Reste comme cela, j'étudie ! »

Pauline sentit ses yeux se remplir de larmes. Pour que Laurence ne s'en aperçût pas (et c'est ce que Pauline craignait le plus au monde dans cet instant), elle s'enfuit dans une autre pièce et dévora d'amers sanglots. Il y avait de la douleur et de la colère dans son âme, mais elle ne savait pas elle-même pourquoi ces orages s'élevaient en elle.

Le soir, Laurence était partie. Pauline avait pleuré en la voyant monter en voiture, et, cette fois, c'était de regret, car Laurence venait de la faire vivre pendant trente-six heures, et elle pensait avec effroi au lendemain. Elle tomba accablée de fatigue dans son lit, et s'endormit brisée, désirant ne plus s'éveiller. Lorsqu'elle s'éveilla, elle jeta un regard de morne épouvante sur ces murailles qui ne gardaient aucune trace du rêve que Laurence y avait évoqué. Elle se leva lentement, s'assit machinalement devant son miroir, et essaya de refaire ses tresses de la veille. Tout à coup, rappelée à la réalité par le chant de son serin, qui s'éveillait dans sa cage, toujours gai, toujours indifférent à la captivité, Pauline se leva, ouvrit la cage, puis la fenêtre, et poussa dehors l'oiseau sédentaire, qui ne voulait pas s'envoler. « Ah ! tu n'es pas digne de la liberté ! » dit-elle en le voyant revenir vers elle aussitôt.

Elle retourna à sa toilette, défit ses tresses avec une sorte de rage, et tomba le visage sur ses mains crispées. Elle resta ainsi jusqu'à l'heure où sa mère s'éveillait. La fenêtre était restée ouverte, Pauline n'avait pas senti le froid. Le serin était rentré dans sa cage et chantait de toutes ses forces.

III

Un an s'était écoulé depuis le passage de Laurence à Saint-Front, et l'on y parlait encore de la mémorable soirée où la célèbre actrice avait reparu avec tant d'éclat parmi ses concitoyens ; car on se tromperait grandement si l'on supposait que les préventions de la province sont difficiles à vaincre. Quoi qu'on dise à cet égard, il n'est point de séjour où la bienveillance soit plus aisée à conquérir, de même qu'il n'en est pas où elle soit plus facile à perdre. On dit ailleurs que le temps est un grand maître ; il faut dire en province que c'est l'ennui qui modifie, qui justifie tout. Le premier choc d'une nouveauté quelconque contre les habitudes d'une petite ville est certainement terrible, si l'on y songe la veille ; mais, le lendemain, on reconnaît que ce n'était rien, et que mille curiosités inquiètes n'attendaient qu'un premier exemple pour se lancer dans la carrière des innovations. Je connais certains chefs-lieux de canton où la première femme qui se permit de galoper sur une selle anglaise fut traitée de cosaque en jupons[1], et où, l'année suivante, toutes les dames de l'endroit voulurent avoir équipage d'amazone jusqu'à la cravache inclusivement.

À peine Laurence fut-elle partie, qu'une prompte et universelle réaction s'opéra dans les esprits. Chacun voulait justifier l'empressement qu'il avait mis à la voir en grandissant la réputation de l'actrice, ou du moins en ouvrant de plus en plus les yeux sur son mérite réel. Peu à peu on en vint à se disputer l'honneur de lui avoir parlé le premier, et ceux qui n'avaient pu se résoudre à l'aller voir prétendirent qu'ils y avaient fortement poussé les autres. Cette année-là, une diligence fut établie de Saint-Front à Mont-Laurent, et plusieurs personnages importants de la ville (de ces gens qui possèdent quinze mille francs de rente au soleil, et qui ne se déplacent pas aisément, parce que, sans eux, à les entendre, le pays retomberait dans la barbarie) se risquèrent enfin à faire le voyage de la capitale. Ils revinrent tous remplis de la gloire de Laurence, et fiers d'avoir pu dire à leurs voisins du balcon ou de la première galerie, au moment où la salle *croulait*, comme on dit, sous les applaudissements : « Monsieur, cette grande actrice a longtemps habité la ville que j'habite. C'était

---

1. « Voilà par quel concours de circonstances toutes naturelles j'arrivai à scandaliser effroyablement les commères mâles et femelles de la ville de La Châtre, rappelle Sand dans *Histoire de ma vie* (IVe partie, chap. 5). À cette époque, aucune femme du pays ne se permettait de monter à cheval, si ce n'est en croupe de son *valet* des champs. Le costume, non seulement de garçon pour les courses à pied, mais encore l'amazone et le chapeau rond étaient une abomination […]. »

l'amie intime de ma femme. Elle dînait quasi tous les jours *à la maison*. Oh ! nous avions bien deviné son talent ! je vous assure que, quand elle nous récitait des vers, nous nous disions entre nous : "Voilà une jeune personne qui peut aller loin !" » Puis, quand ces personnes furent de retour à Saint-Front, elles racontèrent avec orgueil qu'elles avaient été rendre leur devoir à la grande actrice, qu'elles avaient dîné à sa table, qu'elles avaient passé la soirée dans son magnifique salon… Ah ! quel salon ! quels meubles ! quelles peintures ! et quelle société amusante et honorable ! des artistes, des députés ; monsieur un tel, le peintre de portraits ; madame une telle, la cantatrice ; et puis des glaces, et puis de la musique… Que sais-je ? la tête en tournait à tous ceux qui entendaient ces beaux récits, et chacun de s'écrier : « Je l'avais toujours dit qu'elle réussirait ! Nul autre que moi ne l'avait devinée. »

Toutes ces puérilités eurent un seul résultat sérieux, ce fut de bouleverser l'esprit de la pauvre Pauline, et d'augmenter son ennui jusqu'au désespoir. Je ne sais si quelques semaines de plus n'eussent pas empiré son état au point de lui faire négliger sa mère. Mais celle-ci fit une grave maladie qui ramena Pauline au sentiment de ses devoirs. Elle recouvra tout à coup sa force morale et physique, et soigna la triste aveugle avec un admirable dévouement. Son amour et son zèle ne purent la sauver. Madame D… expira dans ses bras environ quinze mois après l'époque où Laurence était passée à Saint-Front.

Depuis ce temps, les deux amies avaient entretenu une correspondance assidue de part et d'autre. Tandis qu'au milieu de sa vie active et agitée, Laurence aimait à songer à Pauline, à pénétrer en esprit dans sa paisible et sombre demeure, à s'y reposer du bruit de la foule auprès du fauteuil de l'aveugle et des géraniums de la fenêtre, Pauline, effrayée de la monotonie de ses habitudes, éprouvait l'invincible besoin de secouer cette mort lente qui s'étendait sur elle, et de s'élancer en rêve dans le tourbillon qui emportait Laurence. Peu à peu le ton de supériorité morale que, par un noble orgueil, la jeune provinciale avait gardé dans ses premières lettres avec la comédienne, fit place à un ton de résignation douloureuse qui, loin de diminuer l'estime de son amie, la toucha profondément. Enfin les plaintes s'exhalèrent du cœur de Pauline, et Laurence fut forcée de se dire, avec une sorte de consternation, que l'exercice de certaines vertus paralyse l'âme des femmes, au lieu de la fortifier. « Qui donc est heureux, demanda-t-elle un soir à sa mère en posant sur son bureau une lettre qui portait la trace des larmes de Pauline ; et où faut-il aller chercher le repos de l'âme ? Celle qui me plaignait tant au début de ma vie d'artiste se plaint aujourd'hui de sa réclusion d'une manière déchirante, et me trace un si horrible tableau des ennuis de la solitude, que je suis presque tentée de me croire heureuse sous le poids du travail et des émotions. »

Lorsque Laurence reçut la nouvelle de la mort de l'aveugle, elle tint conseil avec sa mère, qui était une personne fort sensée, fort aimante, et qui avait eu le bon esprit de demeurer la meilleure amie de sa fille. Elle voulut la détourner d'un projet qu'elle caressait depuis quelque temps : celui de se charger de l'existence de Pauline en lui faisant partager la sienne aussitôt qu'elle serait libre. « Que deviendra cette pauvre enfant désormais ? disait Laurence. Le devoir qui l'attachait à sa mère est accompli. Aucun mérite religieux ne viendra plus ennoblir et poétiser sa vie. Cet odieux séjour d'une petite ville n'est pas fait pour elle. Elle sent vivement toutes choses, son intelligence cherche à se développer. Qu'elle vienne donc près de nous ; puisqu'elle a besoin de vivre, elle vivra.

— Oui, elle vivra par les yeux, répondit madame S..., la mère de Laurence ; elle verra les merveilles de l'art, mais son âme n'en sera que plus inquiète et plus avide.

— Eh bien ! reprit l'actrice, vivre par les yeux lorsqu'on arrive à comprendre ce qu'on voit, n'est-ce pas vivre par l'intelligence ? et n'est-ce pas de cette vie que Pauline est altérée ?

— Elle le dit, repartit madame S... Elle te trompe, elle se trompe elle-même. C'est par le cœur qu'elle demande à vivre, la pauvre fille !

— Eh bien ! s'écria Laurence, son cœur ne trouvera-t-il pas un aliment dans l'affection du mien ? Qui l'aimerait dans sa petite ville comme je l'aime ? Et, si l'amitié ne suffit pas, croyez-vous qu'elle ne trouvera pas autour de nous un homme digne de son amour ? »

La bonne madame S... secoua la tête.

« Elle ne voudra pas être aimée en artiste », dit-elle avec un sourire dont sa fille comprit la mélancolie.

L'entretien fut repris le lendemain. Une nouvelle lettre de Pauline annonçait que la modique fortune de sa mère allait être absorbée par d'anciennes dettes que son père avait laissées, et qu'elle voulait payer à tout prix et sans retard. La patience des créanciers avait fait grâce à la vieillesse et aux infirmités de madame D… ; mais sa fille, jeune et capable de travailler pour vivre, n'avait pas droit aux mêmes égards. On pouvait, sans trop rougir, la dépouiller de son mince héritage. Pauline ne voulait ni attendre la menace, ni implorer la pitié ; elle renonçait à la succession de ses parents et allait essayer de monter un petit atelier de broderie.

Ces nouvelles levèrent tous les scrupules de Laurence et imposèrent silence aux sages prévisions de sa mère. Toutes deux montèrent en voiture, et, huit jours après, elles revinrent à Paris avec Pauline.

Ce n'était pas sans quelque embarras que Laurence avait offert à son amie de l'emmener et de se charger d'elle à jamais. Elle s'attendait bien à trouver chez elle un reste de préjugés et de dévotion ; mais la vérité est que Pauline n'était pas réellement pieuse. C'était une âme fière et jalouse de sa propre dignité. Elle trouvait dans le catholicisme la nuance qui convenait à son caractère, car toutes les nuances possibles se trouvent dans les religions vieillies ; tant de siècles les ont modifiées, tant d'hommes ont mis la main à l'édifice, tant d'intelligences, de passions et de vertus y ont apporté leurs trésors, leurs erreurs ou leurs lumières, que mille doctrines se trouvent à la fin contenues dans une seule, et mille natures diverses y peuvent puiser l'excuse ou le stimulant qui leur convient. C'est par là que ces religions s'élèvent, c'est aussi par là qu'elles s'écroulent.

Pauline n'était pas douée des instincts de douceur, d'amour et d'humilité qui caractérisent les natures vraiment évangéliques. Elle était si peu portée à l'abnégation, qu'elle s'était toujours trouvée malheureuse, immolée qu'elle était à ses devoirs. Elle avait besoin de sa propre estime, et peut-être aussi de celle d'autrui, bien plus que de l'amour de Dieu et du bonheur du prochain. Tandis que Laurence, moins forte et moins orgueilleuse, se consolait de toutes privations et de tout sacrifice en voyant sourire sa mère, Pauline reprochait à la sienne, malgré elle et dans le fond de son cœur, cette longue satisfaction conquise à ses dépens. Ce ne fut donc pas un sentiment d'austérité religieuse qui la fit hésiter à accepter l'offre de son amie, ce fut la crainte de n'être pas assez dignement placée auprès d'elle.

D'abord Laurence ne la comprit pas, et crut que la peur d'être blâmée par les esprits rigides la retenait encore. Mais ce n'était pas là non plus le motif de Pauline. L'opinion avait changé autour d'elle ; l'amitié de la grande actrice n'était plus une honte, c'était un honneur. Il y avait désormais une sorte de gloire à se vanter de son attention et de son souvenir. La nouvelle apparition qu'elle fit à Saint-Front fut un triomphe bien supérieur au premier. Elle fut obligée de se défendre des hommages importuns que chacun aspirait à lui rendre, et la préférence exclusive qu'elle montrait à Pauline excita mille jalousies dont Pauline put s'enorgueillir.

Au bout de quelques heures d'entretien, Laurence vit qu'un scrupule de délicatesse empêchait Pauline d'accepter ses bienfaits. Laurence ne comprit pas trop cet excès de fierté qui craint d'accepter le poids de la reconnaissance ; mais elle le respecta, et se fit humble jusqu'aux larmes, pour vaincre cet orgueil de la pauvreté, qui serait la plus laide chose du monde si tant d'insolences protectrices n'étaient là pour le justifier. Pauline devait-elle craindre cette insolence de la part de Laurence ? Non ; mais elle ne pouvait s'empêcher de trembler un peu, et Laurence, quoiqu'un peu blessée de cette méfiance, se promit et se flatta de la vaincre bientôt. Elle en triompha du moins momentanément, grâce à cette éloquence du cœur dont elle avait le don ; et Pauline, touchée, curieuse, entraînée, posa un pied tremblant sur le seuil de cette vie nouvelle, se promettant de revenir sur ses pas au premier mécompte qu'elle y rencontrerait.

Les premières semaines que Pauline passa à Paris furent calmes et charmantes. Laurence avait été assez gravement malade pour obtenir, il y avait déjà deux mois, un congé qu'elle consacrait à des études consciencieuses. Elle occupait avec sa mère un joli petit hôtel au milieu de jardins où le

bruit de la ville n'arrivait qu'à peine, et où elle re-
cevait peu de monde. C'était la saison où chacun
est à la campagne, où les théâtres sont peu
brillants, où les vrais artistes aiment à méditer et à
se recueillir. Cette jolie maison, simple, mais décorée avec un goût parfait, ces habitudes élégantes,
cette vie paisible et intelligente que Laurence avait
su se faire au milieu d'un monde d'intrigue et de
corruption, donnaient un généreux démenti à toutes les terreurs que Pauline avait éprouvées autrefois sur le compte de son amie. Il est vrai que
Laurence n'avait pas toujours été aussi prudente,
aussi bien entourée, aussi sagement posée dans sa
propre vie qu'elle l'était désormais. Elle avait ac-
quis à ses dépens de l'expérience et du discernement, et, quoique bien jeune encore, elle avait été
fort éprouvée par l'ingratitude et la méchanceté.
Après avoir beaucoup souffert, beaucoup pleuré
ses illusions et beaucoup regretté les courageux
élans de sa jeunesse, elle s'était résignée à subir la
vie telle qu'elle est faite ici-bas, à ne rien craindre
comme à ne rien provoquer de la part de l'opinion, à sacrifier souvent l'enivrement des rêves à
la douceur de suivre un bon conseil, l'irritation
d'une juste colère à la sainte joie de pardonner. En
un mot, elle commençait à résoudre, dans l'exercice de son art comme dans sa vie privée, un pro-
blème difficile. Elle s'était apaisée sans se refroidir,
elle se contenait sans s'effacer.

Sa mère, dont la raison l'avait quelquefois irri-
tée, mais dont la bonté la subjuguait toujours, lui
avait été une providence. Si elle n'avait pas été

69

assez forte pour la préserver de quelques erreurs, elle avait été assez sage pour l'en retirer à temps. Laurence s'était parfois égarée, et jamais perdue. Madame S... avait su à propos lui faire le sacrifice apparent de ses principes, et, quoi qu'on en dise, quoi qu'on en pense, ce sacrifice est le plus sublime que puisse suggérer l'amour maternel. Honte à la mère qui abandonne sa fille par la crainte d'être réputée sa complaisante ou sa complice ! Madame S... avait affronté cette horrible accusation, et on ne la lui avait pas épargnée. Le grand cœur de Laurence l'avait compris, et, désormais sauvée par elle, arrachée au vertige qui l'avait un instant suspendue au bord des abîmes, elle eût sacrifié tout, même une passion ardente, même un espoir légitime, à la crainte d'attirer sur sa mère un outrage nouveau.

Ce qui se passait à cet égard dans l'âme de ces deux femmes était si délicat, si exquis et entouré d'un si chaste mystère, que Pauline, ignorante et inexpérimentée à vingt-cinq ans comme une fille de quinze, ne pouvait ni le comprendre, ni le pressentir. D'abord, elle ne songea pas à le pénétrer ; elle ne fut frappée que du bonheur et de l'harmonie parfaite qui régnaient dans cette famille : la mère, la fille artiste et les deux jeunes sœurs, ses élèves (ses filles aussi), car elle assurait leur bien-être à la sueur de son noble front, et consacrait à leur éducation ses plus douces heures de liberté. Leur intimité, leur enjouement à toutes, faisaient un contraste bien étrange avec l'espèce de haine et de crainte qui avaient cimenté l'attachement réciproque de Pauline et de sa mère. Pauline en fit la remarque avec une souffrance intérieure qui n'était pas du remords (elle avait vaincu cent fois la tentation d'abandonner ses devoirs), mais qui ressemblait à de la honte. Pouvait-elle ne pas se sentir humiliée de trouver plus de dévouement et de véritables vertus domestiques dans la demeure élégante d'une comédienne, qu'elle n'avait pu en pratiquer au sein de ses austères foyers ? Que de pensées brûlantes lui avaient fait monter la rougeur au front, lorsqu'elle veillait seule la nuit, à la clarté de sa lampe, dans sa pudique cellule ! et maintenant, elle voyait Laurence couchée sur un divan de sultane, dans son boudoir d'actrice, lisant tout haut des vers de Shakespeare[1] à ses petites sœurs attentives et recueillies, pendant que la mère, alerte encore, fraîche et mise avec goût, préparait leur toilette du lendemain et reposait à la dérobée sur ce beau groupe, si cher à ses entrailles, un regard de béatitude. Là étaient réunis l'enthousiasme d'artiste, la bonté, la poésie, l'affection, et au-dessus planait encore la sagesse, c'est-à-dire le sentiment du beau moral, le respect de soi-même, le courage du cœur. Pauline pensait rêver, elle ne pouvait se décider à croire ce qu'elle voyait ; peut-être y répugnait-elle par la crainte de se trouver inférieure à Laurence.

1. Célébré à l'époque romantique comme le maître de l'esthétique théâtrale moderne, Shakespeare fut particulièrement apprécié par Sand. *Hamlet* et *La Nuit des rois* figurent parmi ses œuvres favorites. Elle composa également pour le théâtre une adaptation de *Comme il vous plaira*.

Pauline devient serviteur (se rendre utile)

Malgré ces doutes et ces angoisses secrètes, Pauline fut admirable dans ses premiers rapports avec de nouvelles existences. Toujours fière dans son indigence, elle eut la noblesse de savoir se rendre utile plus que dispendieuse. Elle refusa avec un stoïcisme extraordinaire chez une jeune provinciale les jolies toilettes que Laurence lui voulait faire adopter. Elle s'en tint strictement à son deuil habituel, à sa petite robe noire, à sa petite collerette blanche, à ses cheveux sans rubans et sans joyaux. Elle s'immisça volontairement dans le gouvernement de la maison, dont Laurence n'entendait, comme elle le disait, que la synthèse, et dont le détail devenait un peu lourd pour la bonne madame S... Elle y apporta des réformes d'économie, sans en diminuer l'élégance et le confortable. Puis, reprenant à de certaines heures ses travaux d'aiguille, elle consacra toutes ses jolies broderies à la toilette des deux petites filles. Elle se fit encore leur sous-maîtresse et leur répétiteur dans l'intervalle des leçons de Laurence. Elle aida celle-ci à apprendre ses rôles en les lui faisant réciter ; enfin elle sut se faire une place à la fois humble et grande au sein de cette famille, et son juste orgueil fut satisfait de la déférence et de la tendresse qu'elle reçut en échange.

Cette vie fut sans nuage jusqu'à l'entrée de l'hiver. Tous les jours, Laurence avait à dîner deux ou trois vieux amis ; tous les soirs, six à huit personnes intimes venaient prendre le thé dans son petit salon et causer agréablement sur les arts, sur la littérature, voire un peu sur la politique et la philosophie sociale. Ces causeries, pleines de charme et d'intérêt entre des personnes distinguées, pouvaient rappeler, pour le bon goût, l'esprit et la politesse, celles qu'on avait, au siècle dernier, chez mademoiselle Verrière[1], dans le pavillon qui fait le coin de la rue Caumartin et du boulevard. Mais elles avaient plus d'animation véritable ; car l'esprit de notre époque est plus profond, et d'assez graves questions peuvent être agitées, même entre les deux sexes, sans ridicule et sans pédantisme. Le véritable esprit des femmes pourra encore consister pendant longtemps à savoir interroger et écouter ; mais il leur est déjà permis de comprendre ce qu'elles écoutent et de vouloir une réponse sérieuse à ce qu'elles demandent.

Le hasard fit que, durant toute cette fin d'automne, la société intime de Laurence ne se composa que de femmes ou d'hommes d'un certain âge, étrangers à toute prétention. Disons, en passant, que ce ne fut pas seulement le hasard qui fit ce choix, mais le goût que Laurence éprouvait et manifestait de plus en plus pour les choses et, partant, pour les personnes sérieuses. Autour d'une femme remarquable, tout tend à s'harmoniser et à prendre la teinte de ses pensées et de ses

1. Dans *Histoire de ma vie* (Ire partie, chap. 2), Sand évoque son arrière-grand-mère, Marie Rainteau (1730-1775), qui se faisait appeler mademoiselle de Verrières. Actrice de son état, elle eut une liaison avec le maréchal Maurice de Saxe ; en 1748, elle accoucha d'une fille, Aurore, grand-mère de Sand, qu'elle fit reconnaître quinze ans plus tard.

sentiments. Pauline n'eut donc pas l'occasion de voir une seule personne qui pût déranger le calme de son esprit ; et ce qui fut étrange, même à ses propres yeux, c'est qu'elle commençait déjà à trouver cette vie monotone, cette société un peu pâle, et à se demander si le rêve qu'elle avait fait du *tourbillon* de Laurence devait n'avoir pas une plus saisissante réalisation. Elle s'étonna de retomber dans l'affaissement qu'elle avait si longtemps combattu dans la solitude ; et, pour justifier vis-à-vis d'elle-même cette singulière inquiétude, elle se persuada qu'elle avait pris dans sa retraite une tendance au spleen que rien ne pourrait guérir.

Mais les choses ne devaient pas durer ainsi. Quelque répugnance que l'actrice éprouvât à rentrer dans le bruit du monde, quelque soin qu'elle prît d'écarter de son intimité tout caractère léger, toute assiduité dangereuse, l'hiver arriva. Les châteaux cédèrent leurs hôtes aux salons de Paris, les théâtres ravivèrent leur répertoire, le public réclama ses artistes privilégiés. Le mouvement, le travail hâté, l'inquiétude et l'attrait du succès envahirent le paisible intérieur de Laurence. Il fallut laisser franchir le seuil du sanctuaire à d'autres hommes que les vieux amis. Des gens de lettres, des camarades de théâtre, des hommes d'État, en rapport par les subventions avec les grandes académies dramatiques, les uns remarquables par le talent, d'autres par la figure et l'élégance, d'autres encore par le crédit et la fortune, passèrent peu à peu d'abord, et puis en foule, devant le rideau sans couleur et sans images où Pauline brûlait de voir le monde de ses rêves se dessiner enfin à ses yeux. Laurence, habituée à ce cortège de la célébrité, ne sentit pas son cœur s'émouvoir. Seulement, sa vie changea forcément de cours, ses heures furent plus remplies, son cerveau plus absorbé par l'étude, ses fibres d'artiste plus excitées par le contact du public. Sa mère et ses sœurs la suivirent, paisibles et fidèles satellites, dans son orbe éblouissant. Mais Pauline !... Ici commença enfin à poindre la vie de son âme et à s'agiter dans son âme le drame de sa vie.

IV

Parmi les jeunes gens qui se posaient en adora-
teurs de Laurence, il y avait un certain Montgenays, qui faisait des vers et de la prose pour son
plaisir, mais qui, soit modestie, soit dédain, ne
s'avouait point homme de lettres. Il avait de l'esprit, beaucoup d'usage du monde, quelque instruction et une sorte de talent. Fils d'un banquier,
il avait hérité d'une fortune considérable, et ne
songeait point à l'augmenter, mais ne se mettait
guère en peine d'en faire un usage plus noble que
d'acheter des chevaux, d'avoir des loges aux théâtres, de bons dîners chez lui, de beaux meubles,
des tableaux et des dettes. Quoique ce ne fût ni un
grand esprit ni un grand cœur, il faut dire à son
excuse qu'il était beaucoup moins frivole et moins
ignare que ne le sont pour la plupart les jeunes
gens riches de ce temps-ci. C'était un homme sans
principes, mais par convenance ennemi du scandale ; passablement corrompu, mais élégant dans
ses mœurs, toutes mauvaises qu'elles fussent ; capable de faire le mal par occasion et non par
goût ; sceptique par éducation, par habitude et par

ton, porté aux vices du monde par manque de bons principes et de bons exemples, plus que par nature et par choix ; du reste, critique intelligent, écrivain pur, causeur agréable, connaisseur et dilettante dans toutes les branches des beaux-arts, protecteur avec grâce, sachant et faisant un peu de tout ; voyant la meilleure compagnie sans ostentation, et fréquentant la mauvaise sans effronterie ; consacrant une grande partie de sa fortune, non à secourir les artistes malheureux, mais à recevoir avec luxe les célébrités. Il était bienvenu partout, et partout il était parfaitement convenable. Il passait pour un grand homme auprès des ignorants, et pour un homme éclairé chez les gens ordinaires. Les personnes d'un esprit élevé estimaient sa conversation par comparaison avec celle des autres riches, et les orgueilleux la toléraient parce qu'il savait les flatter en les raillant. Enfin, ce Montgenays était précisément ce que les gens du monde appellent un homme d'esprit, les artistes, un homme de goût. Pauvre, il eût été confondu dans la foule des intelligences vulgaires ; riche, on devait lui savoir gré de n'être ni un juif[1], ni un sot, ni un maniaque.

Il était de ces gens qu'on rencontre partout, que tout le monde connaît au moins de vue, et qui connaissent chacun par son nom. Il n'était point de société où il ne fût admis, point de théâtre où il

1. L'antisémitisme ordinaire du XIXᵉ siècle utilise le mot de « juif » comme synonyme d'avare. Sand ne fait pas exception sur ce point.

n'eût ses entrées dans les coulisses et dans le foyer des acteurs, point d'entreprise où il n'eût quelques capitaux, point d'administration où il n'eût quelque influence, point de cercle dont il ne fût un des fondateurs et un des soutiens. Ce n'était pas le dandysme qui lui avait servi de clef pour pénétrer ainsi à travers le monde ; c'était un certain savoir-faire, plein d'égoïsme, exempt de passion, mêlé de vanité et soutenu d'assez d'esprit pour faire paraître son rôle plus généreux, plus intelligent et plus épris de l'art qu'il ne l'était en effet.

Sa position l'avait, depuis quelques années déjà, mis en rapport avec Laurence ; mais ce furent d'abord des rapports éloignés, de pure politesse, et, si Montgenays y avait mis parfois de la galanterie, c'était dans la mesure la plus parfaite et la plus convenable. Laurence s'était un peu méfiée de lui d'abord, sachant fort bien qu'il n'est point de société plus funeste à la réputation d'une jeune actrice que celle de certains hommes du monde. Mais, quand elle vit que Montgenays ne lui faisait pas la cour, qu'il venait chez elle assez souvent pour manifester quelque prétention, et qu'il n'en manifestait cependant aucune, elle lui sut gré de cette manière d'être, la prit pour un témoignage d'estime de très bon goût, et, craignant de se montrer prude ou coquette en se tenant sur ses gardes, elle le laissa pénétrer dans son intimité, en reçut avec confiance mille petits services insignifiants qu'il lui rendit avec un empressement respectueux, et ne craignit pas de le nommer parmi ses amis véritables, lui faisant un grand mérite d'être beau, riche, jeune, influent, et de n'avoir aucune fatuité.

La conduite extérieure de Montgenays autorisait cette confiance. Chose étrange cependant, cette confiance le blessait en même temps qu'elle le flattait. Soit qu'on le prît pour l'amant ou pour l'ami de Laurence, son amour-propre était caressé. Mais, lorsqu'il se disait qu'elle le traitait en réalité comme un homme sans conséquence, il en éprouvait un secret dépit, et il lui passait par l'esprit de s'en venger quelque jour.

Le fait est qu'il n'était point épris d'elle. Du moins, depuis trois ans qu'il la voyait de plus en plus intimement, le calme apathique de son cœur n'en avait reçu aucune atteinte. Il était de ces hommes déjà blasés par de secrets désordres, qui ne peuvent plus éprouver de désirs violents que ceux où la vanité est en cause. Lorsqu'il avait connu Laurence, sa réputation et son talent étaient en marche ascendante ; mais ni l'un ni l'autre n'étaient assez constatés pour qu'il attachât un grand prix à sa conquête. D'ailleurs, il avait bien assez d'esprit pour savoir que les avantages du monde n'assurent point aujourd'hui de succès infaillibles. Il apprit et il vit que Laurence avait une âme trop élevée pour céder jamais à d'autres entraînements que ceux du cœur. Il sut, en outre, que, trop insouciante peut-être de l'opinion publique, alors que son âme était envahie par un sentiment généreux, elle redoutait néanmoins et repoussait l'imputation d'être protégée et assistée par un amant. Il s'enquit de son passé, de sa vie intime : il s'assura que tout autre cadeau que celui d'un bouquet serait repoussé d'elle comme un sanglant affront ; et en même temps que ces découvertes lui donnèrent de l'estime pour Laurence, elles éveillèrent en lui la pensée de vaincre cette fierté, parce que cela était difficile et aurait du retentissement. C'était donc dans ce but qu'il s'était glissé dans son intimité, mais avec adresse, et pensant bien que le premier point était de lui ôter toute crainte sur ses intentions.

Pendant ces trois ans, le temps avait marché, et l'occasion de risquer une tentative ne s'était pas présentée. Le talent de Laurence était devenu incontestable, sa célébrité avait grandi, son existence était assurée, et, ce qu'il y avait de plus remarquable, son cœur ne s'était point donné. Elle vivait repliée sur elle-même, ferme, calme, triste parfois, mais résolue à ne plus se risquer à la légère sur l'aile des orages. Peut-être ses réflexions l'avaient-elle rendue plus difficile, peut-être ne trouvait-elle aucun homme digne de son choix... Était-ce dédain, était-ce courage ? Montgenays se le demandait avec anxiété. Quelques-uns se persuadaient qu'il était aimé en secret, et lui demandaient compte, à lui, de son indifférence apparente. Trop adroit pour se laisser pénétrer, Montgenays répondait que le respect enchaînerait toujours en lui la pensée d'être autre chose pour Laurence qu'un ami et un frère. On redisait ces paroles à Laurence, et on lui demandait si sa fierté ne dispenserait jamais ce pauvre Montgenays d'une déclaration qu'il n'aurait jamais l'audace de lui faire. « Je le crois modeste, répondait-elle, mais pas au point de ne pas savoir dire qu'il aime, si jamais il vient à aimer. »

Cette réponse revenait à Montgenays, et il ne savait s'il devait la prendre pour la raillerie du dépit ou pour la douceur de l'indifférence. Sa vanité en était parfois si tourmentée, qu'il était prêt à tout risquer pour le savoir, mais la crainte de tout gâter et de tout perdre le retenait, et le temps s'écoulait sans qu'il vît jour à sortir de ce cercle vicieux où chaque semaine le transportait d'une phase d'espoir à une phase de découragement, et d'une résolution d'hypocrisie à une résolution d'impertinence, sans qu'il lui fût jamais possible de trouver l'heure convenable pour une déclaration qui ne fût pas insensée, ou pour une retraite qui ne fût pas ridicule. Ce qu'il craignait le plus au monde, c'était de prêter à rire, lui qui mettait son amour-propre à jouer un personnage sérieux. La présence de Pauline lui vint en aide, et la beauté de cette jeune fille sans expérience lui suggéra de nouveaux plans sans rien changer à son but.

Il imagina de se conformer à une tactique bien vulgaire, mais qui manque rarement son effet, tant les femmes sont accessibles à une sotte vanité. Il pensa qu'en feignant une velléité d'amour pour Pauline, il éveillerait chez son amie le désir de la supplanter. Absent de Paris depuis plusieurs mois, il fit sa rentrée dans le salon de Laurence un certain soir où Pauline, étonnée, effarouchée de voir le cercle habituel s'agrandir d'heure en heure, commençait à souffrir du peu d'ampleur de sa robe noire et de la raideur de sa collerette. Dans ce cercle, elle remarquait plusieurs actrices toutes jolies ou du moins attrayantes à force d'art ; puis, en se comparant à elles, en se comparant à Laurence même, elle se disait avec raison que sa beauté était plus régulière, plus irréprochable, et qu'un peu de toilette suffirait pour l'établir devant tous les yeux. En passant et repassant dans le salon, selon sa coutume, pour préparer le thé, veiller à la clarté des lampes et vaquer à tous ces petits soins qu'elle avait assumés volontairement sur elle, son mélancolique regard plongeait dans les glaces, et son petit costume de demi-béguine commençait à la choquer. Dans un de ces moments-là, elle rencontra précisément dans la glace le regard de Montgenays, qui observait tous ses mouvements. Elle ne l'avait pas entendu annoncer ; elle l'avait rencontré dans l'antichambre sans le voir lorsqu'il était arrivé. C'était le premier homme d'une belle figure et d'une véritable élégance qu'elle eût encore pu remarquer. Elle en fut frappée d'une sorte de terreur ; elle reporta ses yeux sur elle-même avec inquiétude, trouva sa robe flétrie, ses mains rouges, ses souliers épais, sa démarche gauche. Elle eût voulu se cacher pour échapper à ce regard qui la suivait toujours, qui observait son trouble, et qui était assez pénétrant dans les sentiments d'une donnée vulgaire pour comprendre d'emblée ce qui se passait en elle. Quelques instants après, elle remarqua que Montgenays parlait d'elle à Laurence ; car, tout en s'entretenant à voix basse, leurs regards se portaient sur elle. « Est-ce une première caMériste ou une demoiselle de compagnie que vous avez là ? demanda Montgenays à Laurence, quoiqu'il sût fort bien le roman de Pauline.

— Ni l'une ni l'autre, répondit Laurence. C'est mon amie de province, dont je vous ai souvent parlé. Comment vous plaît-elle ? »

Montgenays affecta de ne pas répondre d'abord, de regarder fixement Pauline ; puis il dit d'un ton étrange que Laurence ne lui connaissait pas, car c'était une intonation mise en réserve depuis longtemps pour faire son effet dans l'occasion : « Admirablement belle, délicieusement jolie !

— En vérité ! s'écria Laurence toute surprise de ce mouvement, vous me rendez bien heureuse de me dire cela ! Venez, que je vous présente à elle. » Et, sans attendre sa réponse, elle le prit par le bras et l'entraîna jusqu'au bout du salon, où Pauline essayait de se faire une contenance en rangeant son métier de broderie. « Permets-moi, ma chère enfant, lui dit Laurence, de te présenter un de mes amis que tu ne connais pas encore, et qui depuis longtemps désire beaucoup te connaître. »

Puis, ayant nommé Montgenays à Pauline, qui, dans son trouble, n'entendit rien, elle adressa la parole à un de ses camarades qui entrait ; et, changeant de groupe, elle laissa Montgenays et Pauline face à face, pour ainsi dire tête à tête, dans le coin du salon.

Jamais Pauline n'avait parlé à un homme aussi bien frisé, cravaté, chaussé et parfumé. Hélas ! on n'imagine pas quel prestige ces minuties de la vie élégante exercent sur l'imagination d'une fille de province. Une main blanche, un diamant à la chemise, un soulier verni, une fleur à la boutonnière, sont des recherches qui ne brillent plus en quelque sorte dans un salon que par leur absence ; mais qu'un commis-voyageur étale ses séductions inouïes dans une petite ville, et tous les regards seront attachés sur lui. Je ne veux pas dire que tous les cœurs voleront au-devant du sien, mais du moins je pense qu'il sera bien sot s'il n'en accapare pas quelques-uns.

Cet engouement puéril ne dura qu'un instant chez Pauline. Intelligente et fière, elle eut bientôt secoué ce reste de *provincialité* ; mais elle ne put se défendre de trouver une grande distinction et un grand charme dans les paroles que Montgenays lui adressa. Elle avait rougi d'être troublée par le seul extérieur d'un homme. Elle se réconcilia avec sa première impression en croyant trouver dans l'esprit de cet homme le même cachet d'élégance dont toute sa personne portait l'empreinte. Puis cette attention particulière qu'il lui accordait, le soin qu'il semblait avoir pris de se faire présenter à elle retirée dans un coin parmi les tasses de Chine et les vases de fleurs, le plaisir timide qu'il paraissait goûter à la questionner sur ses goûts, sur ses impressions et ses sympathies, la traitant de prime abord comme une personne éclairée, capable de tout comprendre et de tout juger, toutes ces coquetteries de la politesse du monde, dont Pauline ne connaissait pas la banalité et la perfidie,

Montgenays n'a pas les intentions sincéres pour Pauline

la réveillèrent de sa langueur habituelle. Elle s'excusa un instant sur son ignorance de toutes choses ; Montgenays parut prendre cette timidité pour une admirable modestie ou pour une méfiance dont il se plaignait d'une façon cafarde. Peu à peu Pauline s'enhardit jusqu'à vouloir montrer qu'elle aussi avait de l'esprit, du goût, de l'instruction. Le fait est qu'elle en avait extraordinairement eu égard à son existence passée, mais qu'au milieu de tous ces artistes brisés à une causerie étincelante, elle ne pouvait éviter de tomber parfois dans le lieu commun. Quoique sa nature distinguée la préservât de toute expression triviale, il était facile de voir que son esprit n'était pas encore sorti tout à fait de l'état de chrysalide. Un homme supérieur à Montgenays n'en eût été que plus intéressé à ce développement ; mais le vaniteux en conçut un secret mépris pour l'intelligence de Pauline, et il décida avec lui-même, dès cet instant, qu'elle ne lui servirait jamais que de jouet, de moyen, de victime, s'il le fallait. *✶*   *✗ "toy"*

Qui eût pu supposer, dans un homme froid et nonchalant en apparence, une résolution si sèche et si cruelle ? Personne, à coup sûr. Laurence, malgré tout son jugement, ne pouvait le soupçonner, et Pauline, moins que personne, ne devait en concevoir l'idée.

Lorsque Laurence se rapprocha d'elle, se souvenant avec sollicitude qu'elle l'avait laissée auprès de Montgenays troublée jusqu'à la fièvre, confuse jusqu'à l'angoisse, elle fut fort surprise de la retrouver brillante, enjouée, animée d'une beauté inconnue, et presque aussi à l'aise que si elle eût passé sa vie dans le monde.

« Regarde donc ton amie de province, lui dit à l'oreille un vieux comédien de ses amis ; n'est-ce pas merveille de voir comme en un instant l'esprit vient aux filles ? »

Laurence fit peu d'attention à cette plaisanterie. Elle ne remarqua pas non plus, le lendemain, que Montgenays était venu lui rendre visite une heure trop tôt, car il savait fort bien que Laurence sortait de la répétition à quatre heures ; et, depuis trois jusqu'à quatre heures, il l'avait attendue au salon, non pas seul, mais penché sur le métier de Pauline.

Au grand jour, Pauline l'avait trouvé fort vieux. Quoiqu'il n'eût que trente ans, son visage portait la flétrissure de quelques excès ; l'on sait que la beauté est inséparable, dans les idées de province, de la fraîcheur et de la santé. Pauline ne comprenait pas encore, et ceci faisait son éloge, que les traces de la débauche pussent imprimer au front une apparence de poésie et de grandeur. Combien d'hommes, dans notre époque de romantisme, ont été réputés penseurs et poètes, rien que pour avoir l'orbite creusée et le front dévasté avant l'âge ! combien ont paru hommes de génie qui n'étaient que malades !

Mais le charme des paroles captiva Pauline encore plus que la veille. Toutes ces insinuantes flatteries que la femme du monde la plus bornée sait apprécier à leur valeur, tombaient dans l'âme aride et flétrie de la pauvre recluse comme une pluie bienfaisante. Son orgueil, trop longtemps privé de satisfactions légitimes, s'épanouissait au souffle dangereux de la séduction, et quelle séduction déplorable ! celle d'un homme parfaitement froid, qui méprisait sa crédulité, et qui voulait en faire un marchepied pour s'élever jusqu'à Laurence !

V

La première personne qui s'aperçut de l'amour insensé de Pauline fut madame S… Elle avait pressenti et deviné, avec l'instinct du génie maternel, le projet et la tactique de Montgenays. Elle n'avait jamais été dupe de son indifférence simulée, et s'était toujours tenue en méfiance de lui, ce qui faisait dire à Montgenays que madame S… était, comme toutes les mères d'artistes, une femme bornée, maussade, fâcheuse au développement de sa fille. Lorsqu'il fit la cour à Pauline, madame S…, emportée par sa sollicitude, craignit que cette ruse n'eût une sorte de succès et que Laurence ne se sentît piquée d'avoir passé inaperçue devant les yeux d'un homme à la mode. Elle n'eût pas dû croire Laurence accessible à ce petit sentiment ; mais madame S…, au milieu de sa sagesse vraiment supérieure, avait de ces enfantillages de mère qui s'effraye hors de raison au moindre danger. Elle craignit le moment où Laurence ouvrirait les yeux sur l'intrigue entamée par Montgenays, et, au lieu d'appeler la raison et la tendresse de sa fille au secours de Pauline, elle essaya seule de dé-

tromper celle-ci et de l'éclairer sur son imprudence.

Mais, quoiqu'elle y mît de l'affection et de la délicatesse, elle fut fort mal accueillie. Pauline était
enivrée ; on lui eût arraché la vie plutôt que la
présomption d'être adorée. La manière un peu
aigre dont elle repoussa les avertissements de madame S… donna un peu d'amertume à celle-ci. Il
y eut quelques paroles échangées où perçaient
d'une part le sentiment de l'infériorité de Pauline,
de l'autre l'orgueil du triomphe remporté sur Laurence. Effrayée de ce qui lui était échappé, Pauline
le confia à Montgenays, qui, plein de joie, s'imagina que madame S… avait été en ceci la confi-
dente et l'écho du dépit de sa fille. Il crut toucher
à son but, et, comme un joueur qui double son en-
jeu, il redoubla d'attentions et d'assiduités auprès
de Pauline. Déjà il avait osé lui faire ce lâche men-
songe d'un amour qu'il n'éprouvait pas. Elle avait
feint de n'y pas croire ; mais elle n'y croyait que
trop, l'infortunée ! Quoiqu'elle se fût défendue
avec courage, Montgenays n'en était pas moins
sûr d'avoir bouleversé profondément tout son être
moral. Il dédaignait le reste de sa victoire, et attendait, pour la remporter ou l'abandonner, que Laurence se prononçât pour ou contre.

Absorbée par ses études et forcée de passer
presque toutes ses journées au théâtre, le matin
pour les répétitions, le soir pour les représenta-
tions du répertoire, Laurence ne pouvait suivre les
progrès que Montgenays faisait dans l'estime de
Pauline. Elle fut frappée, un soir, de l'émotion

avec laquelle la jeune fille entendit Lavallée, le vieux comédien, homme d'esprit, qui avait servi de patron et pour ainsi dire de répondant à Laurence lors de ses débuts, juger sévèrement le caractère et l'esprit de Montgenays. Il le déclara vulgaire entre tous les hommes vulgaires ; et, comme Laurence défendait au moins les qualités de son cœur, Lavallée s'écria : « Quant à moi, je sais bien que je serai contredit ici par tout le monde, car tout le monde lui veut du bien. Et savez-vous pourquoi tout le monde l'aime ? C'est qu'il n'est pas méchant.

— Il me semble que c'est quelque chose, dit Pauline avec intention et en lançant un regard plein d'amertume au vieil artiste, qui était pourtant le meilleur des hommes et qui ne prit rien pour lui de l'allusion.

— C'est moins que rien, répondit-il ; car il n'est pas bon, et voilà pourquoi je ne l'aime pas, si vous voulez le savoir. On n'a jamais rien à espérer et l'on a tout à craindre d'un homme qui n'est ni bon, ni méchant. »

Plusieurs voix s'élevèrent pour défendre Montgenays, et celle de Laurence par-dessus toutes les autres ; seulement, elle ne put l'excuser lorsque Lavallée lui démontra par des preuves que Montgenays n'avait point d'ami véritable, et qu'on ne lui avait jamais vu aucun de ces mouvements de vertueuse colère qui trahissent un cœur généreux et grand. Alors Pauline, ne pouvant se contenir davantage, dit à Laurence qu'elle méritait plus que personne le reproche de Lavallée, en laissant accabler un de ses amis les plus sûrs et les plus dévoués sans indignation et sans douleur. Pauline, en faisant cette sortie étrange, tremblait et cassait son aiguille de tapisserie ; son agitation fut si marquée, qu'il se fit un instant de silence, et tous les yeux se tournèrent vers elle avec surprise. Elle vit alors son imprudence, et essaya de la réparer en blâmant d'une manière générale le train du monde en ces sortes d'affaires. « C'est une chose bien triste à étudier dans ce pays, dit-elle, que l'indifférence avec laquelle on entend déchirer des gens auxquels on ne rougit pourtant pas, un instant après, de faire bon accueil et de serrer la main. Je suis une ignorante, moi, une provinciale sans usage, mais je ne peux m'habituer à cela… Voyons, monsieur Lavallée, c'est à vous de me donner raison ; car me voici précisément dans un de ces mouvements de vertu brutale dont vous reprochez l'absence à monsieur Montgenays. »

En prononçant ces derniers mots, Pauline s'efforçait de sourire à Laurence pour atténuer l'effet de ce qu'elle avait dit, et elle y avait réussi pour tout le monde, excepté pour son amie, dont le regard, plein de sollicitude et de pénétration, surprit une larme au bord de sa paupière. Lavallée donna raison à Pauline, et ce lui fut une occasion de débiter avec un remarquable talent une tirade du *Misanthrope* sur l'ami du genre humain. Il avait la tradition de Fleury[1] pour jouer ce rôle, et il l'aimait tellement, que, malgré lui, il s'était identi-

---

1. Abraham-Joseph Bénard, dit Fleury (1751-1822). Son jeu dramatique sera imité par plusieurs générations d'acteurs.

fié avec le caractère d'Alceste plus que sa nature
ne l'exigeait de lui. Ceci arrive souvent aux artistes : leur instinct les porte à moitié vers un type
qu'ils reproduisent avec amour, le succès qu'ils
obtiennent dans cette création fait l'autre moitié de
l'assimilation, et c'est ainsi que l'art, qui est l'expression de la vie en nous, devient souvent en
nous la vie elle-même.

Lorsque Laurence fut seule le soir avec son amie,
elle l'interrogea avec la confiance que donne une
véritable affection. Elle fut surprise de la réserve et
de l'espèce de crainte qui régnait dans ses réponses,
et elle finit par s'en inquiéter. « Écoute, ma chérie,
lui dit-elle en la quittant, toute la peine que tu
prends pour me prouver que tu ne l'aimes pas me
fait craindre que tu ne l'aimes réellement. Je ne te
dirai pas que cela m'afflige, car je crois Montgenays
digne de ton estime ; mais je ne sais pas s'il t'aime,
et je voudrais en être sûre. Si cela était, il me semble qu'il aurait dû me le dire avant de te le faire entendre. Je suis ta mère, moi ! La connaissance que
j'ai du monde et de ses abîmes me donne le droit et
m'impose le devoir de te guider et de t'éclairer au
besoin. Je t'en supplie, n'écoute les belles paroles
d'aucun homme avant de m'avoir consultée ; c'est
à moi de lire la première dans le cœur qui s'offrira
à toi, car je suis calme, et je ne crois pas que,
lorsqu'il s'agira de Pauline, de la personne que
j'aime le plus au monde après ma mère et mes
sœurs, on puisse être habile à me tromper. »

Ces tendres paroles blessèrent Pauline jusqu'au
fond de l'âme. Il lui sembla que Laurence voulait

une complexe de pouvoir
    sur Pauline

s'élever au-dessus d'elle en s'arrogeant le droit de la diriger. Pauline ne pouvait pas oublier le temps où Laurence lui semblait perdue et dégradée, et où ses prières orgueilleuses montaient vers Dieu comme celle du Pharisien, demandant un peu de pitié pour l'excommuniée rejetée à la porte du temple. Laurence aussi l'avait gâtée comme on gâte un enfant, par trop de tendresse et d'engouement naïf. Elle lui avait trop souvent répété dans ses lettres qu'elle était devant ses yeux comme un ange de lumière et de pureté dont la céleste image la préserverait de toute mauvaise pensée. Pauline s'était habituée à poser devant Laurence comme une madone, et recevoir d'elle désormais un avertissement maternel lui paraissait un outrage. Elle en fut humiliée et même courroucée à ne pouvoir dormir. Cependant le lendemain elle vainquit en elle-même ce mouvement injuste, et la remercia cordialement de sa tendre inquiétude ; mais elle ne put se résoudre à lui avouer ses sentiments pour Montgenays. *Pauline devient l'enfant*

Une fois éveillée, la sollicitude de Laurence ne s'endormit plus. Elle eut un entretien avec sa mère, lui reprocha un peu de ne pas lui avoir dit plus tôt ce qu'elle avait cru deviner, et, respectant la méfiance de Pauline, qu'elle attribuait à un excès de pudeur, elle observa toutes les démarches de Montgenays. Il ne lui fallut pas beaucoup de temps pour s'assurer que madame S... avait deviné juste, et, trois jours après son premier soupçon, elle acquit la certitude qu'elle cherchait. Elle surprit Pauline et Montgenays au milieu d'un tête-

parallele entre Pauline et Jésus
(dans l'histoire du Pharisien)

à-tête fort animé, feignit de ne pas voir le trouble de Pauline, et, dès le soir même, elle fit venir Montgenays dans son cabinet d'étude, où elle lui dit : « Je vous croyais mon ami, et j'ai pourtant un manque d'amitié bien grave à vous reprocher, Montgenays. Vous aimez Pauline, et vous ne me l'avez pas confié. Vous lui faites la cour, et vous ne m'avez pas demandé de vous y autoriser. »

Elle dit ces paroles avec un peu d'émotion, car elle blâmait sérieusement Montgenays dans son cœur, et la marche mystérieuse qu'il avait suivie lui causait quelque effroi pour Pauline. Montgenays désirait pouvoir attribuer ce ton de reproche à un sentiment personnel. Il se composa un maintien impénétrable, et résolut d'être sur la défensive jusqu'à ce que Laurence fît éclater le dépit qu'il lui supposait. Il nia son amour pour Pauline, mais avec une gaucherie volontaire et avec l'intention d'inquiéter de plus en plus Laurence.

Cette absence de franchise l'inquiéta en effet, mais toujours à cause de son amie, et sans qu'elle eût seulement la pensée de mêler sa personnalité à cette intrigue.

Montgenays, tout homme du monde qu'il était, eut la sottise de s'y tromper, et, au moment où il crut avoir enfin éveillé la colère et la jalousie de Laurence, il risqua le coup de théâtre qu'il avait longtemps médité, lui avoua que son amour pour Pauline n'était qu'une feinte vis-à-vis de lui-même, un effort désespéré, inutile peut-être pour s'étourdir sur un chagrin profond, pour se guérir d'une passion malheureuse… Un regard accablant de

Laurence l'arrêta au moment où il allait se perdre et sauver Pauline. Il pensa que le moment n'était pas venu encore, et réserva son grand effet pour une crise plus favorable. Pressé par les sévères questions de Laurence, il se retourna de mille manières, inventa un roman tout en réticences, protesta qu'il ne se croyait pas aimé de Pauline, et se retira sans promettre de l'aimer sérieusement, sans consentir à la détromper, sans rassurer l'amitié de Laurence, et sans pourtant lui donner le droit de le condamner.

Si Montgenays était assez maladroit pour faire une chose hasardée, il était assez habile pour la réparer. Il était de ces esprits tortueux et puérils qui, de combinaison en combinaison, marchent péniblement et savamment vers un *fiasco* misérable. Il sut durant plusieurs semaines tenir Laurence dans une complète incertitude. Elle ne l'avait jamais soupçonné fat et ne pouvait se résoudre à le croire lâche. Elle voyait l'amour et la souffrance de Pauline, et désirait tellement son bonheur, qu'elle n'osait pas la préserver du danger en éloignant Montgenays. « Non, il ne m'adressait pas une impudente insinuation, disait-elle à sa mère, lorsqu'il m'a dit qu'un amour malheureux le tenait dans l'incertitude. J'ai cru un instant qu'il avait cette pensée, mais cela serait trop odieux. Je le crois homme d'honneur. Il m'a toujours témoigné une estime pleine de respect et de délicatesse. Il ne lui serait pas venu à l'esprit tout d'un coup de se jouer de moi et d'outrager mon amie en même temps. Il ne me croirait pas si simple que d'être sa dupe.

— Je le crois capable de tout, répondait madame S… Demandez à Lavallée ce qu'il en pense ; confiez-lui ce qui se passe : c'est un homme sûr, pénétrant et dévoué.

— Je le sais, dit Laurence : je ne puis cependant disposer d'un secret que Pauline refuse de me confier : on n'a pas le droit de trahir un mystère aussi délicat, quand on l'a surpris volontairement ; Pauline en souffrirait mortellement, et, fière comme elle l'est, ne me le pardonnerait de sa vie. D'ailleurs, Lavallée a des préventions exagérées ; il déteste Montgenays ; il ne saurait le juger avec impartialité. Voyez quel mal nous allons faire à Pauline si nous nous trompons ! S'il est vrai que Montgenays l'aime (et pourquoi ne serait-ce pas ? elle est si belle, si sage, si intelligente !), nous tuons son avenir en éloignant d'elle un homme qui peut l'épouser et lui donner dans le monde un rang qu'à coup sûr elle désire ; car elle souffre de nous devoir son existence, vous le savez bien. Sa position l'affecte plus qu'elle ne peut l'avouer ; elle aspire à l'indépendance, et la fortune peut seule la lui donner.

— Et s'il ne l'épouse pas ! reprit madame S… Quant à moi, je crois qu'il n'y songe nullement.

— Et moi, s'écria Laurence, je ne puis croire qu'un homme comme lui soit assez infâme ou assez fou pour croire qu'il obtiendra Pauline autrement.

— Eh bien ! si tu le crois, repartit la mère, essaye de les séparer ; ferme-lui ta porte : ce sera le forcer à se déclarer. Sois sûre que, s'il l'aime, il saura bien vaincre les obstacles et prouver son amour par des offres honorables.

— Mais il a peut-être dit la vérité, reprenait Laurence, en s'accusant d'un amour mal guéri qui l'empêche encore de se prononcer. Cela ne se voit-il pas tous les jours ? Un homme est quelquefois incertain des années entières entre deux femmes dont une le retient par sa coquetterie, tandis que l'autre l'attire par sa douceur et sa bonté. Il arrive un moment où la mauvaise passion fait place à la bonne, où l'esprit s'éclaire sur les défauts de l'ingrate maîtresse et sur les qualités de l'amie généreuse. Aujourd'hui, si nous brusquons l'incertitude de ce pauvre Montgenays, si nous lui mettons le couteau sur la gorge et le marché à la main, il va, ne fût-ce que par dépit, renoncer à Pauline, qui en mourra de chagrin peut-être, et retourner aux pieds d'une perfide qui brisera ou desséchera son cœur, tandis que, si nous conduisons les choses avec un peu de patience et de délicatesse, chaque jour, en voyant Pauline, en la comparant à l'autre femme, il reconnaîtra qu'elle seule est digne d'amour, et il arrivera à la préférer ouvertement. Que pouvons-nous craindre de cette épreuve ? Que Pauline ne l'aime sérieusement ? c'est déjà fait ; qu'elle ne se laisse égarer par lui ? c'est impossible. Il n'est pas homme à le tenter ; elle n'est pas femme à s'y laisser prendre. »

Ces raisons ébranlèrent un peu madame S… Elle fit seulement consentir Laurence à empêcher les tête-à-tête que ses courses et ses occupations rendaient trop faciles et trop fréquents entre Pauline et Montgenays. Il fut convenu que Laurence emmènerait souvent son amie avec elle au théâtre. On devait penser que la difficulté de lui parler augmenterait l'ardeur de Montgenays, tandis que la liberté de la voir entretiendrait son admiration.

Mais ce fut la chose la plus difficile du monde que de décider Pauline à quitter la maison. Elle se renfermait dans un silence pénible pour Laurence, celle-ci était réduite à jouer avec elle un jeu puéril, en lui donnant des raisons dont elle ne la croyait point dupe. Elle lui représentait que sa santé était un peu altérée par les continuels travaux du ménage ; qu'elle avait besoin de mouvement de distraction. On lui fit même ordonnancer par un médecin un système de vie moins sédentaire. Tout échoua contre cette résistance inerte, qui est la force des caractères froids. Enfin Laurence imagina de demander à son amie, comme un service, qu'elle vînt l'aider au théâtre à s'habiller et à changer de costume dans sa loge. La femme de chambre était maladroite, disait-on ; madame S... était souffrante et succombait à la fatigue de cette vie agitée ; Laurence y succombait elle-même. Les tendres soins d'une amie pouvaient seuls adoucir les corvées journalières du métier. Pauline, forcée dans ses derniers retranchements, et poussée d'ailleurs par un reste d'amitié et de dévouement, céda, mais avec une répugnance secrète. Voir de près chaque jour les triomphes de Laurence était une souffrance à laquelle jamais elle n'avait pu s'habituer ; et maintenant cette souffrance devenait plus cuisante. Pauline commençait à pressentir son malheur. Depuis que Montgenays s'était mis en tête l'espérance de réussir auprès de l'actrice, il laissait percer par instants, malgré lui, son dédain pour la provinciale. Pauline ne voulait pas s'éclairer, elle fermait les yeux à l'évidence avec terreur ; mais, en dépit d'elle-même, la tristesse et la jalousie étaient entrées dans son âme.

VI

Montgenays vit les précautions que Laurence prenait pour l'éloigner de Pauline ; il vit aussi la sombre tristesse qui s'emparait de cette jeune fille. Il la pressa de questions ; mais, comme elle était encore avec lui sur la défensive et ne pouvait plus lui parler qu'à la dérobée, il ne put rien apprendre de certain. Seulement il remarqua l'espèce d'autorité que, dans la candeur de son amitié, Laurence ne craignait pas de s'arroger sur son amie, et il remarqua aussi que Pauline ne s'y soumettait qu'avec une sorte d'indignation contenue. Il crut que Laurence commençait à la faire souffrir de sa jalousie ; il ne voulut pas supposer que ses préférences pour une autre pussent laisser Laurence indifférente et loyale.

Il continua à jouer ce rôle fantasque, décousu avec intention, qui devait les laisser toutes deux dans l'incertitude. Il affecta de passer des semaines entières sans paraître devant elles ; puis, tout à coup, il redevenait assidu, se donnait un air inquiet, tourmenté, montrant de l'humeur lorsqu'il était calme, feignant l'indifférence lorsqu'on pou-

she became more + more bitter

vait lui supposer du dépit. Cette irrésolution fatiguait Laurence et désespérait Pauline. Le caractère de cette dernière s'aigrissait de jour en jour. Elle se demandait pourquoi Montgenays, après lui avoir montré tant d'empressement, devenait si nonchalant à vaincre les obstacles qu'on avait mis entre eux. Elle s'en prenait secrètement à Laurence de lui avoir préparé ce désenchantement, et ne voulait pas reconnaître qu'en l'éclairant on lui rendait service. Lorsqu'elle interrogeait Montgenays, d'un air qu'elle essayait de rendre calme, sur ses fréquentes absences, il lui répondait, s'il était seul avec elle, qu'il avait eu des occupations, des affaires indispensables ; mais, si Laurence était présente, il s'excusait sur la simple fantaisie d'un besoin de solitude ou de distraction. Un jour, Pauline lui dit devant madame S…, dont la présence assidue lui était un supplice, qu'il devait avoir une passion dans le grand monde, puisqu'il était devenu si rare dans la société des artistes. Montgenays répondit assez brutalement : « Quand cela serait, je ne vois pas en quoi une personne aussi grave que vous pourrait s'intéresser aux folies d'un jeune homme. »

En cet instant, Laurence entrait dans le salon. Au premier regard, elle vit un sourire douloureux et forcé sur le visage de Pauline. La mort était dans son âme. Laurence s'approcha d'elle et posa la main affectueusement sur son épaule. Pauline, ramenée à un sentiment de tendresse par une souffrance qu'en cet instant du moins elle ne pouvait pas imputer à sa rivale, retourna doucement la tête et effleura de ses lèvres la main de Laurence. Elle semblait lui demander pardon de l'avoir haïe et calomniée dans son cœur. Laurence ne comprit ce mouvement qu'à moitié, et appuya sa main plus fortement, en signe de profonde sympathie, sur l'épaule de la pauvre enfant. Alors Pauline, dévorant ses larmes et faisant un nouvel effort : « J'étais, dit-elle en crispant de nouveau ses traits pour sourire, en train de reprocher à *votre ami* l'abandon où il vous laisse. »

L'œil scrutateur de Laurence se porta sur Montgenays, il prit ce regard de sévère équité pour un élan de colère féminine, et, se rapprochant d'elle : « Vous en plaignez-vous, madame ? dit-il avec une expression qui fit tressaillir Pauline.

— Oui, je m'en plains, répondit Laurence d'un ton plus sévère encore que son regard.

— Eh bien, cela me console de ce que j'ai souffert loin de vous », dit Montgenays en lui baisant la main.

Laurence sentit frissonner Pauline.

« Vous avez souffert ? dit madame S…, qui voulait pénétrer dans l'âme de Montgenays ; ce n'est pas ce que vous disiez tout à l'heure. Vous nous parliez de *folies de jeune homme* qui vous auraient un peu étourdi sur les chagrins de l'absence.

— Je me prêtais à la plaisanterie que vous m'adressiez, répondit Montgenays. Laurence ne s'y fût pas trompée. Elle sait bien qu'il n'est plus de folies, plus de légèretés de cœur possibles à l'homme qu'elle honore de son estime. »

En parlant ainsi, son œil brillait d'un feu qui donnait à ses paroles un sens fort opposé à celui d'une paisible amitié. Pauline épiait tous ses mouvements ; elle vit ce regard, et elle en fut atteinte jusqu'au cœur. Elle pâlit et repoussa la main de Laurence par un mouvement brusque et hautain. Laurence eut un moment de surprise. Elle interrogea des yeux sa mère, qui lui répondit par un signe d'intelligence. Au bout d'un instant, elles sortirent sous un léger prétexte, et, enlaçant leurs bras l'une à l'autre, firent quelques tours de promenade sur la terrasse du jardin. Laurence commençait enfin à pénétrer le mystère d'iniquité dont s'enveloppait le lâche amant de Pauline. « Ce que je crois deviner, dit-elle à sa mère avec agitation, me bouleverse. J'en suis indignée, je n'ose y croire encore.

— Il y a longtemps que j'en ai la conviction, répondit madame S… Il joue une odieuse comédie ; mais ses prétentions s'élèvent jusqu'à toi, et Pauline est sacrifiée à ses orgueilleux projets.

— Eh bien ! répondit Laurence, je détromperai Pauline ; pour cela, il me faut une certitude ; je le laisserai s'avancer, et je le dévoilerai quand il sera pris au piège. Puisqu'il veut engager avec moi une intrigue de théâtre si vulgaire et si connue, je le combattrai par les mêmes moyens, et nous verrons lequel de nous deux sait le mieux jouer la comédie. Je n'aurais jamais cru qu'il voulût se mettre en concurrence avec moi, lui dont ce n'est pas la profession.

— Prends garde ! dit madame S... ; tu t'en feras un ennemi mortel, et un ennemi littéraire, qui plus est.

— Puisqu'il faut toujours avoir des ennemis dans le journalisme, reprit Laurence, que m'importe un de plus ? Mon devoir est de préserver Pauline, et, pour qu'elle ne souffre pas l'idée d'une trahison de ma part, je vais, avant tout, l'avertir de mes desseins.

— Ce sera le moyen de les faire avorter, répondit madame S... Pauline est plus engagée avec lui que tu ne penses. Elle souffre, elle aime, elle est folle. Elle te haïra quand tu l'auras fait.

— Eh bien ! qu'elle me haïsse s'il le faut, dit Laurence en laissant échapper quelques larmes ; j'aime mieux supporter cette douleur que de la voir devenir victime d'une infamie.

— En ce cas, attends-toi à tout : mais, si tu veux réussir, ne l'avertis pas. Elle préviendrait Montgenays, et tu te compromettrais avec lui en pure perte. »

Laurence écouta les conseils de sa mère. Lorsqu'elle rentra au salon, Pauline et Montgenays avaient échangé aussi quelques mots qui avaient rassuré la malheureuse dupe. Pauline était rayonnante ; elle embrassa son amie d'un air où perçaient la haine et l'ironie du triomphe. Laurence renferma le chagrin mortel qu'elle en ressentit, et comprit tout à fait le jeu que jouait Montgenays.

Ne voulant pas s'abaisser à donner une espérance positive à ce misérable, elle imita son air et ses manières, et s'enferma dans un système de bizarreries mystérieuses. Elle joua tantôt la mélancolie inquiète d'un amour méconnu, tantôt la gaieté forcée d'une résolution courageuse. Puis elle semblait retomber dans de profonds découragements. Incapable d'échanger avec Montgenays un regard provoquant, elle prenait le temps où elle était observée par lui et où Pauline avait le dos tourné, pour la suivre des yeux avec l'impatience d'une feinte jalousie. Enfin, elle fit si bien le personnage d'une femme au désespoir, mais fière jusqu'à préférer la mort à l'humiliation d'un refus, que Montgenays transporté oublia son rôle, et ne songea plus qu'à deviner celui qu'elle avait pris. Sa vanité l'interprétait suivant ses désirs, mais il n'osait encore se risquer, car Laurence ne pouvait se décider à provoquer clairement une déclaration de sa part. Excellente artiste qu'elle était, il lui était impossible de représenter parfaitement un personnage sans vraisemblance, et elle disait un jour à Lavallée, que, malgré elle, sa mère avait mis dans la confidence (il avait, d'ailleurs, tout deviné de lui-même) : « J'ai beau faire, je suis mauvaise dans ce rôle. C'est comme quand je joue une mauvaise pièce, je ne puis me mettre dans la situation. Il te souvient que, quand nous étions en scène avec ce pauvre Mélidor, qui disait si tranquillement les choses du monde les plus passionnées, nous évitions de nous regarder pour ne pas rire. Eh bien ! avec ce Montgenays, c'est absolument de même ; quand tu es là que mes yeux rencontrent les tiens, je suis au moment d'éclater ; alors, pour me conserver un air triste, il faut que je pense au malheur de Pauline, et ceci me remet en scène naturellement, mais à mes dépens, car mon cœur saigne. Ah ! je ne savais pas que la comédie fût plus fatigante à jouer dans le monde que sur les planches !

— Il faudra que je t'aide, répondit Lavallée ; car je vois bien que, seule, tu ne viendras jamais à bout de faire tomber son masque. Repose-toi sur moi du soin de le forcer dans ses derniers retranchements sans te compromettre sérieusement. »

Un soir, Laurence joua Hermione dans la tragédie d'*Andromaque*. Il y avait longtemps que le public attendait sa rentrée dans cette pièce. Soit qu'elle l'eût bien étudiée récemment, soit que la vue d'un auditoire nombreux et brillant l'électrisât plus qu'à l'ordinaire, soit enfin qu'elle eût besoin de jeter dans ce bel ouvrage toute la verve et tout l'art qu'elle employait si désagréablement depuis quinze jours avec Montgenays, elle y fut magnifique, et y eut un succès tel qu'elle n'en avait point encore obtenu au théâtre. Ce n'était pas tant le génie que la réputation de Laurence qui la rendait si désirable à Montgenays. Les jours où elle était fatiguée et où le public se montrait un peu froid pour elle, il s'endormait plus tranquillement, dans la pensée qu'il pouvait échouer dans son entreprise ; mais, lorsqu'on la rappelait sur la scène et qu'on lui jetait des couronnes, il ne dormait point et passait la nuit à machiner ses plans de séduction. Ce soir-là, il assistait à la représentation, dans une petite loge sur le théâtre, avec Pauline, madame S… et Lavallée. Il était si agité des applaudissements frénétiques que recueillait la belle tragédienne, qu'il ne songeait pas seulement à la présence de Pauline. Deux ou trois fois il la froissa avec ses coudes (on sait que ces loges sont fort étroites) en battant des mains avec emportement. Il désirait que Laurence le vît, l'entendît par-dessus tout le bruit de la salle ; et Pauline s'étant plainte avec aigreur de ce que son empressement à applaudir l'empêchait d'entendre les derniers mots de chaque réplique, il lui dit brutalement : « Qu'avez-vous besoin d'entendre ? Est-ce que vous comprenez cela, vous ? »

Il y avait des moments où, malgré ses habitudes de diplomatie, Montgenays ne pouvait réprimer un dédain grossier pour cette malheureuse fille. Il ne l'aimait point, quelles que fussent sa beauté et les qualités réelles de son caractère, et il s'indignait en lui-même de l'aplomb crédule de cette petite bourgeoise, qui croyait effacer à ses yeux l'éclat de la grande actrice ; et lui aussi était fatigué, dégoûté de son rôle. Quelque méchant qu'on soit, on ne réussit guère à faire le mal avec plaisir. Si ce n'est le remords, c'est la honte qui paralyse souvent les ressources de la perversité.

Pauline se sentit défaillir. Elle garda le silence ; puis, au bout d'un instant, elle se plaignit de ne pouvoir supporter la chaleur ; elle se leva et sortit. La bonne madame S…, qui la plaignait sincèrement, la suivit et la conduisit dans la loge de Laurence, où Pauline tomba sur le sofa et perdit connaissance. Tandis que madame S… et la femme de chambre de Laurence la délaçaient et tâchaient de la ranimer, Montgenays, incapable de songer au mal qu'il lui avait fait, continuait à admirer et à applaudir la tragédienne. Lorsque l'acte fut fini, Lavallée s'empara de lui, et, se composant le visage le plus sincère que jamais l'artifice du comédien ait porté sur la scène : « Savez-vous, lui dit-il, que jamais notre Laurence n'a été plus étonnante qu'aujourd'hui ? Son regard, sa voix, ont pris un éclat que je ne leur connaissais pas. Cela m'inquiète.

— Comment donc ? reprit Montgenays. Craindriez-vous que ce ne fût l'effet de la fièvre ?

— Sans aucun doute ; ceci est une vigueur fébrile, reprit Lavallée. Je m'y connais ; je sais qu'une femme délicate et souffrante comme elle l'est n'arrive point à de tels effets sans une excitation funeste. Je gagerais que Laurence est en défaillance durant tout l'entracte. C'est ainsi que cela se passe chez ces femmes dont la passion fait toute la force.

— Allons la voir ! dit Montgenays en se levant.

— Non pas, répondit Lavallée en le faisant rasseoir avec une solennité dont il riait en lui-même. Ceci ne serait guère propre à calmer ses esprits.

— Que voulez-vous dire ? s'écria Montgenays.

— Je ne veux rien dire », répondit le comédien de l'air d'un homme qui craint de s'être trahi.

Ce jeu dura pendant tout l'entracte. Montgenays ne manquait pas de méfiance, mais il manquait de pénétration. Il avait trop de fatuité pour voir qu'on le raillait. D'ailleurs, il avait affaire à trop forte partie, et Lavallée se disait en lui-même : « Oui-da ! tu veux te frotter à un comédien qui, pendant cinquante ans, a fait rire et pleurer le public sans seulement sortir ses mains de ses poches ! tu verras ! »

À la fin de la soirée, Montgenays avait la tête perdue. Lavallée, sans lui dire une seule fois qu'il était aimé, lui avait fait entendre de mille manières qu'il l'était passionnément. Aussitôt que Montgenays s'y laissait prendre ouvertement, il feignait de vouloir le détromper, mais avec une gaucherie si adroite, que le mystifié s'enferrait de plus en plus. Enfin, durant le cinquième acte, Lavallée alla trouver madame S… « Emmenez coucher Pauline, lui dit-il ; faites-vous accompagner de la femme de chambre, et ne la renvoyez à votre fille qu'un quart d'heure après la fin du spectacle. Il faut que Montgenays ait un tête-à-tête avec Laurence dans sa loge. Le moment est venu ; il est à nous : je serai là, caché derrière la psyché ; je ne quitterai pas votre fille d'un instant. Allez, et fiez-vous à moi. »

Les choses se passèrent comme il l'avait prévu, et le hasard les seconda encore. Laurence, rentrant dans sa loge, appuyée sur le bras de Montgenays, et n'y trouvant personne (Lavallée était déjà caché derrière le rideau qui couvrait les costumes accrochés à la muraille, et la glace le masquait en outre), demanda où étaient sa mère et son amie. Un garçon de théâtre qui passait dans le couloir, et à qui elle adressa cette question, lui répondit (et cela était malheureusement vrai) qu'on avait été forcé

109

d'emmener mademoiselle D…, qui avait des convulsions. Laurence ne savait pas la scène que lui ménageait Lavallée ; d'ailleurs, elle l'eût oubliée en apprenant cette triste nouvelle. Son cœur se serra, et, l'idée des souffrances de son amie se joignant à la fatigue et aux émotions de la soirée, elle tomba sur son siège et fondit en larmes. C'est alors que l'impertinent Montgenays, se croyant le maître et le tourment de ces deux femmes, perdit toute prudence, et risqua la déclaration la plus désordonnée et la plus froidement délirante qu'il eût faite de sa vie. C'était Laurence qu'il avait toujours aimée, disait-il ; c'était elle seule qui pouvait l'empêcher de se tuer ou de faire quelque chose de pis, un suicide moral, un mariage de dépit. Il avait tout tenté pour se guérir d'une passion qu'il ne croyait pas partagée, il s'était jeté dans le monde, dans les arts, dans la critique, dans la solitude, dans un nouvel amour ; mais rien n'avait réussi. Pauline était assez belle pour mériter son admiration ; mais, pour sentir autre chose pour elle qu'une froide estime, il eût fallu ne pas voir sans cesse Laurence à côté d'elle. Il *savait* bien qu'il était dédaigné, et dans son désespoir, ne voulant pas faire le malheur de Pauline en la trompant davantage il allait s'éloigner pour jamais !... En annonçant cette humble résolution, il s'enhardit jusqu'à saisir une main de Laurence, qui la lui arracha avec horreur. Un instant elle fut transportée d'une telle indignation, qu'elle allait le confondre ; mais Lavallée, qui voulait qu'elle eût des preuves, s'était glissé jusqu'à la porte, qu'il avait à dessein recouverte d'un pan de rideau jeté là comme par hasard. Il feignit d'arriver, frappa, toussa et entra brusquement. D'un coup d'œil, il contint la juste colère de l'actrice, et, tandis que Montgenays le donnait au diable, il parvint à l'emmener, sans lui laisser le temps de savoir l'effet qu'il avait produit. La femme de chambre arriva, et, tandis qu'elle rhabillait sa maîtresse, Lavallée se glissa auprès d'elle et en deux mots l'informa de ce qui s'était passé. Il lui dit de faire la malade et de ne point recevoir Montgenays le lendemain ; puis il retourna auprès de celui-ci et le reconduisit chez lui, où il s'installa jusqu'au matin, lui montant toujours la tête et s'amusant tout seul, avec un sérieux vraiment comique, de tous les romans qu'il lui suggérait. Il ne sortit de chez lui qu'après lui avoir persuadé d'écrire à Laurence ; et à midi il y retourna et voulut lire cette lettre que Montgenays, en proie à une insomnie délirante, avait déjà faite et refaite cent fois. Le comédien feignit de la trouver trop timide, trop peu explicite.

« Soyez sûr, lui dit-il, que Laurence doutera de vous encore longtemps ; votre fantaisie pour Pauline a dû lui inspirer une inquiétude que vous aurez de la peine à détruire. Vous savez l'orgueil des femmes ; il faut sacrifier la provinciale et vous exprimer clairement sur le peu de cas que vous en faites. Vous pouvez arranger cela sans manquer à la galanterie. Dites que Pauline est un ange peut-être, mais qu'une femme comme Laurence est plus qu'un ange ; dites ce que vous savez si bien écrire dans vos nouvelles et dans vos saynètes. Al-

VII

Huit jours se passèrent sans que Montgenays pût être reçu chez Laurence et sans qu'il osât demander compte à Lavallée de ce silence et de cette consigne, tant il était honteux de l'idée d'avoir fait une école[1], et tant il craignait d'en acquérir la certitude.

Pendant qu'elles étaient ainsi enfermées, Pauline et Laurence étaient en proie aux orages intérieurs. Laurence avait tout fait pour amener son amie à un épanchement de cœur qu'il lui avait été impossible d'obtenir. Plus elle cherchait à la dégoûter de Montgenays, plus elle irritait sa souffrance sans hâter la crise favorable dont elle espérait son salut. Pauline s'offensait des efforts qu'on faisait pour lui arracher le secret de son âme. Elle avait vu les ruses de Laurence pour forcer Montgenays à se trahir, et les avait interprétées comme Montgenays lui-même. Elle en voulait donc mortellement à son

1. Vx. Terme de tric-trac : oublier de marquer les points qu'on gagne ; plus généralement, commettre une erreur telle que l'on est digne de retourner à l'école.

amie d'avoir essayé et réussi à lui enlever l'amour
d'un homme que, jusqu'à ces derniers temps, elle
avait cru sincère. Elle attribuait cette conduite de
Laurence à une odieuse fantaisie suggérée par l'ambition de voir tous les hommes à ses pieds. « Elle a
eu besoin, se disait-elle, d'y attirer même celui qui
lui était le plus indifférent, dès qu'elle l'a vu s'adresser à moi. Je lui suis devenue un objet de mépris et
d'aversion dès qu'elle a pu supposer que j'étais re-
marquée, fût-ce par un seul homme, à côté d'elle.
De là son indiscrète curiosité et son espionnage
pour deviner ce qui se passait entre lui et moi ; de
là tous les efforts qu'elle fait maintenant pour l'empêcher de me voir ; de là enfin l'odieux succès
qu'elle a obtenu à force de coquetteries, et le lâche
triomphe qu'elle a remporté sur moi en boulever-
sant un homme faible que sa gloire éblouit et que
ma tristesse ennuie. »

Pauline ne voulait pas accuser Montgenays d'un
plus grand crime que celui d'un entraînement involontaire. Trop fière pour persévérer dans un
amour mal récompensé, elle ne souffrait déjà plus
que de l'humiliation d'être délaissée ; mais cette
douleur était la plus grande qu'elle pût ressentir.
Elle n'était pas douée d'une âme tendre, et la colère faisait plus de ravages en elle que le regret.
Elle avait d'assez nobles instincts pour agir et penser noblement au sein même des erreurs où l'en-
traînait l'orgueil blessé. Ainsi elle croyait Laurence
odieuse à son égard ; et dans cette pensée, qui
par elle-même était une déplorable ingratitude, elle
n'avait pourtant ni le sentiment ni la volonté d'être

ingrate. Elle se consolait en s'élevant dans son esprit au-dessus de sa rivale et en se promettant de lui laisser le champ libre, sans bassesse et sans ressentiment. « Qu'elle soit satisfaite, se disait-elle, qu'elle triomphe, je le veux bien. Je me résigne à lui servir de trophée, pourvu qu'elle soit forcée un jour de me rendre justice, d'admirer ma grandeur d'âme, d'apprécier mon inaltérable dévouement, et de rougir de ses perfidies ! Montgenays ouvrira les yeux aussi, et saura quelle femme il a sacrifiée à l'éclat d'un nom. Il s'en repentira, et il sera trop tard ; je serai vengée par l'éclat de ma vertu. »

Il est des âmes qui ne manquent pas d'élévation, mais de bonté. On aurait tort de confondre dans le même arrêt celles qui font le mal par besoin et celles qui le font malgré elles, croyant ne pas s'écarter de la justice. Ces dernières sont les plus malheureuses ; elles vont toujours cherchant un idéal qu'elles ne peuvent trouver, car il n'existe pas sur la terre, et elles n'ont point en elles ce fonds de tendresse et d'amour qui fait accepter l'imperfection de l'être humain. On peut dire de ces personnes qu'elles sont affectueuses et bonnes seulement quand elles rêvent.

Pauline avait un sens très droit et un véritable amour de la justice ; mais entre la théorie et la pratique il y avait comme un voile qui couvrait son discernement : c'était cet amour-propre immense, que rien n'avait jamais contenu, que tout, au contraire, avait contribué à développer. Sa beauté, son esprit, sa belle conduite envers sa mère, la pureté de ses mœurs et de ses pensées, étaient sans cesse

l'exemple de "Bovarysme" même si "Madame Bovary" vient après cet texte là devant elle comme des trésors lentement amassés dont on devait sans cesse lui rappeler la valeur pour l'empêcher d'envier ceux d'autrui ; car elle voulait être quelque chose, et plus elle affectait de se rejeter dans la condition du vulgaire, plus elle se révoltait contre l'idée d'y être rangée. Il eût été heureux pour elle qu'elle pût descendre en elle-même avec la clairvoyance que donne une profonde sagesse ou une généreuse simplicité de cœur ; elle y eût découvert que ses vertus bourgeoises avaient bien eu quelque tache, que son christianisme n'avait pas toujours été fort chrétien, que sa tolérance passée envers Laurence n'avait jamais été aussi complète, aussi cordiale qu'elle se l'était imaginé ; elle y eût vu surtout un besoin tout personnel qui la poussait à vivre autrement qu'elle n'avait vécu, à se développer, à se manifester. C'était un besoin légitime et qui fait partie des droits sacrés de l'être humain ; mais il n'y avait pas lieu de s'en faire une vertu, et c'est toujours un grand tort de se donner le change pour se grandir à ses propres yeux. De là à la vanité d'abuser les autres sur son propre mérite, il n'y a qu'un pas, et, ce pas, Pauline l'avait fait. Il lui était impossible de revenir en arrière et de consentir à n'être plus qu'une simple mortelle, après s'être laissé diviniser.

Ne voulant pas donner à Laurence la joie de l'avoir humiliée, elle affecta la plus grande indifférence et endura sa douleur avec stoïcisme. Cette tranquillité, dont Laurence ne pouvait être dupe, car elle la voyait dépérir, l'effrayait et la désespérait. Elle ne voulait pas se résoudre à lui porter le dernier coup en lui prouvant la honteuse infidélité de Montgenays ; elle aimait mieux endurer l'accusation tacite de l'avoir séduit et enlevé. Elle n'avait pas voulu recevoir la lettre de Montgenays. Lavallée lui en avait dit le contenu, et elle l'avait prié de la garder chez lui toute cachetée pour s'en servir auprès de Pauline au besoin ; mais combien elle eût voulu que cette lettre fût adressée à une autre femme ! Elle savait bien que Pauline haïssait la cause plus que l'auteur de son infortune.

Un jour, Lavallée, en sortant de chez Laurence, rencontra Montgenays, qui, pour la dixième fois, venait de se faire refuser la porte. Il était outré, et, perdant toute mesure, il accabla le vieux comédien de reproches et de menaces. Celui-ci se contenta d'abord de hausser les épaules ; mais, quand il entendit Montgenays étendre ses accusations jusqu'à Laurence, et, se plaignant d'avoir été joué, éclater en menaces de vengeance, Lavallée, homme de droiture et de bonté, ne put contenir son indignation. Il le traita comme un misérable, et termina en lui disant : « Je regrette en cet instant plus que jamais d'être vieux ; il semble que les cheveux blancs soient un prétexte pour empêcher qu'on ne se batte, et vous croiriez que j'abuse du privilège pour vous outrager sans conséquence ; mais j'avoue que, si j'avais vingt ans de moins, je vous donnerais des soufflets.

— La menace suffit pour être une lâcheté, répondit Montgenays pâle de fureur, et je vous renvoie l'outrage. Si j'avais vingt ans de plus, en fait de soufflets j'aurais l'initiative.

— Eh bien ! s'écria Lavallée, prenez garde de me pousser à bout ; car je pourrais bien me mettre au-dessus de tout remords comme de toute honte en vous faisant un outrage public, si vous vous permettiez la moindre méchanceté contre une personne dont l'honneur m'est beaucoup plus cher que le mien. »

Montgenays, rentré chez lui et revenu de sa colère, pensa avec raison que toute vengeance qui aurait du retentissement tournerait contre lui ; et, après avoir bien cherché, il en inventa une plus odieuse que toutes les autres : ce fut de renouer à tout prix son intrigue avec Pauline, afin de la détacher de Laurence. Il ne voulut pas être humilié par deux défaites à la fois. Il pensa bien qu'après le premier orage ces deux femmes feraient cause commune pour le railler ou le mépriser. Il aima mieux se faire haïr et perdre l'une, afin d'effrayer et d'affliger l'autre.

Dans cette pensée, il écrivit à Pauline, lui jura un éternel amour, et protesta contre les trames ignobles que, selon lui, Lavallée et Laurence auraient ourdies contre eux. Il demandait une explication, promettant de ne jamais reparaître devant Pauline si elle ne le trouvait complètement justifié après cette entrevue. Il la fallait secrète, car Laurence voulait les séparer. Pauline alla au rendez-vous ; son orgueil et son amour avaient également besoin de consolation.

Lavallée, qui observait tout ce qui se passait dans la maison, surprit le message de Montgenays. Il le laissa passer, résolu à ne pas abandonner Pauline à son mauvais dessein, et, dès cet instant, il ne la perdit pas de vue ; il la suivit comme elle sortait le soir, seule à pied, pour la première fois de sa vie, et si tremblante, qu'à chaque pas elle se sentait défaillir. Au détour de la première rue, il se présenta devant elle et lui offrit son bras. Pauline se crut insultée par un inconnu, elle fit un cri et voulut fuir.

« Ne crains rien, ma pauvre enfant, lui dit Lavallée d'un ton paternel ; mais vois à quoi tu t'exposes d'aller ainsi seule la nuit. Allons, ajouta-t-il en passant le bras de Pauline sous le sien, tu veux faire une folie ! au moins fais-la convenablement. Je te conduirai, moi ; je sais où tu vas, je ne te perdrai pas de vue. Je n'entendrai rien, vous causerez, je me tiendrai à distance, et je te ramènerai. Seulement, rappelle-toi que, si Montgenays se doute le moins du monde que je suis là, ou si tu essayes de sortir de la portée de ma vue, je tombe sur lui à coups de canne. »

Pauline n'essaya pas de nier. Elle était foudroyée de l'assurance de Lavallée ; et, ne sachant comment s'expliquer sa conduite, préférant, d'ailleurs, toutes les humiliations à celle d'être trahie par son amant, elle se laissa conduire machinalement et à demi égarée jusqu'au parc de Monceaux, où Montgenays l'attendait dans une allée. Le comédien se cacha parmi les arbres, et les suivit de l'œil tandis que Pauline, docile à ses avertissements, se promenait avec Montgenays sans se laisser perdre de vue, et sans vouloir lui expliquer l'obstination qu'elle mettait à ne pas aller plus loin. Il attribua cette persistance à une pruderie bourgeoise qu'il trouva fort ridicule, car il n'était pas assez sot pour débuter par de l'audace. Il se composa un maintien grave, une voix profonde, des discours pleins de sentiment et de respect. Il s'aperçut bientôt que Pauline ne connaissait ni la malheureuse déclaration ni la fâcheuse lettre, et, dès cet instant, il eut beau jeu pour prévenir les desseins de Laurence. Il feignit d'être en proie à un repentir profond et d'avoir pris des résolutions sérieuses ; il arrangea un nouveau roman, se confessa d'un ancien amour pour Laurence, qu'il n'avait jamais osé avouer à Pauline, et qui de temps en temps s'était réveillé malgré lui, même lorsqu'il était aux genoux de cette aimable fille, si pure, si douce, si humble, si supérieure à l'orgueilleuse actrice. Il avait cédé à des séductions terribles, à des avances délirantes, et, dernièrement encore, il avait été assez fou, assez ennemi de sa propre dignité, de son propre bonheur, pour adresser à Laurence une lettre qu'il désavouait, qu'il détestait, et dont cependant il devait la révélation textuelle à Pauline. Il lui répéta cette lettre mot à mot, insista sur ce qu'elle avait de plus coupable, de moins pardonnable, disait-il, ne voulant pas de grâce, se soumettant à sa haine, à son oubli, mais ne voulant pas mériter son mépris. « Jamais Laurence ne vous montrera cette lettre, lui dit-il ; elle a trop provoqué mon retour vers elle pour vous fournir cette preuve de sa coquetterie ; je n'avais donc rien à craindre de ce côté, mais je n'ai pas voulu vous perdre sans vous faire savoir que j'accepte mon arrêt avec soumission, avec repentir, avec désespoir. Je veux que vous sachiez bien que je me rétracte, et voici une nouvelle lettre que je vous prie de faire tenir à Laurence. Vous verrez comme je la juge, comme je la traite, comme je la méprise, elle ! cette femme orgueilleuse et froide qui ne m'a jamais aimé et qui voulait être adorée éternellement. Elle a fait le malheur de ma vie, non pas seulement parce qu'elle a déjoué toutes les espérances qu'elle m'avait données, mais encore parce qu'elle m'a empêché de m'attacher à vous comme je le devais, comme je le pouvais, comme je le pourrais encore, si vous pouviez me pardonner ma lâcheté, mon crime et ma folie. Partagé entre deux amours, l'un orageux, dévorant, funeste, l'autre pur, céleste, vivifiant, j'ai trahi celui qui eût relevé mon âme pour celui qui la tue. Je suis un misérable, mais non un scélérat. Ne voyez en moi qu'un homme affaibli et vaincu par les longues souffrances d'une passion déplorable ; mais sachez bien que je ne survivrai pas à mes remords : votre pardon eût seul été capable de me sauver. Je ne puis l'implorer, car je sais que je ne le mérite pas. Vous me voyez tranquille, parce que je sais que je ne souffrirai pas longtemps. Ne craignez pas de m'accorder au moins quelque pitié ; vous entendrez dire bientôt que je vous ai fait justice. Vous avez été outragée, il vous faut un vengeur. Le coupable, c'est moi ; le vengeur, ce sera moi encore. »

Pendant deux heures entières, Montgenays tint de tels discours à Pauline. Elle fondait en larmes ;

elle lui pardonna, elle lui jura d'oublier tout, le supplia de ne pas se tuer, lui défendit de s'éloigner, et lui promit de le revoir, fallût-il se brouiller avec Laurence : Montgenays n'en espérait pas tant et n'en demandait pas davantage.

Lavallée la ramena. Elle ne lui adressa pas une parole durant le chemin. Sa tranquillité n'étonna point le vieux comédien ; il pensa bien que Montgenays n'avait pas manqué de belles paroles et de robustes mensonges pour la calmer. Il pensa qu'elle était perdue s'il n'employait les grands moyens. Avant de la quitter, à la porte de Laurence, il glissa dans sa poche la première lettre de Montgenays, qui n'avait pas encore été décachetée.

Laurence fut fort surprise le soir, au moment de se coucher, de voir entrer dans sa chambre, d'un air calme et avec des manières affectueuses, Pauline, qui, depuis huit jours, ne lui avait adressé que des paroles sèches et ironiques. Elle tenait une lettre qu'elle lui remit, en lui disant que c'était Lavallée qui l'en avait chargée. En reconnaissant l'écriture et le cachet de Montgenays, Laurence pensa que Lavallée avait eu quelque bonne raison pour la charger de ce message, et que le moment était venu de porter aux grands maux le grand remède. Elle ouvrit la lettre d'une main tremblante, la parcourant des yeux, hésitant encore à la faire connaître à son amie, tant elle en prévoyait l'effet terrible.

Quelle fut sa stupéfaction en lisant ce qui suit :

« Laurence, je vous ai trompée ; ce n'est pas vous que j'aime, c'est Pauline ; ne m'accusez pas, je me suis trompé moi-même, tout ce que je vous ai dit, je le pensais en cet instant-là ; l'instant d'après, et maintenant, et toujours, je le désavoue. C'est votre amie que j'adore et à qui je voudrais consacrer ma vie, si elle pouvait oublier mes bizarreries et mes incertitudes. Vous avez voulu m'égarer, m'abuser, me faire croire que vous pouviez, que vous vouliez me rendre heureux ; vous n'y eussiez pas réussi, car vous n'aimez pas, et, moi, j'ai besoin d'une affection vraie, profonde, durable. Pardonnez-moi donc ma faiblesse comme je vous pardonne votre caprice. Vous êtes grande, mais vous êtes femme ; je suis sincère, mais je suis homme ; au moment de commettre une grande faute, qui eût été de nous tromper mutuellement, nous avons réfléchi et nous nous sommes ravisés tous deux, n'est-ce pas ? mais je suis prêt à mettre aux pieds de votre amie le dévouement de toute ma vie, et vous, vous êtes décidée à me permettre de lui faire ma cour assidûment, si elle-même ne me repousse pas. Croyez qu'en vous conduisant avec franchise et avec noblesse, vous aurez en moi un ami fidèle et sûr. »

Laurence resta confondue ; elle ne pouvait comprendre une telle impudence. Elle mit la lettre dans son bureau sans témoigner rien de sa surprise. Mais Pauline croyait lire au-dedans de son âme, et s'indignait des mauvaises intentions qu'elle lui supposait. « Il y avait une lettre outrageante contre moi, se disait-elle en se retirant dans sa chambre, et on me l'a remise ; en voici une qu'on suppose devoir me consoler, et on ne me la remet pas. » Elle s'endormit pleine de mépris pour son amie, et, dans la joie dont son âme était inondée, le plaisir de se savoir enfin si supérieure à Laurence empêchait l'amitié trahie de placer un regret. L'infortunée triomphait lorsque elle-même venait de coopérer avec une sorte de malice à sa propre ruine.

Le lendemain, Laurence commenta longuement cette lettre avec Lavallée. Le hasard ou l'habitude avait fait qu'elle était absolument conforme, pour le pli et le cachet, à celle que Montgenays avait écrite sous les yeux de Lavallée. On demanda à Pauline si elle n'avait pas eu deux lettres semblables dans sa poche lorsqu'elle avait remis celle-ci à Laurence. Triomphant en elle-même de leur désappointement, elle joua l'étonnement, prétendit ne rien comprendre à cette question, ne pas savoir de qui était la lettre, ni pourquoi ni comment on l'avait glissée dans sa poche. L'autre était déjà retournée entre les mains de Montgenays. Dans sa joie insensée, Pauline, voulant lui donner un grand et romanesque témoignage de confiance et de pardon, la lui avait envoyée sans l'ouvrir.

Laurence voulait encore croire à une sorte de loyauté de la part de Montgenays. Lavallée ne pouvait s'y tromper. Il lui raconta le rendez-vous où il avait conduit Pauline et se le reprocha. Il avait compté qu'au sortir d'une entrevue où Montgenays aurait menti impudemment, l'effet de la lettre sur Pauline serait décisif. Il ne pouvait s'ex-

elle contribue énormement à sa propre victimization

pliquer encore comment Pauline avait si merveilleusement aidé sa perversité à triompher de tous les obstacles. Laurence ne voulait pas croire qu'elle aussi s'entendît à l'intrigue et y prît une part si funeste à sa dignité.

Que pouvait faire Laurence ? Elle tenta un dernier effort pour dessiller les yeux de son amie. Celle-ci, éclatant enfin et refusant de croire à d'autres éclaircissements que ceux que Montgenays lui avait donnés, lui déchira le cœur par l'amertume de ses reproches et le dédain triomphant de son illusion. Laurence fut forcée de lui adresser quelques avertissements sévères qui achevèrent de l'exaspérer ; et, comme Pauline lui déclarait qu'elle était indépendante, majeure, maîtresse de ses actions, et nullement disposée à se laisser enchaîner par les volontés arbitraires d'une personne qui l'avait indignement trompée, elle fut forcée de lui dire qu'elle ne pouvait donner les mains à sa perte, et qu'elle ne se pardonnerait jamais de tolérer dans sa maison, dans le sein de sa famille, les entreprises d'un corrupteur et d'un lâche. « Je réponds de toi devant Dieu et devant les hommes, lui dit-elle ; si tu veux te jeter dans un abîme, je ne veux pas, moi, t'y pousser.

— C'est pourquoi votre dévouement a été si loin, répondit Pauline, que de vouloir vous y jeter vous-même à ma place. »

Outrée de cette injustice et de cette ingratitude, Laurence se leva, jeta un regard terrible sur Pauline et, craignant de laisser déborder le torrent de sa colère, elle lui montra la porte avec un geste et une expression de visage dont elle fut terrifiée. Jamais la tragédienne n'avait été plus belle, même lorsqu'elle disait, dans *Bajazet*, son impérieux et magnifique *Sortez*[1] *!*

Lorsqu'elle fut seule, elle se promena dans sa chambre comme une lionne dans sa cage, brisant ses vases étrusques, ses statuettes, froissant ses vêtements et arrachant presque ses beaux cheveux noirs. Tout ce qu'elle avait de grandeur, de sincérité, de véritable tendresse dans l'âme, venait d'être méconnu et avili par celle qu'elle avait tant aimée, et pour qui elle eût donné sa vie ! Il est des colères saintes où Jéhovah est en nous, et où la terre tremblerait, si elle sentait ce qui se passe dans un grand cœur outragé. La petite sœur de Laurence entra, crut qu'elle étudiait un rôle, la regarda quelques instants sans rien dire, sans oser remuer ; puis, s'effrayant de la voir si pâle et si terrible, elle alla dire à madame S... : « Maman, va donc voir Laurence ; elle se rendra malade à force de travailler. Elle m'a fait peur. »

Madame S... courut auprès de sa fille. Dès que Laurence la vit, elle se jeta dans ses bras et fondit en larmes. Au bout d'une heure, ayant réussi à s'apaiser, elle pria sa mère d'aller chercher Pauline. Elle voulait lui demander pardon de sa violence, afin d'avoir occasion de lui pardonner elle-

---

1. Adressé par Roxane à Bajazet, le mot conclut la scène 4 de l'acte V de la pièce « turque » de Racine, représentée pour la première fois en 1672.

même. On chercha Pauline dans toute la maison, dans le jardin, dans la rue… On revint dans sa chambre avec effroi. Laurence examinait tout, elle cherchait les traces d'une évasion ; elle frémissait d'y trouver celles d'un suicide. Elle était dans un état impossible à rendre, lorsque Lavallée entra et lui dit qu'il venait de rencontrer Pauline dans un fiacre sur les boulevards. On attendit son retour avec anxiété : elle ne rentra pas pour dîner. Personne ne put manger ; la famille était consternée ; on craignait de faire un outrage à Pauline en la supposant en fuite. Enfin, Lavallée allait s'informer d'elle chez Montgenays, au risque d'une scène orageuse, lorsque Laurence reçut une lettre ainsi conçue :

« Vous m'avez chassée, je vous en remercie ; il y avait longtemps que le séjour de votre maison m'était odieux ; j'avais senti, dès le premier jour, qu'il me serait funeste. Il s'y était passé trop de scandales et d'orages pour qu'une âme paisible et honnête n'y fût pas flétrie ou brisée. Vous m'avez assez avilie ! vous avez fait de moi votre servante, votre dupe et votre victime ! Je n'oublierai jamais le jour où, dans votre loge au théâtre, trouvant que je ne vous habillais pas assez vite, vous m'avez arraché des mains votre diadème de reine, en disant : "Je me couronnerai bien sans toi et malgré toi !" Vous vous êtes couronnée en effet ! Mes larmes, mon humiliation, ma honte, mon déshonneur (car vous m'avez déshonorée dans votre famille et parmi vos amis), ont été les glorieux

la nuance dans leur relation
une narratrice infiable
(unreliable narrator)

127

fleurons de votre couronne ; mais c'est une royauté de théâtre, une majesté fardée, qui n'en impose qu'à vous-même et au public qui vous paie. Maintenant, adieu ; je vous quitte pour jamais, dévorée de la honte d'avoir vécu de vos bienfaits ; je les ai payés cher... »

Laurence n'acheva pas cette lettre ; elle continuait sur ce ton pendant quatre pages : Pauline y avait versé le fiel amassé lentement durant quatre ans de rivalité et de jalousie. Laurence la froissa dans ses mains et la jeta au feu sans vouloir en lire davantage. Elle se mit au lit avec la fièvre, et y resta huit jours, accablée, brisée jusque dans ses entrailles, qui avaient été pour Pauline celles d'une mère et d'une sœur.

Pauline s'était retirée dans une mansarde où elle vécut cachée et vivant misérablement du fruit de son travail durant quelques mois. Montgenays n'avait pas été long à la découvrir ; il la voyait tous les jours, mais il ne put vaincre aisément son stoïcisme. Elle voulait supporter toutes les privations plutôt que de lui devoir un secours. Elle repoussa avec horreur les dons que Laurence faisait glisser dans sa mansarde avec les détours les plus ingénieux. Tout fut inutile. Pauline, qui refusait les offres de Montgenays avec calme et dignité, devinait celles de Laurence avec l'instinct de la haine, et les lui renvoyait avec l'héroïsme de l'orgueil. Elle ne voulut point la voir, quoique Laurence fît mille tentatives ; elle lui renvoyait ses lettres toutes cachetées. Son ressentiment fut inébranlable, et la généreuse sollicitude de Laurence ne fit que lui donner de nouvelles forces.

Comme elle n'aimait pas réellement Montgenays, et qu'elle n'avait voulu que triompher de Laurence en se l'attachant, cet homme sans cœur, qui voulait en faire sa maîtresse ou s'en débarrasser, lui mit presque le marché à la main. Elle le chassa. Mais il lui fit croire que Laurence lui avait pardonné, et qu'il allait retourner chez elle. Aussitôt elle le rappela, et c'est ainsi qu'il la tint sous son empire pendant six mois encore. Il s'attachait à elle de son côté par la difficulté de vaincre sa vertu ; mais il en vint à bout par un odieux moyen bien conforme à son système, et malheureusement bien propre à émouvoir Pauline. Il se condamna à lui dire tous les jours et à toute heure que Laurence était devenue vertueuse par calcul, afin de se faire épouser par un homme riche ou puissant. La régularité des mœurs de Laurence, qu'on remarquait depuis plusieurs années, avait été souvent, dans les mauvais mouvements de Pauline, un sujet de dépit. Elle l'eût voulue désordonnée, afin d'avoir une supériorité éclatante sur elle. Mais Montgenays réussit à lui montrer les choses sous un nouveau jour. Il s'attacha à lui démontrer qu'en se refusant à lui, elle s'abaissait au niveau de Laurence, dont la tactique avait été de se faire désirer pour se faire épouser. Il lui fit croire qu'en s'abandonnant à lui avec dévouement et sans arrière-pensée, elle donnerait au monde un grand exemple de passion, de désintéressement et de grandeur d'âme. Il le lui redit si souvent, que la

129

malheureuse fille finit par le croire. Pour faire le contraire de Laurence, qui était l'âme la plus généreuse et la plus passionnée, elle fit les actes de la passion et de la générosité, elle qui était froide et prudente. Elle se perdit.

Quand Montgenays l'eut rendue mère et que toute cette aventure eut fait beaucoup de bruit, il l'épousa par ostentation. Il avait, comme on sait, la prétention d'être excentrique, moral par principes, quoique, selon lui, il fût roué par excès d'habileté et de puissance sur les femmes. Il fit parler de lui tant qu'il put. Il dit du mal de Laurence, de Pauline et de lui-même, et se laissa accuser et blâmer avec constance, afin d'avoir l'occasion de produire un grand effet en donnant son nom et sa fortune à l'enfant de son amour.

Ce plat roman se termina donc par un mariage, et ce fut là le plus grand malheur de Pauline. Montgenays ne l'aimait déjà plus, si tant est qu'il l'eût jamais aimée. Quand il avait joué la comédie d'un admirable époux devant le monde, il laissait pleurer sa femme derrière le rideau, et allait à ses affaires ou à ses plaisirs sans se souvenir seulement qu'elle existât. Jamais femme plus vaine et plus ambitieuse de gloire ne fut plus délaissée, plus humiliée, plus effacée. Elle revit Laurence, espérant la faire souffrir par le spectacle de son bonheur. Laurence ne s'y trompa point, mais elle lui épargna la douleur de paraître clairvoyante. Elle lui pardonna tout, et oublia tous ses torts, pour n'être touchée que de ses souffrances. Pauline ne

130

put jamais lui pardonner d'avoir été aimée de Montgenays, et fut jalouse d'elle toute sa vie.

Beaucoup de vertus tiennent à des facultés négatives. Il ne faut pas les estimer moins pour cela. La rose ne s'est pas créée elle-même ; son parfum n'en est pas moins suave parce qu'il émane d'elle sans qu'elle en ait conscience ; mais il ne faut pas trop s'étonner si la rose se flétrit en un jour, si les grandes vertus domestiques s'altèrent vite sur un théâtre pour lequel elles n'avaient pas été créées.

Paris

la Rose = Pauline ♡

des épines,

quand la Rose a quitté sa place, son jardin, elle est morte

un sens de justice parce que Pauline est misérable dans son mariage → ce n'était pas sa faut (elle était du province)...?

une rose qui ne dure pas longtemps

ANNEXE

NOTICE DE 1852

Le projet d'œuvres complètes chez l'éditeur Michel Lévy en 1852 poussa George Sand à reprendre l'ensemble de ses publications et à rédiger des notices pour celles qui n'en comprenaient pas. Celle qu'elle rédigea pour Pauline *rappelle les circonstances singulières de sa rédaction.*

J'avais commencé ce roman en 1832, à Paris, dans une mansarde où je me plaisais beaucoup. Le manuscrit s'égara : je crus l'avoir jeté au feu par mégarde, et comme, au bout de trois jours, je ne me souvenais déjà plus de ce que j'avais voulu faire (ceci n'est pas mépris de l'art ni légèreté à l'endroit du public, mais infirmité véritable), je ne songeai point à recommencer. Au bout de dix ans environ, en ouvrant un *in-quarto* à la campagne, j'y retrouvai la moitié d'un volume manuscrit intitulé *Pauline*. J'eus peine à reconnaître mon écriture, tant elle était meilleure que celle d'aujourd'hui. Est-ce que cela ne vous est pas souvent arrivé à vous-même, de retrouver toute la spontanéité de votre jeunesse et tous les souvenirs du passé dans la netteté d'une majuscule et dans le laisser-aller d'une ponctuation ? Et les fautes d'orthographe que tout le monde fait, et dont on se corrige tard, quand on s'en corrige, est-ce qu'elles ne repassent pas quelquefois sous vos yeux comme de vieux visages amis ? En relisant ce manuscrit, la mémoire de la première donnée me revint aussitôt, et j'écrivis le reste sans incertitude.

Sans attacher aucune importance à cette courte peinture de l'esprit provincial, je ne crois pas avoir faussé les caractères donnés par les situations ; et la morale du conte, s'il faut en trouver une, c'est que l'extrême gêne et l'extrême souffrance sont un terrible milieu pour la jeunesse et la beauté. Un peu de goût, un peu d'art, un peu de poésie ne seraient point incompatibles, même au fond des provinces, avec les vertus austères de la médiocrité ; mais il ne faut pas que la médiocrité touche à la détresse ; c'est là une situation que ni l'homme ni la femme, ni la vieillesse ni la jeunesse, ni même l'âge mûr, ne peuvent regarder comme le développement normal de la destinée providentielle.

30 mars 1852

G. S.

Appendices

Éléments biographiques

1804. En juillet, naissance à Paris d'Amantine-Aurore-Lucile Dupin, fille de Maurice Dupin, lieutenant de chasseurs à cheval, et de Sophie Delaborde. L'un et l'autre parents d'enfants illégitimes, les jeunes gens viennent de régulariser une liaison de plusieurs années.

1808. En juillet, arrivée de la famille à Nohant après un séjour à Madrid où Maurice Dupin a suivi les armées de Murat. En septembre, mort du petit Louis, âgé de quelques mois, puis de Maurice Dupin d'une chute de cheval. Quelques mois plus tard, afin de conserver sa petite-fille, la mère de Maurice propose à Sophie un marché : sur la promesse d'une belle pension, elle est invitée à regagner Paris et à laisser à la grand-mère de l'enfant le soin de son éducation à Nohant. Aurore recevra d'abord un enseignement assez libre sous la houlette de Deschartres qui a été le précepteur de son père ; en 1818, elle sera placée comme pensionnaire au couvent des Dames anglaises à Paris où elle restera près de deux ans.

1821. Mort de Mme Dupin, née Marie-Aurore de Saxe. Sa petite-fille hérite de tous ses biens, dont une imposante « maison de campagne » du XVIII⁰ siècle à Nohant et deux cents hectares de terres. L'année suivante, Aurore Dupin épouse Casimir Dudevant. Maurice naît en 1823, Solange en 1828 (Stéphane Ajasson de Grandsagne en est vraisemblablement le père).

1831. Après quelques voyages et de nombreuses querelles, Aurore Dudevant obtient de son mari d'aller vivre à Paris une partie de l'année. Elle y suit son amant, Jules Sandeau, avec lequel elle commence à écrire des romans et à publier des articles dans le journal satirique *Figaro*.

1832. En mai, publication d'*Indiana*, écrit à Nohant pendant l'hiver. Le roman est signé « G. Sand ». Le succès est immédiat et considérable. La même année, rédaction inachevée de *Pauline* ; publication de *Valentine* et d'une nouvelle, *La Marquise*.

Dans les années qui suivent, George Sand va publier un grand nombre de romans, nouvelles et articles. Sa route va croiser celle de Marie Dorval fin 1832, de Musset en 1833, puis de Chopin en 1838 (elle partagera son existence pendant neuf ans) ; les époux Dudevant se sont séparés en 1836. George Sand se liera notamment d'amitié avec Franz Liszt et Marie d'Agoult, la cantatrice Pauline Garcia, Félicité de Lamennais et Eugène Delacroix. À partir des années 1840, elle prend une part plus active aux débats politiques. Avec ses amis Pierre Leroux et Louis Viardot, elle fonde *La Revue indépendante* en 1841 puis finance la création de *L'Éclaireur de l'Indre*, journal d'opposition. Publication du *Compagnon du Tour de France*, du *Meunier d'Angibault*, du *Péché de Monsieur Antoine*.

1848. En février, George Sand est appelée à Paris par ses amis républicains dont Lamartine, Louis Blanc et Armand Barbès. Elle participe aux *Bulletins de la République*, publie à ses frais plusieurs brochures et lance *La Cause du peuple*. En mai, déçue par la tournure que prennent les événements, elle regagne Nohant. Elle revient alors à ses « bergeries », romans champêtres dans lesquels elle exprime ses idées politiques tout en travaillant à la constitution d'un Berry utopique : *La Mare au Diable*, *La Petite Fadette*, *François le Champi*, *Les Maîtres Sonneurs*.

1852. Sous le Second Empire, l'activité de George Sand se diversifie. Si elle continue à publier des romans, elle s'intéresse aussi au théâtre, au théâtre de société et aux marionnettes. Nohant, où elle réside désormais la plupart du temps, devient un lieu d'intense création artistique, parfois en collaboration. Flaubert, Tourgueniev, les Viardot, Alexandre Dumas fils, le prince Napoléon, Pierre Bocage et Eugène Fromentin y séjournent. George Sand rédige son autobiographie (*Histoire de ma vie*), compose notamment des romans « psychologiques » (*La Filleule*, *La Confession d'une jeune fille*) ou d'admirables « fantaisies » (*L'Homme de neige, Les Dames vertes, Laura*). Quelques-unes de ses pièces connaissent un vif succès, dont *Le Marquis de Villemer*, qui triomphe à l'Odéon en 1864. Solange a épousé le sculpteur Clésinger dont elle se sépare rapidement. De son côté, Sand est liée depuis 1849 au graveur Alexandre Manceau, qui sera son compagnon jusqu'à sa mort en 1865.

1870. Après la chute du Second Empire, Sand continue d'écrire des romans, dont *Nanon*, mais livre aussi ses impressions sur la guerre (*Journal d'un voyageur pendant la guerre*) ainsi que quelques textes autobiographiques, tel *Impressions et souvenirs*. Pour les petites filles de son fils Maurice, marié à la fille du sculpteur Luigi Calamatta, elle écrit les *Contes d'une grand-mère*.

1876. Elle meurt à Nohant, vraisemblablement d'un cancer de l'intestin. Aujourd'hui la grande maison de Nohant est un musée, comme la petite maison de Gargilesse, dans la Creuse, dont Manceau avait fait l'acquisition en 1858.

Repères bibliographiques

Œuvres de George Sand

À l'occasion du bicentenaire de la naissance de George Sand en 2004, un nombre conséquent de romans ont été réédités, notamment en Folio, au Livre de Poche et dans la collection « Babel » d'Actes Sud. Une édition des œuvres complètes est actuellement en chantier chez l'éditeur Champion. Seuls quelques volumes de correspondance et textes autobiographiques sont signalés ici.

Correspondance, éd. Georges Lubin, Paris, Garnier, 1964-1991, 25 vol.

FLAUBERT Gustave / SAND George, *Correspondance*, éd. Alphonse Jacobs, Flammarion, 1993.

Histoire de ma vie, éd. Martine Reid, Paris, Gallimard, « Quarto », 2004.

Le Roman de Venise [édition critique de la correspondance de Sand et Musset], éd. José-Luis Diaz, Arles, Actes Sud, « Babel », 1999.

Lettres d'une vie, éd. Thierry Bodin, Paris, Gallimard, « Folio », 2004.

Lettres retrouvées, éd. Thierry Bodin, Paris, Gallimard, 2004.

MUSSET Alfred de / SAND George, *« Ô mon George, ma belle maîtresse… ». Lettres*, éd. Martine Reid, Paris, Gallimard, « Folio 2 € » n° 5127, 2010.

Œuvres autobiographiques, éd. Georges Lubin, Paris, Gallimard, « Bibliothèque de la Pléiade », 1980-1981, 2 vol.

Sur l'œuvre de George Sand

DIDIER Béatrice, *George Sand écrivain*, « *Un grand fleuve d'Amérique* », Paris, Presses universitaires de France, 1998.

LAFORGUE Pierre, *Corambé. Identité et fiction de soi chez George Sand*, Paris, Klincksieck, 2003.

MOZET Nicole, *George Sand écrivain de romans*, Saint-Cyr-sur-Loire, Christian Pirot éditeur, 1997.

NAGINSKI Isabelle, *George Sand. L'écriture ou la vie*, Paris, Champion, 1999.

REID Martine, *Signer Sand. L'œuvre et le nom*, Paris, Belin, 2003.

Divers

BARRY Joseph, *George Sand ou le scandale de la liberté*, Paris, Seuil, 1982.

L'ABCdaire de George Sand, éd. Bertrand Tillier et Martine Reid, Paris, Flammarion, 1999.

Album Sand, éd. Georges Lubin, Paris, Gallimard, 1973.

BERNADAC Christian, *George Sand. Dessins et aquarelles*, Paris, Belfond, 1992.

George Sand. L'œuvre-vie, sous la dir. de Martine Reid, Paris, Éditions Paris-Bibliothèque, 2004.

Composition Nord Compo
Impression Novoprint,
á Barcelona, le 1ᵉʳ août 2016
Dépôt legal: août 2016
1ᵉʳ depôt légal dans la collection : janvier 2007

ISBN 978-2-07-034208-5 /Imprimé en Espagne.

307329

MEREDITH DURAN

WICKED
BECOMES YOU

POCKET BOOKS

New York London Toronto Sydney

Pocket Books
A Division of Simon & Schuster, Inc.
1230 Avenue of the Americas
New York, NY 10020

This book is a work of fiction. Names, characters, places, and incidents either are products of the author's imagination or are used fictitiously. Any resemblance to actual events or locales or persons, living or dead, is entirely coincidental.

First Pocket Books paperback edition May 2010

POCKET and colophon are registered trademarks of Simon & Schuster, Inc.

For information about special discounts for bulk purchases, please contact Simon & Schuster Special Sales at 1-866-506-1949 or business@simonandschuster.com.

The Simon & Schuster Speakers Bureau can bring authors to your live event. For more information or to book an event contact the Simon & Schuster Speakers Bureau at 1-866-248-3049 or visit our website at www.simonspeakers.com.

Designed by Peng Olaguera
Cover illustration by Gene Mollica
Hand lettering by Dave Gatti

Manufactured in the United States of America

10 9 8 7 6 5 4 3 2 1

ISBN 978-1-4165-9312-6
ISBN 978-1-4319-0095-0 (ebook)

For Rob, Betsey, and Stella,
with all my love.

ACKNOWLEDGMENTS

My heartfelt gratitude to those whose aid, encouragement, and faith saw me through the writing of this book: Margaret and Bob McGuire; Steven Kosiba, who crossed continents to plot with me on Rajasthani rooftops; Stephanie Rohlfs; Liz Carlyle; Megan McKeever and the production team at Pocket Books, who rolled so gracefully with the punches; and Lauren McKenna, whose incredible resourcefulness became all the more evident from half a world away. All of you made this possible, and to each one of you, I give my grateful thanks.

WICKED
BECOMES YOU

Prologue

1886

England was a wicked bitch who wished him ill. Thunder had greeted him at the pier in Southampton. On the journey north, trees split by lightning had toppled across the tracks like dominos. This morning's swim had turned into a wrestling match with the undertow. Only now, when a storm might have been fitting, did the sun finally emerge. All the stained-glass windows lit at once, flooding the stone church with light. It seemed a minor wonder to Alex that he did not burn to ash where he stood.

The brass fixtures on the coffin sparkled like children's toys.

He went down on one knee. The kneeling cushion sighed, exhaling the scent of lavender. His hands fitted together by some old, dusty habit, fingers clasped as though to pray. But no prayer came to mind. He felt curiously removed from the scene.

It was ironic. All through his childhood he'd fought to throttle his emotions, to silence them lest they suffocate him—but only now, his illness long abated, did he finally master the skill. Even grief could not touch him. The thoughts passing through his head felt unattached. He listened impassively as a distant voice in his head spoke of rage.

This was a useless death.

Damn Richard's idiocy.

You're the one to blame.

Which was nonsense, of course.

He watched his fingers tighten, knuckles whitening against skin still brown from the Italian sun. Very well, melodrama would serve where prayer could not. Richard's last amicable words to him, he could not recall. They had been drunk. But the next day's anger—Richard's accusations, and his cold replies, and the acrid scent of Gwen's letter burning in the hearth—he remembered that quite clearly. He'd been sober, after all.

So there was no excuse for what he'd done next.

Knowing Richard to be a wide-eyed puppy, Alex had given him directions to a wolf pit. For days, Richard had been clamoring for adventure; when he'd offered to partner in the shipping firm, he'd not realized, perhaps, that business entailed actual work. *What's the point in making a profit if we can't spend any of it?* Restless, irritable, he'd been searching for the sort of easy, stupid antics favored by bachelor travelogues.

Then go, Alex had told him. That casino was not in any guidebook. It operated outside the law. *But you go alone. If you think I mean to seduce your sister, you'll prefer other company.* And with that dismissal, he'd returned his attention to a litter of financial reports—as if such bloodless affairs had required more of his concern than the clawless idealist he sent off to play with wolves.

Richard had gone into that casino to prove a point. *You have nothing to be proud of,* he'd said as he'd left. *For all your high-flying ideals, it's simple cowardice that drives you. Anybody can make a pound, Ramsey. Anybody can play the rebel.*

For that piece of naïveté, he'd received a knife in the ribs.

"You were a damned fool," Alex whispered.

And also, no doubt, the best friend any man could hope for.

The only boy who'd bothered to speak to him during his first term at Rugby, that year before his body had remembered how to breathe and grow.

The only one who had encouraged him when he'd vowed to make something of himself. *You're a daft, dreaming idiot,* his brother had sneered at him. *How far do you imagine you'll possibly go, without the family connections?*

Bully for you, Richard had said. *Let's build an empire! Shall we?*

Alex laid his hand on the coffin, cool wood polished to the smoothness of silk. So soon the worms would make a meal of it. But Richard was already gone.

"You were better than all of us," he said quietly. He took a long breath and retrieved his hand. "Your sister will be safe."

He had left her alone too long now.

The thought brought him to his feet. Gwen stood on the far side of the nave, her dark red hair a bloody corona in the crimson wash of light falling from a window overhead. Alex's twin sisters flanked her elbows, but vultures were circling: mourners reached for her attention, eager to condole her, to impress their faces in her memory so it might work to their advantage later.

He picked his way through the crowd. Very few people he recognized, but as usual, most seemed to know him. Eyes followed his passage, whispers accumulating. The snatches of conversation that reached his ears made him sigh. His sins were numerous and novel, no doubt, but they were also heavily fictionalized.

Other remarks came to him, too: whispers about invitations to Ascot, the Eton-Harrow match at Lord's. These were Gwen's friends, all of them. Richard had never gone out of his way to collect lofty acquaintances, but only a month into her first season, his sister drew them with a crook of her finger.

The mourners' grief was not wholly feigned, Alex supposed. Her brother's death would remove Gwen from the marriage market for a year at least. Estates would continue to molder, lands to go to auction, as her fortune sat vexingly out of reach.

Halfway across the nave, Alex's sister intercepted him. The sight of Belinda's reddened eyes made something in him tighten. It caused that distant anger to intensify and draw nearer.

He took a deep breath. How irrational that his anger

should focus on Bel. *You'd prefer to be an outcast*, Richard had told him once—admiringly, as Alex recalled. But Richard had missed the obvious point. No matter how far Alex traveled, his sisters' love tethered him more firmly than chains. Their chiding letters followed him across the globe. They seemed to imagine that his presence would be a comfort to them—a *boon*, even—if only he would settle in England. Even now, after all of this, they probably still believed it.

This anger he felt made no sense to him. He never looked to his sisters for an example of good sense.

He took Belinda's hand. It was too cold and limp for his liking. His grip tightened. "Are you all right?"

She nodded, then stepped closer. "Gwen was sick in the coach," she whispered. "She needs to sit down."

He glanced past her. Some stern-faced dowager was addressing Gwen, lightly touching her arm. In reply, Gwen's lips turned up in a neat, mechanical smile.

Really, there was something perversely impressive in how doggedly she pursued her role. Puke in the coach, smile in public; she would swallow her vomit now even if it choked her. Condolers were flouting convention to approach her in church because it was the height of the season and their social schedules left no time for the burial or the reception thereafter. She would never acknowledge this, though. If she noted their unusual behavior, she would ascribe it to a kindness so large that it transcended convention.

He didn't know how she managed to fool herself. She wasn't stupid.

"Alex . . ." Belinda was giving him a searching look. "Are you *certain* you're fine?"

Her meaningful tone puzzled him until he noticed her fingers brushing her throat. Ah. He gently loosed her hand. Thirteen years since he'd last gasped like a fish brought to beach, but that made no difference. His sisters doted by habit, fierce as nursemaids. "I'm well," he said, deliberately gentle, because this concern grew wearing and his fatigue and addled emotions urged him to snap. "You're right, though. Gwen needs to rest before the burial."

Belinda sighed. "Your turn to try, then. When I asked her, she said the mourners might think it rude if she withdrew."

Christ. "Your mistake was in asking," he said and walked forward.

The dowager was stepping away. Motioning his other sister aside, Alex touched Gwen's elbow. "Miss Maudsley," he said, speaking formally for the sake of the onlookers, whose worthless opinions she so valued. "A word?"

She turned. "Mr. Ramsey." Her smile for him looked as blank as any other, her large brown eyes not quite focusing on his. "How are you faring?"

"As best as can be expected."

Some quiver crossed her mouth, breaking apart her smile. "How hard this must be for you," she said unsteadily. "Of all people here, I know you share my grief. Richard was so . . . blessed for your friendship."

"And I for his. Step aside with me for a moment."

When she looked hesitant, he took her hand and placed it on his arm. "I have something from your brother," he said. "I meant to give it to you later, but perhaps it will lend you strength."

As he led her through the black-clad mourners, the twins falling into step behind them, he found himself growing acutely aware of her hand on his forearm. A light touch. It focused his senses like a match struck in darkness. That letter she'd sent had been innocuous, a polite courtesy to a family friend. But Richard had not bothered to read it. Finding it on the desk in Alex's suite had been all the proof he'd required of suspicions that must have been brewing—so Alex realized now—for months. *You encourage her interest*, Richard had shouted. *You will keep your eyes off her!*

The force of his own amazement had made Alex less than tactful in reply. *Sweet God. I have no interest in schoolgirls.* And then: *She's a very nice girl who smiles at everyone and disagrees with nobody. That will make her a prize on the marriage mart, but for myself, I can think of no better recipe for boredom.*

His denials had been factual. Alas, they had not been honest.

He glanced briefly at her profile, so serenely composed despite the dark circles beneath her eyes. *Not a thought in her head but for dresses and weddings*, Richard once had laughed. But during their rare encounters over the past few years—during Christmas holidays at his sisters' houses, or autumn fortnights in Scotland—Alex had noticed other things in her. She read a great deal but never spoke of it. She saw far more than she acknowledged. Her sunny optimism was not oblivious but deliberate. She had trained herself into it with such soldierly discipline that even her own brother had been fooled.

Alex understood such discipline. He knew the rarity of it, and the cost. And on the rare occasions when he happened to touch her, he did wonder what else she might have been, if she had not been so determined to be typical. If she had not been Richard's sister. If she had not been respectable.

He appreciated curiosities. He would have enjoyed stripping away the layers of her pretense, finding out what lay beneath her smile. Coaxing her brow into a frown and encouraging her, in the dark, to whisper all the wicked, vulgar thoughts that she tried so hard not to think. He would tell her to be easy with him: he had no use for pretty manners or useless virtues. There was something far more interesting in her, and such potential in her self-control. What was she trying to deny in herself? *Show me*, he would have murmured. *Let's see what we can make of it.*

But she was determined to be typical. And he had no interest in a lasting connection. He'd spent his entire childhood tied, limited, trapped; he would not willingly submit to that again.

He'd spoken the truth to Richard: he had never encouraged her.

They stepped into a little room off the arcade. Gwen released his arm. He knew no ceremony for such moments. Perhaps there wasn't one. Wordless, he reached into his pocket and withdrew the ring.

Her eyes widened, filling with tears. "I . . ." Pressing her lips together, she took the ring from his hand. It slipped into the cradle of her palm, the simple gold band glittering in the cold white light from the window above. "I thought it was stolen," she whispered.

"The Italian police recovered it." Richard's killer had met justice at the end of a noose yesterday morning; that news, Alex would consult with the twins before deciding how to share. "I received it only this morning."

Her fingers closed into a fist. Such a small fist. Her head bowed. "Oh," she said, and a tear slipped off her cheek to the floor.

The sight sank a knife through his chest, releasing some pure strain of grief, untainted by regret or doubt. It buffeted him so violently that he pressed a palm against the stone wall for balance. *Idiot*, he thought, the silent word flavored by astonishment, a touch of wonder. So, people really could be staggered: it was not simply a figure of speech.

By old habit, he took a testing breath. His lungs responded as they should.

Another tear fell to the ground. Why the hell didn't his sisters embrace her? Bel and Caro were looking away, no doubt out of some misguided notion that Gwen's grief needed privacy. Even Alex knew that this was the wrong approach.

He cleared his throat. "Forgive me, Gwen. The timing was ill judged."

She shook her head fiercely. Her fist, the ring clutched within it, moved to her breast. "No," she said hoarsely. "This is—the most *precious* thing, Alex. It was my father's, before. And Richard wore it . . ."

"Always," he finished, when it became clear she could not go on.

She nodded. Then, with a muffled sob, she turned into Caroline's arms.

Good. He nodded to his sisters, then stepped back outside. Several mourners now craned to see into the anteroom. A smile twisted his lips. It must have looked . . . unpleasant, for most of the gawkers turned hastily away.

For all the attention he received, it was nothing compared to this avid curiosity for her. Amazing. With his shipping concerns, he had built something approaching a fortune, but he'd also made a reputation that discouraged men in search of easy pickings. Gwen, on the other hand, was a blank white page: pretty, fabulously rich, descended from nobodies. Now that her brother's death left her without family, she must seem to this lot like a prize made for pirates, begging to be seized.

He propped his shoulder against the doorway to block the view to the interior. One of these people would have her, of course. Richard had seen to that. *Promise you will look after her*, he had gasped. *See her . . . well settled. For my sake.*

Alex remained uncertain if it had been punishment or pardon that Richard had granted by asking this promise. Either way, he understood what was meant by the request. The Maudsleys had never made a secret of their plans for Gwen. Her marriage would be their final triumph. Failing a prince, only a title would do. The Maudsleys had not leapt and clawed their way up in the world for less.

Well, he had taken the vow, and he would keep it. He had no designs on her.

But God save him if he had to help her find a husband.

Chapter One

Fridays were not Gwen's favorite; they too often rained. But in April of 1890, they turned lucky for her. On the first Friday of the month, a note arrived from an anonymous admirer, delicately sprinkled with rose-scented tears. On the second Friday, she supervised the placement of the final pagoda in the garden at Heaton Dale. And on the third Friday, beneath an unseasonably bright sun, three hundred of London's most fashionable citizens filed into church to witness her marriage to Viscount Pennington.

Gwen waited on her feet, in a little antechamber off the nave, a wholly unnecessary fire crackling in the hearth. The ceremony should have started half an hour ago, but (so Belinda had told her, in a brief visit to ensure that her veil still sat straight) the guests were too busy consorting to be seated. The brightest lights of society were convening, some for the first time since last season; according to one of the social columns this morning, "Only the angelic Miss Mauds-

ley, whom everybody adores," could gather a crowd of
such numbers before Whitsuntide.

Gwen took a deep breath and cast her eyes to the
window above her. It was not odd, really, that she
wished she were in the pews, exchanging greetings. Or
outside, even. In the park. The air in here felt stifling,
far too warm.

The walls seemed to be closing in.

What am I doing?

She bit her lip. Her discomfort was only the fault
of the fire, of course, and the boy who fed it too much
wood. And perhaps a *bit* of it was owed to the memory
of that other time, and that other fiancé. It had taken
months of brilliant successes to persuade the papers
to describe her as anything other than "the much-
beleaguered Miss M——, so dreadfully disappointed
by the treacherous Lord T——."

Still, for all that she was now a shining success
set to achieve her greatest triumph, this corset was
strangling the life from her. And her gown, encrusted
with innumerable pearls, weighed thirty pounds at
the least. One might drown in such a gown! And these
heeled shoes pinched her toes awfully.

She took a deep breath. *This is the happiest day of my life.*

Of course it was. Her feet throbbed, regardless.
The stool to her right began to beckon like a siren. An
evil siren. The bustle of her train would not survive a
crushing.

Giggles exploded from across the room. Four bridesmaids in pink and ivory ribbons clustered by the door,

their noses pressed to the crack. "Oh, Lord," Katherine Percy squealed. "I *died*! She matched peacock feathers with plaid!"

"That's appalling," said Lady Anne. "One would cut her, but she's evidently too blind to take note of it."

Gwen cleared her throat. "Lady Embury has arrived?"

Four faces turned toward her, mouths agape. "You're a marvel," Katherine said. "How did you guess? Yes, it was she!"

Gwen pressed her palm to her stomach, which was jumping so violently that it seemed a wonder her hand could not detect the commotion. She had told the baroness not to add the feathers. An entire morning they had spent designing that hat! What was the point of soliciting counsel if one refused to heed it?

"Oh!" Lucy clutched Katherine's shoulder. "Look now! Gwen, your groom is passing by!"

Lady Anne's back went rigid as a poker. Gwen, meanwhile, felt a startling wave of relief. She realized that some secret part of her had been braced for another debacle like the one with Lord Trent.

Well, perhaps her nerves would settle now. This was the day she'd dreamed of for years. Surely she could manage to enjoy it!

Charlotte Everdell glanced toward her. "He's so handsome, Gwen! Why, I think the viscount is the most attractive man in London!"

She managed a smile. Thomas was not *so* handsome. That word better fitted the angelic blondness of Mr.

Cust, or, at the darker end of it, Alex Ramsey, whose blue eyes worked to such striking effect against his dark hair and angular cheekbones. But what of it? A wise woman did not place much import on looks. Mr. Cust, after all, was a mean-tempered scalawag, and Alex a notorious rogue; she rarely passed five minutes in his company before biting her tongue lest she reply to some rude quip in kind. Indeed, Alex proved the point: looks mattered little without a manner to match them.

Happily, Thomas's manner was just like his face: pleasant through and through. He lacked a chin but made up for it with a fine beard, black as the hair on his head. His green eyes were kind and his thin lips, given to smiling. And he loved her! That was most important of all. He had told her so a hundred times. In an hour at most, she would once again have a family of her own—a real family, not just one made of friends and paid companions.

"He's gone," Katherine said. "Boohoo."

"Up the aisle?" Gwen asked softly.

"No, not yet. Oh, Gwen, what a brilliant match. I'm so happy for you!"

"We all are," said Lucy. "The nicest girl in England, and the handsomest heir in the realm! Why, it's like some fairy tale."

Charlotte clapped. "Oh, do tell us, Gwen—don't you love him *awfully*?"

"Of course she does," snapped Lady Anne. "Really, what an absurd question to ask at her wedding."

Charlotte shrank. Lucy, patting her arm, sent a knowing look to Gwen.

Gwen pretended not to see it, but she took the meaning. Lady Anne had nursed a terrible crush on Thomas last season. She couldn't afford him, of course; her father's magnificent estates near Lincoln were as heavily mortgaged as his. But her eyes had followed him across the floor at every ball.

Gwen felt very bad for her. Only four weeks ago, she'd felt utterly wretched. But then she'd learned that Lady Anne had volunteered her to knit ten sweaters for Lady Milton's orphanage before its spring excursion to Ramsgate. Ten sweaters in a month! Gwen was not a loom! *It's a marvelous opportunity to prove your dedication*, Lady Anne had told her. But this was not the first time she'd made impossible promises on Gwen's behalf. Last season, shortly after Thomas had paid his first call, it had been thirty embroidered handkerchiefs for Lady Milton's charity bazaar, not three weeks away. It seemed clear that these sweaters were Lady Anne's latest attempt to sabotage Gwen's bid for a seat on the charity committee.

All the same, Gwen had smiled and thanked her and put in an order for merino. Madness was forgivable in the heartbroken. (Why, after Lord Trent had jilted her, she'd briefly taken an interest in learning *Latin*!) Still, when the newspapers claimed that she was "everyone's bosom friend" on account of her "inborn good cheer," they missed how much work the position actually required—not to mention the toll it took on her wrists.

Perhaps, she thought, she would give up knitting after marriage.

And embroidery, while she was at it.

What a thrilling notion. Did she dare?

A knock came at the door. The bridesmaids leapt back. Aunt Elma entered, smiling. When Uncle Henry appeared behind her, Gwen's mouth went dry. "Is it time?" she whispered.

"So it is," Elma said warmly. "I've come for your bridesmaids, dear."

They turned to Gwen, clapping, crying out encouragement, blowing her kisses as they hurried out.

And then the door closed, and it was only she and Uncle Henry who remained.

Silence filled the room. Without her friends' chatter to oppose it, the noise filtering through the door from the nave seemed much louder, like the roaring of the crowd at a circus. Surely three hundred people wasn't *that* many?

That's six hundred eyes.

"Well," she said brightly.

Henry Beecham was not given to garrulity. He cleared his throat, nodded at her, ran a hand over his silver mustache, and then resumed his inspection of his shoes.

She smiled, remembering that the first time she'd arrived on his doorstep, he'd greeted her just so, with a stroke of his mustache and a snuffle. His wife, Elma, had told him to say something lest Gwen think him a mute. "All right then," he'd said, and that had been the last Gwen had heard from him for a day or two.

As a thirteen-year-old, she'd found his silence quite puzzling. Frightening, even. Now, ten years later, she would not have the first idea what to do if he began to soliloquize. Call for a doctor, maybe.

She was glad he would walk her up the aisle. Her brother had paid the Beechams to raise her, but their affection had long since grown genuine. Since Richard's death, they were the closest thing she had to family.

But not in half an hour. By noon, I will have a real family.

It would still be purchased, though.

The thought was dark and evil and skittered across her brain like a big black beetle. She shook her head to cast it out—mindful to do so carefully, lest she disturb the veil. This was not *at all* like the arrangement her brother had struck with the Beechams. The viscount *loved* her. And if she admired his station, that was only natural. His family tree was old and much distinguished, whereas hers . . . well, hers was more in the way of a very stumpy shrub. That it also happened to be gilded in gold—or the dyes her father had invented; no difference, really—made her more attractive to Thomas than she would have been otherwise. She knew that. Still, she was not *paying* him to be her husband. And as for his motives . . . well, her fortune hadn't persuaded Lord Trent to the altar, had it?

"Auspicious day," Henry muttered.

"Yes."

He looked up sharply. "Bit nervous?"

Her voice failed her. She nodded.

He chuckled. "Should've seen me. Shaking in my shoes. Best man had to hold my head over a chamber pot. I'll tell you what he told me: 'So long as you lay the cornerstone straight, Providence will build the house.'"

She managed a smile but found the adage ominous. Thomas had thirteen houses, all of them in terrible disrepair; another would only add to the expense.

Now came another knock, and Uncle Henry straightened and extended his elbow to her. She realized only belatedly, from the pain in her loosening fingers, that she'd been squeezing her hands into fists.

But he loves me, she thought. *That is all that matters. He loves me, and I want* this. *What was all of it for, if not for this? I've wanted this forever.*

And so did Mama and Papa and Richard. They wanted this for me, too. We all did.

I want this.

She cleared her throat. "Yes," she said. She laid her hand on Henry's arm. "I'm ready."

Alex arrived without warning, flustering his brother's butler with his refusal to be announced. There was a mystery here, and in his experience, ambushes were the most expedient way to uncover the truth.

He walked toward Gerard's study on legs still braced for the unsteady sway of a ship. He could smell the widow's perfume rising from his skin, and the scent compounded on his fatigue, making his stomach churn. The lady had slipped into his cabin last night after thirty days of idle flirtation, but this headache was enough to make him regret having entertained her. The attraction between them had been more the product of boredom than true interest. *What harm?* he'd reasoned. Left to his own devices, he wouldn't have managed to sleep anyway. He barely remembered what a sound sleep felt like.

Odd to think that the insomnia had seemed a blessing, at first. So much useful time no longer squandered on unconsciousness. But after five months, the nights were beginning to stretch into dry-eyed eternities. The widow's company had not made the time pass more quickly for him.

At least her perfume would lend him the illusion of having bathed.

As he turned the corner, he willed himself to focus on the task at hand. It would be convenient to find an obvious explanation for his brother's actions, but nothing in the house spoke of want. The threadbare Aubussons had not been replaced by newer, plusher, cheaper rugs. The wallpaper bore no darkened patches where frames had been removed. In the box stalls in the mews, which he had checked upon arrival, a new pair of chestnuts now gave company to the matched grays. The carriages showed no signs of neglect. Everything looked exactly the same, which made Gerry's decision all the more baffling.

The door to the study stood open. For an uncanny

second, as Alex paused in the doorway, he had a sense of looking onto a scene long dead: his father, sitting ramrod-straight at his desk, industriously scrutinizing the household accounts. With the déjà vu came other, equally dead impulses—to stay quiet; to walk on by; to avoid a fight that could not be won. The weariness that touched him was not all from the insomnia, nor the long journey either. As a boy, he'd had to work very hard to believe in possibilities.

He exhaled. It was only Gerard at the desk, of course. His older brother was the picture of the Earl of Weston before him, lantern-jawed and stocky, as well-fleshed as a bull. Came home more frequently in the evenings, though. And there were other small differences—such as the fact that their father would have shot himself before surrendering any title to family land.

Of course, it would have been a waste of a bullet, in Alex's view. He had no interest in the patrimony. It wasn't his, anyway.

Why the bloody hell am I here, then?

He sighed. He was heartily sick of this question, having asked it of himself all the way from Gibraltar. Little else to do in the early hours before dawn. Best answer: his sisters had asked it of him. It would be his favor to them, then—enough to purchase twelve months' freedom from additional pestering. "Cheers," he said from the doorway.

Gerard looked up. "What—Alex!" He started to rise, then caught himself. "You're back! We had no idea!"

"Neither did I," said Alex. "A sudden decision when I reached Gibraltar. The whole place reeks of blood pudding—brought the motherland to mind."

In fact, he'd received several telegrams during his stop there: two outraged screeds from his sisters, and a half-dozen cautions from friends who had seen Christopher Monsanto dining in Buenos Aires with the Peruvian trade minister. It seemed that the Yank now had his overbearing eye on Alex's contracts with the Peruvian government.

The thought seemed to add weight to his exhaustion. He would probably regret not having turned back for Lima at once.

"Well." Gerry was making a swift, critical inspection, his gaze raking Alex from head to toe. "I must say, this is a splendid surprise."

As always, the inspection grated. As always, Alex produced a smile. "Will I live?" he asked. "Or does the deathbed draw nigh?"

His brother had the grace to redden. "You look whole enough. Do sit, then."

Alex picked up an armchair on his way across the carpet.

"Careful," Gerry said sharply. "That's heavy."

Sweet Christ. Alex dropped the chair in front of the desk and took his seat. "It weighs no more than a ten year old," he said. "Really, Gerry, has it escaped your notice that I outstrip you by a head?" Since his fourteenth birthday, he'd been outrunning and outfighting his brother in any number of arenas. But if he picked up a toy poodle, Gerry would probably feel the need to call out a warning.

"Bulk, not height," Gerry said critically. "Bulk is what matters."

Alex eyed his brother's ever-expanding gut. "Yes, I suppose that's one view of it."

"You look as if you could use a meal. And some sleep."

He made a one-shouldered shrug. "Writing something, were you?"

"Ah . . . yes." Gerard fingered the corner of the page. "Speech for tomorrow. This nonsense with the Boers . . ." He sighed. "Half the Lords wants a war."

"How novel."

Frowning, his brother peered at him. "Actually, Alex, we fought in the Transvaal in '81."

Gerry had never had an ear for irony. "Did we? Never a dull moment, then."

The frown was slow to clear. "Mm, yes. When did you arrive, then? Have you seen the twins yet?"

Had Alex not been listening for it, he might have missed the note of anxiety flavoring this last question. Gerry did not know, then, that the twins had already informed him about the Cornwall estate. "Not yet, no."

"They'll be over the moon to see you, then. Worry about you terribly."

"Still?" He'd hoped that having children would redirect their focus, but his siblings seemed to have a marvelous capacity for multidirectional anxiety.

He reached out and retrieved Gerry's pen, flipping it through his fingers. The tortoiseshell was second rate, a poor imitation of Chinese loggerhead, probably from Mauritius. It was exactly the sort of product that Monsanto, until now, had specialized in trading.

From the periphery of his vision, he saw Gerry's fingertips come together into a steeple. This was the sign of imminent moralizing. Alex set down the pen and smiled.

"You can't blame them," his brother said. "You would not believe the rumors we hear about you."

"Oh, I might," said Alex.

Gerry took no note of this comment. "Listen, hell," he continued in disgust. "Read, more like. The bloody newspapers are full of it! Dreck masquerading as financial news. And what do you expect? That spectacle with the showgirl—I'm surprised you weren't prosecuted."

Showgirl? Dimly, Alex recalled an acquaintance in New York twitting him over something along these lines. Bizarre. Some of these stories he started himself; his notoriety usefully eliminated most of the tedious social obligations to which he otherwise would be bound. But the showgirl belonged to that sizeable group of rumors that other people were kind enough to fabricate for him. Had he paid these faceless benefactors, they could not have served him better.

"Disgraced her, did I?" He was curious despite himself.

"I don't know how else to describe such behavior in public!"

In public, no less. That did not sound impressive so much as stupid. How typical of Gerard to believe it of him. "Yes, well, the lung power," Alex said with a shrug. "Foolish of me to underestimate her. She said she was a contralto, but to be honest with you, I think her range goes higher. Perhaps she'd lacked the proper . . . tutelage."

Gerard made a scornful noise. "Is that meant to shock me?"

"No. If my aim was to entertain people, I'd have gone into the theater."

No doubt Gerard's glare made his soft, wheezing opposition in the Lords cower and tremble. Once or twice, in their childhood, it had made Alex tremble, too. Then Alex had mastered it himself. In his experience, it also worked well on foreign trade boards and corporate men desperate for investment. Paired with a smile, women fell before it like dominos—although, alas, he'd never tried it on a showgirl. They generally preferred coins to smiles, whereas Alex used money to buy goods; he did not buy people.

At any rate, the glare was useful. It also strained the eyes. "You're going to give yourself an aneurysm," he said mildly.

Gerard reached up to rub his brow. "Tell me this. Do you really think I waste my breath out of priggishness?"

The silence wanted an answer. Christ. Did they have to do this *every time* he came home? "No," Alex said. "I think you waste it out of stubbornness." Had it fallen to his family, Alex would have joined the church. The world was changing; grain from the Americas, meats and wools from the Continent, had sliced into the profitability of English agriculture. But the Ramseys still fared very well, and no son of Lord Weston, his father had often informed him, would dirty his hands in trade. In other words: the Ramseys would cling to the past and ignore the present so long as they could afford it.

Even as a boy, Alex had found this philosophy absurd. He'd spent his entire childhood buried in the country—for his own good, they'd said; for the sake of his health. He'd had no intention of hiding from the world as a man.

"You may call it whatever you like," Gerard said. "Stubbornness or stupid optimism, I don't even know. But I am certain of one thing: you keep leading this bohemian lifestyle, you're bound to pay for it one day. Cross the wrong man and you'll have a bullet in your brain. And in the meantime, it's damned embarrassing for *us*."

Alex rubbed his eyes. Dry as sand. Perhaps, in the first years out of Oxford, he'd derived an idle amusement in scandalizing stuffed shirts—but even then, he'd done it only by happy accident, never as a deliberate goal. "The bit about the showgirl is rubbish," he said. "I don't misbehave in public, Gerry. It's bad for business."

Gerard snorted. "Oh, indeed, God save the profit margin. And even if it's rubbish, what of it? Do you think it matters, now, whether these stories are true or not? The way you live, who can tell? Who's even bothered to wonder? Either way, it's *we* who pay the price!"

Alex nodded and reached inside his jacket.

"Yes? A *nod*? Is that *all* you have to say for yourself?"

Alex laid the bank draft atop the desk.

Gerard leaned forward to examine the draft, then looked up, scowling. "What's the meaning of this?"

"You need money, don't you?"

"According to whom?"

Alex sat back and kicked out his legs, crossing them comfortably at the ankle. "The trade winds." He glanced around the room. He'd been gone for seven months, first in the United States and then in Peru and Argentina. In that time, his sister-in-law had redecorated. The bust of some dead Roman now glared blankly from one corner. An entire wall had been consumed by an oil of some eighteenth-century massacre, replete with gleaming swords, anguished grimaces, and riderless horses, wild-eyed. "New painting," he remarked.

A pause. "Yes," Gerry said gruffly. "Picked it up from auction. I expect you don't like it."

"No, it's quite impressive."

"I know what you prefer."

"So you do. Children's scribbles, I believe you've called it."

Gerry tried out a smile. "Well, you have to admit it, Alex. Very little talent required."

Alex shrugged. What modern art required was an imagination drawn to possibilities, rather than braced by smug presumptions. Certainly the work of Gaugin did nothing to flatter a British imperialist's vision of his role in the world. "But I meant it," he said. "The painting is striking. I particularly admire the discreet pools of blood. Came cheaply, I assume?"

Gerard's jaw firmed. "I can well afford the purchase, but clearly you think otherwise. I'll thank you to tell me who's maligning my name."

"Your sisters. You mustn't blame them. It was a natural assumption, upon learning that you'd sold the Cornwall estate to Rollo Barrington."

Gerry slowly lowered his hand. "Oh."

Alex waited, but that seemed to be the extent of Gerry's reaction, which in itself seemed significant. His brother so rarely declined an opportunity to hear his own voice. Requirement of a nobleman, that healthy self-regard. "Interesting man, Barrington," he said casually. "Never met, but I've seen him in passing. Heard a good deal as well. He's making quite the reputation with these purchases of English land. Curious thing, though: nobody can say where he gets the money for it."

Silence.

"What puzzles me," Alex said, "is why you didn't come to me first."

His brother flushed. "Because I don't require your help."

He laughed softly. If Gerry were dying of thirst and spotted Alex two feet from a well, he still would not think he required his younger brother's help. It simply would never occur to him that Alex might be able to provide it. "Right. So you sold it for, what . . . a lark?"

"That estate was an albatross round my neck, and well you know it. Rent rolls falling for five years straight. There was barely a household left to me by the end."

"True." But since when had Gerard cared for financial wisdom? He was a creaking anachronism who spent his free time in musty gentlemen's clubs, raging against the nation's decline into capitalist barbarism. His only comfort, he often opined, was that most of England's soil still rested in civilized hands. That he had sold a good deal of this sacrosanct substance suggested a variety of possibilities, but nothing so rational as a sound economic decision.

Gerard was growing redder. "What do *you* lot care, anyway? The twins never spent a night there. And God knows I've never heard you speak fondly of the place."

"No, I've no particular love of Heverley End." It had been little more than a prison to Alex as a child—the echoing house to which he'd been banished for months on end when his lungs had grown contrary. "But you must admit, the decision seems peculiar. Moreover, Bel and Caro had to learn of it from the gossips. If you wish to discuss awkwardness, I imagine that gave the showgirl a run for her money."

Gerard looked back to his half-finished speech, his stubby fingers linking together atop the page, then separating again and clenching into fists. He pulled them abruptly into his lap, out of Alex's sight, like secrets to be hidden.

The gesture raised some unpleasant feeling that Alex did not want to examine. If Gerry required his pity, he did not want to know the cause. Unlike his siblings, he did not enjoy worrying. It was a pointless exercise by which nothing was gained. "Tell me the problem," he said flatly. "I'll fix it." This, after all, was the reason he'd come when he should have been halfway around the world, attending to his own business.

"Listen to me: you will let it alone."

"If only I could. Alas, I've promised the twins to buy back the land." And he was determined not to have made this trip for nothing.

His brother gazed stonily up toward the painting.

Alex took a breath, leashing his impatience. "Barrington stands to make quite a profit by selling to me," he said evenly. "My last bid was double what he paid you. Yet he proves remarkably difficult to contact. Four letters I've sent now, and I've still to receive a reply. I was hoping you might facilitate our acquaintance."

"Alex." Gerard looked into his eyes. "I said, *let it alone*."

What the hell was going on here? "Perhaps I will," he said with a shrug. "Lazy by nature, you know." At his brother's snort, he gave up a lopsided smile. "Only give me a reason for it, Ger."

Gerard's snort flattened into a sneer—that same

damned sneer inherited by every firstborn brat Alex had ever had the misfortune to meet. "It seems I must remind you of a very basic fact," he said through his teeth. "I do not explain myself to you—"

"Thank God for that," said Alex. "I've little enough time as it is."

Gerry's palm slammed onto the desktop. "Amusing," he bit out. "You are very amusing, Alex, never doubt it. A veritable family clown. But much as it pains you, *I* am the head of this family. The land is *mine* to dispose of. You may remind the twins of that, if you please. And *you* may interfere in my business the same day you hand me the reins of your little business." He gave a nasty little laugh, sounding, for a moment, exactly like the schoolyard bully he'd once been. "God knows, *that* would be rich. Bilking Chinamen of their tea. Wheedling teak from coolies in India! Christ, but you do the family proud."

Alex inclined his head. "No prouder than you do in the Lords. Fine show, shaking your fists at the Boers for daring to take land that you'd prefer to steal yourself." He rose. "Shall I find lodgings, then?"

Gerry eyed him, clearly struggling to remember the less autocratic obligations of the head of the family. "Don't be an idiot," he said finally, gruffly. "You're always welcome to stay here."

It was a marked sign of Alex's fatigue that he almost found this statement touching. "And it would look rather awkward for you if I didn't," he said dryly. Well, he'd take a week to poke around in Gerry's files, see what he could uncover. The mystery would irritate him now until he solved it.

His brother tried out an unsuccessful smile. Or perhaps he had a moment's pain from indigestion. The twist of his mouth supported either hypothesis. "How long are we blessed with your company?"

"Not long." Never long. Anywhere. *Be restful, and rest will come:* so spake the doctor in Buenos Aires. Very easy advice to give, a nice play on words, and as medical advice, useless. Alex took a breath. "I've a few showgirls waiting on the Continent, in fact." An acquaintance in Gibraltar had mentioned that Barrington favored springtime in Paris. He glanced toward the clock. "Luncheon is still at half past?"

"Yes, but not today, of course." Gerard rose. "Or do you intend to miss the wedding? If you're in town, you might as well come."

It took a moment to recover his smile. "Ah, yes. My brilliant timing." He'd known mystics in India who'd predicted destinies based on the pull of the moon on the tide. Had his ship only met with an opposing current or a fractious wind, he would not be here. A mere hour's delay into port this morning, and he still would have been in Southampton, free to miss this *auspicious* event.

Gwen noticed nothing on her walk down the aisle, so absorbed was she in negotiating the flagstones in her spindly, pinching heels. The altar seemed to leap up out of nowhere. Uncle Henry abandoned her with no ceremony, which rattled her; she'd expected a kiss on the cheek or, at the least, the press of his hand on her arm. Thomas was smiling at her and taking her hand, and for a moment she couldn't breathe; the corset had tightened further and was about to finish her off. And then she saw her brother's ring shining on Thomas's finger, her betrothal gift to him.

The breath returned to her lungs. Of course she wanted this. Who would not want this? Everybody liked him. He was handsome and well-born and always joking. He was the nicest man she knew.

She stepped forward. The minister began to speak.

Gwen tried to attend, but an itch started in her nose. How maddening! If she wrinkled her nose it would go, maybe—but she didn't dare.

The itch intensified.

Thomas glanced away toward the audience, and she took that as permission to do so as well. *Do not wrinkle. Do not.* What a profusion of flowers Elma had ordered! Roses over the chancel, orchids dangling from the rafters, lilies overflowing the baptismal font—good heavens, no wonder she wanted to sneeze! London's bushes must have been stripped bare. It was a pity that people proved so ferociously single-minded about flowers; sprigs of pine and honeysuckle would have looked just as lovely, but of course nobody would have been impressed, since tree boughs came for free.

She turned her attention back to Richard's ring, staring so hard at it that it began to blur. *I will not sneeze*, she thought, and risked puffing a small bit of air out through her nostrils. It didn't help. What a monstrous collection; no garden in nature would ever contain such an overpowering combination of scents.

The minister droned onward. She forced herself to think of something, anything but the itch. Thomas's hair was such a handsome, true black. She hoped it would overpower her own contribution. While her hair was acceptably close to auburn, Richard and her mother had looked like torches on fire. She did not want her children to accrue nicknames like "Carrot-top."

Oh, stars above. If she sneezed, Aunt Elma would never forgive her.

Why did Thomas keep looking off to the side?

Gwen followed his glance again. Candlelight flickered over jeweled hat pins, skipping in flashes and gleams across the shifting rainbow of satins. She had the vague impression of smiles, of tears being dabbed discreetly. Warmth flushed through her, and the urge to sneeze subsided. All these dear, dear people! They had come today to rejoice for her. How she loved them for it!

She glanced back to Thomas. He looked very solemn now. But his hand turned under her palm so their fingers could thread together.

She found herself blinking back tears. She would be so good to him, better even than he dreamed. He could have anything he liked; she would not withhold a penny, no matter what her solicitors had advised.

"Do you, Thomas John Whyllson Arundell, take Gwendolyn Elizabeth Maudsley—"

A door closed at the back of the church. Thomas's glance flickered away again.

"—to protect her and cherish her—"

His face went white. She darted a glance toward the back of the church but saw nothing.

"—as long as you both shall live?"

He opened his mouth.

His mouth closed.

But he hadn't spoken. Had he?

Surely she hadn't . . . *missed* it somehow?

She peered at his lips. They twitched and compressed, forming a flat, hard seal. His fingers began to slip free.

She tightened her grip and looked an urgent question at him.

His eyes slid away.

At Thomas's elbow, Mr. Shrimpton, the best man, was now frowning. Her heart quickened. The oddity of this pause was not in her imagination, then.

The minister cleared his throat. "Sir?"

A faint wheeze whistled through Thomas's nose.

Heavens above. *The flowers.* Of course! They must have been affecting him, too.

She sent a pleading glance to the minister. *Give him a chance to breathe*, she willed him.

The minister, ignoring her, sent a puzzled look toward the best man.

Mr. Shrimpton's shoulders squared. He stepped forward, shoes squeaking in the pin-drop silence, to lean near Thomas's ear.

He spoke too softly for Gwen to hear, but Thomas closed his eyes and inhaled deeply, his throat working in an effort to swallow. Oh, the poor man! How awful for him! Would he faint?

A whisper rose from the audience. Her heartbeat escalating, Gwen directed a bright smile toward the crowd. *It's all fine,* she thought. Should she say it aloud? *Really, it's nothing. Only the flowers.*

An abortive movement yanked her attention back to Thomas. His shoulders jerked, and she almost laughed from relief. Goodness, he was only gathering himself to speak, overcoming a brief bout of allergies. What an amusing story this would be to tell at dinner parties! *We were both battling a sneeze, you see . . .*

Then she realized the source of his movement: the best man had planted his fist in Thomas's back.

This isn't happening.

Over Thomas's shoulder, Henry Shrimpton flashed her a panicked, horrified look. "Say it," he whispered to Thomas.

I am dreaming.

"Sir," said the minister.

I will wake now.

"Speak," Mr. Shrimpton hissed.

Thomas made a choking noise.

"Nicest girl in town," someone murmured, and something cold welled up in the pit of Gwen's stomach. A million times she had heard herself described so, but never in a voice full of *pity*.

She looked out to the crowd, but it was impossible

to find the source of the remark. All of a sudden, a great many other people were whispering, too, their soft remarks and speculative rustling blending into a mounting hum.

Good heavens. Gwen swallowed. She recognized this noise in her bones—had encountered it in her nightmares—but she'd never thought to hear it in truth. Not this time. Not when the groom had actually shown up!

She glanced back to Thomas. "Sir," she whispered. "They—they think that you're—"

But her throat closed. A chill danced over her spine. She could not finish that statement. She could not put it into words. Surely he must know what they thought!

He gave her a desperate, pop-eyed look. She could not interpret it. She shook her head—helplessly, frantically.

His bloodshot eyes rolled again toward the crowd.

What was he *looking* at? She tracked his stare but could see nothing remarkable, save a sea of gaping mouths that sharpened and dimmed in time to the roar in her head. Her eye landed on the second-to-last row, and the sight of four brown heads, the Ramseys, briefly penetrated her panic—Caroline hiding her face against Belinda's neck; Belinda, bright red, twisting away to speak into her husband's ear (oh, she had no patience for shenanigans, she would not forgive Thomas for this); Lord Weston scowling; and in the aisle seat, Alex, lifting his hand to disguise a yawn.

The sight jolted her. Alex was back in London?

He was *yawning*?

Was he *bored* by this?

Their eyes met. His hand dropped. He gave her a slight, one-shouldered shrug, as if to say, *What of it?*

Her thoughts jumbled. Did he mean that gesture to be comforting?

Why, no, he did not. He simply looked *sleepy*. Did nothing surprise him? Her brother had always claimed so. Unaccountably, Richard had loved him precisely for that—his unflappable, inhuman cool.

He transferred his gaze to Thomas. His mouth curled.

She drew a startled breath. The sight of his scorn acted like ice water on her sleeping wits. Because— really, why shouldn't he sneer? The buzz was mounting to a clamor. Thomas was having cold feet *at the altar.*

What sort of woman let this happen to her *twice*?

She pivoted back to Thomas. Sandy hair and a ruddy complexion grown ruddier for his sudden, slack-jawed madness. "I will," she hissed. "Say *I will*."

His lashes fluttered rapidly. Someone in the audience called out, "Say it!"

From the *audience*! It was beyond humiliating; their wedding had turned into a sideshow! Yet all he did was *stand* there like some gawking chicken!

She cleared her throat. Her knees were trembling. "Viscount," she managed. *Oh dear Lord only make him say it and I will knit a hundred sweaters! And never again sleep till noon, or think a single unkind thought about anyone*—"Will you not answer the vow?"

Thomas stumbled back a pace. "Forgive me," he choked, and turned on his heel. Turned—*away* from her.

Mr. Shrimpton made a lunge for his arm, but Thomas shoved free and bolted past his groomsmen, then leapt the rail into the nave.

The crowd rose amidst a great communal shriek. "Swine!" someone shouted, and "Catch the cad!"

Thomas sprinted across the nave and cut a sharp left toward the arcade. Someone made a grab for him; he ducked into a somersaulting roll, shot to his feet, and bounded out of sight behind a row of pillars.

At her side, Mr. Shrimpton gave a low whistle. She turned, the world trailing sluggishly past her eyes, to look at him.

His brows were at his hairline. "Had no idea he could run like that," he said.

Vises clamped onto her arms. She glanced down. Hands, they were—pale, slim fingers, wrists bound in fluttering ribbons and white tea roses. *Oh*, she thought. Her bridesmaids were trying to draw her away from the altar. *Again.*

God above. It had happened *again.*

He actually let me walk up the aisle.

Even Lord Trent didn't do that.

"Oh," she said, and the sound startled her. "Oh," she whispered, as she tripped over her train and the candles seemed to brighten and the scent of flowers sharpened, pricking her eyes and making her nose run. She shook off the grasping hands. This was new;

it really was. At least Lord Trent had the decency to have jilted her before the wedding day, to let *her* cry off the betrothal. A terrible mess, informing four hundred guests that their attendance would not be required; the number of notes she'd penned had left her hand cramped for weeks. But this?

Oh, this was *quite* different. *Twice*, now.

She stumbled back a pace, and then another.

The altar began to recede.

There could be no recovery from this.

Chapter Two

❦

"Please, miss. Madam is determined that you come downstairs."

Gwen pulled her knees closer to her chest. She was buried beneath the covers, with a pillow atop her face, but it still wasn't enough. What she needed was a shell. Then she could crawl into it and hide, no matter where she found herself. How lucky turtles were, in that regard. "Once again," she mumbled, "I send my regrets."

"Miss, she insists! There is company!"

It was only the Ramseys, who would forgive her. Nevertheless, the maid's wheezing voice made her lift the pillow for a peek. An unhealthy flush blotched Hester's cheeks. No wonder! Aunt Elma had sent her scrambling up the staircase five times in the last half hour.

Gwen threw off the pillow and sat up. "The next time my aunt sends for me, you're to pay her no heed. Just wait a bit in the hall, then tell her I refused again." When Hester looked hesitant, she rose to her feet for the added air of authority. "I assure you, that's exactly what I'd do if you came anyway."

The maid gave a little panting moan, then ducked a curtsy and withdrew. As the door closed, the room sank again into darkness.

Gwen swayed indecisively. There was no desire in her to do anything. Her whole body ached. But she did not think she would manage to go back to sleep now.

She crossed to the window and pulled open the curtains.

Surprise stopped her breath. Bits of mild blue sky showed through the green leaves that brushed the glass. Still daylight! How was that *possible*? It felt as though the day should have been over years ago.

She glanced disbelievingly to the clock on the mantel. Only a quarter after five! Why, people were strolling through the park still! They hadn't taken their afternoon tea yet, while already she'd woken, breakfasted, nearly been married, cried herself to sleep, and been roused five times by an aunt who wished her to go downstairs and contemplate, amongst company, her public humiliation.

Quite a lot to fit into a day, really.

Tears pricked her eyes. Not again! She dashed them away. *Stop crying*, she thought. *You did not love him*. She had liked him very much, and she had hoped and vowed to grow to love him, but these endless tears were not for the life they would have shared. They were for humiliation, she thought. And betrayal, and shock. And they had already given her an awful headache and she didn't want it to worsen.

Her hand fell from the drapes. With a sigh, she

turned away from the window. A piece of paper lay discarded on the carpet. After a startled moment, she recognized it: her anonymous admirer had sent another note today; it had been waiting on her return from the church. Had she read it earlier? It looked as if she had, but she couldn't remember doing so.

She took it up and sat down in an easy chair. Yes, there was a tearstain near the top. She swallowed and decided to ignore that. The script was very elegant, wasn't it? Oh, she would not fool herself. With her luck, the author probably had gout, six children, and no hair.

For fear of offending you I have hesitated to write another letter, but my ardent admiration overwhelms the bounds of propriety. Herein I intend to contemplate a question that has haunted me for some time: How could I not have fallen in love with you, Miss Maudsley?

Her admirer needed to have a chat with Thomas. Thomas could advise him on this question. For that matter, Lord Trent could as well.

What was *wrong* with her? Jilted *twice*!

She laid down the letter and stared blankly at the window. Some awful flaw lurked inside her. That was the obvious conclusion.

But the obvious conclusion made no sense! It was not immodest to acknowledge herself passably pretty, reasonably charming, and very well liked. Moreover, she had done everything right. Everything! Obeyed every rule. Smiled at insults. Charmed all the snobbish gorgons who'd caviled at her lowly background.

Refused every second glass of wine! Forgone cycling because it required split skirts, refrained from singing in company, declined all wicked parlor games. Cheered up sourpusses and swallowed retorts, forgiven ill tempers, and never—not once!—taken the Lord's name in vain. Embroidered thirty handkerchiefs in three weeks! Why, she'd been stitching in her sleep by the end of that!

And for what?

Not for this.

The lump was forming in her throat again. Very well, if she wanted to cry, she would cry for her parents. They had given up so much to ensure her prospects! They had given *her* up. After she'd gone to school, all she'd had of them were letters and the holidays—so brief, never enough. They'd claimed to want a different fate for her than their own. Having come into wealth as adults, her parents had lost their old friends—some of whom had no longer felt comfortable with them, others of whom had sought to take advantage. But new friends of equal fortune had not lasted, either. Their manners, customs, attitudes and interests had been too different to support true friendship.

In these tribulations, her parents had seen a lesson for her. A girl dowered so richly would have to associate with her peers—the best and wealthiest members of society. But in such circles, a girl raised in Leeds, with a northern accent and rustic ways, would never flourish. Thus they had sent her to school, and after their deaths, according to their wishes, Richard had found a well-born family to raise her during holidays and guide her successfully through her debut.

And she *had* succeeded. She had! For her parents' sake as much as her own, she had tried her best and triumphed in every way.

Every way but one.

A choked laugh escaped her. Only one matter remained outside of her control. And Thomas had seemed such a safe choice for it! So gentlemanly, so reliable, so . . . desperate. Oh, the monster! The sight of him bounding away from the altar was stuck in her head; in her half-sleep, it had unfolded over and over, as taunting as a snippet from some irksome song. He loved her, did he? She'd prayed it to be true, but had feared that he loved her fortune better. And in the end—how odd!—neither idea had proved right.

Three million pounds he had left at that altar! It was beyond a fortune. And he was *dead broke*! What else could he want from a woman?

It was very difficult not to believe that something was wrong with her.

Some flicker of movement caught her attention. She realized it had been her own reflection in the looking glass, as she'd shoved her fist against her mouth. Why, she looked like a madwoman—chignon collapsing, eyes wide and crazed, her simple green morning dress rumpled beyond repair.

She lowered her fist, exhaled, and forced her attention back to the letter.

Of course, I do not need to mention your kindness. Your benevolence to the orphanages is legendary; you are a bosom friend to all who have the good fortune to know you. The entire town praises your chaste, moral rectitude and your unshakable good temper. Even the wicked columnists in the newspapers can find no wrong in you.

A wild feeling tightened her throat. Yes, any number of anonymous journalists had testified in print that she was a paragon. How would they describe her now? Not only "dreadfully disappointed by the treacherous Lord T——," but also "abominably abused by the perfidious Lord P——." They would run out of ink for her, maybe. Or adjectives.

But no, of course they wouldn't. *Pitiable*: that was the word they would use. It was the next step up from beleaguered; it conjured a more permanent condition. One broken engagement was shocking. Two spelled damaged goods.

She pushed the letter to the floor. Anonymously penned—what did it signify? It was only another piece of cowardice from another penniless blackguard.

Men! All of them, spineless.

Springing to her feet, she began to pace. Well, she had no use for spineless curs. In fact, she *pitied* the poor girl who purchased Thomas. That girl would not get value for her money! When Gwen thought of all the objections she had swallowed during their courtship—his habit of leering at ladies' bosoms, which Elma had persuaded her was natural for a man; his execrable fondness for bad puns, which she'd told herself she found charming; his taste for gambling, although the roof on his country estate had fallen in for lack of funds to repair it; his snobbery toward the lower classes, as if her parents hadn't once belonged to them—why, she felt quite *lucky* that he'd jilted her!

She came to a stop. How astonished he would be to learn that. He probably imagined her prostrate with grief, wailing and rending her hair. As if *he* were such a prize to lose! A man who bolted from church like a rat from the light!

Perhaps she should inform him of this. Yes, what a brilliant idea! She could write him this very instant, chronicling the many reasons she was *so* glad not to be wed to him.

She threw herself down at the writing table.

You fancied yourself a fine dancer, but you stepped on my feet at every turn.

The scratch of pen across the paper sounded pleasingly violent.

Your breath so often reeked of onions that I wondered if you ate aught else.

She did not think her handwriting had ever slanted so boldly!

I nearly gagged every time you kissed me. In fact, I think you the <u>worst</u> kisser I have ever encountered.

That was saying something, for although she only had one other kisser to go by, Lord Trent's performance had not recommended itself either. Very . . . slobbery, had been Lord Trent. Paired with all the nipping, he had put her in mind of a terrier.

Oh, surely she could . . . extrapolate a little?

In fact, with all your slobbering, you put me in mind of a terrier.

There. That would make him wonder!

Also, you talked of all the things you would do for us, as if "doing" were tantamount to "purchasing." You never acknowledged that it was my money you spent so freely in your imagination—and your own desires, not mine, that you intended to gratify. Why should I desire the addition of a smoking room to your country house? Moreover, why would you not wish first for a roof?

Some delicious feeling was sparkling to life inside her. It made her breath come quicker and the fog clear from her brain. Her heart was pounding and her skin tingling in the very same manner as when she'd taken that balloon ride across Devonshire last summer.

As for me, do not think I am crying into my pillow for what happened today. As you wanted my money, so I wanted your name. It was a fair trade, I thought, to achieve my parents' dream for me.

Good luck with the roof at Pennington Grange, by the way. I will hope it does not rain too much this season.

No, no. That sounded too bitter. Also, she had no interest in defending herself through reference to her parents' hopes. She did not need to excuse herself to him.

In fact, I will admit that I very much liked the idea of being a viscountess. It seems I am as shallow and vain as you. But at least I can acknowledge it! Besides, I have an excuse: I had no true understanding of how empty and insignificant a title might be, until its worthlessness was demonstrated by <u>*your*</u> *unmanly cowardice.*

Nevertheless, you may persist in thinking me grasping: I simply <u>*don't care*</u>.

"I don't care," she whispered. What an astonishing statement. She laid down the pen. Was it true? "I *don't* care." Had she ever said those words before?

She hoped they were true, for she knew what would come next. All the pity in the world would be directed toward her. After all, she was so very, very *nice*.

How undignified. How unbearable! She could not tolerate it again. And it would be worse this time, for she was clearly the victim now.

Perhaps she should take out an advertisement in the paper: *Do not waste your sympathy on me. I don't require it. I am glad to be rid of the swine.* Why not? Surely there was more dignity in being thought rude than wretched. She had spent a great deal of time at Lady Milton's orphanage; she had seen how the wretched lived, and she had seen with what distaste the other ladies ministered to those children. There was nothing worse than being thought wretched. And she was not wretched! The roof over her head wasn't collapsing.

She reached again for the pen, and the shine of the gold band at its base struck some chord in her. She frowned at it, trying to think—

She sat bolt upright in the chair. He had Richard's ring! Her father's ring!

She cupped a hand over her mouth. Horror prickled over her, hot and mortifying. What had she been thinking? She had agreed to marry him with no love in her heart, but she'd given him her most precious relic! Even with Trent she'd shown more caution.

It was unforgivable. Oh, she was low and rotten. And he had worn it at the altar! Bile rose into her throat. He had bounded out of the church wearing her ring!

She would demand it back instantly. If he dared to give it away or pawn it, she would—why, she would set the police on him!

The thought astonished her. Police chasing a viscount. A laugh bubbled in her throat. Why, she was not so nice, after all.

She looked down at the words, scrawled so fiercely that one might think a man had penned them. A terrier! It made her laugh again. Maybe wickedness was more her native talent. After all, where had niceness gotten her? From beleaguered to pitiable, that was where! Slobbered on and nipped by beastly men!

The *deuces* with being nice, then! It profited her nothing. It was exhausting! And here was proof: only five minutes ago she'd been exhausted, while now she felt like skipping into the hallway and—yelling! No, yelling wasn't enough. She felt like *smashing* something!

She made a fist and smacked it experimentally against the desktop. Yes, she could smash something. She looked around. The clock? No, no, Aunt Elma admired that clock.

The mirror? It seemed a bit gothic. Madwomen too

often smashed mirrors. She wouldn't want to give the wrong impression.

The flower vase? Yes! Yes, she *could* smash that!

Over his *head*!

Just imagining it made her queer exhilaration redouble. It swelled up so fast and fiercely that she had to swallow to keep herself from—screaming something, maybe. It felt just like that balloon ride, *exactly* like it: all the strings falling away, and then the sudden giddy lift into the ether.

Why, she would *not* knit those sweaters! Lady Anne had made the promise. Let *her* knit them! Gwen would even supply her with the yarn. Fifty skeins of quality merino currently sat in her dressing room, simply *longing* for the tender touch of an earl's daughter.

What else wouldn't she do? Heavens above, the possibilities seemed dazzling. All the nasty small thoughts that she hid away—why not share them?

No more purchasing gowns she disliked simply to placate sad-eyed shopkeepers.

No more patronage of charity events when she suspected the profits were going straight into the host's pocket.

And no more ignoring the sly allusions to her background! Ten years, now—she was done with it! *Why, Lady Featherstonehaugh, do you mean to remind these ladies that my father was once a chemist, a shopkeeper of the most common order? How kind. Let me return the favor. May I remind them of how your husband halved your allowance when he found you in bed with Mr. Bessemer?*

No more feigned obliviousness when a gentleman rubbed his hand over her breast during a dance. *Did you misplace your fingers? I will misplace mine into your eye.*

No more levees at court! She always came home sore from wrists to shoulders, thanks to the nasty women who stuck pins into people's arms to force them out of the way on the stairs. The Queen's concerts were dead boring anyway.

And no more kissing *any* man who slobbered. Really, there *had* to be something more to kissing, or else why would ladies giggle over it? Well, bother it, she supposed she would simply have to find out! If she wasn't going to be nice anymore, why not be fast?

In fact, now that being nice didn't matter, perhaps she should also make a list of things she *would* do.

But first, she must finish the task at hand. Retrieving the pen, she wrote in that deliciously aggressive and unfamiliar hand, *You will return my brother's ring immediately*.

Despite the underlining, it did not look quite complete to her.

Ah! In giant block-print, she added:

OR ELSE.

Alex was beginning to wish he'd brought his own bottle of liquor. Alcohol—so said the doctor he'd consulted in Buenos Aires—interfered with natural sleep. But an hour now he'd sat listening to this nonsense, and it was beginning to wear on his patience.

Meanwhile, Henry Beecham, who was Gwen's de facto guardian and should have been out for blood, instead grew ever more cheerful. He reclined in the easy chair by the fireplace, flicking drops of his fourth or fifth whisky into the flames. With every sizzling pop, he smirked into his sleeve like a boy with a secret.

"But Fulton Hall won't do," said Belinda. She sat in a nearby chair, outwardly composed; heavy lids lent her blue eyes a deceptive air of placidity, and her chestnut hair had been trammeled into a viciously tight chignon. But Alex knew her nature, so he knew where to look. Her right hand had broken free of her left, which still sat demurely in her lap; the rogue digits were squeezing the armrest in a fierce and regular rhythm. She was imagining herself in possession of Pennington's throat. Alex would wager money on it. Already she had told him to wring Gerard's throat for the sin of selling a musty house she'd never bothered to visit.

Had a good deal of snap, did Belinda. Put her down in Manhattan's Five Points, and by nightfall, half the citizens would be pouring into church to repent their evil ways.

"But Fulton Hall is lovely," said Elma Beecham. She cast a hopeful look toward the settee, where Caroline was languishing.

As suited the twins' respective roles, Belinda had shrieked in the church, while Caro had wept. Now Caro offered a regretful smile, along with a shake of the head.

Elma sighed. "No, I suppose not, then. It's too near to Pennington's estate."

"Then keep her in London," Alex said flatly. He rubbed his eyes. "I told you the viscount is bound for the Continent." Henry Beecham might have come home directly from the church, but Alex had not. He'd found Pennington's town house in a state of disarray. The master had fled to the railway station, intent on the Dover-bound train.

Elma gaped at him. "But she's not *invited* to anything, Mr. Ramsey. Everybody thought she would be on her honeymoon."

"Besides," said Belinda, "it doesn't matter. His mother is still in town."

Caroline gave a visible shudder. "She's even worse."

"Right," he said. "The dragon might slay her with an unkind look, I suppose. Who bloody cares?"

Elma gasped.

Most of the world could not tell his sisters apart. He'd no trouble on that account, but it never failed to amaze him how identically they delivered a glare.

"Watch your language," Belinda bit out. "And please, do *not* illuminate us with one of your trenchant social commentaries."

All right, he was usually a bit subtler in his approach, but this conversation was going in circles. "I illuminate, do I? And here I thought I idled, ignored, and absconded." *Absconded.* Almost, he sighed with longing. It sounded like an excellent idea.

Belinda launched into a lecture to which he did not

bother to listen. His attention wandered to the empty sofa across the room, an overstuffed piece of maroon brocade. Hideous. Unusually long, too. Almost as long as a bed.

It looked quite comfortable.

Sleep. The doctor in Buenos Aires had warned him against napping. That was very easy advice to give, no doubt.

Belinda grew louder. He nodded agreeably, and she rewarded him by modulating her voice to a less strident pitch. ". . . *you* may find civility tedious, Alex, but Gwen cares about her place in society."

"Certainly," he said. "But if actions bespeak character, as you have so often told me"—he gave her a flattering smile—"then I consider this morning a lucky escape for her. Don't you?"

Belinda sighed. "Well, I am tempted to agree." She wrinkled her nose. "What a toad the viscount is!"

"I just can't understand it," Elma murmured. As she took a deep breath and launched back into her pacing, Caroline sat up and sent him a mischievous look.

He lifted a brow in acknowledgment. Since vanity did not permit Elma to wear spectacles, her progress across the carpet was proving dramatic. Three times already she'd collided with the centre table, and now she looked bound for a fourth.

"I still don't see why Trumbly Grange won't do," Elma grumbled. "The peace and quiet would do her good."

Bel and Caro gave speaking snorts. Unaccustomed

to their synchronized contempt, Elma halted. The centre table held its ground, four inches away. Alex shook his head at Caro, who grimaced apologetically.

"It's a sad little house located on the edge of the moors, isn't it?" Belinda was never one to mince words, even when the property she maligned was her host's. "There's not a neighbor in miles. Would *you* like to stay at Trumbly Grange?" When Elma looked at her blankly, Belinda added, "You'll be accompanying her, of course. She can't travel alone!"

"Oh!" Clearly it had not occurred to Elma that the itinerary she proposed would be her own. "Yes, of course I'll accompany her. Trumbly Grange . . ." She turned to consult with her husband. "Hal, hadn't you planned to go north and have a look at that filly for the Yorkshire Oaks?" When no reply came from the fireplace, she put her hands on her hips and lifted her voice. "Mr. Beecham. I am addressing you!"

"What's that?" Snuffling, Beecham wiped his nose and set down his drink. "North? No, no, changed my plans. Bad strain of the back sinew. She's done for."

"Ah!" Elma turned back to the twins. "Well, I suppose the north will serve, then. Indeed, why not? Have you noticed how young everyone looks there? It's for want of sun, I expect." She sounded positively warm now. "Yes, what a good idea. The north will do nicely!"

Alex swallowed a laugh. Elma had a remarkable ability to judge anything by its possible effect on her looks. Moreover, since her faith in her beauty still thrived at age fifty, this worked to create an attitude in her of unshakable optimism. The gray in her blond hair only made it look blonder. The wretched failures of her cook benefited her bone structure by melting away "that puppy fat about my jaw." Three summers ago, when taken with fever during a weekend at Caro's country house, she had observed to Alex, in a tone too syrupy for his comfort, that the flush on her face made her hazel eyes look radiantly green. Didn't he agree?

He'd agreed, but he'd also taken care not to find himself alone with her again. She had the alarming habit of speaking to him as though she were twenty, and raised in a bordello. Worse yet, on the rare occasions when her husband was present for it, he tended to stand behind her and nod vehemently, as if to say, *Give it a go, then. I don't mind.*

"The lack of sun is a sound point," Belinda decided. "What Gwen needs is someplace cheerful."

"Hmm," Alex said. "Rules out England, then, doesn't it?"

Belinda flashed him a sharp look.

"Not the north, then," Elma said hesitantly.

"Not the north," Belinda confirmed.

Sighing, he tipped his head back to study the ceiling. It was an interesting geography they were assembling, here. For shame, Gwen could not stay in London. For pride, she could not go south. For spirits, north was out of the question. East lay the ocean, of course.

His eyes had shut.

Forcing them open, he said, "There's always west."

His sarcasm was lost on Elma. "Wales, do you mean?"

The syrupy note. He pulled his head down to confirm it. Yes, she was posing for him. Her hand strategically stroked the neckline of her gown. He did not wish to glance onward toward her husband.

Belinda cleared her throat. She looked dubious, and he did not think it all for Wales. "Herefordshire, perhaps."

"Ireland!" cried Caroline. "Whisky cheers a lady as well as a man." She cast a pointed look toward Henry Beecham, who had not offered to share his joy.

"Boston?" Elma frowned. "Do we know anyone in Boston?"

"Newfoundland," said Alex. "San Francisco—bit foggy, no doubt, but most Londoners would call it tropical. Or why not China? Keep going west and you're bound to hit it eventually. Usually works for me."

"You might wish to reconsider that," Caro said. "You got kicked out of China last year, if I recall."

"Did I? Well, that explains the rude reply to my greeting at the port authority. I thought I was in Japan."

"Your flippancy helps no one," Belinda informed him.

He shrugged. "You propose to hide her away like a broken toy. London is her home, and you want to hound her out of it. Is that the act of a friend?"

Caroline leaned forward. "Alex, you *must* try to understand. It's not at all like last time! The *groom* cried off. And in such a horrible way—when he needed her money so badly! People will assume he discovered something awful about her at just the last moment." She faltered, going pale. "I really do fear she is . . ."

"Ruined," Belinda whispered.

Elma flinched.

"For God's sake." Hearing the edge in his voice, he caught himself. "It isn't as if she were caught *in flagrante delicto.* This is London's darling you're talking about. I hope you won't feed her this nonsense; she's silly enough to believe it."

"You're so naïve," Belinda said pityingly. "How do you manage that with all these foreign places you visit?"

He sighed. In an argument, Bel was like a dog with a bone: she would never let go of her point. "Naïveté is imagining that doors will stand closed to her after this. Naïveté, Belinda, is your *vast* underestimation of the power of three million pounds. Preach all you like about what people will *say.* In Shanghai, they gossip if a woman's feet are too large—in Valparaiso, if her mantilla clings too tightly to her breast. But no matter where you are, money makes every sin disappear. It's better than vinegar that way."

She gaped at him. "You can't really believe that," she said. "If you do, then you've been away from civilization for far too long."

"Civilization," he said dryly. "Half the guests in that church this morning were using the opportunity to pray that land prices will rise so they can sell their forty thousand acres and pay off their debts before creditors seize their town houses and ruin their season. *That* is your civilization. As venal as any other."

Belinda tipped her chin mutinously but did not reply.

"Oh, and let me tell you," he added helpfully. "Land prices are not going to rise. Not that much. Not anytime soon."

The silence extended. It seemed to him a minor miracle. Finally, his sisters were listening to sense.

He decided to take advantage of it, for the occasion came only once in a blue moon. "And from now on, instead of standing by while she stumbles into an engagement with the first rotten bounder who bothers to smile at her, I suggest that you take an *active* hand in the business. Find a man who will make a proper husband for her—or at least manage to stick it out at the altar."

Belinda huffed. "Oh, Alex."

Of course there was an objection. "Let's have it."

"What do you propose? That we pick a man and instruct her to love him?"

He snorted. "Love? Have you not—"

"Paris!" Elma gasped.

"No," Caroline said, "the viscount will be certain to pass through. The Dover-bound train, you know—"

"Guernsey, then?"

"Guernsey," Belinda echoed.

"Yes, it's perfect! What do you think? Sunshine, fresh air, and absolutely nobody of note!"

He fell back in his chair. This was useless. What they *should* be discussing was how Gwen always managed to pick the worst of a very large lot. First Trent, now this one. For poor taste in husbands, her judgment rivaled Anne Boleyn's.

Then again—he shook his head as Caroline countered Guernsey with Cornwall, and the debate of various hidey-holes picked up steam again—perhaps he had it wrong, and the reason Gwen kept picking duds was because her counsel came from this lot. He would swallow knives for his sisters' sakes, but if his life or even his lunch depended on it, he would not turn to them for advice. *Love*, Bel said. Gwen's aim had nothing to do with love. She wanted status, a title, and so long as everyone around her encouraged her to disguise that ambition and play the nearsighted romantic, her search for golden princes would unerringly turn up toads.

Damn it. He'd promised Richard to look after her. But he'd resisted taking a direct hand in this courtship. His failure had led to the fracas today.

Black humor settled over him. Did he have time for this nonsense? No. But how hard could it be to find a tenable husband? Surely there was *one* unmarried, titled idiot who did not have a violent temper, or syphilis, or a consuming thirst for drink, or a destructive appetite for cards, or, for that matter, any perversions either illegal or extraordinary.

Almost, Alex could picture this paragon: balding, perhaps, with a pronounced belly accrued during

afternoons sitting on his arse in the Lords and evenings relaxing at his club, drinking port and dining
on steak while raging with his cronies at the gall of
upstart foreigners. Irascible to abstract foes, yes, but
also indubitably good-humored with friends, chiv-
alrous with women, fond of his dogs, given to bad
jokes that rhymed, and—above all—loyal through
and through to those with the good taste to admire
him. And Gwen would admire him. If she'd managed
to admire Trent, she could manage it with anybody.

All right, so he'd draw up a list of candidates. Hire
a man to research them. That should take two, three
weeks at most; these MP types were never discreet.
He'd dispatch the list to his sisters, instruct them to
set Gwen in front of these men, and drop mention
of her assets and marital intent. A month more until
someone proposed? Yes, just about.

If he got on with it, they could have her engaged
within eight weeks. He'd be halfway around the world
by the time the next wedding day came. Would send a
cable by way of congratulations. Perhaps he wouldn't
even remember the date, and someone, his secretary,
would have to remind him when the event was drawing near. *Yes*. That sounded like an excellent plan.

What he needed, he thought, was a copy of Debrett's
Peerage. And a very strong cup of coffee.

He came to his feet. "If you will excuse me, ladies."

Chapter Three

One foot into the lobby, Alex came to a stop. Elma had assured them that Gwen was flattened by grief, but here she was picking her way down the stairs, an oversized valise clutched to her chest. More to the point, she had an envelope between her teeth.

The sight arrested him. It seemed historic. He could probably sell tickets to it. Proper Gwen Maudsley, carrying a letter in her mouth for convenience's sake.

In fact, now that she'd embraced creativity, he could think of several other uses he might suggest for her lips.

It was a hot, predictable thought, irritating and useless, and, above all, *bewildering*. With so many willing, complex women in the world, he had little respect for men who fixated on girlishness. Innocence was, by definition, an absence of experience—character— knowledge. To *desire* that absence seemed rather deviant. Certainly it reflected a terrible laziness, or else the same failure of imagination that drove Gerry to

patronize artists who challenged none of his precon-
ceptions about the world.

Come to think of it, pity that Gerry was already
married. He needed so badly to be admired, and
Gwen, of all women, was determined to be nothing
but agreeable. A more boring goal, Alex could not
imagine.

It said nothing good of him that he found himself
watching her all the same. She paused mid-step, lifting
her shoulder to catch the edge of the letter, readjust-
ing her toothy grip.

He glanced up again and discovered that she had
paused to torque her shoulder toward her mouth and
was using this shoulder as leverage to readjust her
toothy grip on the letter.

How long since he'd seen her so close? Last
autumn, he thought—in the garden at Heaton Dale.
The breeze had carried away her shawl, and the late
afternoon light, falling through the oak leaves, had
strewn a delicate filigree of gold across her smooth,
pale shoulders—

Well, yes, she'd always been pale, hadn't she? Many
girls were, nothing special there. Her current pallor
probably owed to shock.

Since she'd had a difficult morning, he stepped
backward into the hall, out of sight, to wait until
she'd exited. No doubt the realization that someone
had witnessed her indecorum would serve her the
death blow.

A panicked squeak reached his ears. He leaned

back into the lobby in time to spot her bobbling. She caught her balance, barely, but that valise was almost too large for her to see over. Another round of toothy acrobatics, and she was going to fall on her head before she made it to the landing.

Muttering a curse beneath his breath, he approached the staircase. "May I help?"

"Oh!" The valise plummeted to her feet. The envelope pursued a more leisurely descent, floating down to the first step, glancing off its edge, then sliding down several more. It was addressed, but he could not make out the name.

"Alex!" Her eyes rose from the envelope, which was nearer now to him than her; as she gave him a very wide smile, he had the curious impression that she meant to distract him from this knowledge. "How do you do this afternoon? So glad to see you back in town!"

This good cheer seemed a bit unlikely, even from her. "I'm tolerably well," he answered slowly. Her eyes looked a bit bloodshot. Someone needed to rub the color back into her cheeks, but not him. Some titled xenophobe would do it. He cleared his throat. "And how are you?"

She set a slipper atop the valise and lifted her chin. The posture put him in mind of explorers staking their sovereign's flag in new ground. "I'm splendid," she declared.

A smile pulled at his mouth. Really, somebody needed to cast a trophy for her. *In Recognition of Her*

Tireless Dedication to Utterly Groundless Good Cheer. "I'm impressed," he said. "I expected you'd have a headache at least."

Her auburn brows knitted. "Oh." Only now did she appear to recall a cause for distress. "Well, not *splendid*, I suppose. Of course not. How silly would that be! But I am better, thank you. I slept a good deal. Sleep is restorative!" Her words came more and more quickly. "And how good of you to call. I do appreciate your concern. I'm much better. And your sisters, of course." Her lashes fluttered. "Ah—their concern, I mean. I appreciate it. I hope they're well?"

Beyond the price of a ticket. For Gwen Maudsley to bungle such a basic social courtesy seemed no less likely to him than the failure of a prima ballerina to lift her leg above her waist. But she'd bungled it, all right. She'd butchered it. "They're quite well," he replied, straight-faced by an effort. Because it suddenly seemed wise to ask, he added, "What's in the luggage?"

"Oh, the—the valise? Just some . . ." She brushed a hand over her brow. Her chignon was slumping toward imminent collapse. Another first. He had never seen her hair in any state other than viciously domesticated. "Sweaters," she said brightly. She gave a light, atrociously fake laugh. "Sweaters for Lady Milton's orphanage. She asked me to deliver them today."

He held his tongue, hoping that a brief silence might highlight for her the patent absurdity of that claim. But her expression did not waver; she regarded him quite earnestly. Or was it defiantly? No, he could not square that sentiment with what he knew of her. "Deliver them," he repeated. "Today."

"Yes, today."

He gave her a disbelieving smile. "Before or after your wedding? Did she specify?"

"I know, I should have dispatched a footman with them, but . . ." She gave a helpless shrug. "The orphans, you know."

"No," he said. "Don't know any, unless you and I count."

"Orphaned *children*." Then, apparently reading into his expression a sympathy he did not feel—for he doubted that these particular orphans existed—she added, "I know, it's quite horrible, isn't it? I've been knitting sweaters for all those poor tots. Every single one."

"How virtuous," he said dryly.

She did not appear to have heard him. "And now they're finished, finally, so I thought to drop them by and have the joy of watching the sweaters be . . . donned." From behind her ear, a red tress sprang to freedom, tickling her chin.

Portentous, that lock of hair. He found himself riveted by it. Its message seemed clear: he was witnessing the total collapse, mental and physical, of London's golden girl. If it sent all her hair tumbling, he would not even oppose it.

He released the image on a long breath. Now she was making *his* brain misfire. If she collapsed, he'd have a much harder time finding a man willing to marry her. Lunatics lacked cachet.

Her hand rose to tuck the curl away. "Terribly tragic," she said absently. "Little boys and girls, with no . . ." She glanced toward her valise and frowned.

"Sweaters," he said helpfully. Generally she was a much better liar than this, persuasively complimenting any number of people for virtues they did not possess. Were it otherwise, she would never have been so popular with her set.

"Sweaters, yes!" With another bright smile for him, and a covert glance for the letter, she bent to retrieve the valise. Judging by how easily she lifted it, it might even contain children's sweaters. In which case, he was going to conclude that she'd lost her mind.

As she straightened, the smile flickered briefly, then strengthened again. "But how kind of you to drop by," she said. "After that dreadful scene, no less. I hope you weren't too discomfited. I expect we will see each other before you go abroad again?"

That was a very clumsy attempt at dismissal. Yielding to alarm, he took two steps up the stairs. Her pupils looked to be normal, so she hadn't been administered a sedative. "Did you take a knock to the head today?"

She blinked. "No, of course not. Why do you ask?"

He tipped his head. "Would you call this behavior typical of you, then?"

She shifted her weight, clearly uncomfortable with the question. "Everyone is in the drawing room, you know." Her eyes stole again to the letter, which now sat by his foot.

"Yes, I just came from there. Won't you join us?" Certainly he couldn't let her run off in this . . . state. Whatever it was. He supposed it did not speak well of him that he found it rather fascinating. Gwen Maudsley, come undone. He'd always had a fascination with how things came apart—clocks, telephones, the whatnot. But until now, he'd drawn the line at the dismantling of people. "Surely the orphans can wait an hour?"

She opened her mouth. He lifted a brow. She sighed and took a quick peek beyond him, then said in a lowered voice, "I will speak frankly, then. I don't wish to attend the campaign session."

"Campaign session." He was beginning to feel like a parrot.

"Yes, you know, the Campaign to Save Gwen from Eternal Humiliation, *again*." She produced a wry smile. This one proved less stable than her cheerful mien; it slipped quickly away. "But you mustn't let me keep you from it. I expect you will be quite useful to them. They already used up their best ideas the last time."

She descended a step. He laid a hand on either banister, blocking her path. "And what of your attendance? Should you not be rather interested in the outcome?"

She eyed his hands. "Not really. I have decided my path."

"Oh? How intriguing. Where does it lead?"

She gave him a blank look. "To the orphanage."

Right. He bent down to pick up the letter. A

gasp came from above him. "That's mine!" she cried.

"I'll just hand it up—"

A large, soft weight smacked into his head, throwing him off his balance. He staggered sideways, letter in hand; missed a step, cursed, and took a great leap clear of the stairs.

Safely on his feet, he straightened and looked up. She stood wide-eyed, her hands cupped over her mouth, her brown eyes huge. The valise now lay several steps below her, having split open to disgorge a great mess of... yarn.

His brain balked. "You didn't—did you *throw* that at me?" No. It was inconceivable.

About as inconceivable as a valise that fell horizontally.

Her hands dropped to fist at her waist. "I want my letter!"

He laughed in astonishment. "You *did* throw it. Why, Miss Maudsley. You naughty girl."

"It slipped!"

"The law of gravity disagrees with you."

She sniffed. "Do not bring science into this."

"Right, very bad of me," he said. "I always forget to leave it at the door with my hat. All right, then, tell me this: did you forget to actually *knit* the sweaters?" He nodded toward the valise. "Or were you planning to have the orphans do it for you?"

"Never," she said heatedly. Another red lock collapsed, this one unfurling all the way to her waist. "I will *buy* sweaters for those orphans."

"Of course," he murmured. Her hair was such an unusual color. The shade of a fine pinot noir, he thought, when struck by the sun.

"I will buy a hundred sweaters," she said. "A thousand! But I shan't knit them, and I shan't pretend I did!"

In fact, she'd pretended it only a minute ago, but now did not seem the opportune time to remind her. "Right," he said. "Well done. And why should you?"

The question was rhetorical, but she took it seriously. "Lady Milton and Lady Anne want me to do it. They're both hypocrites, you know. They care nothing for those orphans. Lady Milton isn't even joining the excursion—why go to Ramsgate when one can holiday in Nice!" She crossed her arms and rolled her shoulders, as though to physically shed such thoughts of duplicity. "Hypocrites," she repeated. "*I* care for the orphans."

Oh ho, a quarrel. No doubt it involved a great lot of silk-clad women with diamonds in their ears, arguing about who cared more for poor little Oliver—pausing only to allow the footman to refresh their champagne. "Naturally, you care."

Her eyes narrowed. "You don't believe me? Perhaps I'll open my own orphanage. And I will feed them something more than gruel, you may count on it!"

The shrill note in her voice dimmed his amusement. All right, the lack of tears and screams had thrown him off, but clearly she was hysterical. On consideration, it seemed typical that Gwen would permit herself to exhibit only the mildest, most pleasant symptoms of the malady. "Beef every night," he agreed. "Why not? You've certainly got the funds for it."

A line appeared between her brows. "Don't humor me."

"Did I ever?" The idea surprised him. "If so, it was only by accident. No need to pile on to that effort."

She hesitated, then gave him a smile. "That's true. You've never gone out of your way to be nice."

He smiled back at her; for all that she was babbling nonsense, hysteria looked charming on her. "Open the orphanage," he said. "You can do anything you like. Your options were not limited by today's events."

"Oh?" She came marching down the steps, hand extended. "Then I will ask you to return my property."

He glanced at the envelope. *The Right Honble. The Viscount Pennington.* "Oh, good God. What—"

She lunged for it, and he caught her wrist. Her pulse thrummed like the drum in some wild jungle dance. Hot skin, soft beneath his thumb. "That's *mine*," she said. He hadn't imagined her brown eyes could be put to a glare, but they looked nothing doe-like to him now. She gave a futile yank against his grip. "Let go of me!"

"Writing to Pennington," he said. The sound of his own words focused him. He opened his fingers, shedding the feel of her. "What in God's name is this?" Her optimism went too far if she hoped that bastard would change his mind.

Her jaw squared. "That is not your concern."

He did not recall the irksome discovery of a backbone being one of hysteria's symptoms. "I made a promise to your brother," he reminded her. Alas, alas, for deathbed promises. "I'm afraid it's very much my concern."

Mention of Richard seemed to throw her. She hesitated. "All right, then. It's a list of reasons I hate him."

"I'll have the truth," he said flatly.

"That is the truth!" Her finger caught up a loose strand of hair, twining it around her knuckle. Biting her lip and peering up at him, she looked like a very good approximation of a barroom flirt.

A more annoying development he could not imagine. He relied on her to look prim and untouchable. "Leave your hair alone," he snapped.

Her hand dropped. She gave him a marveling look. "You're quite beastly, you know."

"You're only now realizing this? I would have assumed the gossips might inform you. Failing them, Belinda."

"Yes, but . . ." Her eyes narrowed. "Alex," she said. "Belinda tells me all the time how much you loathe when Lord Weston tries to bully you. Why should you do the same to me? Let me have my letter."

He laughed, surprised by this devious turn. "Oh, that's well done, Gwen. Yes, it's true, of all the roles I might play, the bully is not my favorite. But when you're determined to play the idiot—"

"I am *not* playing the idiot!" She grabbed again for the letter.

He stepped backward, holding the envelope above

her reach. "It doesn't matter anyway," he said. "Pennington's run off. He's not here to receive your notes."

The news visibly stunned her. Mouth agape, she retreated a pace toward the stairs. "Run off?" she whispered.

"Train to Dover, bound for the Continent. I'm sorry," he added. "He's a piece of filth."

"But he has my ring!"

He felt a brief flicker of amazement: she had purchased the wedding bands? Had the viscount done nothing for this match?

Why had she been content to sell herself so cheaply?

And then, looking at her face, a new possibility occurred to him. "Richard's ring."

"Yes!"

Christ. He remembered all too clearly her face as he had placed that ring in her palm. He sighed. "I'll get it back, then."

Her wide eyes looked dazed. She seemed to look through him at some disastrous scene, miles distant. "But if he's taken it abroad with him—"

"His first stop will be Paris, no doubt, and I'm bound for there tomorrow." And then, because she was still staring in that broken, addled way that put him disturbingly in mind of a vacant-eyed doll, he added, "Don't fret, sweetheart. You'll have it back soon enough. And for the man himself, consider yourself well rid of him."

She blinked and focused on him. A curious look

crossed her face. The sudden slant of her mouth seemed almost ... calculating.

"All right," she said slowly. "You want to read the letter? I'll read it to you myself, if you like. But only if you promise to do a favor in return."

His instincts stirred, bidding caution.

How ridiculous. Hell, maybe hysteria was catching. Gwen was as harmless as a rabbit. "Ask away," he said and started to break the seal.

"Not here!" She threw a quick glance around. Now she looked almost feverish—bright spots of color on her pale cheeks, and an odd glitter in her eyes. "Discretion, Alex! The library will do."

The strange smile she gave him before turning on her heel made his instincts rise up again, clanging.

Misfiring, misfiring. *Rabbit*, he told himself and fell in step behind her for the library.

Chapter Four

Striding down from the corridor toward a new and better chapter in her life, Gwen felt transformed. For one thing, she was striding. Before, she had only drifted. Secondly, she was leading—and leading Alex Ramsey, no less! Alex never followed anybody's lead. It seemed a considerable accomplishment, akin to hooking a bull by the nose.

In fact, by the time she threw open the door to the library, she felt well underway to becoming a smashing success at this routine. On the table in the center of the room lay a volume on womanly virtues that Elma had been reading to her as she'd knitted in the evenings. She would throw it into the street! That map of the world against the left wall, full of so many empty spaces—she would travel to those spaces and document them!

Why not? Her giddiness showed no signs of abating. Perhaps this attitude was not a temporary impulse but a true expression of her nature, long trammeled by tight lacing and endless worrying and abstention from all the many delicious foods that Elma had warned her would make her fat.

Alex walked into the room, sparing her one of those cool head-to-toe looks that, only a day ago, would have made her feel summarized and dismissed as tediously conventional. She slammed the door shut. "I think we should ring for scones," she said. "And a great boat-load of cream! A decadent high tea in the library! What do you say?"

He put his hands into his pockets and tilted his head. Mildly he said, "Perhaps you need something stronger. A dose of laudanum, say."

"Or brandy!" she exclaimed. "Yes, what a brilliant idea! Why not?"

He hesitated briefly. "Order whatever you like," he said. "I won't be distracted from the letter, but I am willing to wait."

Ah, this was more the tone she was accustomed to hearing from him: amused and a touch condescending. In such tones did Lady Milton explain to orphans that it was more important for food to be nourishing than appetizing.

"Oh, I would never wish to inconvenience you," she said sweetly. "So many countries to visit, so much profit to be made! Very important business; I'll gladly forgo my brandy for it. Now open the letter, quick as you please."

His blue eyes widened as he placed his hand to his heart. "Sarcasm, Miss Maudsley?"

She held her smile by sheer dint of will. "I've no idea what you mean."

He shook his head and turned away. She followed him across the carpet, taking a seat near the window as he shook out the letter and propped his shoulder against the sash.

His lounging attitude made her cognizant of her own, sadly proper posture. She tried a slump of her shoulders, but her corset would not allow it.

As he began to read, the light of the setting sun illuminated his face in detail. She kept her eyes on him; she did not want to miss a single nuance of his reaction. He was, after all, the expert at rude behavior—a fact that, all of a sudden, made him very interesting. Educational, even. Did he, too, experience this lovely sense of freedom from flouting convention?

His expression remained disappointingly impassive as he read. She recalled her thoughts of him this morning, in the church. He was handsomer than Mr. Cust, she decided. Even if one preferred blonds, Mr. Cust was merely . . . pretty. But Alex's face was all angles, as though some mad sculptor had hacked him in a few strokes from a block of wood. His jaw was sharp, his chin squared off, his nose high-bridged but perfectly straight, save the slight thickening in the middle. The last bit didn't look quite so well on Belinda and Caroline, but since it counterbalanced the way his face winnowed beneath his cheekbones, it made Alex deadly.

His mouth curved. "This is quite . . ."

"Oh!" She sat forward. "Which line?"

He shook his head.

"No, really, you must tell me!"

He made a shooing gesture, as if she were some bothersome six-year-old.

She sat back again, irritated. How useful for him that he happened to be handsome. After all, a rake without looks would require charm, and Alex had none whatsoever.

Rake. She turned the word over in her mind, curious. His reputation had always seemed to her a sort of dreadful affliction, as unnerving as terminal illness or disfigurement, albeit far more distasteful because he had chosen to acquire it. Bel agreed, of course, but Caroline defended him. She said the women with whom he consorted had no interest in marriage. *Artists, actresses, and suffragettes,* Caro had told her over tea one day. *Radicals.* And then, in a whisper: *Do you know, I think I would prefer it if he seduced the debutantes! Then perhaps some marriage-minded girl would trap him.*

Remembering her own titillated shock, Gwen felt irked. Three years ago, now. How smug she'd been, with her wedding to Lord Trent scheduled and the invitations dispatched. How inevitable marriage had seemed to her, then. She'd decided that the women Alex entertained must be unnatural for not wanting to marry—and that, in turn, Alex was unnatural for admiring them.

Now she wondered if these women didn't have something to teach her. At any rate, none of them would have agreed to marry either of the swine she'd picked.

Alex cleared his throat and refolded the note. "This

is . . ." His lips folded together briefly, as if he were biting back a smile. "Not what I expected, shall we say."

"Oh? What did you expect?" It might be instructive to learn what he thought her capable of doing. He'd visited Heaton Dale last autumn to say farewell to his sisters before leaving for New York, and once or twice she'd caught him looking at her quite peculiarly—as though expecting her at any moment to do something awful, like burst into a cancan.

Learn to cancan! That was an excellent addition to her list of things to do now that she no longer cared what anybody thought of her. Better yet, Paris was the place to try it.

"Does it matter?" Alex gave a one-shouldered shrug as he slipped the letter into his jacket. "I suppose I assumed it was a plea for him to return to you. But bully for you, Gwen. You certainly gave him what-for."

The praise might have encouraged her had it not dripped with condescension. She frowned as he straightened off the window frame. The reddening sunlight spread down the length of his body, and she felt her temper sharpen. Drat it. Her criticism of Thomas had not been nearly as comprehensive as she'd hoped. He prided himself on his height, but Alex was taller. His shoulders had been adequate, but Alex's shoulders were broader. Indeed, their breadth seemed all the more striking for the slimness of Alex's waist and hips.

She supposed his odd athletic habits must account for that. Everybody knew that he spent an hour each

morning hopping about and kicking things like a mad-
dened rabbit. In France they apparently considered
this a proper sport of some sort, but then, French-
men were an odd lot. Alex was probably one of ten
people on the entire island who gave the nation credit
for anything besides its wine. At any rate, she did not
recall encountering other similarly shaped gentlemen
among English society.

The rarity suddenly struck her as regrettable.

He was speaking. "—stay right here and stand your
ground. Although the decision is yours, of course."

She opened her mouth, but her reply fell away as
she noticed something: he'd unbuttoned his jacket
at some point between lobby and library, and it had
fallen open. His belly beneath his dark waistcoat was
perfectly flat. How had she never noticed that before?
Katherine Percy, her horse-mad bridesmaid, would
have likened him to a good racehorse, all height and
lean muscle.

He was certainly a *serviceable* specimen.

"Gwen," he said. "Are you all right?"

She blinked. He lifted a brow in question. A hot
feeling prickled over her, alarm and excitement
at once. She'd been ogling him like a trollop. Alex
Ramsey, London's most dedicated bachelor. Astonishing to behold how one was blinded by his lack of eligi-
bility. Bohemian ladies must be positively gleeful that
no respectable lady got a crack at him!

"I'm perfectly well," she replied. She *felt* very well,
as if an electrical charge had gripped her. What other

new things would she see, now that she no longer cared to be virtuous? "May I have the letter back?"

"I'm afraid not." He put a hand on his hip, knocking his jacket back farther. "You can't post this, you know."

The temptation was too much to resist. She took another quick glance downward. "Why not?" Good heavens, ogling was addictive. How did one ever stop once one formed the habit? One might go on ogling for days, there were so many points of interest. His lips, for instance! What a long, well-formed mouth he had. She had noted that before, of course. Thomas's lips were quite thin.

His lips spoke. "Several reasons," they said. "Surely you can deduce them. First and foremost, you have no idea what he'd do with this note."

Alex would know how to kiss properly. Bohemian women would not endure slobbering. Only ladies determined to marry would tolerate such indignities.

Not that she would kiss him, of course. The very idea made her feel itchy. He seemed so old, although in fact he was only four years her senior, and—why, two years younger than Thomas! Thomas seemed so young, in comparison. He had not traveled so widely, though. He'd never done nothing awful or extraordinary (until today, of course). He had not made piles of money (although his family required it more than the Ramseys did), or visited Argentina, or courted suffragettes who had no intention of marrying. Such wide and varied experiences probably made the prospect of kissing a respectable girl only a fraction more interesting than staring at a wall.

Besides, what of *her* view on kissing *Alex*? He'd been so close with her brother that it would be like kissing her brother!

Well, not really. But probably Alex would think kissing her was like kissing one of his sisters.

She felt nervous, suddenly. Which was silly. It was only Alex—rude, amused, and condescending as usual.

"Gwen," he drawled. "Do try to attend. Shall I speak more slowly?"

"I heard you," she said. "You asked what he would do with the note. I expect he'd read it."

"And share it with friends," he said dryly, "and then sell it to the papers, no doubt. God knows he needs the money, and the sale of private correspondence is nothing so shocking as dirtying one's hands through actual work." He paused to smirk. "Indeed, I expect it would fetch a pretty penny. Certain of the details you included, such as the—" He cleared his throat. "The—" His smirk now twisted into a grimace. He averted his face, and his shoulders jerked.

She had the panicked thought that he was having some sort of attack—his lungs, the old boyhood ailment—and she leapt forward to take his arm. "Are you all—"

"Oh, good God," he said rapidly, and burst into laughter.

Her hand fell away. A fit might have astonished her less. He had laughed at her before, certainly, but this was true laughter, low and husky and unrestrained. She backed up a pace, beginning to smile, too; his hilarity was somehow infectious.

He put a fist to his mouth, and after evident struggle, seemed to grow calmer. "The—" He cleared his throat. "The terrier," he managed, but when she nodded, this prompted him to snort, which turned into another peal.

She surrendered to laughter as well. Gratification spread in a warm, heady rush. Finally, he acknowledged it: the terrier bit had been brilliant!

After a ragged breath, and another, he finally calmed. Clearing his throat, he met her eyes. "Forgive me," he said hoarsely, and wiped the corner of his eye with a knuckle. "You really do have quite a way with—" The corner of his mouth kicked up; he pressed his lips together and drew an audible breath through his nose. "Quite a way with words. I confess, I didn't suspect it."

"Thank you! But you see, for that very reason, Thomas would never let the letter become public. It's clever *and* rude. And he's very vain." She paused, eyeing him. "Although I can't understand why."

He grinned. "Ah, from the mouths of babes," he said. As if he were so much older! "And perhaps you're right, but it's a calculation, you see. And in this case, the risk wouldn't be worth the possible profit."

She frowned. "What risk?"

He pushed a hand through his hair. All the Ramseys had such wonderfully thick hair. Lord Weston's

couturiers in most of the ports I visit? And flowers are not always pretty. Some of them try to eat you."

"I don't even favor flowers," she said. "I don't have an interest in little box gardens, Alex; I am thinking of *landscapes*. I have a talent for designing them, I think— you should see Heaton Dale at present; it's brilliant! Why—"

She fell abruptly silent. He was looking at her with an expression of mild, tolerant incredulity.

"Well," she said. "The point is, I'm done with the conventional routine."

His head tilted just a fraction. "So. No need to make that list, then. Yes?"

"Exactly right," she said encouragingly. "You may keep doing absolutely"—she flapped her hand— "nothing. It quite suits you! In regard to me, that is. Of course you do a great deal, generally speaking."

"I see," he murmured. "Well, that's a relief. I must say, I wasn't relishing playing the matchmaker." After a brief pause, and another curious inspection of her, he added, "The day has been inordinately taxing, so I suppose I should leave you to rest. Let's revisit this conversation another time, shall we?"

Her stomach sank. She'd been feeling encouraged, but this last remark did not bode well at all. "No," she said. "I told you to keep doing what you always do! And may I remind you, only once in a year do you make plans to converse with me. Otherwise, we meet only by accident, generally at the holidays, and we exchange nothing so substantial as might be counted conversation!"

His answering smile was benign. Not a trace of mockery! "True enough, Gwen. I will bid you good afternoon, now." And then—horror of horrors—he bowed to her.

Dear God! There: she had taken the Lord's name in vain, and the occasion well deserved it. Alex was playing the *gentleman*.

He did not believe her in the least. He still planned to make that list.

It could not stand.

As he turned for the door, she said sharply, "Alex, I mean it. I am not joking."

He glanced back over his shoulder as he laid his hand to the door latch. "Splendid," he said mildly. "Be as wild as you like. God knows I'm no advocate for the straight and narrow. Now, if you don't mind, I really must be—"

"Could I go to Paris with you, then?"

Slowly he turned back, his expression frozen into comical dismay. "Paris," he said. "With me. Are you serious?"

"Absolutely," she said. "You could show me the sights!"

His laughter sounded openly disbelieving now. "Show you the sights. Take you on a tour of the Louvre, do you mean? Oh, wouldn't that be smashing. Perhaps we could have a tea party in the Tuileries afterward, and press flowers into our scrapbooks."

She pulled a face. "The Tuileries is nothing original, and museums aren't my aim. That is—I want to give

Pennington what-for! And after that, well, I've seen all the proper bits already. The Opera, the Exhibit, that new tower they put up—it sways in the wind, utterly ghastly. But I didn't see any of the *fun* bits. The bits that proper girls never see!"

His hand slipped away from the door. "You're a heathen," he said. "The Eiffel Tower's a miracle of engineering. As for the rest—I've no idea what bits you mean. The fish market, say? The workhouses?"

"The wicked places! The Bal Bullier, the Moulin Rouge, the places where ladies dance the cancan all night—"

He choked. "Italy, Gwen. I suggest you go there. *Ever* so much more fun. Pesto, Rome, the Medicis— who can resist? You can purchase a fine poison ring, propose a swap with the viscount."

"But he cannot have gotten to Italy yet," she said patiently. "Paris will be his first stop if he's going anywhere on the Continent. And I already explained that I *must* get the ring back."

"And I told you I'd get it back for you," he said with a hint of sharpness. "So don't worry your pretty little head."

"My head is not little and I'm not particularly concerned. Where *did* you pick up all this dreadful slang, Alex? You should really have a care around Americans!"

He shook his head as if to clear it. "Right. Gwen, as I said—we'll discuss it later. For now, do go rest."

It was the smile with which he concluded these

remarks that punctured her patience. That smile did not sit naturally on his lips. It was conciliating. Coddling.

He did not believe a word of what she was saying.

Well, she knew a quick way to prove her intentions. Suffragettes and actresses had tested the method. He was going to mock her, no doubt, but at least he would have to take her seriously afterward. "Wait," she said as he pulled open the door.

He sighed and turned back. "For God's sake. *What?*"

She took a deep breath. She could do this. Why not? "You promised to do me a favor, earlier."

"I am not taking you to Paris," he said flatly. "I am not your bloody chaperone."

"No! That wasn't what I meant to ask."

Closing the door again, he put his hands into his pockets and waited, although the impatient tap of his boot suggested he would not give her long. "Fire away."

She was tall for a woman, but as she eyed his mouth, it seemed unwise to leave things to chance. "Perhaps you should sit, first."

He lifted his eyes to the ceiling, then moved to the nearest chair. Taking a seat, he said somberly, "I am braced."

She ignored the sarcasm, nodded once, lifted her skirts, and marched toward him.

His brows lifted a fraction.

She smiled.

At two paces' distance, he tilted his head.

"Stay still," she warned.

When her skirts hit his knee, his eyes narrowed and he looked as though he would speak. She planted her hands on his upper arms and pressed her mouth to his.

Well. He was made of lean muscle, all right; beneath her hands, his biceps contracted into stone. His lips were warm and motionless. He smelled of soap, very clean, barely a trace of sweat. He'd recently taken a bath, she supposed. Or: he'd recently lowered this long body of his into a bathtub, completely naked.

The thought did something awful and lovely to the pit of her stomach. Her hands slid of their own accord up to his shoulders, and she pressed her mouth harder to his. See a man naked. Good Lord: did she actually intend to add that to her list?

Very softly, his breath hot on her mouth, he spoke. "Gwen. You're hysterical."

Her cheeks burning, she pulled back. He sat perfectly still, his blue eyes locked onto hers, his expression impenetrable. What thick, dark eyelashes he had. She wanted to touch them, out of gratitude or wonder: for some reason, he was not laughing at her. "No," she said, "as I told you, I am done with convention. Also, I am pursuing a question in the scientific fashion. I can't believe every man kisses like a terrier."

His nostrils flared. "And?"

She stepped back. "Well, you didn't slobber. In no way was it canine."

He came suddenly to his feet, forcing her to look up at him. "Not canine," he repeated in grim tones. "Gwen. You need to *rest* now."

No wonder he hadn't laughed. He really thought her in the grip of some madness. "I feel quite alert. Besides, actions speak louder than words, so please consider my kiss to be proof—"

He made a queer noise, something between a scoff and a grunt. "That was hardly a kiss."

"—proof that I'm quite done with behaving myself." And done with male judgment, too! The whole smug species could toss themselves out a window. "So please don't waste your time on that silly list, for I won't marry even if you put a gun to my head—a policy that I think *you*, of all people, should understand." Her sore vanity compelled her to add, "And if that wasn't a proper kiss, it's not my fault, is it? One would think a man of *your* reputation might know it requires a bit of effort on your part!"

His lips parted. Finally, for the first time in the ignoble history of their acquaintance, she'd surprised him! Or were his feelings hurt?

What an odd and fascinating idea. It made her feel generous. "Don't worry about it," she added. "I'm sure you can do much better than that. Even without proper notice, you rank on par with Trent."

She turned away, but his strong grip on her elbow pulled her back. "I beg your pardon?"

Why—now his vanity was pricked! The laugh that escaped her was born of sheer astonishment. Alex Ramsey, the jaded sophisticate—how easy he was to rile in this matter! "I said you rank on par with Trent. And far above Pennington! And I'm sure—"

His thumb stroked down her forearm, and her voice faltered. Had that been deliberate? "I'm sure other men will rank below you, too, if it makes you feel any better."

"Oh, much better," he said sarcastically, and tugged her toward him. His free hand cupped and lifted her chin, and he laid his lips against hers.

Amazement immobilized her. This was a brilliant triumph! Goading Alex into kissing her after he'd tried to play the brother! She'd never imagined she might have a talent for seduction, but for her first day as an unconventional woman, she was doing splendidly! As far as his performance, he was not doing too badly, either. His mouth was stroking over hers, which felt unobjectionable. Now his teeth caught hold of her upper lip, which, in fact, seemed very much like what a terrier would do—

His tongue followed his teeth. It traced a hot path along the seam of her mouth. Her stomach fell away. She shut her eyes. *Oh.* He was tasting her, his lips molding hers lightly, persuasively. She cupped his cheek and found it hot, slightly rough beneath the stroke of her thumb. His hand pressed her waist, drawing her into his body, his chest hot against hers; she drew a startled breath and his tongue slipped inside her mouth.

Strange parts of her startled awake—her nape, her belly, the place between her legs. He tasted of Aunt Elma's tea; she would never drink a cup so casually again. Her fingers found the soft abundance of his hair, winding into it and tightening. Such things she could do, now that she'd stopped worrying! She leaned against him, giving him all her weight, so much larger he was. On her toes, she rubbed against him. He made some muffled sound, and his mouth slipped to her neck. The light scrape of his teeth was followed by a soft, hot sucking; she felt herself dissolving like sugar into tea.

He turned her by the waist, his hands urging her downward. A seat cushion pressed against her bottom. Goodness, he was . . . kneeling down over her, his hands braced on either side of the chair, his mouth moving up her neck, returning now to her mouth. Her languor took a twist into something sharper and more demanding; she tightened her grip on him and opened her mouth again, hoping, perhaps, that his tongue—

He pulled out of her reach so abruptly that her open hands lingered in the air a moment before falling to her lap.

"There," he said curtly. "That should satisfy your curiosity."

Dazed, she peered up at him. The stony set of his jaw puzzled her. He'd enjoyed the kiss, hadn't he? His chest was rising and falling rather rapidly. In all the novels she'd read, that was the hallmark of passion, and her own shortened breath seemed to confirm it.

Maybe he felt as though he'd betrayed her brother. Yes, that made sense. "I'm sorry," she said hesitantly. "I baited you, I admit it. Surely Richard will know this was my fault."

For a moment, he said nothing. And then, on a

fierce exhalation, he said through his teeth, "Go back to *bed*, Gwen. You're out of your cheery little mind."

Turning on his heel, he strode for the door and slammed out.

Goodness! She'd never seen Alex lose his temper before.

Then again, *she* had never kissed a rake.

A smile formed under her hand. "O brave new world," she murmured, and came to her feet. With or without companionship, she had a ticket to book for Paris.

Chapter Five

"You waste my time!" Bruneau yelled.

Somebody in the corner laughed. "*Fais gaffe à toi!*" Watch yourself.

In all fairness, Alex thought, Bruneau had solid cause for complaint. They'd been circling each other for a good three minutes, right arms braced over their chests, elbows angled out to create a shield of muscle and bone. In proper form, Bruneau held his other arm high behind his head, aiding his balance as he kept his weight on his back foot in preparation to kick. But his arm was beginning to shake. Apparently he was not accustomed to opponents who proved loath to engage.

Then again, few men who practiced savate loathed fighting as much as Alex did.

He took a deep breath of the hot, sweat-soaked air in the *salle d'armes*. When in Paris, he never permitted himself to miss the opportunity to train here. Had never done it in this state, though. Five days now, and not more than ten hours' rest between them. He knew whom to blame.

He broke form, offering Bruneau a deliberate invitation.

Bruneau made an abortive lunge. It was transparently a ploy, and Alex did not flinch.

"Bloody *boy*," the man growled in gutter French. "I do not come to play!"

He might have saved his breath; Alex hadn't responded to a taunt since his first year at Rugby. That year, Richard's background had made him, and any of his friends, a target for bullies. Richard had fought like a wildcat and raged against Alex's reserve. *Why don't you fight back? Didn't your brother teach you? They say he could thrash George Steadman himself!*

In reply, Alex had offered shrugs. Explaining had felt too complicated. He'd not known, then, how to fight without being angry—and the anger and the physical exertion combined would have defeated his lungs before the older boys could even raise a hand to him. Between wheezing and passing out, or learning to endure the pain, he'd chosen the latter.

The second year, of course, things had changed.

Alex shifted direction, circling counterclockwise now. The way one fought revealed one's character, and yesterday morning, he'd seen Bruneau destroy three men in record time. The man was hot-tempered, confident, and impatient—not to fight, but to win. Victory was his sole purpose. In that regard, he was not dissimilar from Alex. If one was able to win, there was no point in fighting to lose.

The difference, then, lay in their approaches. For

Bruneau, the effort of securing victory seemed like an irritating delay. Alex, on the other hand, was inclined to discount a victory that did not require a bit of hard work. One fought to prove oneself to one's opponent, and a fight too quickly concluded often left the defeated party confused about the reasons for his defeat. He might be inclined to blame himself rather than to give credit solely to the man who had beaten him.

Alex sprang forward, just to see Bruneau jump. Recovering, Bruneau struck out his foot, but Alex had already skipped backward.

"Pathetic," Bruneau sneered.

"Mm." The other men in the *salle* had withdrawn to the walls to watch now, and their murmurs formed a distant, irrelevant background to the tremendous thunder of his heart. He was not going to lose this match. Bruneau had begun his training while still a boy, testing himself in the roughest lanes of the Latin Quarter; he also stood an inch taller, and savate favored the long-limbed.

Alex had his own advantage, however. He bloody *loathed* fighting. Nine years he had been coming to this studio, and each time, when he crossed the threshold, he still fought the urge to vomit, just as he had that first year at Rugby whenever he'd seen Reginald Milton coming round the corner. Nothing like fear to sharpen a man's reflexes. For useful effect, even anger could not rival it.

"Are you a coward?" Bruneau sneered.

Alex grinned. "Yes," he said.

This remark snapped Bruneau's patience. He sprang forward. Alex dodged the foot flashing past his head and spun to return the kick. Bruneau blocked it with a blow to his shin. As Alex fell back, grunting, the man whirled. His reverse kick smashed into Alex's chest.

More sleep would have helped, here. *Damn you*, *Gwen*.

He tried to shove her from his mind. For a week now, her memory had proved harder to shake than an African parasite—one of those worms, say, that rendered men blind.

He let the impact carry him, staggering a pace before he managed to regain his balance. As he pivoted, he found Bruneau's fist heading toward his face. Mistake. Alex blocked the punch and slammed his elbow into Bruneau's throat. The man lurched backward, wheezing.

Wouldn't Gerry be proud. He always insisted that when it came to fists, Englishmen knew no rivals.

Bruneau recovered more quickly than the average giant. As he threw out his rear foot, Alex took a backward leap, saving his kneecap but sacrificing his balance. Here, as always in moments where defeat became a distinct possibility, he experienced a momentary clarity, an accord between body and mind that seemed to stop time itself. No choice but to fall. Didn't mean he was down for good. He surrendered to gravity but managed to stagger just long enough for Bruneau to get the idea and come after him. Then he let himself plummet like a stone. His palms slammed into the floor.

Bruneau's comprehension flashed across his bulbous face a split second before Alex swept out his foot and hooked the man's ankles. The Parisian toppled backward. His head cracked against the floor.

For some curious reason, Parisians always assumed that Englishmen didn't know that trick.

Alex shoved himself to his feet. God above, he felt good. It was a far finer start to the morning than coffee. He made a bow to acknowledge the applause, then stepped up to Bruneau, who was blinking muzzily at the ceiling. "All right?" he asked.

The man sat up, shook his head, then offered Alex a bleary smile. "You try that again," he said, "and I will be waiting for it."

"Tomorrow, then?" He seized Bruneau's hand and hauled him to his feet. *Or perhaps now*, he almost added, for all at once, as adrenaline ebbed, an awareness of the larger world pressed in on him again: the salon with its swords strapped into crosses against the wall; the clatter of carts and the screams of street vendors filtering in through the single-paned windows; the irritating telegram from Belinda that had been delivered to his hotel suite this morning.

GWEN TO PARIS WITH ELMA STOP FEAR SHE SEEKS VISCOUNT STOP ELMA OBLIVIOUS STOP PLEASE REASON WITH HER STOP

This development was beyond irritating. Rightfully Gwen should be opening wedding gifts right now. Penning her thank-you notes. Alex had imagined receiving such a note from her. He'd looked forward to it. It would be the moment, he'd decided, that would mark the conclusion of his obligation to Richard.

Instead, she had popped up in Paris, a turn of events that unleashed some irrational foreboding in him. *Foreboding*. It was the lowest and most pathetic order of worry, based on nothing more solid than a twinge in the gut. A cousin to indigestion. But there was no other word for the feeling encroaching upon him. Rightly Gwen belonged to the same lot of obligations that included his sisters and nieces—an easily managed group, requiring only gifts at the holidays, notes on birthdays, and the occasional postcard (preferably something with a horse or kitten: so Caroline's littlest had recently informed him). She should not be in Paris. *He* should not be in Paris. He did not need to be checking on her, or playing his brother's keeper. If Gerard had sold the lands to Rollo Barrington, let Rollo Barrington have his joy of them. Where Alex needed to be was in Lima, uncovering the plans that Monsanto was hatching.

But no. He was half a world away, tracking down a man named *Rollo*, for God's sake, and plagued by a bunch of lunatics in the process. Gerry refused to account for his behavior. Nothing in Pennington's background suggested that he could *afford* to flee such a sum of money. And Gwen—well, Jesus Christ. If she thought he kissed *about as well* as Trent, she'd suffered a serious blow to the brain, somewhere.

Bruneau delivered the obligatory slap to his back. (And now Gwen had him *daydreaming*, Alex realized with disgust.) Dutifully, he pounded the man in return. The Frenchman retreated a pace and uttered some respectful remark.

Properly it fell now to Alex to suggest a drink at the bar across the street, where they would trade stories of good fights and unfair opponents, and exchange jibes that would add spice to their rematch tomorrow. He would have been glad to buy a round—except, God damn it, he now had to track down not only Barrington but also one naïve heiress and her feather-brained chaperone.

He cursed the invention of the telegram.

All the life in the world teemed on the boulevards, jostling beneath tree limbs laden with lilacs. On the green benches that lined the pavement, dandies lounged in white coats with fur collars, their long mustaches framing cigarettes that they smoked with frowning care. Smartly dressed ladies hopped fearlessly from omnibuses, and servants shuffled past with their various charges—nannies escorting little boys in velvet knickerbockers and cuffs of Belgian lace; maids dragged by tonsured poodles, which lunged at the olive peddlers and made the girls selling fresh carnations shriek and jump away. Every lamppost in view was plastered with colorful playbills, and the boy at the newspaper kiosk cried the headlines continuously, with a voice long since grown hoarse.

Gwen sat beneath the striped awning of a charming little café, sipping a glass of wine and marveling. Twice before she had visited Paris, but she remembered none of this. Previously, her mornings had been swallowed by the dark corridors of the Louvre, her afternoons suffocated in the satin boudoirs of Laferrière, Redferns, and Worth. Yesterday Elma had insisted they waste the evening in some dark little box at the Opera. But the truth of Paris was not to be found indoors. It was *here*, parading by for her enjoyment as the gentleman at the next table drank his curaçao and spared her not so much as a single look. The waiter had offered her absinthe, even!

She felt enormously pleased with herself. Her Baedeker's guide decreed that the cafés on the south side of the boulevards were suitable for ladies, but the author certainly hadn't assumed that she would be drinking her coffee *unchaperoned*.

Smiling, she looked back to the newspaper spread open before her. *Galignani's Messenger* printed a daily list of English newcomers to Paris; on Fridays, the list expanded to include notable departures to other spots on the Continent. A scan yielded no sign of Thomas's name. He was probably still here, then. But where he might be skulking remained a mystery. Her concierge at the Grand Hôtel du Louvre had made discreet inquiries on her behalf, so she knew that he was not lodged there, nor at the Maurice, the Brighton, the Rivoli, or the Saint James and Albany. He had not even stopped in for a chop at Richard-Lucas. For an Englishman, he was proving remarkably unpredictable.

"Enjoying yourself?"

She twisted around from the waist, heart thumping. What on *earth*? "Alex!"

"None other," he said. He made an excellent impression of a well-heeled Parisian: gray suit, gray waistcoat, gray felt hat, gray suede gloves—even a gray necktie, appropriately loosened in the manner of the locals. He looked expensive and sophisticated and, thanks to the dark circles beneath his eyes, utterly debauched to boot: a man who enjoyed his nights as thoroughly as his days.

He gestured toward the empty chair opposite her. She nodded. What else was she to do?

As he sat down, the cramped quarters forced his knee into her skirts. He gave her a startlingly broad smile. Perhaps his temperament changed with the country, just like his wardrobe. She tried to look away from his throat, but the sight drew her back again. Since her arrival to Paris yesterday, she'd witnessed a hundred gentlemen with ties thus draped. But on Alex, the effect was... startling. As if he'd been interrupted while undressing.

It occurred to her that the last time she had seen him, he'd just finished kissing her with expert skill. She felt her face warm.

He threw one long leg over the other and glanced around, utterly at ease, as though he had not just ambushed her in a foreign country. She held very still, overly conscious of her breathing, of the way her fingers itched to fidget. His cheekbones had a dramatic slope to them.

Loose ladies probably had fever dreams about his lips. Those lips showed no signs of moving in speech.

"What are you *doing* here?" she burst out.

He lifted one brow as he looked back to her. "What a disingenuous question. I told you I was coming to Paris." The smile that curved his mouth seemed to weigh a variety of improper possibilities. "Perhaps I should ask if you were following me."

"What a silly question that would be," she said irritably, "as I had *also* already expressed my intention to come here during our last conversation."

His eyes narrowed. "I believe I stated mine first."

"Yes, but *my* idea was born separately. It had nothing at all to do with you."

"You—" He ran a hand over his face and muttered something beneath his breath which she could not make out. Then he sat back in the chair and pasted on a lazy smile. "Ah, what does it matter. Paris is big enough for the both of us."

"Then why are you here at my café?"

A muscle ticked briefly in his jaw. "An excellent question," he said finally. "My sisters have no faith in your chaperone, and apparently their suspicions are correct. She is napping beneath cucumber slices while you are wandering about collecting wine carafes."

"So there's my answer," Gwen said triumphantly. "You found the note I left her."

The corner of his mouth lifted, but it did not appear to be a sign of good humor. "Yes," he said. "I found the note."

"Well, I hope you haven't come to harass me back to London. I believe I made my opinion very clear with regard to that ridiculous plan on being married by autumn."

"Yes," he said. "I have no intentions of inflicting you on anyone, Miss Maudsley. I only wish my sisters felt the same. I've come to Paris strictly on a holiday." As if to illustrate this, he tipped his face up to the sun. A breeze swept over the table, and he closed his eyes and slid lower in his chair, stretching out like some giant, basking house cat.

"Hmm," she said, wanting him to take note of her skepticism. To her knowledge, Alex had never gone anywhere for a motive as profitless as holidaying.

But his lashes did not so much as flicker at the sound. He covered a yawn with his palm. Perhaps he was telling the truth, then. Certainly she'd never seen him look so . . . carefree.

Indeed, this unusual repose freed her, for once, to look as closely as she liked at him. She decided that his lower lip should give her hope. It looked full enough to pull off a good pout—far too sensitive to belong to a bully.

Despite herself, she leaned forward. Really, his mouth was remarkable. Were men supposed to have such lips? They were a shade darker than his tanned skin, the upper a fraction longer than the lower, but not quite as full. The edges were so precisely defined that she could have traced them, given rice paper and a pen.

He spoke without opening his eyes, his sleepy voice giving her a dreadful start. "Have you found the viscount?"

She jerked back in her seat. "Not yet."

His eyes opened directly on hers. "I told you I would find him for you. Do you think me incapable?"

Strange that she did not recall being unnerved by his eyes in the past. But they were a startling light blue and seemed to catch her like a fist around the throat. "I don't doubt your skill," she said. "And I know my brother would have appreciated your offer. But as I said, I have come to Paris for a variety of purposes, one of which is to make known to the viscount my *immense* distaste for his actions." She paused. "I *had* written a letter about it, but somebody rudely intercepted it and forbade me to mail it."

"Forbade you?" He looked amused. "Do you always listen to what others tell you to do? Seems rather *conventional*, to me."

"I am a fledgling free spirit," she said with a shrug. "My wings are still sprouting. But you're quite right; I shall endeavor to ignore you *completely* in the future." When he laughed, she added, "Even if you do persist in following me about in this brotherly mode."

He laughed and sat up. "Brotherly? *Brotherly?* What lies have my sisters been telling you? I believe the last time I was properly *brotherly*, it was 1876, and Belinda had just skinned her knee." The corner of his mouth lifted. "Do you need me to inspect your knees, Miss Maudsley?"

She lifted her chin. "My knees are quite fine."

"Ah, good to know." He laid his index finger on the carafe of burgundy sitting by her glass, drawing an idle path through the collected condensation. "One hopes they'll remain so," he said, "for I suspect you have very pretty knees, and running off can be dangerous. One tends to slip."

She watched his hands. His fingers were long and elegant, well suited to musical instruments; she had seen them stroke piano keys with exquisite finesse. Apparently they could just as easily pummel a man until his jaw broke—or so people liked to whisper, when neither he nor the unfortunate Mr. Reginald Milton were in the room. As for Lady Milton, Reginald's mother, she thought Alex the devil incarnate. But probably even she would admire his hands, so long as she did not know to whom they attached.

Gwen looked to her own fingers, knotted together limply in her lap. They were stubby, the hands of a washerwoman, not even figuratively: her paternal grandmother had been a scullery maid at an estate of the Roland family. She did not advertise this fact when supping with Baron and Lady Roland, of course.

The next time she saw them, perhaps she *would* mention it. "I do not 'run off,'" she said firmly. "I am twenty-three years of age, you know. I suppose you could say that I have the right to simply *go*—when and wherever I please."

"Admirable philosophy," he murmured. His nail tapped the carafe. "You may want to try it sober, at first."

She frowned. He glanced past her and jerked his chin. This somehow managed to draw the approach of the waiter, a skinny lad who wore his sandy hair parted horizontally, brushed forward over a set of enormous, winglike ears.

Alex's request for *une bock* seemed to delight him. "Boum!" he cried, and blew away again.

Gwen scowled. Her order had not merited such enthusiasm.

"Have you had a falling out with Mrs. Beecham?" Alex asked idly.

She looked at him blankly. "What? Of course not. Only last night we went to the Opera to see a show." She grimaced. "Rather tragic, in fact."

"Grim play, was it?"

"Oh, not at all. But neither she nor I could make sense of the French—this colloquial variety is dreadfully confusing—and then we ran out of small change for all the pourboires. It wasn't our fault at all! The attendants in the cloakroom insisted on installing us in the seats with these rickety little footstools that used up all our coins. So when the ouvreuse came around to sell a playbill, we tried to deny her. Only apparently she was not asking a purchase so much as *demanding* it, and she made an awful scene. Such rudeness!" She shook her head. "I told Elma I shan't go back. And I mean it, although she *will* try to convince me."

He laughed. "She was not concerned about the opera so much as your refusal to accompany her on calls."

"I thought she was napping."

"Yes, but she briefly deigned to lift one of the cucumber slices."

Gwen sighed and picked up her wine. A sip for courage, perhaps. "Elma has a hundred friends here and wishes to visit all of them. She has made a list, in fact, and it goes on for three pages, organized by location: today she works her way through the Faubourg Saint-Germain. Tomorrow, it is Rue de Varenne and Rue de Grenelle. Twelve, fifteen families at a time." As the wine went down, she did her best not to grimace; the warmth of the sun had soured the burgundy. "At any rate, I count it a favor to leave her be. Everyone will want the latest gossip from London, and since I *am* the gossip, she could hardly share it with me by her side."

"Very generous of you," he said dryly. "Where have you been going, then?"

She tried out a one-shouldered shrug, the sort that he favored. All it did was awaken a cramp in her neck. "All the places one might think to find an Englishman in Paris."

The waiter reappeared with a tall glass of beer. She

wanted to try one, and she was finished with disguising her desires. She said to the boy, "Une canette, s'il vous plaît."

"That would be the larger size," Alex said mildly.

"Yes," she said. "That's why I ordered it. Only a brother would mention that," she added.

"A brother would also carry you back to the hotel when you passed out, but you may rest easy on that count: I won't bother."

She smiled despite herself. Alex was the only man she'd ever known who seemed to positively *invite* one's rudeness. Before, this had always unnerved her about him; the obligation had been upon her to ignore his provocations. But now, for the first time, she could answer with equal flippancy, and the effect was strangely heady, more intoxicating even than the wine had been. "I have a good head, you know."

"Yes, I hear you once drank two whole glasses of the stuff."

"And *I've* heard that sarcasm is no substitute for cleverness."

"Have you heard this? Kidnapped heiresses are not just the stuff of novels."

"Kidnapped?" A laugh escaped her. "Wouldn't that be a lovely piece of irony! Abandoned by two men, and kidnapped by a third!"

He paused. "You shouldn't be out on your own," he said in a different, more serious tone. "That's all I mean. The world is not so kind as it looks in Mayfair."

"Does it look kind in Mayfair?" she asked blandly.

"Perhaps I had a bad view, last week, when I found myself standing alone at the altar."

"I'm not speaking of wounded feelings," he said quietly. "Things do happen. You need only think on your brother to realize that."

She glanced up at him, startled. He held her look, but his very impassivity betrayed an awareness of the moment's significance. They had never spoken of Richard's death. All the details about it had come through the twins.

She wanted to be flippant again, to turn the mood back into banter. But instead she found herself saying, "I miss him."

"Yes," he said at length. "So do I."

The sobriety of his reply further dampened her spirits. Richard had been dear to him as well.

It was Alex who had returned the ring to her.

She had felt so grateful to him for it that day. Even amidst all the other mad, grieving ideas that had raced through her head, she had still wanted to hug him, to cry onto his shoulder, for the favor of returning the ring.

"I can't believe I gave it away," she whispered.

He shrugged. Apparently he did not even need to ask what she meant. "You thought to wed the man, Gwen."

There was no censure in his tone. And Elma and the twins had said the same. But perhaps that was the worst part: she *had* felt justified in giving Thomas the ring.

How willingly she had deluded herself! She'd not

even had the courage to recognize her own hypocrisy. Thinking on it turned her stomach now. It was like that childhood game, in which one whirled in circles, round and round, until one managed to convince oneself that the sky and earth had switched places and the horizon was so close that one could touch it. But when one came to a stop, the world caught up and everything slammed into place, stolid and unchanged. Everything returned to the way it had been. Nothing new at all. And the nausea in one's stomach was born half of wonder, half of fear: *How did I convince myself, even for a moment, that things were different? I knew the truth all the time.*

Her order arrived, jarring her from her thoughts. The beer foam presented her with a bit of a dilemma. She decided to plow through it, and ended up wiping suds from her nose.

Alex was smiling faintly. "*Oui?*"

"*Oui,*" she said, because she liked the smile, and the fact that he was not chiding her. It tasted like rotgut, though.

He spoke slowly. "I sense that you're on somewhat of a larger mission, here in Paris."

She gave him a bland smile. "I do intend to try new things, if that's what you mean. Life is too short to spend simply *behaving* oneself, don't you think?" On a laugh, she added, "But perhaps you've never tried that, Alex. Maybe *you* should be my example."

He propped his elbow on the table and cupped his chin in his hand. "I would advise you to look elsewhere, for I can lead you nowhere good."

"Perhaps I don't want to go anywhere good."

His smile slipped into something more contemplative. "But the only place I'd have a use for you is in bed."

She froze, glass pressed to her mouth. Surely he didn't mean . . .

"Oh, you have it right," he said. "I mean that in a purely sexual way. Nothing brotherly about it."

The word registered like a physical shock. She put her glass down hastily lest she drop it, then cast a panicked glance around. Nobody looked to be eavesdropping.

His laughter snapped her attention back to him. "You don't have it in you to do this, Gwen."

The sound of her name went through her like an electric current. He had a lovely voice, low and smooth. *Gwen*. She'd never realized how pretty her name could sound. "What—what do you mean?" Good Lord! What would his sisters have said if they'd been able to hear this conversation? Alex, interested in her in a purely sexual way! "I don't have it in me to do what?"

"To rebel," he said.

"You're mistaken. I intend to live for myself now."

He inclined his head. "I don't debate your motives," he said. "But living for yourself requires you to stop caring about what others expect from you."

"Yes," she said. "I know. Perhaps I *want* to be judged." Last night, Elma had been abuzz with news of some duke, newly widowed—a fact less startling when one learned he was seventy. But his age had not

stopped Elma from formulating a grand plan to reha-
bilitate Gwen into a duchess. Nor would it stop the
man from courting her, probably. Elma assured her
that his ancient-and-doddering grace was simply *desperate* for funds. "Perhaps ruin would please me," she
said. She was done with purchasing grooms.

What would it take to drive off these men, anyway?
A scandal of Hippodrome proportions? Only something truly heinous would counteract the appeal of
her three million pounds. Poison, murder, devil wor-
ship. The sight of an altar.

"If it's done right, ruin would surely please you,"
Alex said with open amusement. "But the consequences
wouldn't. You're a kitten, Gwen, and I say that with no
censure whatsoever. You live to be smiled at, to charm
people. There's nothing wrong with that, of course, so
long as you choose the right people to charm. It's the
choice that has been your failing to date."

The words stung, but only because, until so
recently, they had been true. Why charm anyone?
What a futile exercise it seemed now! People blew
away like dandelion thistles, carried off by death or
indifference or sheer, inexplicable whim. Why bother
to grasp at them? One would only be disappointed
eventually.

And of all people, *Alex* certainly understood this.
He'd spent his entire adult life avoiding his home and
family. What hypocrisy for him to encourage her to do
what he never bothered with! "I am telling you right
now," she said fiercely. "I no longer care."

He sat back in his chair, setting his fist to his mouth as he studied her. "All right," he said at length. "Let's test it, shall we?"

"Yes," she said immediately. "Why not? Give me your fiercest frown. Chastise me as harshly as you please."

"Oh, but I'm the last person to disapprove of you. I'm a blackguard, aren't I? No, what we need"—here he glanced around the café—"is a group of fine, upstanding citizens for you to offend. There," he said, and lifted his brow and chin to indicate someone over her shoulder.

She twisted in her seat. A family of American tourists had taken the table behind them. The balding man was puffing comfortably on his cigar as he flipped through *The World*, utterly ignoring the glare from his portly wife, whose jowls and thick pearl choker gave her the look of a collared dog. Their daughter, a snub-nosed beauty in a walking gown made of ribbed bengaline silk, heaved a long-suffering sigh and looked off toward the pavement. Her dress was very fashionable in cut and cloth, but its quality was disguised by its color—an unfortunate, vulgar purple.

Gwen turned back. "What do you propose? Shall I . . . approach them and apologize? My father invented that dye, you know. It never did favors to anyone's complexion."

"Dear God, Gwen. The point is to be *shocking*. Not to invent new ways to ingratiate yourself."

"But it *would* be shocking! A conversation without

first being properly introduced . . ." She trailed off as his smile took on an unkind edge. "All right," she said on a deep breath. He wanted shocking?

She plucked up her soiled serviette and tossed it over her shoulder.

Heart thundering, she waited for an outcry. She'd tossed a dirty napkin onto them—fifty years ago, such offenses had started duels.

A long moment passed. No exclamation rose from the offended party. Alex yawned into his palm. Frowning, she peeked over her shoulder.

Her napkin sat directly behind the young girl's chair. The girl, oblivious, inspected the hem of her glove.

"Works better when you aim," said Alex. "Shall I demonstrate?" He pulled a handkerchief from his pocket and dipped it into her wine, then began to ball it up.

"No! You can't do that. Wine stains fabric!" When he grinned and opened his hand, letting the handkerchief drop onto the table, she felt her patience snap. "This is very childish," she said, "and pointless to boot. I said I wished to live freely, not to throw things at people. "

"No," he said evenly, "you said you no longer cared for others' censure."

"One entails the other."

He inclined his head. "Precisely my point. So, can you follow through with it? Try the wineglass."

"The wineglass? But it would break!"

"True," he said thoughtfully. "And quite loudly, to boot." He picked up her glass and extended his hand into the aisle.

His fingers opened.

The glass shattered.

"Oh, dear," she heard the American girl murmur. The other patrons glanced over, some of them blushing with vicarious embarrassment.

It wasn't so bad, really. Gwen looked at him and shrugged.

He smiled back at her and lifted his glass as though in a toast. "To waking the dead," he said, and then dropped it onto the ground as well.

Shouts went up. The matron at the table behind her said in a very loud voice that he had done it deliberately. The man with the curaçao shot to his feet, cursing in language Gwen could not follow, although she did gather he was offended by the splatter on his pant leg.

"You're quite red," Alex said mildly. "Feeling a bit... uncomfortable?" With a casual rap of his knuckles, he knocked her water glass off the table.

At this point, people on the pavement began to stop and gawk.

Gwen sat frozen. Alex propped his forearms on the table, leaning in confidentially. "We seem to have run out of minor glassware. There's always the pitcher, of course. Or if it's real drama you want, I can tip over the table."

"No," she snapped.

"Oh, I do beg your pardon—would you like to give it a go yourself?"

"This is not *rude*. This is wanton destruction!"

He shrugged. "A table, a glass, a lady's character . . . all of them break so easily. Pity, that."

A clawlike grip caught her arm. The waiter ranted incoherently down at her, spittle flying from his lips.

Alex reached over and took hold of the waiter's wrist, saying something sharp and short.

The waiter spat back a guttural curse.

Alex's knuckles whitened, and the waiter gasped, his fingers loosening. Gwen inched out of his grip and Alex's hand dropped. He sat back in his chair.

The waiter clutched his wrist to his chest now, launching into a flurry of agitated French that she could not follow—save the mention of *les gardes municipaux*.

Police.

That meant police.

She came to her feet, clawing at the chatelaine bag clipped to her waist, wherein sat all her money. Her stammered apology did not assemble grammatically. "Get up!" she cried at Alex. Why was he *smiling*? "He's going to summon the police!"

He tipped his head to listen. "Why, yes, so he is. Apparently we're a public nuisance." He nodded once. "I always did suspect you'd be a nuisance, Gwen."

Pounds. Pence. Francs, yes, finally! She shoved a banknote into the waiter's hand. He took a look at it, fell abruptly quiet, and began to bow to her profusely as he backed away.

Murmurs went up from the crowd on the pavement. Suddenly everybody was looking at her very queerly.

Alex began to laugh.

"What?" She felt near to stamping her foot. To *strangling* him. "What is so funny? I should say he was owed fifty francs for this mess!"

"Then you overpaid him tenfold," he said as he rose. "That was a five-hundred-franc note. Seems we'll have to work on your bribery skills."

By God, she was sick of being laughed at! "Oh yes?" She turned and snatched up the pitcher of mazagran from the Americans' table, ignoring the sharp *"Hey!"* from the man with the newspaper.

Alex lifted his brows.

Holding his eye, she threw it at his head.

He ducked, and the crowd behind the railing followed suit. The pitcher exploded against the pavement.

Utter silence.

"That was a bit much," Alex said helpfully. "But at least you did take aim this time."

A tap came at her shoulder. The young waiter, brow lifted, held out his hand imperiously.

"Another five hundred, do you think?" The amusement in Alex's voice did nothing to cool her temper. In a minute she would not *believe* she'd just done this.

"One hundred," she said to the boy, and dared him with her eyes to refuse the note.

He was not a fool. Sketching her another deep bow, he retreated once more, the note clutched in his hand.

She turned back to Alex. "I don't require your help," she said.

The dimple in his cheek betrayed his sober expression: he was biting back a smile. "*Mais non*," he said. "If you're going to do this, you'll do it right. Next time, fifty francs should do nicely."

Chapter Six

Le Highlife du Westend. Among fashionable French society, this was the sardonic term used to describe the annual influx of Englishmen to Paris. It also applied to their clumsy forms of amusement: their insatiable appetite for champagne (which no true Parisian would touch, save during Carnival); their ardent pursuit of the plump-cheeked *cocottes* who worked the music halls and cafés of the Latin Quarter; and their long lunches over haunches of beef at Richard-Lucas. In short, the phrase was a mocking acknowledgment that the well-heeled English came to Paris to do the very same things they liked to do in London, only with the added entertainment of being able to gawk at foreign ways that convinced them ever more deeply of their own country's superiority.

It surprised Alex, then, to discover that Barrington had managed to set up camp in the Rue de Varenne. Generally speaking, the neighborhood jealously guarded its aristocratic provenance, making exceptions only for select Americans. To have found a house here, Barrington must have well-connected friends in very high places.

But connections were not the only resource Barrington could claim. He also had a surprisingly large number of guards posted about his property. As Alex loitered on the corner, pretending to smoke a bulldog pipe—no better way to look like an English tourist, and thereby provide passersby with a reason to dismiss the importance of any other detail of his person—he noticed that a deliveryman and a mail carrier were both stopped and questioned before being allowed up to the front door. The mail carrier did not disappoint, voicing considerable outrage at this violation of his dignity. Said outrage prompted another man in a bowler hat to emerge from the shadows of the ground story, and a third to lean out the window.

Three men set to guard the entry. It seemed curious. English real estate barons generally did not require such security.

After a half hour or so, Alex decided against attempting to approach. Better to find out as much as possible about the man. The first and most obvious idea was to discover who had secured him that house.

And who better to ask than the doyenne of gossip herself? Today, Alex recalled, had been Elma Beecham's social tour of the Rue de Varenne.

"No," Elma said absently, "I don't know who owns that house." They were standing in the marble-floored lobby of the Grand, beneath the chandelier at the base of the grand staircase, waiting for Gwen to make her descent to dinner. "I can find out, of course," she added.

"I would appreciate it if you did," Alex said. "A discreet inquiry, of course. Elsewhere, I would have contacts, but I do very little business in Paris . . ."

He trailed off as he realized that for once, Elma was not curious for explanations, nor intent on keeping his attention. Indeed, her blue eyes continually broke from his to dart toward the staircase. She reached up to run a nervous hand over her smooth blond coiffure, and then set her fan to rapping an arrhythmic tattoo against the inside of her gloved wrist. "Where is she?" she muttered.

"And how is Gwen faring?" he asked slowly.

"Oh, she—here she comes," she exclaimed.

He followed her look toward the stairs, and found Gwen drifting down toward them.

I'm an idiot, he thought. He had forgotten the most basic tenet of business: to issue no challenges one was unprepared to see met.

Yesterday afternoon, Gwen's enthusiasm had seemed relatively harmless. The glee with which she'd ordered beer had put him in mind of his nieces playing dress up in Caroline's jewelry. Where two bracelets would suffice, Madeleine and Elizabeth always insisted on twenty, stacking bangles right up to their armpits.

But in the past twenty-four hours, Gwen appeared to have moved past bracelets and beer and fallen headlong into a pot of rouge. To be sure, she still looked like a child who had gotten into her mother's ward-robe—but only if her mother was a high-class pros-titute whose taste ran to pink satin and necklines far lower than the hour permitted.

"Did you take her shopping?" he asked. *In a bordello?*

Elma shot him a nervous smile. "Oh, a short stroll through the arcades on the ground floor. We picked up a great many joking gifts. I must have missed the moment when she chose this particular . . . Well, she'd never wear such a thing in London, of course! But she took a liking to it, and I—you know how Parisians are. Nobody will notice."

"Right," he said slowly.

Gwen swept up. "Mr. Ramsey," she said. She was wearing a tiny pink rose tucked behind her ear, and another—he did a double take—in her décolletage.

Probably no one else would remark it, though. In her ears swung a pair of diamond eardrops so large that it was a wonder her lobes were not sagging to her shoulders. Their sale might have fed the populace of a small nation for a year.

"So," he said. "Where shall we go, ladies? I placed a call to the Maison Dorée, and it seems we're in luck: a cabinet particulier is available this evening."

Gwen's mouth pulled in disapproval. "How old-fashioned," she said. "Can we not dine in public? I've no wish to be shut up alone in some stuffy little room."

Elma flashed him a significant look, which he had no idea how to interpret. "But Gwen, dear!" she said. "The Maison Dorée is the finest restaurant on the

Continent. It's practically impossible to get reservations there. If Mr. Ramsey has been so kind—"

"It's no trouble," he said with a shrug. "I've connections at Le Lyon d'Or as well, if you'd prefer that. I know the man who fills some of their more arcane orders for spices."

Gwen glanced past them, her eyes following a group of gentlemen in top hats and capes. "No," she said decisively. "I've seen so many interesting-looking foreigners in the lobby. Let's dine at the *table d'hôte.*"

And on this note, she casually brushed past Alex toward the dining room.

He turned, watching the roll of her hips with disbelief. Was she *sashaying?*

"Well, all right," Elma said, and took Alex's arm, towing him forward to catch up with her charge. "But do look for the Italians, Gwen. They are the best gentlemen to flirt with! I flirted with several when I did the grand tour as a girl. They're *ever* so educational."

And so it was that twenty minutes later, he sat at one of the long, communal tables in the hotel dining room, enduring the first course of excruciatingly average fare as he slowly suffocated in a cloud of toxic perfume. To the left, he had an excellent view of Gwen's complicated chignon: she had turned away from him entirely, wholly engaged with the blond—Italian— lad at her left. Opposite sat two graying Germans who had introduced themselves as Austrians, probably to avoid spittle in their food; they were either deaf or melancholy, and kept their attention fixed on their plates. To the right, somewhere inside the noxious cloud of odor, sat Elma. Overhead, the clash of a dozen languages echoing off the gilded ceiling made the line of chandeliers tremble.

Alex rather envied those chandeliers. At least the air up there was free of the reek of Bouquet Impérial Russe.

"She's looking well, isn't she?" Elma still sounded nervous. "Mr. Beecham was staunchly opposed to this trip, but see how cheerful she seems!"

"Certainly," he said dryly. Gwen seemed about as cheerful as one of those maniacal mechanized puppets that terrorized children at Madam Montesque's House of Wonders. Meanwhile, the poor Italian looked as if he was being slowly beaten down by a hailstorm. What on earth was she saying to him? Probably a dizzying mix of compliments to his person and declarations regarding her own liberation. *Yesterday I threw a napkin and broke a glass. Today I painted my face. Tomorrow, one never knows, I might spit on the pavement . . .*

If she did, she would wipe it up afterward. Alex would place money on it.

"Mr. Beecham felt certain we shouldn't humor her," Elma said a little desperately. Dear God, she was coming closer. He averted his face for a long breath. "But I tell you, he has so little understanding for the heart of a woman. Last winter I thought I would *die* of melancholy, the weather was so dull. Not a spot of sun for weeks. But he wouldn't even consider a holiday. 'You can have card games in the conservatory,' he told me.

Well, for Gwen's sake, I put my foot down this time. I told him, what harm can Paris do? Even if she runs across the viscount, *he* knows better than to approach her. And now *you're* here. Why, we haven't a thing to worry about! Do we?"

He refrained from comment. He saw a number of things to worry about. He had yet to receive a reply from the Peruvian minister. The woman he'd just asked to perform a *discreet* inquiry with regard to the house on Rue de Varenne was now telling him tales about her husband. And the *vin ordinaire* at this table tasted thicker than ox-blood.

This last might not have bothered him so much, had both women not been drinking with the enthusiasm of hardened sailors.

He reached for his glass of soda water. "Here's a fine Parisian custom," he said, and splashed half the glass into Elma's wine. He reached over Gwen's elbow to empty the other half into hers. The Italian sent him a beseeching look. He smiled maliciously.

"... buy *all* the flowers in Paris," Gwen was saying, "and fill an entire hotel with them! Wouldn't that be the most horrid good fun? I expect everybody would be forced to evacuate for sneezing! *You* would not sneeze, though, would you? You seem *far* too masculine to sneeze."

God above. Someone really needed to teach her how to flirt.

Elma's breath gusted across his ear. "Yes, soda water, a very good idea. That's her third glass this evening, you know; she ordered one to the room beforehand. I *would* stop her, that is, I did *try* to stop her, but she told me that there was no harm in a glass, which I suppose is true. They do say that wine thickens the blood, don't they? And jiltings *do* wear on the constitution." A hint of anxiety flashed across her face. "I only want her to enjoy herself," she added softly. "Lord knows that once she's married, Parisian holidays may come few and far between."

And on that note, she drank her wine straight down.

Alex sighed, suddenly divining the larger picture. Gwen was not the only one who had come to Paris to cut loose. Mr. Beecham apparently wore on the constitution as well.

Bloody good luck that none of this was his concern. Gwen was right: he had not promised Richard to make her behave, nor to play her caretaker while her actual chaperone wallowed in nostalgia for her own lost youth. If his sisters had sent that telegram hoping *he* would oversee this mess, they'd been badly mistaken. He didn't have the energy. He barely had the attention span. Dear God, he needed some sleep.

In fact, he had no idea why he'd agreed to stay for dinner. He should excuse himself and go find a meal that actually proved edible, and perhaps a dose of laudanum for dessert. He'd resisted drugs until now; God knew he'd gotten his fill of medicine in his youth. But at some point, one had to concede the inevitable—

A radish flew past, launched from somewhere down

the table by a fork made unsteady by too much wine. It landed in Elma's glass, drawing a multinational cry from up and down the table: *Oh lá lá*, *Youpi*, *Gut gemacht!*

Flushing, Elma lifted the glass in a triumphant toast. The balding gallant at her right promptly offered his own in exchange. She turned toward her admirer, leaving all Alex's attention for Gwen, who was still laughing.

It was a lovely, uninhibited sound, and it turned the heads of the glowering Austrians, who unbent and gave her a smile. Alex smiled a little himself. Her laughter held an elated note, expressive of more than simple amusement. Listening to her, one had the impression that she was thrilled to be in the world, and saw no shortage of wonders to delight her.

She glanced to him as she fell silent, but her dark eyes still sparkled with mirth. "I like these flying radishes," she said. Her cheeks glowed from the wine, and in the dim lighting, her hair looked the russet shade of autumn leaves. She looked invitingly, irresistibly warm, a bonfire on a frozen winter night. "I don't think I'd approve of flying cabbage," she added, "but radishes, I'll gladly encourage."

He cleared his throat. "Live wildly," he said. "Throw one yourself."

"Perhaps I will." Her expression was arch. "Certainly I proved that I was capable of it yesterday."

There were a dozen obvious places to touch her. The hollow of her throat. The curve of her brow.

Beneath her lower lip—that faint shadow in the shape of a downturned half-moon, marking the spot where her pointed chin began to jut outward.

He'd counted them all before. They made an excellent list of reasons to keep the hell away from her.

"Yesterday proved that you know how to buy your way out of trouble," he said. "Not much else."

"Oh?" Lifting her brow, she reached out and put one slim finger beneath his chin.

He'd not been expecting it. His breath caught from sheer surprise.

For other reasons, every muscle in his body tightened as well.

"I know how to flirt," she murmured. "The Italian has been teaching me."

He reached up and caught hold of her hand. If he stood up now, he'd become the sort of spectacle more often provided by fourteen-year-old boys. "You're drunk," he said. "Enjoying it?"

She laughed softly. Her eyes were a warm, rich brown, the color of loam upturned in the planting season. "I haven't decided yet."

His thumb discovered its own will, pressing slowly into the warm, soft cavern of her palm. Hot and soft, slightly moist; her sweat would be more fragrant than any perfume. "You'll have to let me know," he said, and his own hushed voice startled some distant part of him; he sounded drunk himself.

Her eyes dilated slightly as he stroked her palm. He was watching for it. He was watching for everything and anything in her: his senses felt like strands suddenly twined together and snapped taut with great force, anchored somehow into her flesh, so every small movement she made reverberated along his nerves. Which was . . .

Which was unnerving as hell.

I know how to flirt, she had told him. Warned him, more like.

"This is not flirting." His voice was laconic enough to focus his mind. He dropped her hand abruptly and ran his own over his mouth. He looked toward Elma—ostensibly. But in truth, he was simply testing his ability to look at, to focus on, anything other than Gwen.

Jesus Christ.

The insomnia was rotting his brain.

When her hand touched his sleeve, he had to restrain himself from knocking it away. "What?" he asked curtly. Now would be a good time for Elma to become anxious again, but she was too busy being admired by the American at her elbow.

"What did I do wrong?"

He turned back in disbelief. Gwen did not look at all rattled by what had passed between them. Far from it. Christ, she was *grinning*.

"You said it wasn't flirting," she said earnestly. "I wish to know where I went wrong. Did I not seem drawn to you? Was I not complimentary enough?"

"It wasn't flirting," he said curtly, "because you gave the impression that if I slapped a coin down on the table, you'd lift your skirts directly."

A second too late, he regretted the words. They were born of an anger that he was too old to misinterpret: his goddamned *vanity* was pricked by how unaffected she seemed.

She stiffened and went pale.

"I'm sorry," he said quietly. "Forgive me, Gwen. That was a spiteful remark."

"Yes," she said. Her lower lip trembled.

"Which would have been fine," he added, "if it had been clever, but it wasn't. You flirted very well. I'll admit it."

Her attempt at a smile failed. "Don't patronize me, Alex. We are not *all* born knowing how to be sophisticated. Some of us must learn these tricks." She stared at her plate now. "I don't—I'm not looking to seduce anyone, of course. But I told you, I just want to . . . have a bit of fun."

The words made him feel suddenly impatient. *Fun.* What a naïve little goal. By some witchy stroke of luck, she was able to get under his skin; perhaps if he were twenty, he'd enjoy becoming her entertainment for a week or two. If he were a different man entirely, he might make good use of her innocence, turning her desire against her and netting three million pounds for his trouble.

The thought lingered, troubling him. Taking advantage of her would be so easy. "Gwen," he began, but when she glanced up, he trailed off. *Be careful*, he wanted to say. *Of everyone.*

But what purchase would such a warning have? He

remembered too well the sharp little laugh she'd given yesterday at the idea of being kidnapped.

His conscience stirred. Uncomfortable, creaking sensation. When he found the viscount, he was going to show that piece of shit exactly what happened to men who betrayed their word.

Well, it all came down to the ring. Once he got it back, there would be no excuse for Gwen to linger in Paris. Back under his sisters' aegis, she'd be fine.

She tipped her chin defiantly. "Mr. Carrega has offered to take me onto the town tonight."

The Italian lad? Why did she bother to inform him of this? Did she want him to play the brother and forbid her to go? She really needed to make up her mind about that.

"I am considering accepting his invitation," she added.

"How intelligent of you," he said courteously.

Her jaw squared. "Nobody else has offered."

"What a pity. Did you want somebody to offer? Perhaps you should hold up a placard in the lobby to advertise."

Her sigh sounded impatient. "*You* have not offered."

"I have other things to do with my time than squire around debutantes," he said. "However, if you would muster the courage to ask me, I might just take you anyway. I imagine it would be amusing, watching your eyes pop like saucers." Indeed, the experience would serve her well when it came to picking another groom. Strip away a bit of that naiveté, and she would not go into the next match so blindly.

Her eyes did not pop. They narrowed. "I'm not sure I want your company."

"Then *viva l'italia*," he said, and took a long drink of his wine. Of course, there was no way in hell that Elma would let her go with the Italian, and Gwen knew it.

"But yes," she said. "If you'd take me out for a bit of fun, I would be grateful."

He nodded and set down the glass, then looked around the room, this collection of various over-moneyed European riffraff eating and drinking themselves into a stupor. "This isn't the right place to begin," he said. "We'll go to Pigalle, shall we?" Why not? Wasn't as if he needed to sleep.

Her smile caught him off-guard. It made something curious and sweet stir in his chest. "Brilliant! Pigalle it is. But—" She leaned to whisper, and he caught the scent of her, the warm stir of air from her décolletage, and as simple as that, he was hard again. "Let's tell Elma we're going to the boulevards instead."

Gwen took Alex's arm and stepped down from the carriage into a tremendous din—screams clashing with whistles and clanging bells, snatches of rollicking music, drunken choruses of song. A girl in bicycle bloomers went running past, inserting herself between two gentlemen, grabbing an elbow from each and then shrieking with laughter as they swung her off her feet. The air smelled of tobacco smoke and roasting chestnuts from the street vendors' braziers. A lilac petal drifted past, pink as a rose in the livid glare.

"Wrong way," Alex said mildly, and steered her by the elbow to look behind her.

Her jaw dropped.

Above her towered the red-thatched windmill of the Moulin Rouge, its great, electrified blades slowly revolving against a backdrop of low-hanging, scarlet-tinged clouds. Red bulbs flashed along the blades' edges, and blinked in multilayered strings along the windows and doorways. The combined force of these lamps cast a crimson glare over the crowd passing beneath them, throbbing across the white cutaway jackets and spats of young men, drawing glitter from the stoles and beaded feathers of the women who loitered by the entrance.

"Good heavens," she said. She felt as electrified as the lights.

"Gwen. Can you not think of a less pious exclamation?"

She slanted a glance at him. "Stars?"

He laughed. "Hopeless. Onward, then." He proffered his elbow.

Strange that she should feel a moment of shyness as she took it. She stole a glance at his profile as he led her forward. The twins always insisted that he not wear a beard; they admired his jaw greatly, and Gwen supposed they weren't wrong. It had a sharp, square definition, and made a pleasant frame for his long, mobile, very wicked mouth. But his looks were not what held her interest now. It was his agreement to take her here, although he clearly hadn't wanted to— and perhaps, also, the stroke of his hand over hers at dinner—that seemed to have set off this fever in her. Every time she looked at him now, some hot, pulsing feeling seized her.

It felt curiously like jealousy.

He doesn't try to be scandalous, Caroline had once said. *He simply can't be bothered with worrying about what's proper.*

Even now, navigating this chaos—two boys careened past, hooting; a bicycle swerved out of their way—he seemed so at *ease*. He was not pretending, she realized. His composedness operated at some muscular level. It made sense, in a way: a man who traveled the world must make a home of his body. Alex carried his certainty, his sense of belonging, in his bones.

Like a turtle carrying its shell, she thought. The silliness of the comparison made her swallow a giggle. Still, how comfortable it must be to live as he did! She had no idea how to acquire such confidence, but he made her realize that *this* was her aim.

They passed under the archway into a hot, cloistered hall done up in red velvet and brass gilding. A false redhead wearing a bored grimace sat inside a glass-boxed booth, collecting money. Alex surrendered two francs for broad cards. The music from the interior was very loud, a vigorous schottische punctuated by muffled cries and laughter.

Alex handed her a card, then stood looking down

at her, a slight smile playing over his lips. "All right," he said. "Chin up, Maudsley. Your fall from grace draws nigh."

She laughed. "What fall? I intend to jump."

Two steps onward, the corridor opened abruptly onto a grand dance floor encircled by small tables, flanked by tiers of boxed seating that rose up several stories. Electric chandeliers glared onto the crush of people filling the floor. The blasting music made the floor vibrate. The gleam of lurid red satin drew her attention, and then the sparkle of champagne flutes, the shine of black silk tall-hats, skipping flashes of light across paste jewelry at throats and wrists. At the left, on a stage festooned by scarlet silk drapery and long yellow banners, several women formed a dance line, twirling so madly that their ruffled skirts lifted over their legs, exposing ribboned socks that ended at their bare knees. The denizens of the orchestra pit beneath them were very gentlemanly, Gwen thought, not to look up.

They stepped a foot into the crowd, and a shattering explosion pierced the din, followed immediately by another. She startled before realizing that someone nearby must be throwing glasses against the wall.

"How fortunate," she began, laughing, and then realized she would need to raise her voice considerably. "How fortunate," she shouted, "that I practiced breaking things yesterday!"

Alex cupped his ear. "What's that?" he yelled.

She took a deep breath. "I said *how fortunate*—"

His laughter brought her to a halt. He'd heard her perfectly. She stuck out her tongue at him.

He leaned down and put his mouth against her ear. The touch startled her to a dead stop. "Watch out," he said, his voice low and startlingly quiet, his breath hot. "Someone's going to take that as an invitation."

Goose bumps broke out on her arms. It sounded less like a warning than a promise.

As he straightened, a shiver moved through her. She touched her tingling ear and looked blankly away— and then blinked and peered harder at the stage. One by one, each of the dancers gave a great whoop, threw up her arms, and—Gwen went on tiptoes to confirm it—slid straight down to the floor, one leg stretched flat before her, the other extended behind.

Oh, no. If *that* was what the cancan required, she would not be learning it.

Without warning, Alex yanked her into his body. A high-kicking dancer pranced past, her slippered foot sailing past Gwen's ear. "What a dangerous dance," Gwen said in bewilderment. "Someone will lose an eye!"

He sputtered out a laugh, then nodded and yelled, "Outside, then, before we're blinded by chorus girls."

She started to protest, and then realized he did not mean for them to leave; he was leading her past the bandstand, toward a set of doors that opened onto a garden.

She took a grateful breath as they stepped into the warm night air. Strings of colored lanterns illuminated the grounds, and as a mild breeze blew over her, it loosed the sound of a thousand tiny bells, shivering and silvery, strung from the lime trees at the garden's edge. She took a step, and then stopped dead, too startled even to squeak: a *monkey* had just raced past her skirts.

"They're tame," Alex said. "But I wouldn't try to pet one."

She gave him an astonished look—then did a double take. "There is an elephant behind you," she whispered. The giant stucco beast towered over the small stage to its right. Save for its height—it might have outmatched a three-story building—it looked startlingly lifelike, its hide painted in mottled shades of gray, its great, drooping wrinkles scored by the hand of a very talented sculptor.

"Yes," he whispered back. "A very overburdened elephant, with an orchestra in his rib cage and an Egyptian dancer in his belly. Alas, ladies are not allowed inside." The flash of his white teeth lent this piece of information a pleasurable air of scandal.

"How unjust," she murmured. At the front feet of the elephant, a fortune-teller was cooing destinies. Tucked under his tail was a refreshment stand. Nearby, a small queue was forming to play a machine made of painted wooden dials. A young lady pulled the lever on the side of the box; the wooden wheels spun round, coming to rest on various images: an apple, a pig, a tree. The result disappointed the audience, who hissed sympathetically.

"Beer?" Alex asked.

She nodded mutely.

They procured two glasses of Allsopp from the stand, but when they turned away, a freckled girl in a blue gown that barely covered her breasts bounded up and caught hold of Alex's sleeve. She spoke in a colloquial patter that Gwen could not follow, and he replied at an unintelligible clip, sounding polite but amused. From the vehement shake of her curling black head and the tug she gave to his cuff, the girl disagreed. But she was having trouble maintaining her pout; it continually broke into a smile.

He glanced at Gwen, one brow lifting apologetically, and then stepped sharply free of the girl's grasp. The girl spared her a glare before whirling away and stalking back into the ballroom.

"What did she want?" Gwen asked.

His lips canted as he handed her a glass. "Company."

"Oh." To her irritation, she felt a blush heat her face. "But—she knew I was with you!"

"I don't think that bothered her," he said, laughing.

It took a moment to follow the implication of this statement. Then, as she followed him to a nearby table, her hand flew to her mouth. No! Surely she was misunderstanding him!

To hide her shocked expression, she pretended a close interest in the vase of orange tulips sitting atop the tablecloth. Such a strangely domestic appointment amidst this bohemian scene. Her eyes rose again to the spectacle of the elephant, from which spilled a peculiar, foreign melody. A few cou-

ples were twirling to the song on the small, cano-
pied dance floor.

A curious amazement washed over her. *I am doing
this. I am drinking beer at a Parisian pleasure club*. And
yes, it *was* Alex who had pressed a *bock* upon her and
was now sitting at her side, watching her with evident
curiosity but no visible judgment whatsoever.

Her disbelief shifted into something giddier. How
generous of him to take her at her word—to respect
her desire for adventure despite his obvious skepticism at dinner! She found herself smiling up at him,
utterly afire with gratitude. "Have you come here
often, then?"

He shook his head slightly. His eyes fell to her
mouth briefly before he looked back to the dancers.
"Never, in fact."

"How do you know it so well, then?"

His laughter seemed to brush against her skin, a
tangible thing that made her stomach contract. He
smiled at her, and it was a gypsy's smile, taunting her
for the staidness of her own small world. "They're all
very much the same, Gwen. The Bal Bullier, the Moulin, the Pere Chateau . . ."

"Well, thank you for agreeing to escort me," she
said. "I know you didn't wish to do so. All this must
be very routine and boring for you."

He made an impatient noise. "If you mean to be
wicked, here's my first piece of advice: never fish for
compliments by demeaning yourself. Assume there is
no place I'd rather be than by your side."

"But I know that's not true."

"It doesn't matter what *my* truth is. Know your worth and assume others do, too. Modesty, if you consider it, is the most unforgivable sort of falsehood: it's a lie that does damage to no one but yourself."

She laughed. "Damage? I like that. Of course, you're a heretic by profession. Most gentlemen consider modesty very becoming to a lady."

"No doubt they do," he agreed. He reached out to cup a tulip blossom. "The same gentlemen who liken ladies to flowers, no doubt." He urged the blossom gently upward, as tenderly as a man might tip up a lady's chin for a kiss, and stroked it with one long finger.

A peculiar dizziness struck her. She tried to take her eyes off his hand, but they would not budge.

"Others of us," he said courteously as his hand dropped, "do not believe a woman's main aim is to decorate a room."

She looked up into his eyes. Her mouth felt dry. How odd. This was only Alex. And yet—hints of exotic mysteries seemed suddenly to cling to his shirtsleeves. Every time he came back from abroad, bits of strange new worlds clung to him.

"Modesty is useless," he said with a shrug. "And, as I said, offensive. Cast it away for tonight." He gave a wave of fluttering fingers, as though to illustrate the evaporation of this virtue.

The gesture struck a curious chord in her. It seemed like a flourish in some exotic dance, decidedly foreign.

As he leaned back, propping his elbow atop the back of the chair, the close fit of his jacket emphasized the flatness of his belly. His black-clad shoulder was a hair's breadth from her own.

The silence seemed to thicken, a weird, electric charge bridging the space between them, so she felt that only a breath separated their skin. She had a visceral sense of how far he had traveled, all the distant lands he'd seen—dark adventures and sultry nights she would never know about. Her hand curled at the sudden memory of how he had felt to touch, the hew of his muscle. She had dug her fingers into his arms as he'd kissed her. He'd felt so solid.

Why hadn't he kissed her again? He had no care for morals.

She turned her face into her beer, taking a very large swallow.

"Give it a go," he said.

"What?"

"Practice makes perfect. Say something immodest."

She took a deep breath and looked up. "I want to touch you," she said.

He smiled. "Very good. But perhaps the first lesson should concern the avoidance of beer foam." His hand lifted, brushing across her cheek.

Did he not realize she was serious? Some wild impulse winged up through her. She grabbed his wrist.

His smile widened. "You have foam," he said patiently. "On your cheek. I only meant to brush it away."

She could feel his pulse beneath her thumb. She opened her mouth, but words dried up. His wrist was solid and hot. There was such density to him. Her fingers tightened, testing it.

His face changed. Such an indefinable shift: only the expansion of his pupils, the slight loosening of his lips. But her body understood it. The wild instinct made her thumb press harder. Strange, predatory thought: *I've caught you.*

He exhaled through his nose. "Let go."

"No." The whisper felt drawn from her by some power outside herself. As he met her eyes, she did not even feel embarrassed. The dim glow of the fairy lights, the violinists' abrupt segue into a waltz, made the scene surreal, dreamlike.

She required a scandal to drive suitors away? *He* could be her scandal.

Chapter Seven

Alex's eyes reflected the flicker of the lamp behind her. His mouth slipped into a half smile, but it looked unwilling, not true amusement. "All right," he said calmly. "You've mastered immodesty. Now let's aim for something a bit more sophisticated."

Why, she thought, he was not misunderstanding her at all. He was only *pretending* to do so. A flush moved through her; instinctively she recognized that his descent into pretense spelled a triumph for her. "And what—" Her mouth had gone dry. She licked her lips, and as he glanced down to watch her tongue, his own mouth seemed to harden. "What if I asked you to kiss me again?"

His free hand rose, knuckles brushing lightly down her jaw. "An interesting approach," he said. His thumb settled against her lower lip, exerting the slightest pressure. Her lips parted. She tasted the salt of his skin, and her entire body seemed to contract to the awareness of it. She leaned forward, instinctively, and touched the tip of her tongue to his thumb.

The breath hissed from him. He removed his hand and sat back. "Bit risky, though, for your first night of adventure." His voice sounded strained.

"I am in the mood for risk," she whispered.

His eyes narrowed. "I suggest something subtler."

"I'm not playing," she said.

He gripped her chin with sudden, startling firmness. "Better to play," he said. "Between us, at least."

She did not move, did not lower her eyes. "Why?"

He let out a breath that bordered on a laugh. "Surely I needn't list all the reasons. You know me well enough. You think I have an interest in debutantes?"

"No," she said. "But I am no longer a debutante."

"There's also the small matter of your brother."

"Richard?" The name was like a slap. She sat back out of his grip. "What does *he* have to do with this?"

His eyes held hers, steady and unflinching. "If we're not pretending," he said, "then we must be speaking honestly, no? I told my sisters the full story of my quarrel with him the night he died. They must have told you."

"Yes," she said. "But he was wrong, of course—"

"Oh, you and I both know that. But we also know, then, what he wished for you—and what he most ardently did *not* wish."

"Meaning you," she said.

"Meaning anyone like me," he said impatiently. "Richard knew me well. He knew you well. And while his alarm was mistaken, it would certainly have been justified, were his suspicions correct."

"So you mean to say that I . . . disrespect his memory somehow? By asking you to *kiss* me?" The thought was outrageous. "Richard wanted me to be happy, Alex. That was *all* he wanted. And I'm pursuing my happiness, right here, now. If a scandal is what it requires, then surely he would prefer me to pursue one with you than with some no-name stranger!"

"I see," he said at length. "You think to use me as your avenue to ruin, then?"

"You yourself said it: three million pounds." Her voice sounded suddenly bitter. But what woman in the history of the world had ever had to justify her own seduction to convince a man like this to take advantage of her? It seemed so unjust. He must be *trying* to embarrass her. "It will take a great deal to undo my appeal. A man with your reputation would come in handy."

His eyes narrowed. "How charming. To which aspect of my reputation do you refer?"

"Recall, we are being honest," she bit out. "I refer to the fact that you are a well-known rake."

"Ah, yes." He sat back in his chair, smiling unpleasantly. In his hand he turned the beer glass back and forth, making the barest pause after each twirl, lending the movement a contemplative flavor. "It's true, I suppose. And of all my accomplishments, I am of course flattered that you deign to find useful this one, oh-so-impressive achievement. But if it's sex you want, there are several men in London who can't keep their trousers up. No need to follow me to Paris for it."

Her cheeks ached with the force of her blush. "Do not mock me," she managed. "You have *earned* your reputation."

"No, no, I don't mock you," he said soberly. "Indeed, as a businessman, I applaud your strategy; very economical, very thrifty. No doubt a mere brush against my coattails would blacken the halo of a saint. But you must forgive me if I have no interest in being used to suit your purposes. As you point out, I have a name to uphold, and falling victim to a virgin's machinations would put me in very poor company."

She glared at him. "What do you mean? What sort of company?"

He tossed back the rest of his beer. "Trent," he said when he'd swallowed. "Pennington. Every sad toff whom you've contemplated purchasing in order to have your title."

"*Purchasing—*"

"Do you deny it? I thought we were being honest."

She could match his sarcasm. "I tell you now, if a title appealed to me, it was merely because I knew that once I had one, no one would *dare* to speak to me like this."

He shocked her by laughing. "Nobody ever speaks to you like this, Gwen." He carefully placed his glass onto the table. "You've taken pains to ensure that. These smiles you don't mean, these compliments you waste on people who don't deserve them, even this sad little habit of devaluing your own worth—you're as manipulative as any financier. Only your method is different."

"And my motive," she said furiously. "Unlike you,

Mr. Ramsey, we do not all appraise a person like some commodity from which we might stand to make a profit. I wanted a family; I wanted a home. But I never tried to undertake a marriage that would benefit only me. Now my aims have changed, but I am no less committed to a fair exchange. If you don't wish to help me, I will simply find someone who does."

"The hell you will," he said grimly.

"I should like to see you stop me."

He spoke slowly. "Perhaps you haven't been attending to my reputation as closely as you claim. Otherwise I don't think you would imagine yourself a match for me."

The breath hissed through her clenched teeth. "I hardly think myself a match for you. I have a far better regard for myself."

"Oh? As I said, I could argue that point."

"I do not want to hear it."

"I'm certain you don't." He glanced beyond her, as if bored with the conversation, and his expression suddenly shifted, his eyes narrowing before his face went absolutely blank.

The transformation was dramatic enough that a thread of curiosity fractured her anger. She turned to follow his regard. He was looking at the girl in the low-cut blue gown. The girl had found a new object for her attentions now—a handsome blond man in a well-cut tail coat. Together with his companions, he was twitting her into giggling, teasing the hem of her skirts with the tip of his gold-knobbed cane.

"Stay here a minute," Alex said. And then, with a hard look: "I mean it. Do not leave this seat."

With no further explanation, he rose and walked away.

In disbelief, she twisted to follow his progress. He made directly for the blond man, but his path was impeded by the man's friends, who stepped forward and exchanged words with him. Meanwhile, the blond took the girl's arm and strolled around this scene, onward in Gwen's direction.

Alex took a step after him. The other men interceded. One of them gestured toward the interior of the building. After a visible hesitation and a brief, unreadable glance toward Gwen, Alex pivoted and followed them.

Take her here and *abandon* her, would he?

She looked wildly around. Alone, in the Moulin Rouge! Amidst all these people!

She jerked up her chin, staring fixedly at the elephant. She would be fine. She did not need Alex's company, or anybody else's, for that matter. She could manage very well on her own.

The elephant's face looked sad. Why had the artist chosen to paint it that way? Its great, dark eyes fixed woefully on some point in the distance, enduring without enthusiasm the antics of stupid boys climbing in and out of its belly. Poor, dumb creature! It looked so resigned. And so lonely.

A terrible wave of pity rose in her. Tears came to her eyes, which seemed *beyond* stupid; impatiently she pressed her fingertips to her eyelids. What nonsense. It was only a statue. Those eyes were the work of a very talented artist.

Still, something about the scene suddenly felt unbearable. The knot in her throat was growing. She came to her feet, planning to go after Alex, or to leave and hail a cab herself—

—and as she turned, she bumped directly into the blond man whom Alex had tried to approach. The girl clinging to his arm flashed Gwen a hostile look, but the gentleman stopped immediately and sketched a short bow. "Pardon me, mademoiselle," he said in English. "I didn't see you there."

"No, no, it was my fault," Gwen said. She should have realized he was a fellow countryman when he'd given Alex the cut. He had the ruddy, wholesome good looks that bespoke the playing fields at public schools, and summers spent scrambling across the countryside with howling hounds in tow. "Please accept my apologies, sir."

His brow lifted. Her accent startled him, maybe. One didn't expect to hear such posh tones emerging from an unaccompanied woman—not here, at least.

This realization revived her anger. Her hand closed over the visceral memory of her stinging palm, all those endless raps from the ruler. *We do not say "tha," Miss Gwendolyn. We say "you."*

Why, she thought, *I have been a trained, talking dog.* No wonder Alex showed contempt to her. For all her life, she had done as she was told, and when she had yapped for attention, it had taken but a word to make her sit quietly.

"Perhaps you can tell me," the gentleman said, "since my companion seems to know no English." He glanced at said companion, releasing her elbow with a smile, ignoring her quick protest. "Was there not meant to be singing, tonight?"

Gwen felt the girl's glower as a hot pressure on her cheek. "Yes, but not until midnight." It seemed unnecessary to add that this information came from her guidebook rather than any firsthand knowledge.

He nodded slowly. "What a pity," he said. "I shall have to find something else to occupy my time."

His accent wasn't quite as good as hers. She heard it now—some buried, rural inflection that wormed up through his vowels, sabotaging him at the occasional syllable. For some reason, the realization emboldened her. "I have a very nice singing voice," she said. "Alas, I know no lyrics for this sort of music."

"Oh?" The Englishman turned his body just enough to give the French girl his back. This marked signal made her cross her arms over her chest, then whirl and stalk away. "Allow me to introduce myself," he said pleasantly. "I am Mr. Rollo Barrington, of Manchester."

"Far from home," she said lightly.

"And all the better for it," he said, eyeing her. "I don't know if you've ever been to Manchester, but I always say that *escape* is the only verb that properly describes one's departure from it."

She laughed. "And how does one term one's departure from Paris, then?"

"Punishment," he said with a smile. "I say, mademoiselle—might I make a bold proposal? The surroundings certainly encourage it."

Through the double doors standing open to the ballroom, she spied Alex wending his way back through the crowd. Her heartbeat stuttered, then quickened. "You may attempt boldness, sir. I do not promise to encourage it."

He had a charming laugh, light and free of malice. "Then I will gather up my courage, and ask if I might have the honor of watching you drink a glass of champagne."

She hesitated. Alex expected to find her exactly where he had left her. Of course he did. Trained dogs did not wander, after all.

Fresh anger lurched through her. It felt stronger and even headier than the beer she'd been drinking.

She produced a smile. "I suppose you may watch me drink champagne," she said. "But I have two conditions."

Mr. Barrington sketched a bow. "I pray I may meet your terms."

"Oh, my terms are very simple," she said. Amazing how well her smile worked! The gentleman leaned toward her, now, his manner attentive and intrigued. She felt another heady rush—of satisfaction; of power; perhaps of relief. Alex would learn he did not know her as well as he thought. "First, you must allow me the same honor, for champagne is never meant to be drunk alone. And second, you must guarantee that we drink to celebrate an achievement."

He laughed. "And what achievement might that be, dare I ask?"

"Why, your success in smuggling me into that elephant."

A bribe of five francs satisfied the lad standing guard by the elephant's trunk. Gwen entered first. The short flight of iron stairs led to a carpeted platform lit by bluish gas lamps, with a red velvet love seat at the center. Exotic silks covered the walls, shades of scarlet and teal and saffron embellished with silver embroidery and fringed with gold coins. At the end of the platform stood a large wooden screen, intricately carved, concealing the remainder of the space. From somewhere behind it came the rhythmic jingling of bells.

"Not yet," Mr. Barrington called out. The smell of pomade and cigars surrounded her, and then his gloved hand closed over her elbow, giving her heart a startled lurch. "Careful," he murmured. "The floorboards are uneven."

Alone, in the dark, with a stranger: this was certainly a proper adventure. Gwen stepped forward, out of Mr. Barrington's grasp, but only to examine the lamps set into the walls: cunning brass sconces, inlaid with squares of red and yellow glass. Remembering how Alex had trailed his finger down the wine bottle at the café, she put her fingertip to the lamp, tracing the pattern engraved into the brass. Casting Mr. Barrington a flirtatious glance over her shoulder, she asked, "What is this space for? Do you know?"

He lifted his brows. "In the natural order of things? Digestion, I believe."

She laughed and turned back, put at ease by the joke. "And in the unnatural order? Or can't we speak of it?" Oh, that was *very* daring, she thought.

"Oh, we may speak of anything you like, mademoiselle. But first, tell me whom I have the honor of escorting into this pachyderm."

Her smile lingered. Once again she felt the full measure of courage she'd experienced at dinner, before Alex had sunk all her fun. "A woman who isn't afraid of beasts." *Or brutes*, she added silently.

Mr. Barrington had a fine, square chin, with a cleft that became visible when he laughed. "Have you encountered so many, then?"

"Oh, every day! Beasts have a taste for young ladies, you know."

"But one can't blame them when the young lady is so fetching." He took a step toward her. "I hope none have taken a bite from you, here in Paris?"

"You would not believe how well I wield a parasol."

"Yet I don't think you carry one tonight," he said. "Defenseless as you are, a monster might get ideas."

A nervous laugh escaped her. "How lucky I am to have the escort of a gentleman, then."

"A *gentleman*," he repeated, and now he sounded distinctly amused. "Was it in search of civilization, then, that you walked into the belly of this creature?"

She stared at him. On a deep breath, she said, "No. It was not."

His eyes narrowed. He meant to kiss her now; she could see it in the firming of his mouth. Well, she'd succeeded, then. Why else had she come up here with him if not to have a kiss? She was not a nice girl anymore; she was out to satisfy her curiosity. She could kiss as many gentlemen as she liked, provided they cooperated.

But did she want to kiss him? She couldn't even say. It seemed a daring thing to do—to kiss a man inside the elephant at the Moulin Rouge, the most notorious dance hall on the Continent. Such things only happened to wild women, heroines in novels, somebody's wicked cousin; her friends would never believe it. She would have to work hard, tomorrow, to believe it herself. Perhaps it would change her understanding of herself. She would look in the mirror and see the stamp of this bravery, this absolute sophistication.

His hand cupped her jaw. She wished his fingers did not feel so damp. He wore his pomade too thick, as well; the sweet scent was overpowering in this small space. Her heart tripped and beat faster as he lifted her chin. He had a mole at the corner of his nose, just behind the curve of his nostril. A racing heart was the hallmark of passion but all she felt was terribly, terribly anxious.

A dark hair was beginning to sprout from his mole. She screwed her eyes shut. She need not look. She could imagine he was someone else. Alex, perhaps—but with a different and far superior personality.

After a moment, when nothing happened, she opened her eyes again. To her puzzlement, Mr. Barrington had not drawn any closer. He turned her face now toward the light, examining her with a frown. "Do I know you from somewhere?" he asked.

Oh, goodness. He might well have seen her picture in the London newspapers. There had been a photograph published when her engagement had been announced—each of them. "No," she said.

"Yes," he said slowly, his fingers tightening, "I feel certain I do."

"Mr. Barrington," she said. How clumsy his grip was; it had become a hair shy of painful, now. "I think it very likely we move in different circles."

"But you look so familiar . . . what did you say your name was?"

She sighed. What ailed these men that made them tarry and waffle, so? Gentlemen in novels seized ladies and ravished them directly. But Alex hemmed and hawed and then stalked away, and *this* one insisted on babbling. Couldn't he simply kiss her and be done with it? The longer she had to look at him, the more stray hairs became apparent. "I didn't say. But my name is—Lily." That was the name of the girl in the novel she'd read, who had kissed a stranger beneath the stars and fallen in love. The hero, of course, had not sported a mole.

"Lily," he echoed. "Miss Lily . . . ?"

"Goodrick," she finished promptly. The surname of the author.

His eyes narrowed. "Lily Goodrick," he said, as though testing the syllables. "Miss Lily Goodrick."

"Mr. Rollo Barrington," she said helpfully. "There. Now we are acquainted."

He recovered his smile. His thumb stroked down her chin. Nothing ailed him, really, that a pair of tweezers would not cure. "Miss Goodrick, you're an enchanting little piece. Do you know that?"

"Remove your hand."

She started violently at the sound of Alex's voice. But Mr. Barrington did not look away from her. "Mr. de Grey," he said lightly. *Mr. de Grey?* "Did my men not make it clear to you? I am in Paris for pleasure. I have no interest in discussing business."

"Fair enough," Alex replied calmly. "However, if you do not remove your hand, we'll soon be discussing how you might reattach it to your wrist."

"Oh?" Mr. Barrington released her with a curious little smile. He stepped backward and brushed down his jacket, then slid his hands into his pockets. "Prior claim, is it?"

Alex stepped between them, a tall, broad-shouldered bulwark, but the hard look he gave her seemed less than reassuring. "Yes," he said curtly. A muscle ticked in his jaw.

Mr. Barrington nodded agreeably. "And you, Miss Goodrick—are you in accord with this claim? I confess, I was thinking to propose that we take a tour of

Montmartre in the moonlight. But if you bid me, I will abandon that hope."

She opened her mouth, then closed it. *Montmartre.* Was there any other word better able to kindle the imagination? Here she was, in the epicenter of everything scandalous in Paris! Who would not wish for a tour?

Alex took her elbow and delivered a slight, prompting squeeze. A quick glance upward revealed him to be scowling in the very brotherly manner he professed not to own. She did *so* love a white knight who abandoned her, then acted very ill-tempered upon discovering that she'd found other pursuits to occupy herself.

"Answer him," he said softly.

She gave him a wide-eyed, innocent look. "But what shall I say, monsieur? After all, it isn't as if I can claim to have had any *long* acquaintance with"— glancing toward Mr. Barrington, she delicately cleared her throat—"Mr. *de Grey*."

"Oh, not any long acquaintance," Alex said, "but certainly a thorough one." His hand slid around her waist and curved firmly over her hip, turning her toward him. She jerked upright from surprise, and he pressed his mouth to hers.

His lips took hers softly, suggestively. They clung, teasing her mouth to open to him.

He was kissing her *in front of Mr. Barrington*.

He broke away, delivering a soft, hot kiss to the side of her neck, dragging his mouth up to her ear on a hot breath. His teeth closed gently on her lobe. "*Behave*," he whispered.

As he withdrew, he gave her a smile. *Such* a smile—amused, playful, thoroughly wicked. She had never seen it before. *This* was the smile he gave the women he seduced.

It knocked all possible responses straight from her mind.

Only one certainty remained: she was most definitely not going to behave. The results of that were *far* more boring.

"I suppose," she said on a sigh to Mr. Barrington, "that I will admit to *some* knowledge of Mr. de Grey, now that he reminds me of it. But his attentions are so inconstant, he can hardly blame me for forgetting."

Mr. Barrington's face cleared. He gave her a sunny smile of perfect understanding. "I am hard-pressed to imagine any man so foolish as to neglect you, Miss Goodrick."

Alex's warm palm cupped her neck, his fingertips dragging lightly down her nape. "Oh, she isn't neglected," he murmured, and the roughness in his voice, combined with his touch, sent a small, involuntary shiver over her skin. "She simply likes to complain."

Mr. Barrington locked eyes with Alex. "In a soprano?" he asked. "Or a mezzo, would you say?"

Alex's hand paused. She divined that as a sign of his confusion. He had no idea she sang. It was a talent inherited from her mother, and one that Mama had never encouraged. "Neither," she said.

"A contralto?" Mr. Barrington looked delighted,

although it was to Alex that he directed his smile. "Oh, really, Miss Goodrick, now I *must* hear you sing."

Alex matched the smile with one of his own. "Must," he repeated evenly. "That can be a dangerous word, I find."

The brief, fraught silence that followed unnerved Gwen. "I have lately been on tour in the Americas," she said, attempting to restore the atmosphere to a lighter mood. "I meant to give my voice a rest, but perhaps, as a token of friendship . . ."

Alex laughed softly. She slanted him a glance, and his eyes met hers, warm, dancing. "Concluded in San Francisco, didn't it?" he asked. "Your tour, I mean."

His collusion briefly threw her off. She regained her smile. "Of course not," she said warmly. "The cards and drink are rotting your mind, poor man. Absinthe and roulette," she confided to Mr. Barrington. "Terrible plagues. He is thinking of two years ago, when I was crowned Queen of the Barbary Coast. But this season, I went no further than Chicago. Earthquakes do not agree with me."

"And a wise woman, too," Mr. Barrington said approvingly. "Come now, say you'll both accompany me to the Chat Noir. We can leave at once, and perhaps convince Miss Goodrick to take the stage."

Before she could decide how to reply, a jingling stomp sounded. From behind the screen appeared a dark-haired woman who folded her bare arms over her chest—but not before Gwen got a very good glimpse of what lay beneath: in a word, flesh.

The slits in her diaphanous rainbow skirts appeared to stop where her hip bones began.

Goodness. If *that* was what people were coming inside the elephant for, Gwen thought she had a good deal of ground to cover before she even approached the meaning of daring.

"Do I dance?" the woman demanded in heavily accented French. "Or do you go elsewhere? Others are waiting."

"Oh, dear, our most abject apologies," Mr. Barrington said. He reached into his coat and produced a banknote, which she snatched up with a sniff before trouncing back behind the screen. "Well?" he asked them. "I confess, I will perish of curiosity if I do not hear Miss Goodrick's voice now."

"As will I," Alex said, and then defied all her expectations by adding, "but I suppose it is up to the lady."

He looked to her with a slight smile.

Why, he didn't think she could sing. He was counting on her to produce an excuse.

She smiled back at him. "To Le Chat Noir, then."

Paris's most infamous café-chantant was small, dark, and narrow, a maze of protruding knees and misplaced elbows and the glowing heads of cigarettes. The walls were covered with bric-a-brac, old copper pans nailed haphazardly next to rusting suits of fake armor, and between these were pinned various scrawled drawings, prints cut out from magazines,

the occasional dried flower, somebody's handkerchief. In the corner, a young man in a heavily patched
velvet jacket was adding to the collection by drawing
on the wall in charcoal.

Alex accepted a glass of brandy from one of the
waiters, who wore green coats and cocked hats, in a
mocking nod to the outfits of Parisian academics. Age
and the pungent damp had warped the floorboards, so
the three-legged tables sat at drunken slants; when he
sat down his drink, it slid an inch before stopping.

The server loitered at the table a moment to
exchange pleasantries with Barrington, who had been
greeted, on the way inside, by several hearty slaps
from various rough-hewn patrons.

"I do love bohemia," Barrington sighed when the
waiter moved on. "It makes one long to be a boy again,
to begin anew."

Alex didn't judge him a day over thirty-five. A bit
early to be mourning for lost boyhood. "Were you a
bohemian in your youth, then?"

"No, never. But if given the opportunity to revise?
I think I would make a fine vagabond."

"Curious sentiment," Alex said, "coming from a
man who trades in property."

Barrington threw him an amused look. "I told
you, I discuss no business when in Paris." His regard
returned to the piano, where Gwen was conferring
with the accompanist.

Alex was braced for disaster there. It had purchased
him access to the man across from him, but the final

balance between cost and profit would have to calculated later. Elma Beecham had seen them off this evening with a cheery Godspeed, but she had not imagined
their itinerary continuing well into the small hours
of the night. Nor would she have suspected that her
charge would be masquerading as some sort of music
hall temptress, and taking every secret opportunity
to try to wrestle her neckline lower than the milliner
had ever intended.

For that matter, he did not like the way Barrington
watched her. The man showed no evidence of being
dangerous, but he certainly had proven himself to be
acquisitive.

Gwen shook out her skirts, squared her shoulders,
and mounted the stage. Nobody took note of her. The
place was filled to the rafters, but by reputation, the
crowd at Chat Noir proved notoriously difficult to
impress. It had its favorite composers and singers and
poets—those who earned their fame through regular
recitals here—but the rest, it either did a kindness
by ignoring, or a savage cruelty by dismissing, in the
middle of performances, at very high and often pro-
fanity-laced volume.

Sink or swim, Alex supposed: every fledgling
learned the same way.

Gwen's breasts rose and fell on a long breath. Nervous, no doubt. She looked across the crowd at him,
and he barely recognized the smile that curved her
lips. Perhaps it was a trick of the dim light and her
adjusted neckline and this role she'd decided to play,

but it occurred to him, suddenly, that he might not know her as well as he thought.

He lifted his glass to her. A mischievous angle took over her smile. She transferred it then to Barrington, who promptly bowed from the waist and sketched a pretty flourish with his hand.

Bohemian, hell. The man was practically a relic of the Regency, with that gesture.

I really should be in Lima, Alex thought, and he took a long swallow of his drink.

The pianist launched into the first bars of the melody. Bizet—the Habanera aria from *Carmen*. Christ. Unfortunate choice. It required a certain earthiness that she would never manage to pull off.

And then Gwen opened her mouth and began to sing.

Glass to lips, he froze.

From the very first bar, it became clear why she'd kept him, and everyone else, ignorant of her talent: her voice did not belong in drawing rooms.

Table by table, silence spread.

"*Quand je vous aimerai?*" she sang. "When will I love you? Heavens, I've no idea. Maybe never, maybe tomorrow . . . but certainly not today!"

An odd panic fleeted through him—an irrational impulse to stand and leave, or to plug his ears like a frightened boy.

A cheer went up from the back. Her lashes fluttered in startled, gratified reply. Then she threw a wink at the audience.

More cheers, now. God help him, her hand was slipping toward her skirts. She hiked up her hem, flashing an ankle as she launched into the next verse.

"Love is a rebellious bird that nobody can tame. You will call her in vain, if it suits her better to refuse . . ."

As she twirled, her skirts rose higher yet. She was wearing white silk stockings embroidered with scarlet flowers. Her calves were as slim and firm as a can-can dancer's.

He felt certain that he had not needed to know this.

Indeed, he had not needed to know what her voice sounded like, either. It seemed to wrap around him as sinuously as her arms had done, pressing like a palm against his throat, soft and hot, poised equally to caress or to throttle him. There was power in that voice—power too rich and dark for a sheltered, untested debutante.

But she was not untested, of course. How hard he had tried to forget this: that she had lost and suffered, just as he had. If her smiles came easily, that was not a testament to shallowness or inexperience. It was a testament to her peculiar, unfaltering strength.

"My God," Barrington breathed. "Where did you find this girl, de Grey? That's no common music hall voice."

Alex drew a long breath. Oh, the music hall might be a good start. But Barrington was right. A voice such as hers—as low and smoky as an army encampment, able to transform a mildly risqué French aria into a pornographic fantasy—probably deserved a rarer setting. A harem, say.

Or his bed.

He felt a smile twist his lips. Yes, better to think of that—of beds, and bare limbs, and sweat. Wiser, safer, to focus on what he could slot under the common label of lust.

She dropped her skirts and spun, hands lifting in mimicry of a flamenco dancer, her voice low and silken. "Love is the child of Bohemia; it has never, ever recognized any law . . ."

Richard's mother had briefly been an actress.

This piece of information disgorged itself wholesale into his consciousness. He could not recall the conversation in which he'd learned it, or any of the details, but he felt certain he was correct.

A strange sensation passed through him. He looked at Gwen with new eyes now. She was doing more on that stage than having *a little fun*, as she'd put it. She was flaunting something that she had spent most of her life learning to conceal.

His will seemed to split apart beneath the revelation, as neatly halved as beneath a blade.

He rather liked her as she'd been. The Gwen he knew was manageable.

Then again, he'd always thought she could be a great deal more.

He cleared his throat and massaged one wrist. His pulse was banging like a jackhammer. *Idiot*. All right, bully for Gwen; she was cutting up her heels now in a very fine fashion. But her talents, her courage, had nothing to do with him.

As the pianist segued into the passage that would rightly be sung by the opera chorus, Gwen lifted her hand and curled her fingers in invitation to the crowd. First one man, and then another, picked up the lyrics; as they sang, her eyes found his, sly humor tipping her smile to one side.

The smile jarred him. For a brief moment, he felt thoroughly disoriented—as on those rare occasions when he looked into a window pane and realized, between one blink and the next, that what he had mistaken for a reflection was, in fact, the true scene behind the glass. He forced his attention away from her, though it balked and wanted to linger; he focused on mundane moorings, on the words the drunkards were singing at her bidding. And as he listened with ferocious single-mindedness, understanding suddenly dawned on him.

He laughed out loud. No wonder this song appealed to her. "If you don't love me, then I love you," the men were singing, "and if I love you, you'd best beware!" It made a fine summary of Gwen's love life, to date.

She took a visible breath and slid back into the song, her voice spinning effortlessly through the scales, rough and sweet as raw sugar. "The bird you thought you had in your palm beat its wings and soared away," she purred. "Wait for love, and she remains ever distant; stop waiting, and she's there beside you."

Monsanto, Alex thought. What was Monsanto up to, in Peru? Had he managed to steal the shipping contracts, yet?

What the hell. I can afford to lose them.

Christ. That was not the damned point. He bolted half his glass as the song came to a thunderous close. Frenzied applause broke out. "I say," Barrington said, raising his voice over the racket, "that was splendid!"

Alex suddenly could not muster the energy to reply. Gwen was bowing, laughing, her face brighter than the gaslights behind her. He watched her as he took another drink. Had he just finished running a dozen miles at full speed, he would have felt precisely as he did just now: exhausted, dry-mouthed, and also wholly awake, thrummingly alive, his every vein invigorated by a fresh current of rushing blood.

Idiocy. *Idiot.* He should feel nothing like invigorated. He was losing. *Fight*, *then.* He never submitted gracefully to defeat.

Losing? Losing *what*? Irritated with himself, he set down his glass. He was done with liquor for the night.

"You two really must come down to Côte Bleue," Barrington said. "A small estate I picked up on the Riviera, recently."

"Perhaps," Alex said absently. Gwen started down the stairs, and several of the young poetic sorts piled forward to meet her.

Not surprising. Even he could admit to admiring her. Her intention, here, did not seem so dissimilar to those of the rogue artists whom he sponsored. Having glimpsed a vision of something different and better, she wanted to transform that vision into reality. But the invention she was undertaking was herself.

It was, perhaps, the only damned thing she could have done that would have won his instant and entire interest.

"Really, I must insist you come," Barrington said. "I'm having a small house party this weekend; I think you'd find the company quite enjoyable."

Alex made a noncommittal noise. He would sit here. No need to rise, to go to her. She would cast him a look if she required his help. "Policy of mine, Barrington: I travel to escape British company, not chase it down."

"Oh, but I'm quite of the same mind," Barrington said. "I've in mind a few Italians, and an artist or two from Paris should be hanging about. Very small, as I said. Select."

One of the poets went down on his knee before Gwen. The sound of her laughter traveled across the room, as musical as her singing. How had he not realized she could sing? Her laughter alone should have betrayed her.

"Do think about it," Barrington pressed. "And if Miss Goodrick would consent to sing a song or two, she'd be well rewarded for it."

At that, Alex looked Barrington in the eyes. "She is not available for purchase."

Barrington tempered his smile. "Genius is never for sale. And never fear, sir; I see how closely she holds you in her affection." The remark raised Alex's hackles; it seemed, to him, to carry a note of underlying sarcasm. "However, talent does require nourishment, and if Miss Goodrick has an eye for beauty, she'll find Côte Bleue a natural wonder. Only an hour from Monte Carlo, at that—entertainment abounds for a gambler as well."

Alex bestirred himself to produce a smile. An invitation to the man's house was an ideal opportunity to get to the bottom of Gerry's mystery, and he was never one to waste opportunities—particularly those that would save him a great deal of time in the long run. "I will put the question to Miss Goodrick," he said with a shrug. "Her wish, as you may gather, is my command."

Chapter Eight

Gwen finally wended her way back to the table. With Barrington having extended an invitation to his home, Alex saw no need to linger, but he waited as she drank a glass of wine, and watched with veiled interest as she deftly managed Barrington's compliments.

She had accused him, not without cause, of appraising people like commodities, but it required a deliberate and sustained effort to view her so cold-bloodedly. She would never convince anybody of being a professional courtesan: he was certain of that. Laughter lifted her long face from merely pretty to beautiful, but her blushes came too readily. No one would believe she had professional experience in lovemaking.

Still, she had unexpected talents, and a very unexpected ability to enjoy a masquerade. A bohemian artist . . . he thought she might manage that pretense for a weekend.

He was still undecided when they left the café shortly before dawn. Barrington had offered a ride, which they declined. Gwen floated out ahead of him. She was in the grip of some dreamy silence, but as he helped her into the cab, she leaned back out and spoke abruptly. "You haven't told me what you thought of my performance."

"Perhaps you can guess."

"No," she said. "You must tell me."

He smiled a little. "Or what? You won't let me inside?"

She stared at him, unspeaking, and some quality in her silence lent the moment an uncanny flavor. While the darkness of the interior concealed her body, the streetlight behind them illuminated the pale oval of her face, gilding her cheeks in shades of amber and ghostly blue. The effect was . . . arresting. Vermeer had used natural light to paint women in this way, faces emerging from the shadows, forcing the viewer's eye to focus on what was most important: the look of grace. The mouth firmed in determination. The eyes poised to behold a revelation.

But God knew Gwen was waiting in vain if she looked to him for it. And surely she knew that, too. He rubbed his hand over his chest, which felt strangely tight, no doubt from the smoky air inside. "Didn't get your fill of praise inside, then?"

Her unabashed laugh broke apart the weird mood. "Never," she said.

"Well, at least you've mastered immodesty." He smiled and unbent. "I would say the Barbary Coast chose well."

In response, she flushed and sat back into the vehicle.

A few blocks from her hotel, Alex stopped the driver so they could walk the rest of the way. He wanted to make sure Barrington was not following them; it would not do to have the man discover her identity. "Fresh air," he said as he helped her down to the quay. "Even in this stench, there's a bit of it."

As they strolled beneath the elms that lined the embankment of the river, she drew a long, testing breath. "I rather like the smell," she said as she took his arm. "Somebody's burning . . . dung, I believe? It reminds me of the countryside."

"And that's a good thing?"

She gave him a peering, incredulous look. "You dislike the country?"

"I'm not particularly fond of it."

"But whyever not? You spend the holidays there— and I know you grew up at Weston Hall. That's a beautiful estate."

He paused. "No doubt it is. But the countryside tends to make me feel . . ." *As if I'm suffocating,* he thought. "Bored," he said instead. "Cities are full of life. Ambition." It was to the city men went when inspired by the possibility for change. Conversely, the very appeal of the country, so far as he could gather, rested on ideas of staidness, stability, stagnancy. It came close to his idea of a prison, did English country life—rotting quietly in the middle of nowhere, dining every evening before the same view that he would see from his deathbed, amidst company that had known him from the day he was born.

As a boy, of course, he'd been told that he would be lucky to enjoy such a fate.

"I find the country a very lazy cousin to the city," he continued. "Can you disagree? Had the viscount not come to Paris—had he gone instead to ... Suffolk, say—would you have managed to have such an adventure tonight?"

"Of course not." She made a thoughtful pause. "I suppose you're right. My home is in the country, you know. But I never thought to go there."

"Your home? Do you mean Heaton Dale?"

"Of course," she said in surprise. "Where else?"

He hadn't realized that she thought of that place as home. It was a monstrous, Palladian palace, the construction of which had become the subject of great mockery amongst his mother's friends fifteen years ago. *Some arriviste's attempt at a bourgeois Buckingham*, his mother had called it. *I wonder if Mr. Maudsley plans to cast his own crown?*

"Do you spend much time there?" The place, as far as he knew, had stood empty since her parents' death. Certainly Richard hadn't lived there. He'd mocked its pretensions more viciously than anyone else had.

"Oh, occasionally I spend a day or two. Never long, but I *had* hoped—well." Gwen pulled a face. "I've just redesigned the gardens. Trent adored Tudor mazes, but Thomas preferred the Chinese style. Heavens, I pulled up the entire back lawn for that boor!"

Ah. "You'd planned to live there, after marriage."

"Where else?" She gave a light laugh. "It wasn't as if my fiancés—either of them—had a better option to offer. Odd, isn't it? Both gentlemen had a dozen houses to their names, but not a single one fit to inhabit."

"Hmm. May I suggest, Gwen, that when you next undertake to marry—"

"Oh, please, let's not even speak of it."

"—that you make a requirement," he finished. "Consider nobody who cannot claim at least one roof without holes."

"A good policy, I suppose." She gave her head a little shake. "But why are we even speaking of such matters? We're in Paris, of all places! Paris at sunrise! I'd be terribly greedy to be dreaming about the country when surrounded by this!" She swept out her hands, then did a little twirl down the pavement.

The twirl looked like manufactured good cheer—her first placating routine of the evening, in fact. Almost, he made a sarcastic remark. Paris, for all its charms, was one of the filthier cities of the world. And sunrise was no large wonder: he could testify, first-hand, that it happened every morning.

But then her face did light up, as though the act had become real, and, caught off guard as he was, he felt his damned bloody heart trip; he was grateful that her attention no longer fixed upon him, for he had no idea what she would have seen in his face, had she looked.

Instead, she gazed past him, then around them, turning a slower circle, head tipping in scrutiny. She was admiring the sleeping street, he supposed, the darkened windows in the stony faces of the Gothic and medieval facades—and the bits of trash fluttering along the embankment. Fair enough, they did tangle with some very pretty early wildflowers sprouting through the cracks in the pavement. Rogue flowers. The saffron petals formed a colorful, illicit trail up the walk as far as the eye could see, until one's attention was hijacked by the tower of Notre Dame, demanding the eye follow it upward to the heavens. The night sky was ripening into peach on the eastern horizon, promising a day of warmth ahead. On the Seine, the glow of the rising sun spread in ripples of gold.

A lilac petal was drifting past him. On impulse, he reached out to catch it. "Yes," he murmured. "I suppose it is beautiful."

She turned back, mouth quirked. "Alex, you do not even have to suppose. I will vouch for it—or bribe you to believe it, if you prefer. I do not hesitate to do such things now, you know; I have grown thoroughly wicked in the night."

He laughed. "God help us," he said, and tossed the petal at her. "Wicked becomes you a bit too well, Miss Maudsley."

She laughed back and batted the petal away. "And there's the pot calling the kettle black!" she said before slapping her hand over a jaw-cracking yawn. When her hand dropped, her expression grew serious.

She looked again toward the tower of Notre Dame. "It's not really *so* wicked, though, is it? To want to live like this?"

"Like this?" he echoed.

"To want to live . . . freely," she said. "Even as a woman."

There was a vulnerable note in her voice, longing entwined with the faintest note of fear. She turned her face to him, then, and he saw the hope there, written in her eyes.

She should not trust him with such sights. It would be so easy to crush her now—to laugh at her and say, *You think what you've done is wicked? It was child's play, sweetheart. This is not freedom. This is simply the sort of lark available to a woman with three million pounds.*

He opened his mouth, then closed it.

He would not speak the words to her. It would make him a hypocrite of the lowest order. For all the ways he could pick apart her phrasing, he did know what she meant. What she was feeling . . . it was the same yearning that had driven him away from England the very moment that university had concluded. His first sunrise over the Atlantic, the sea spray in his face, he'd leaned so far over the rail into the wind that a passing sailor had cried out in alarm.

How odd. He'd forgotten that exhilaration. How long since he'd last felt it? Its diminishment had probably been inevitable. In those early years, he'd boarded ships for sheer curiosity about the destination. Now he looked at a map and saw no names unfamiliar to him. His travels had become a matter of routine and obligation.

The sticky strands of fatigue seemed to twine together and constrict around his brain. He set his teeth against a profound tug of exhaustion. *Think. Answer her.*

But his sluggish mind was still stuck on the other matter. How had he come to the point where a week in Paris struck him as nothing more than an irritating delay between various and equally irritating business commitments?

He had a brief flash of a hamster on a wheel. A caged hamster. A hamster in a cage. Round and round and round it ran.

"Won't you answer me?" she asked softly.

He took a long breath. "My apologies. I'm . . . a bit tired. Is it wicked to live like this . . ."

Would it be so wicked if the next time she touched him, he did not stop her?

He cleared his throat. "I suppose the answer depends on whom you ask."

Her eyes were clear and steady. "I am asking you."

"Then here's a lesson for you," he said. He looked toward the sunrise. "The only person to ask is yourself."

By the time Gwen woke, sunlight had conquered the molded ceiling. It put the time at well past noon. The smell of eggs seeped inside from the sitting room, growing steadily stronger, as if they'd started to rot.

She had a fuzzy memory of Elma shaking her awake for breakfast and saying, "We have an appointment at Laferrière at ten o'clock, dear. Why on earth are you still abed?"

Oh, no. Gwen pushed herself upright against the headboard, recalling the full extent of it now.

Thanks to her grogginess, she'd not thought to lie to Elma about what had happened last night. Elma had been furious. For the first time in Gwen's memory, she had lifted her voice. Gwen could not recall the full extent of the lecture, only that it had touched on hoydens, irresponsible bounders who encouraged them, and the horrors of rabble-rousing more generally.

She also recalled the crack of the door as Elma had slammed out of the suite.

She clamped a hand over her eyes. She should apologize, of course. She did not think she could bear having Elma angry with her.

But it would be a lie if she said she regretted a single thing about last night. Even falling asleep to the sunrise had seemed romantic! Cozy beneath the covers, she'd fought to keep her eyes open as long as possible, concentrating on the singing feeling inside her, the wild giddy thrill of everything that had happened. *Remember this*, she had thought. *That I can feel this way! So light and unworried. I never knew it before.*

A knock came at the door. Michaels, her lady's

maid, poked her head into the room. "Mail and the newspaper, miss."

The number of letters surprised her. She flipped through them as the door closed. One from Caroline, who probably wanted expatriate gossip. Another from Belinda, who had been entertaining her by proposing ever more novel forms of persecution for Thomas. Lady Anne had sent a note; her daily condolences were beginning to smack of schadenfreude. *The Earl of Whitson paid me particular attention at the Flintons' ball last night*, she wrote. *Everyone says I am likely to wed before the end of the season. Of course, my only regret would be your inability to attend.*

What a clever way to be disinvited from one's bridesmaid's future, imaginary wedding!

The fourth letter bore an unfamiliar, starkly angular penmanship. When she opened it, she discovered it was from Alex.

Her heart skipped a beat. He had thrown a petal at her this morning, on the banks of the Seine, and when he'd laughed, the sound had stolen her breath. In the golden light of early morning, he had looked impossibly handsome. But also younger—friendlier, somehow—and more playful, too. He had looked, in short, like somebody who might be speaking to her as an equal.

She had not wanted the night to end. She had wanted to keep walking with him along the river. He'd been as much a part of her intoxication as the wine she'd drunk at Le Chat Noir.

Gwen, he had written, *I hope this letter finds you in no lower spirits than did the sunrise. I write to you in lieu of a call because of a pressing appointment with the Peruvian ambassador. However, the contents of this note are no doubt too indelicate to be safely committed to paper, so I hope you will recognize the trust I place in you by committing them to ink. I ask you to destroy the letter after reading it.*

In short, I have a proposition for you. But first, it will require an explanation of my main cause for visiting Paris . . .

By the time she'd finished the letter and cast it into the fire, she was a-thrill again with all the excitement of the evening before. What a wicked and marvelous plan he proposed! And to think that he would ask *her,* of all people, to help him!

But why not? He *needed* her help. What a novel and remarkable idea! He needed her. He would never have won that invitation by himself, and he could not go to Barrington's country home without her.

She wrote her reply immediately, ringing for Michaels to arrange its delivery. After the door closed again, though, it occurred to her that one small fly marred the ointment: Elma.

Elma would forbid such adventures. Indeed, Gwen had no doubt that Elma was complaining of her right now. Lady Lytton, the wife of the English ambassador, was a particular favorite of the Beechams', and Elma was slated for lunch with her in the Palais-Royal. *I brought her all the way to Paris,* Elma would be complaining over oysters, *and now she refuses to accompany me anywhere. Indeed, this morning she refused to leave bed.*

Lady Lytton would not be surprised. She would nod understandingly and pat Elma's hand. Of course, nobody could expect better from a girl who'd been jilted, crushed, flattened, twice now.

Gwen did not feel flattened, though. For the first time in what seemed like ages, she felt positively . . . robust.

Your help would be useful, Alex had written.

With a laugh, she flopped back onto the bed and spread out her limbs. As a girl, she'd visited a museum in Oxford that had displayed a dried sea specimen called a starfish. If one of its limbs got chopped off, the curator had said, another would grow overnight. Something like that had happened to her, perhaps. She felt more cheerful, even, than she had in the days before her jilting.

On an impulse, she lifted her heels into the air. Her nightgown fell down to her thighs. She considered her bare legs with interest; the cancan dancers at the Moulin Rouge had given her material for comparison. Slim ankles, nicely rounded calves. She preferred the dimpled knees she had seen last night; her own looked sadly knobby. But she could kick as well as anyone. She pointed her toe and delivered a solid punt to an imaginary Thomas Arundell. She felt better prepared than ever to give him a bit of what-for. Lily Goodrick was the Queen of the Barbary Coast, after all. She took guff from no man, least of all a spineless toad.

Perhaps today she'd find him.

* * *

Except, of course, for the small fact that Thomas had left Paris already, making him unavailable for the what-for she'd been composing in her head all afternoon. Upon learning these tidings, Gwen nearly dropped the teapot. "Are you certain?" she asked Elma. How on earth had he come and gone so quietly?

"Completely certain," said Elma. She sat across from Gwen in the sitting room, nearly vibrating with good spirits. "I had the news from Lady Lytton herself. He is her second cousin twice removed, you know, and he always pays her a visit before he leaves town. I suppose he thinks of her as he might his own mother, were his mother not such a dragon." Elma paused to give a delicate shudder. "Narrow escape you had there, my dear."

"But where has he gone?" Gwen asked. This was beyond deflating.

"Baden-Baden, says Lady Lytton, and thence to Corfu."

Gwen nodded, now thoroughly confused. Elma had proposed a celebratory tea; were these the tidings they were meant to celebrate? If so, Gwen could not help but think it slightly mean-spirited. Elma knew that she had come here to retrieve the ring. Thomas's absence was no cause to rejoice.

"Never fear," said Elma, seeing the doubt on her face. "I have better news yet. But first, let's raise our glasses."

Wary now, Gwen held out one spindly china cup—cream with a splash of tea, per Elma's preference. It was always possible, she supposed, that Elma was not about to propose that they toast the death of some countess on her wedding night, or the sudden expiry of an heir who'd had the audacity to be married already but whose younger brother yet languished in bachelorhood.

An anticipatory smile slipped free of Elma's lips. "Darling," she said, "first I must apologize for my temper this morning. I know that you've had a very trying time of it, and I should have realized that Paris is no place for a young woman in a troubled state of mind. What you required was rest, not this nervous, constant stimulus."

"Oh no," Gwen said quickly. "Please don't apologize. I am sorry to have worried you, but I assure you, I had a grand time last night."

"No, no, don't forgive me; it wasn't you whom I owed my temper. The blame rests solely with Mr. Ramsey. I confess, I expected a great deal more of him. Of course I know he is not *widely* considered worthy of respectable company, but I supposed our connections to his family would hold him to a better standard of behavior. I was gravely disappointed by what you told me, but as I said, rightfully it is he with whom I should quarrel."

"But I was the one who insisted on going to Chat Noir," Gwen said.

Elma lifted a brow. "Well," she said, after a significant pause. "As I said, you've been through a trial. And one night won't have done you any harm, provided you met no one we knew." She frowned. "Goodness—you didn't, did you?"

"No," Gwen said hastily. "Nobody at all."

Elma exhaled. "Then, as I said, no harm done. But I do think it's time to leave, darling. To the countryside, for a bit of a constitutional, exactly as the Ramsey sisters suggested. Guernsey, we'd proposed, although Cornwall could serve nicely, too. Which do you prefer?"

Guernsey? Good heavens. "Aunt Elma," she said carefully, "I think you misunderstand the situation. I do not feel overwrought in the slightest. Last night—"

"Enough about that. Don't you wish to know what we're celebrating?" Elma's stern expression melted into a twinkle as she reached into her purse. "I have the most lovely surprise for you. First, you are well rid of the viscount, dear. His love is not for one such as you, it seems. You must not blame yourself one whit for his behavior. But while he is a rascal, he is not a dishonorable one—nor a thief, I am glad to say! Just look what he left in the care of dear Lady Lytton."

She opened her hand. In it was Richard's ring.

Gwen's lips parted on a silent breath of surprise.

"Yes, dear," Elma said gently. "Take it, do. I know how much it means to you, and I'm so glad to be the one who managed to return it to you."

Slowly Gwen reached out. For a moment, as her

fingers closed on the band—so much cooler than the air, a hard and alien pressure in her palm—she had a curious sense of déjà vu.

She ran her thumb along the band, finding the familiar striations at each side. It *was* the right ring. The brilliant gleam of the gold surprised her. It seemed as if recent contact with Pennington's finger should have tarnished the metal.

She glanced up and found Elma beaming at her, waiting, no doubt, for some cathartic bout of tears, or, failing that, a fluttering joyous clamor. The occasion deserved it. With the return of the ring, her honor was redeemed, she supposed. And she was glad to have it back—truly. It was a piece of her family; it belonged with her. She would not have rested easily so long as it was missing.

But as she turned it over in her fingers, she realized that somewhere, during these last few days, the blemish that its absence had gouged into her self-regard seemed to have healed.

This ring had traveled farther, and had enjoyed so many more adventures, than she had.

"I wasn't wrong to have given it to him," she said, and this time, she believed it. "It was he who was at fault. I couldn't have known."

"No, of course not," Elma said. "Nobody could have! But now you have it back, you will put him from your mind entirely. So many other men in the world! In London, right now, the bachelors are swarming." She leaned forward, the rope of pearls at her neck swinging free. "Just think," she said mischievously. "Some handsome lad in town is waiting for you, never suspecting the good fortune about to enter his life!"

Gwen laughed. Indeed, to the swarming bachelors, that would be precisely what she signified: a fortune, no more. She doubted Elma was even aware of the irony of the statement. "But I'm afraid my feelings haven't changed, dear." If anything, they had strengthened. "I've no wish to begin that rigmarole again. Indeed, I think I would like to stay in France a while yet."

Elma's mouth pursed. The movement drew into prominence the little lines she so loathed, which fanned out from her lips and the corners of her eyes. "Gwen, do be reasonable. After last night, I can hardly countenance remaining here."

"Yes," Gwen said hesitantly. "I understand; it would not be conscionable." She lifted her own teacup to her nose, breathing deeply of the calming fragrance. The spice from the bergamot rind never failed to put her in mind of her father, who had drunk so much of the stuff that the scent had seemed permanently impressed into his clothes. He'd grown up on bohea, a watery broth made from third-rate scraps; he'd claimed that no luxury had ever startled and delighted him more than discovering the taste of proper tea. *What a miraculous transubstantiation for common water,* he'd often said. *I tell you, Gwen, no man-made chemistry has ever surpassed it.*

Exhaling, she set the cup down. "You needn't stay, of course. I'm old enough to look after myself!"

The other woman's eyes shot wide. "I—good Lord. You cannot mean to say you think to remain here *alone*?"

The incredulity gave her a moment's pause. Yes, it did sound quite outré, didn't it? "But . . . it wouldn't be *so* unusual, would it? That is, I see women of my age all the time unchaperoned! In St. Pancras Station, for one." She paused, struck by that truth. For all the money she had, she'd never experienced any true form of independence. "Why, they stand alone at the refreshment counter—drinking brandy, even! Many of them look quite respectable."

Had she sprouted another head, Elma might have gawked at her so. "*Working* girls," she said. "Typists, Gwen. Postal clerks! Surely you don't mean to compare yourself to *those* people!"

"I—of course not." That would be foolish. Such women did as they must in order to keep a roof over their heads. Perhaps, if they could have afforded it, they would have preferred to be looked after by somebody like Elma. "But that doesn't make them disrespectable, surely. That is—they are no better or worse than my mother, before her marriage."

Elma shook her head slowly, her lips forming an O. "Your mother," she said. "Your mother wanted *better* for you than that!"

Gwen looked down to her tea. "But she would not have wanted me to marry without love," she said.

"Nobody is asking you to do so. God above, what *happened* to you at that altar? Was your brain broken along with your heart?"

"My heart was not broken!" Gwen slammed down her teacup. "I've been trying to tell you that for some time now!"

Elma's eyes narrowed. "Yes, so you have. But *this* is another order entirely." Voice growing cold, she said, "Perhaps I should remind you that when I took you into our household, I vouched for your character. I risked my *own* name to promote you. What you may not know is that my friends warned me against it. They said, Elma, orchids do not grow from common barnyard soil. But I refused to hear a word against you. I told them they did not understand the sweetness, the sterling nature, of your character. Certainly I never *dreamed*—"

She broke off, her lips compressing; violently, she shook her head and looked away.

Gwen watched her miserably. The only response that suggested itself was supremely unkind. The fruits of common barnyard soil had, of course, paid the Beechams' household bills for ten years now. It was not admiration for her character that had prompted Elma to take her in.

Elma's head swiveled back. "No," she said sharply. "I will not permit you to do this. And I shall hear no further debate on it! Do you understand me?"

The door opened without a knock, giving them both a dreadful start.

Alex leaned against the doorway, buttoning up his glove in a casual gesture. "Did I hear yelling?" he inquired pleasantly. "May I be of some assistance?"

Oh, dear God. Gwen shot him an urgent look of warning. Now was not the time!

"*You*," Elma hissed, and came to her feet. "This is all *your* doing."

Chapter Nine

❧⟨⟩❧

"Ta!" Elma called, waving her handkerchief out of the window. "Don't forget to write!"

Gwen grunted as Alex's elbow landed in her ribs. "Every day!" he cried in reply, and then, under his breath, muttered, "wave, damn you, or we'll never make it aboard."

"Oh." Numbly, she lifted her hand. The handkerchief flapped an energetic reply, then retreated into the window, which snapped shut decisively.

With a great sigh, Alex slapped his felt hat back onto his head. "All right," he said. "Quickly, now, before she decides to stick her head back out." He took Gwen's arm and turned on his heel, starting down the platform at a rapid clip.

People scattered from their path, either because he was over six feet and dressed all in black, like a thief with midnight plans, or because there was an innate and intimidating elegance to the way he wore his great caped coat. He drew the attention of every female passing by, eighteen to eighty, and this was *not* simply Gwen's imagination at work: from the corner of her eye, she spied a silver-haired grandmother on a nearby bench twisting at the waist to ogle him as he passed.

"Here we are," he said to her. A hiss came from the train; a great roiling mass of steam spilled out from the warming engines. He leapt up the steps into the carriage and turned back for her just as the carriage lurched and began to roll forward.

Gwen, one foot on the stairs, cried out and lost her balance.

He caught her by the waist and hauled her up inside, directly into his chest. She held very still for a moment, in his arms, breathing in the scent of him— wool and soap and the faint, spicy hint of one of those tonics men used to soothe shaving nicks.

And then she began to smile. She pulled away, laughing. "A dramatic beginning!"

He grinned back at her. "No doubt."

A throat cleared itself very pointedly in their vicinity. They turned. An astonished gray porter stood gawking at them. "Les—les billets, s'il vous plaît?" he asked tentatively.

"Ah, yes," Alex said, and reached into his jacket for the tickets while Gwen sank back against the wall. The train was picking up speed, the floor beginning to shudder beneath her slippers. "I rented the whole damned carriage, so this should work," Alex said in an aside to her. "Even if she decides to wander, she won't be able to come back into our section."

She gazed at him. How . . . cleverly he'd managed all of this.

He glanced briefly toward her, then glanced back again with a frown. "Oh, *Christ*. And what ails *you*? Are *you* about to weep? It's not too late to jump back down, you know."

She found a smile. "Yes, it is." The platform was flying by now. Paris was over.

"The next station, then. I can figure out Barrington myself."

"No," she said quickly. "And I wasn't going to cry. It's only—" She slanted another glance at his angular face and swallowed her next words.

It's only that you're rather frightening, she wanted to say. Alex had come into the room this afternoon and taken the seat next to Elma, ignoring with grave dignity her insistence that he leave or be thrown out by security. Capturing her hand, he had meekly invited her to recite his sins. Meekly! Gwen had never seen him meek in her life.

Naturally, Elma had obliged, unleashing a volley of accusations about his black character and his terrible effect on her charge. In reply, he had nodded, squeezed her hand, and made numerous sympathetic murmurs of accord.

Just when it had looked to Gwen like she was about to be shipped back to London, Alex had introduced, with all apparent amazement, the idea of how trying his behavior must have been for Elma—which insight somehow had led the discussion off-course entirely, traversing various subjects including the misery of a life spent beholden to ingrates, the endless anxieties of keeping face in society, and the woeful injustices to which beautiful women of a certain age proved subject. Another conversational sleight of hand had then narrowed focus specifically to Mr. Beecham, at which point Elma had burst into tears and collapsed onto Alex's shoulder, wailing as he'd patted her arm.

Indeed, Gwen could feel certain of only one thing: by the end of the conversation, Elma had felt convinced that *she* was the one in need of a holiday. "From *every* obligation that troubles you," Alex had specified. "Including Gwen, of course."

Now Elma was four cars ahead of them, on the first leg of her journey to Lake Como, in northern Italy. Before leaving, she had secured their repeated and ardent reassurances that they would not breathe a word of her jaunt to anybody, *most* of all Mr. Beecham. The three of them planned to reunite in Marseilles in five days' time.

"It was just . . ." She paused. "A very sudden departure. I am a bit—addled, I suppose."

"Hmm." He seemed to accept this. "Perhaps you require some dinner."

The carriage Alex had booked contained three sleeping compartments and a small sitting area, where lunch was served atop trays the porter screwed into the floor. The spread was far more impressive than what the English railway might have mustered: first came the prawns, radishes, and chilled Marennes oysters, accompanied by a fine Madeira. The main course, to be delivered in an hour's time, would consist of braised partridges with garnishes of Gruyère cheese and salade à la Romaine. For dessert, they were assured a choice selection of fruits, coffees, and cognacs.

It promised to be a long dinner in which to avoid Alex's eyes.

"Enough," he said curtly after the prawns arrived. "Something ails you. If you're regretting your rashness, *tell* me. I can put you on a returning train at Lyons."

"Nothing ails me," she said for the fifth time. She stared fixedly out the window. They were traveling past breathtaking scenery: ancient manors perched atop cliffs that glowed in the vermilion sunset; stands of woods that rose up suddenly and cast the compartment into a darkness broken only by the dim light of the single lamp above them; and then, as the woods fell away again, great fields of sunflowers, beyond which, in the distance, lay small towns, church spires, and the turrets of crumbling castles, picturesque as any fairy tale.

She felt curiously divided in herself—on the one hand, painfully alive, vibrating in sympathy with the entire universe, so that even the great metal tube in which she rode seemed somehow of a piece with her. The train flew through the countryside, carried by its own unstoppable momentum, unembarrassed by the way its shrieking, clanging, squealing progress scattered flocks of sedate sheep and startled sleepy birds from branches into great cawing clouds of disapproval.

On the other hand, the train had a known destination, whereas she felt strangely unmoored, as if she were hurtling freefall through the sky. Hours before, Alex had pulled Elma into his arms and spoken gently and persuasively to her of possibilities she had not dared imagine for herself. Elma had been persuaded by his speech. Gwen had felt bespelled by it.

Last night, she had not dreamed she would be leaving Paris. This evening, she would be halfway across the country from it. Was this always the way he lived? The freedom of it seemed mad and dangerous and exhilarating. The world stood so *open* to him.

And now he had laid it open to her.

She dared a glance at him. Interrupted in his own study of her, he smiled. That smile, while designed to be an admission—*Yes, you caught me looking*—seemed so companionable and charming that it hit some sweet, painful nerve in her breast. She felt almost breathless, and on the footsteps of that sensation came an odd and unsettling fear.

This fascination she felt for him was clearly unidirectional.

I want to touch you, she'd told him last night, brazen as any harlot. How demoralizing—no, how purely *horrifying* that her desire seemed to have survived his rejection. In all her life to date, she'd never had the bad taste to continue to long for someone who spurned her. The viscount could go spit for all she cared. She'd loathed Trent from the moment she'd opened that note in which he'd begged forgiveness for having to break their engagement. But now, after Alex had replied to her advances with a shrug and some nonsense about his deep regard for her *brother*, what did she do?

She found herself staring again at his lips!

She found herself *envying* a silvering matron the privilege of being cozened by him, simply because it entailed the right to curl up against his chest.

She sighed and tipped up her chin. Beyond Alex, in the mirror affixed to the length of teak that formed a privacy screen dividing the sitting nook from the corridor, a redheaded girl in mauve silk gazed back, her brown eyes a bit ... woeful.

She tried to smile at herself, to put on a saucy expression befitting the Queen of the Barbary Coast. The whole point of this adventure was to seize hold of that glorious, reckless confidence that immunized her to caring for others' judgments.

Her smile faltered. If her aim was to cast off others' opinions, then desiring Alex was more than an inconvenience. For she very much wanted him to approve of her. How not? When he smiled at her, when he offered encouragement, she felt as if anything in the world was possible for her.

Which was absurd, really. Had she not learned her lesson, yet, about hitching her prospects to the good opinion of a man? And of all men, Alex was the last whose notions of admirable behavior should appeal to her. "I feel very bad for what you did to Elma," she said. "She'll feel so foolish when she comes to her senses."

He reached out to select a prawn from the platter. "Why so? I only gave her an excuse to do exactly as she wished. She doesn't enjoy playing the tyrant, Gwen." He paused. "Or has it escaped your notice that the woman's desperately unhappy?"

Gwen cast him a startled glance. "Elma is nothing near to unhappy," she countered. "She adored being in Paris; you should have seen her counting her collection of calling cards. And she was thrilled to think of returning to London—full of talk about the parties, the bachelors, the—"

"Thrilled for you," he said curtly. He bit the head off the prawn. "Thrilled to live, vicariously, through you. She has no children. Her husband doesn't give a damn about her. Alas, he has the bad taste to keep kicking, so she can't search out a replacement. In the meantime, she's growing older. My hope is that she finds a nice Italian bloke in Lake Como. Kick up her heels for the weekend."

"An—affair?" All right, this she could object to most vigorously! "Have you forgotten poor Uncle Henry—"

"Poor Uncle Henry ignores her completely, from what I can tell. God knows I'm no advocate of adultery; if you're idiotic enough to take the vow, you might as well honor it. But he seems to be doing a very poor job of that, so let him pay the piper, for once."

Gwen fixed him with a glare meant to telegraph outrage.

He laughed. "So righteous, are you? Come now, Gwen, what would you have preferred? That we bundle Elma into a trunk and dispatch her screaming to England? *Your* approach left something to be desired. What did you say to her, anyway? *Oh, cheers, Auntie Elma, thanks for the company these last ten years, but now I'm off to flash my knickers to the lads.*"

She flushed. "Of course not! Really, Alex. I always suspected you thought me stupid—"

"Did you?" His brows lifted.

"—but I'm not *that* thick. I simply said I was ready for a bit of independence."

He snorted.

"Manipulation made more sense, I suppose," she said icily.

His smile looked sharp and feline. "Darling, your hypocrisy is a beautiful thing to witness."

"What does that mean?"

"It means that you are not one to moralize when it comes to the gentle art of manipulating affections."

She went still. "I will ask you to clarify."

"You didn't convince London society to adore you by commanding it to do so."

"No," she said, "I didn't. I *befriended* them."

"Certainly. Your friends and admirers felt persuaded to adore you because you made it seem like the most natural and advantageous thing to do." He took a long sip of his wine. "Tell me," he said, "*how* many sweaters did you promise to knit the orphans? It's no wonder you demonstrate a natural talent for bribery; you've been practicing in wool."

"That is not at all the same!"

He tapped his shrimp fork against the rim of the plate, a delicate, considering sound. "You think your success was accidental, then? That your popularity was simply the product of the smiles you give so freely?"

"Of course not." She was hardly so naïve. "As you always point out, there is also the matter of my three million pounds."

The fork went still. "I pointed that out to you once," he said slowly. "In service of a very specific argument. It's you who continue to mention it now. One would almost think you really *do* tally your worth in terms of pounds and pence."

The question stirred some obscure, wounded anger. "Well, it's true, isn't it? If I weren't rich—"

He sighed. "Spare me. If you weren't rich you wouldn't have had a chance of entering high circles— of course that's true. But money is not what won your popularity."

The floor shuddered and set the dishes to rattling as the train slowed for a station. "Oh, please let's not talk about how *nice* I am."

"Wasn't going to," he said. "You're shrewd. And disciplined as hell."

Shrewd and disciplined? This idea startled her into a pause. Soldiers were disciplined; so, too, were religious widows who spent entire nights on their knees in prayer. But she? And as for shrewd—ha! "You were right about that Aubusson in the Beechams' library," she said. "I had it checked before leaving London."

"And?"

"And, you said I was shrewd."

"Not in buying carpets," he said. "But in your social success, yes. Far too complete to be the product of luck and charm and smiles alone."

"Then what?" she asked. "I did not *purchase* my friends, if that's what you mean."

"No," he said. The train had come to a full stop, now, and his voice sounded painfully precise in the new silence. "You gamed them."

"*Gamed* them?" She speared up a prawn. Curious things, prawns. They seemed so peculiarly *naked*, curled around themselves, their delicate veins exposed so plainly. "You make it sound like my life was all a sham."

"Wasn't it?" He made a sound in his throat that managed to convey amusement and skepticism at once. "Don't tell me you believed in it for a moment. You cracked that little world by mastering the rules and using them to suit yourself."

He paused, and she kept her eyes on the prawn, hoping he was finished. Her skin seemed to be crawling. There was something curiously ... *humiliating* ... in hearing him analyze her so cold-bloodedly. She was not so calculating as he painted her, but she could see how a stranger might be persuaded by his view.

Was this really how he saw her?

He spoke more gently as he continued. "Gwen . . . had you taken that world so seriously—had you placed faith in any of the people in it—you'd never have played them so cleverly. You do know that, don't you?"

The flaw in his argument emboldened her to look up. "Everyone knows there are rules," she said. "Everyone, Alex. Otherwise etiquette guides wouldn't be so popular."

His blue eyes held hers steadily. "I'm not speaking of etiquette. I'm speaking of subtler arts. Flattery, for one. And the talent for well-timed obliviousness. You recall the soiree Caroline threw, three years ago? In June, I think it was."

She shrugged and returned her attention to the prawn on her fork, twirling it around once. "There were so many—"

"Vomit in the lobby," he said.

"Oh. Yes," she said reluctantly. Vaguely she remembered it now. An unseasonably muggy day. Caroline had pitched a pretty striped tent in case of rain. For herself, she'd been abuzz with her impending wedding to Lord Trent. But half the guests had gotten sick, her fiancé included, because the shellfish—

She looked askance at prawn, then returned it to her plate. "The shellfish was off," she said. "Thank you for reminding me."

He laughed. "Yes, that was the single time I ever mistook Caro for Belinda. Her rage was extraordinary to behold."

"I didn't realize you were there."

"I had no intention of coming. I was at the docks, overseeing the unloading of some shipment. When the guests started falling ill, Caro fetched me over to help load portly MPs into their carriages." He smiled at some private memory. "Sweet God. Some of those men must *eat*. At any rate, I was there long enough to overhear you speaking to some grande dame or other. She introduced you to her friend as the daughter of a corner-shop apothecary who'd discovered a remarkable talent for capitalism."

"Oh." This sounded familiar. In the way that one sometimes recalled dreams, days or weeks later, it stirred some hazy emotional echo in her. As a policy, she never dwelled on such incidents.

"It was an insult," he said cheerfully. "Undisguised. But your smile never wavered. You thanked her for being so kind as to remember your late father."

"Did I?" She plucked up a radish from the plate and bit down on it. At first taste, these French radishes were mild and sweet, but they fought back with a spicy aftertaste that took the palate by surprise. She was forming quite an appreciation for them. "I don't remember that," she lied.

"No? I'll never forget it." The sudden sobriety of his tone drew her eyes. He held her look. "That was no piece of etiquette. It was a very clever strategy that you used to checkmate a hag." More softly, he said, "You daft girl. Of course I never thought you were stupid."

Her face went warm. The effect of the radish, maybe. "Perhaps I do remember now," she said. "It was Lady Fulton, no?"

"Maybe," he said with a shrug. "You know I take pains to avoid knowing any of that lot."

Yes. It had been Lady Fulton. With the mention of the woman's name, the moment returned to Gwen with perfect clarity. She'd been fretting over the humidity, which had melted the curl from the hair she'd frizzled over her forehead and made her feel like a sausage in overtight casing; such long, tight sleeves fashion had required that year! The remark had come out of nowhere, startling her from her more mundane miseries. She had looked around very quickly before replying, to make certain that Lord Trent had not been near enough to have overheard the slight.

How odd to think on it now. She'd been afraid. Rightly she should have looked to her fiancé to defend her. Instead she'd worried that a stray comment might change his opinion of her.

Well, for all she knew, a stray comment *had* changed his opinion. He'd never given a proper explanation for his defection.

These *men*.

"I loathe Lady Fulton," she said. *Loathe.* What a lovely word. Why had she never used it before? "That woman is a mean-tempered little snob."

"No doubt. As I said, I was greatly impressed by your restraint. Shriveled witch."

"Shriveled," she said. "Yes, that is *exactly* the word

for her. I expect her soul resembles nothing so much as a withered corn husk."

"I was thinking of her face, but I'll concede the other, too."

Together they laughed. It occurred to her that if Alex ever were to marry, his fiancée would not need to conceal such insults from him. He would be glad to step up and parry them for her.

Not that he would ever marry, of course. She turned her thoughts away from this dangerous ground. "But what you're saying, then, is that you've always thought me a very clever hypocrite."

"No. Well, perhaps," he said with a grin. "But if hypocrisy is what the game requires, who am I to judge a hypocrite?"

"How flattering," she said dryly.

"You should be flattered. I adjudged you to be good at the game. Indeed . . ." He gave her a slow smile that seemed to lick down her spine like flame. "I admired your performance enough to invite you to join a game of my own."

She was no proof against that smile. He'd first shown it to her inside the elephant at the Moulin Rouge, and she had yet to build immunity to it. She inhaled slowly. "Tell me what I must do."

"Bluntly put, you're my ticket into the party. That's more than enough. Barrington will certainly ask you to sing, but there's no call to oblige him." He paused, then set aside his wine. "Gwen, you do realize that Barrington is under the impression that we're lovers?"

She could not control her blush, but she held his blue eyes by sheer dint of will. How casually he spoke that word. "Yes," she said.

"So you understand that we'll be sharing rooms, then."

She swallowed. "Yes."

"And most likely there will be only one bed provided."

Her fingers dug into the plush velour of the cushion beneath her. "Of course," she said, attempting nonchalance. But even to her ears, her voice sounded too breathless.

"Good. Simply behave prettily toward me, then, and keep the fictions about the Barbary Queen to a minimum. The fewer lies, the harder to get tripped up."

She nodded, growing conscious of some rising dissatisfaction. The role he was outlining for her was that of a prop. But she wanted to be of *use* to him. "What are you looking for, anyway? Do you think he gulled Lord Weston out of the land, somehow?"

"I don't know," he said quietly. "Would be easier if I had an inkling. Something's not right—certainly Barrington doesn't present as a simple land baron. If he's got the money to buy a house off the old guard on the Rue de Varenne, this entire trip may be a fool's game. Perhaps he's buying up English land just for the hell of it and never replied to my offer because he has no care for the profit he might make." His mouth twisted at this idea. "What a perverse thing to collect," he said softly.

"But how odd," she said hesitantly. "If he's so wealthy, it seems that one of us should have heard of his family, at least. Where did his money come from?"

"Yes, it's damned odd," Alex agreed. "But that still doesn't mean it has aught to do with Gerry." He drummed his fingers lightly atop the table, then shrugged and looked out the window. The train had begun to move again; the iron girders of the station were passing slowly by the window, and faces on the platform were lifting toward the departing train, turning after it like pale flowers toward the sun. "Either way, this is my one attempt to find out. I'll give it two days."

She hesitated. "May I ask why you care?"

He glanced blankly back to her. "About Gerry?"

"No," she said, laughing. "About Heverley End. That is, I'm sure it's lovely—but I thought you had no regard for the countryside. And it was a very minor estate, wasn't it? Never entailed. What matter if he sold it?"

"None to me," he said. "And yes, the estate is minor. But my sisters have taken the sale badly—so there's that. And I can't dismiss the idea that my brother has gotten in over his head, somehow. Not without looking into it, at least."

She began to smile. "And you say you aren't brotherly!"

"Oh, nothing noble to this, Gwen. I'm saddled with a passel of incompetents—a pompous bore of a brother and two shrill, complaining sisters who prefer fretting to fixing things. It's easier this way—take care of the matter and they leave me alone. Until the next matter arises," he added in a mutter.

Until the next matter arises. How reluctantly and matter-of-factly he acknowledged this: whenever the need arose, he would step in, with no hesitation. He would always be there to help, whether he liked it or no.

As always when anyone spoke of family affairs, she became conscious of a stir of fascination. Envy, too: she would admit it, although it spoke ill of her character. Even in their quarrels, the Ramseys belonged to each other, permanently. For all the worry and grief Alex's roaming caused his siblings, they always welcomed him home with open arms. For all the irritation the twins felt at Lord Weston, they still convened at his house on Sunday evenings for dinner. And Alex, who held himself aloof from polite society and preferred to be away from England whenever possible, did not fail to attend those dinners when he was in town.

It was so different than the upbringing Gwen had known. For the sake of their children's advancement, her parents had willingly fractured their family. Sometimes she wondered what life might have been like had they proved less ambitious.

She looked away from that thought, physically. She looked up into Alex's face—blue eyes that made no pretense at generosity or optimism and glinted, always, with a cynical light. His brow rose, questioning, and without conscious direction, her fingers closed very tightly in her lap.

They wanted, she thought, a hand to hold. The

right to reach out for someone, for him, any time she required his aid. Suddenly, with a physical ache in the pit of her stomach, she wanted—impossible things. Not marriage. God, not something so easily broken or betrayed. Something more than marriage—a bond as fierce and unbreakable as a physical embrace. Tight. Even suffocating. She would not struggle.

She'd hoped a wedding would guarantee such a bond. She had looked at Pennington and seen the father of her future children—four, five, six children, enough to begin to fill the bedrooms in that huge, empty, echoing estate her parents had built. Enough children to ensure that she would never be alone, and neither would they.

Instead of a hand, she closed her fingers over Richard's ring, which she had strung on a chain around her neck.

But her eyes would not move from Alex.

She could not have him, of course. But God above, she wanted him.

It was inevitable, perhaps, that any period of extended conversation between them should turn, eventually, to Richard. They remained in the dining nook long after the dishes had been cleared away, sharing memories, swapping tales, laughing together like friends. And by the time the moon rose, round and heavy in the star-strewn sky, Gwen had regained her peace around him. All of this common ground, this love they had shared

for her brother, made it very difficult to feel anxious
in his presence.

How curious, then, that the longing still persisted.
She had always supposed that attraction thrived on
nerves and uncertainty, but the more comfortable she
felt with him, the closer she wished to be.

After they had parted ways and gone to their separate compartments—her unassisted disrobing made
possible by the simple clasps of the Pretty Housemaid
corset she'd purchased in the Galeries du Louvre the
day of her scandalous shopping spree—it occurred to
her that she might be confusing her emotions. Perhaps
what she felt for Alex was only an extension of her love
for Richard.

She tossed the corset onto the floor. It subsided
with a sad, cheap flop, and so did she, into the single
small chair.

She stared at the corset. "Pretty housemaid,"
indeed. What sort of name was that? Certainly it had
succeeded in inspiring her to buy it, but only as a lark;
she'd imagined gifting it to Caroline just to hear her
shriek with laughter. Housemaids could be pretty, and
the corset was priced to appeal to that demographic,
but it seemed rather lewd, associating an undergar-
ment with the wearer's source of income.

And the corset itself was not, in fact, pretty. No
housemaid would wear it if seduction was on her
mind. Indeed, the insert did not even advertise it as
pretty; rather, the manufacturer assured her, it was
both strong and cheap.

She frowned. Was that a lewd reference, as well? A strong, pretty, *cheap* housemaid?

She slid down in her chair and kicked the thing across the small space. It went skidding up against the bed, where it sagged dispiritedly. It knew there were far prettier corsets in the world, far more appealing to men, and stronger, too. She had several lovely corsets to her name, each designed to mold her body slightly differently, the better to flatter the line of particular gowns. She'd often thought, while half-dressed in front of the mirror, that some of her corsets were almost too fetching to be covered up—that somebody should get to see her in them.

But not the Pretty Housemaid. She scowled at it. She should not have abandoned her other corsets in Paris. What had she been thinking? Corsets were not articles to be abandoned lightly; they were the benchmarks of a lady's success, in some circles. Amongst the girls who had debuted with her three years ago, everybody had aspired to marry no later than the age that corresponded to the measurement of their corseted waists. Twenty-four had marked the beginning of proper spinsterhood.

Corsets had shortened in the years since, and lacing had grown more vicious. The current lot probably all wished to marry before they turned twenty-two.

Why . . . she sat up. The very fact that she had not overheard the other debutantes discussing the current equation of waist to marriage age was probably a *sure* sign that her age fell somewhere above the acceptable limit.

Or that her waist was too large!

Heavens. She put her hands to her hips, squeezing lightly. Would she still look pleasing only in her underclothes? Cream puffs and champagne took their toll, of course. If only she had brought her sea-green corset with her, a bit too long now for current gowns, but cunningly trimmed in matching ribbon and ivory lace. If it were with her, *that* was what she would wear into Alex Ramsey's compartment.

She clapped a hand to her mouth.

Good Lord!

She was thinking of undergarments because somewhere, in the course of their conversation earlier, she had made a decision: the Pretty Housemaid would not serve for the seduction she planned to undertake tonight.

She could not have him forever. But she meant to have him now.

Chapter Ten

It took her a good hour, and the rest of her glass of cognac, to build her courage. Then, unbuttoning her white cotton nightgown to the point where the slope of her breasts began, she took a deep breath and slipped into the corridor.

He had the compartment directly next to hers, and the door was not locked. It swung open beneath her hand soundlessly, revealing a direct and immediate view of his bed. He was lying flat on his back, one arm thrown over his head. A clothed arm, by the look of it.

For some reason she had imagined he would be naked.

When it became clear that the clamor of her thundering heart would not wake him directly, she crept forward toward the bed. How did one begin to seduce a man? Did one wake him and announce her intentions? *I have come to ravish you. I will not accept rejection.*

That approach seemed to require a good deal of brute strength. She also suspected that if she told him he could not deny her, he would do so simply to prove her wrong. If she knew anything of him, it was that he was a man who jealously guarded his prerogatives.

The single chair was drawn up by the bed, and lying atop it was a magazine—*The Board of Trade Journal*, great ghosts, how awful—and, more intriguingly, something that glinted. She bent down, squinting, and discovered that the glint came from a pair of wire-rimmed spectacles.

Spectacles! She glanced up at him, lips parting in amazement. She also required them to read comfortably. But like him, she never wore them in public.

So we are both a little bit vain, she thought. The idea made her smile. It was becoming something of an obsession, uncovering the small things which they might have in common. His loyalty to his family. His love for her brother. His disregard for the opinions of idiots and shriveled snobs.

He made a soft noise, and she froze. In the moonlight, in slumber, his face looked boyish, almost innocent. He would need to shave on the morrow; she wished she dared to touch the shadow on his chin, to stroke it simply for the pleasure of the texture beneath her fingertips. But as she reached out, her fingers curled into her palm. Some superstitious conviction came over her: if she woke him the wrong way, everything would go wrong. Fairy tales often emphasized this point. There was only one right way to stir a sleeping person if one wanted them to fall in love.

But I do not want him to fall in love with me, she reminded herself. *I am not here because I am dreaming of a future with him.*

What would a future with him even look like? He had no interest in the country, no taste for England, no care for settling down.

If he fell in love, he would still want to chase the wind. His beloved would simply have to race alongside him.

It did not seem a very restful life.

Some strand of discontent was threading through her resolve now. Of course he would not fall in love. Not with anybody. No need to feel so ill-tempered toward this faceless woman able to race with him when she would never, in fact, exist. Alex was the most determined bachelor known to her.

The thought gave her courage. It was one thing to deny a woman in public. But to find her in his bedroom, at night? Any man would take such an invitation.

Emboldened, she leaned down to inhale the scent of him. Cognac fumes still clung to him, but beneath that was something else—the smell of his bare skin? She pulled in a deeper breath. Yes, that was it. The scent of a warm, healthy, muscular man in his prime. The scent of Alex.

His eyes opened.

She froze.

He studied her for a moment with sleepy, heavy-lidded eyes.

Her heart gave a painful jolt.

The next moment, he came awake. She saw it happen. Saw his expression focus and narrow.

The only sound was the thumping of the wheels over the ties.

Or, no: the breath rasping in her throat seemed embarrassingly loud, too.

"How wicked do you want to be, then?" he murmured.

She had not planned for him to speak. With a single question, he seemed to seize control of the moment. She felt powerless, suddenly, to answer him, or to say anything at all.

His eyes, dark in the shadows falling across his face, rested unblinkingly on hers. He pushed himself up on one elbow, supple and fluid as a cat, and his open shirt parted and fell away. The muscles of his flat abdomen rippled as he moved.

Her mouth went dry.

All right. This was not *at all* a sisterly feeling.

"How wicked?" he asked again softly.

"I—" The word yielded to a breath she hadn't realized her lungs needed. "Very," she said as she exhaled.

"And?"

She hesitated. *And?* And what? "You . . . do you not want to?"

"Gwen." He tilted his head slightly, so his expression was further lost to the shadows. "When you wake to find me watching you, you may begin the discussion by asking what I want. But tonight, it's your turn to speak first. What do *you* want?"

Why must he make this so difficult? Wasn't it clear what she wanted?

Or did he just wish to hear her stutter and stammer for his amusement?

Probably.

Why had she come in here? *Why* hadn't she brought her green corset? "Never mind," she muttered. "Go back to sleep."

His mouth curved slightly. "Gwen," he murmured, and his voice was like a siren's song, a balm, luring her to turn back toward him. His voice addled her, she thought. Low, smooth, steady—everything sounded persuasive, wrapped up in those polished vowels. Such a voice could recite Bible verses to atheists, rally troops to suicidal charges . . . and coax a woman ten meters from the mountaintop into jumping off a cliff.

"What?" she breathed.

"You keep telling me you want to live freely," he said. "But what's the point in breaking free if you don't even know what you want? Why are you here? Do you even know?"

She wrapped her arms around herself. "I *do* know what I want. But you—" *Make it very difficult to get it*, she added silently.

He leaned forward, toward her, bringing one of his large, muscled shoulders into the moonlight flooding the bottom half of the bed. Her eyes fixed on it. She wanted to touch it. She wanted to press her lips to it.

"I know my desires," she said in a whisper. "I do."

"Then you have a choice," he said softly. "Lock

them away and ignore them. Walk out of this room. Or learn to embrace them without shame. For *that* is what people mean when they call a woman wicked, you know." He waited until she looked away from his shoulder, back to his face. "It has nothing to do with the quality of her spirit," he said, "or the measure of her character. In this world, there is nothing more wicked than a woman who is unafraid to acknowledge what she wants."

Still she hesitated. "But I have told you before what I want," she said slowly. "At the Moulin Rouge. You stopped me then."

"Yes," he said. "And maybe I'll stop you now. That's a right I have, and a risk you must take. But even if I stop you, that won't mean you were wrong to have taken the risk."

She stared at him. She could not speak the words. Could she?

He laughed, a soft, rough sound in the darkness. "For God's sake," he murmured. "It's only me, you know. Not some stranger."

A flush moved through her, warming her, heating her stomach, the backs of her knees. No. Not some stranger. Far from it. He had been watching her for years. Even when she had not been watching him, his eyes had rested on her, observing, studying. Forming opinions that nobody else had thought to draw about her. *Disciplined. Shrewd. Clever.*

"I want you to do things to me." She swallowed. "I was to have been a married woman by now. I want to . . . know." On a ragged breath, she said, "And now I have told you what I want. Will you refuse?"

He remained still for a long, agonizing moment. Perhaps he was deliberately tormenting her. She could not say, for the light in the room made his face impossible to read.

And then he rolled up onto his knees in one fluid move. A fine line of dark hair trailed down from his navel, disappearing into the waistband of his trousers, which clung low to his angular hip bones. "No," he said.

For a split second, she did not know whether he was assenting or refusing. And then he rose very lightly from the bed, and from the expression suddenly revealed on his face, the slight, wicked cant to his lips, she understood that he was hers.

Her experience was based on novels. She expected him to lunge, then—to seize her by the waist and toss her onto her back. Instead, he smoothed his hand beneath her hair, cupping the side of her neck in one large, warm palm. Twice, thrice, he smoothed her neck, and then he lifted her hair away and bent his head. His breath wandered up her throat, hot, restless, as if searching for a place to lodge.

"Suppose you try being more specific," he whispered into her ear.

Her eyes drifted shut. "Yes."

His lips brushed the spot beneath her ear, the lightest tease. "You wish me to make love to you? Or shall I make you come?"

She had no idea what the difference was. But she instinctively understood why he asked. He was going to make her own this moment. This choice.

Which was well and good, because the wild resolve in her would not back down now. "I don't know," she said steadily. "You will have to show me the difference. But first, you will kiss me, please."

His laughter was hot, dark velvet. He set his hands on her shoulders. His palms rubbed up the sides of her throat, turned briefly so his knuckles could brush the line of her jaw, and then slid up along her cheeks. He lifted her face to his.

"With pleasure," he said.

The kiss he pressed on her was gentle, inviting somehow, as if his mouth were asking hers some intimate question, a secret between two pairs of lips, not meant for the ears or thoughts above. His tongue moved to the corner of her mouth, touching, retreating, and then touching again: tasting her. It slid along the seam of her lips, and she inhaled, caught by the unexpected tenderness.

His teeth very gently bit her lower lip, in reproof or encouragement. Her lips opened, then, and he moved into the kiss—moved into *her*, his palm sliding around to cradle her skull as he backed her against the wall and his tongue came into her mouth.

He tasted like brandy, like mint toothpaste and lemon water. He tasted like a wild dark night in which girls lost themselves and were lucky to ever resurface—the sort of night that left white streaks in the hair. She kissed him back, trying to arch against him. He made some slight noise and adjusted his body so their torsos could not touch. Only his mouth wooed her, and his hand cupped her head.

She opened her eyes and saw that his had closed. He was concentrating completely and specifically on her mouth, and holding her as if she were made of glass, something unsteady and precious, that otherwise might threaten to break. How lightly and economically he held her. Yet she felt completely surrounded—held, possessed, fixed in place forever.

Something melted in her heart. It had no relation to the desire. It felt more dangerous.

Don't let me go.

The thought alarmed her. Some instinct of self-preservation struck out. She pushed against him and felt his lips curve into a smile. He took one short step toward her and used his entire body to press her against the wall.

Not gentle any longer. *Yes.* She twined her arms around his neck and opened her mouth wider, taking him in, wrapping her leg around his, every cell in her discovering the need to be touched, to be pressed against his skin. His fingers tightened in her hair and his arm slipped to her waist, pulling her by the small of her back away from the wall, more firmly into him. She could feel his hardness pushing into her belly; that would be the part of him that would make this night decisive. She rocked against it on some primitive impulse, and he made a low, guttural noise.

His mouth broke away to trace a hot, wet path to her throat. His thumb brushed across her nipple, causing her to gasp. "Yes?" he whispered.

"*Yes*," she said.

He pulled down the neckline of her nightgown. For a moment, he went very still—so still that she looked down at him, starting to ask a question.

He smiled up at her through long lashes, and closed his mouth over her nipple.

The hot, soft sucking—the sight of his dark head bent over her naked breast—pulled something more out of her than want; her strength seemed to go with it. Her knees folded; she caught herself, barely.

He turned her and laid her down on the bed. His fingertips trailed up her calves, lingering in the tender space behind her knee, smoothing into a flat palm along her inner thigh. She felt the muscles there quiver. He was urging her legs apart. She looked into his face and found him watching her; the moment seemed unbearably intimate, but she refused to let herself close her eyes. It would be cowardly, and she had already invited these acts in words, which was sin enough in the eyes of the world; now she was only bearing out her promise, and this was the easy part, the most pleasurable part, God above, his hand moved upward through the curls between her legs and he stroked and she nearly jumped out of her skin.

His hand lingered there between her legs as he leaned up over her, the muscles in his upper arm springing into prominence as he rested his weight on it for balance.

He looked startlingly grave in the half-light, his fingers moving so gently up and down that wet and wetter part of her. She reached out and laid her palm atop his biceps, then pulled herself up to plant her lips onto his shoulder, which was as smooth and hard and hot as she had imagined. She licked him, for the taste, and maybe to shock him, but she forgot whom she was dealing with; the low, broken thread of his laugh announced only approval. "Bite," he whispered, and she almost wasted time by giving him a look of surprise, but what was the point? Biting was a brilliant idea. She put her teeth gently against his flesh, and below, he pushed one long finger into her, so she inhaled in startlement against his skin, and then broke away to arch up as his thumb hit some sweet nerve that made her light up like the windmill at the Moulin Rouge.

He stroked again, and again, leaning down now to kiss her earnestly, his lips never breaking from hers as she twisted and pushed beneath his touch. There was more to this, she knew there was more to the marriage bed, or the un-marriage bed, the fornication bed they could call it, she did not care, only she knew that the part of him that had grown hard, his erection, was meant to be involved, too, and he was driving her toward some point, his hand setting a purposeful rhythm that tormented her and made pleasure pop through her like champagne bubbles, but his erection remained uninvolved. She groped blindly, finding it, and he hissed into her mouth when she closed her hand over his length. His hips jerked into hers, and she pushed harder back; this was what she wanted, she felt achingly empty, incomplete in a novel and wholly delicious and utterly abandoned way. This couldn't go on, she couldn't go on like this—she felt a lick of anger move through her, and bit his lip to express this. He settled the full weight of his torso against hers while his hand continued to drive her mad and his kisses grew harder and deeper, and she lifted her hips, once, twice, a third time, and, *oh*.

"Oh, oh, oh," she gasped, as her body, her hips, the aching places deep inside her, sprang apart and snapped back together; she felt like one of those wind-up alarm clocks with bells, which rattled and jumped and clanged, *oh*. She felt his lips turn into a smile against her mouth and well he might smile as her head fell back; her mind went blank as the pleasure uncoiled again sharply through her, fading slowly, in deep, pulsing throbs, until the gentle reminder of his hand called them forth once more, briefly now.

Her muscles unwound like overcooked pasta. She lay back, gasping, her eyes blindly fixing on the darkness of the ceiling, the ghostly rippling silhouettes of trees, rising and falling, rising and falling as the train passed onward.

She had never felt so... *replete*... in her life.

A gentle kiss pressed against her cheekbone. She blinked slowly, then turned her sweaty face to him.

One might have thought it would be awkward. His hand was still pressed between her legs. But the sight of him, his angular bones, the long, dramatic sweep of his mouth, seemed so natural to her. As though she should see his face every night in the dark.

Slowly he removed his hand, sliding it gently over her bared hips.

"What of you?" she murmured. Her voice sounded slurred.

A soft breath escaped him. She knew enough now to interpret it: he liked the way her voice sounded, or the remark. It made him hot, as he'd made her.

He was still hot, in fact. The awareness stirred a small bit of anxiety. She was not so naïve as to imagine that *this* was why men visited brothels. She started to sit up. "You haven't—"

"Shh." Delicately he touched her temple, the feathery hair there. "Lie back, Gwen."

"But I wanted—"

"No. We're not going to do that."

No? The words tripped off a flutter of strange panic. Weren't they done with rejection? She'd looked up at him in those moments of immense pleasure and seen him gazing back at her, expression stark, and she'd felt as though they were attuned. Would he refuse her again tomorrow, then? She felt greedy for him now. The very pores of her skin seemed to be opening in order to inhale him, the scent of him. "But why not?" she asked, and her voice emerged so clumsily, sounding as small and petulant as a child's.

He pulled away from her, rose from the bed, crossed to the small ledge built into the teak wall. He had ordered another bottle from the porter. As he splashed brandy into a glass, the moonlight caught his face again, outlining the sculptured contours of his mouth. He glanced up at her, as if sensing her inspection, and his eyes caught the light, glittering beneath the heavy fall of his dark hair.

"I can't do this," he said quietly. He put down the bottle with a thump and kicked around the chair so its back was to the bed. He fell into it, straddling the seat, one muscular forearm propped atop the back, the brandy glittering in the cold light.

She knocked her nightgown back over her legs. Did up the buttons above her waist. *He* sat in all apparent comfort, although he was naked from his trousers up. His torso—well, it distracted her briefly. As a boy, he'd been sent down from the Rugby School for beating Reginald Milton bloody—she knew this from Richard, whom his violent intervention had saved, and the twins besides. She knew, too, that he still studied violent arts, but his manner was so casual and his physicality so indolent that one did not imagine him capable of brutality, until one studied the muscled hew of his arms and chest.

"You can do anything," she said. Her throat tightened; she spoke the next words with difficulty. "But if you don't *want* to, that's another thing."

He leaned forward, quick as a snake, and caught up the chain around her throat. He let a length of it run through his fingers, setting Richard's ring swinging over her breast.

Her stomach fell.

"I meant to take that off," she whispered. She could not believe she'd forgotten.

"Did you?" He sounded contemplative. "We talked of Richard all night, you know." He let go of the chain and took a sip of the drink, then added, "But we never talked of what he would have thought about this."

Cold foreboding stabbed through her—through a body that still felt lethargic, weighted with the remnants of pleasure. The combination dazed her. "Perhaps we did not mention it because my brother is dead. His opinion no longer signifies."

A caustic note entered his voice. "Of course I am aware of that. Let me be clearer: when I am speaking of Richard now, the person I am really speaking of is you. I begin to wonder at your motives, Gwen."

She stared at him, utterly confused. "I have been as frank with you about my motives as I know how. I have told you again and again that I'm in search of a different life. Of something... something that is—"

"Irrevocable," he said. "You are in search of a moment, an experience so irrevocable that you will never be able to turn back."

She pondered this for a moment, looking for traps. But she found none. "Perhaps that's part of it," she said. But not all of it. If it had been, then any man would have served for seduction.

Instead, she only wanted him.

"It's good that you admit it," he said casually. "But as I said, there are always two choices involved. And I won't be your guillotine. Regardless of what happened to Richard."

The words chilled her. She did not understand them, but she recognized their power. They raised a wall that would take an axe to break down. "What happened to Richard has nothing to do with this."

"And yet we've never spoken of it," he said. "An absence so pointed is not an absence at all."

She drew her knees up into her chest. "I have . . . no wish to die, if that's what you mean. This is not some grand, reckless, suicidal lark on my part."

"I don't think he meant his to be, either."

Silence. "He was . . . angry with you," she said finally. "I know."

"I could have stopped him," he said. "So easily."

The rawness in his voice jarred her. "Alex—do you think I *blame* you for his death? I have never done so. Not once."

The corner of his mouth tipped up. He sat back into the shadows, his expression lost to her. "Not *once*," he echoed.

The mocking emphasis filled the air between them longer than she should have allowed. But she knew a challenge when she heard one—and also that old habits were so hard to shake, while new skills took time to sharpen. She did not want to be clumsy in her honesty.

"Perhaps," she began carefully, "in the early days, when he had just . . . left us—"

"Been murdered," he said emotionlessly. "He did not leave us, Gwen. He was violently taken. It is an important distinction: it means there is blame to be apportioned."

"All right," she said softly. "After he was murdered . . . I did think, once or twice, that it was you who taught him to play such games—that it was your path he had followed to the grave."

There. That was the cruelest part, and it was spoken, now.

By a fierce act of will, she restrained herself from rushing onward.

He, in turn, sat impassively, watching her from the dark.

She stared back into his featureless face. She did not need the light; she knew what she was looking at. Chestnut hair, ice blue eyes, broad cheekbones over gaunt cheeks, a strong jaw and high-bridged nose: he was the picture of rugged good looks, and girls did sigh over him, in secret, when their mothers were not listening.

For herself, she had always, usually reluctantly, admired his more intangible qualities—foremost, his unshakable composure.

It was rather unnerving now to be faced with the full force of that composure. He had asked the question; surely he owed her *some* reaction to the answer.

As the silence extended, his impassivity, his unfair use of the darkness, roused a small strain of resentment in her—just enough to remind her of exactly what she *had* thought, in those weeks after Richard's death. After his *murder.*

"At the funeral, you were so cold," she said. So composed. It had unnerved her. Unnerved and angered her, too. She had lost the last person remaining to her, but he still had so many people to love him, for all that he took them for granted, rebuffing their every sign of care.

"I was in shock," he said evenly.

"Yes." That had been her later conclusion. But at the time, locked in her own shock, she had thought that maybe it was not composure so much as inhumanity that aided him—in which case, people would do better to admire him as they might a tiger at the zoo: from a distance, with no ambitions.

She did not believe that now. She saw him more clearly.

"Here's something," she said quietly. "I thought to myself that you put a spell on people—inadvertently, of course. Sometimes I still think it. Your wit and charm seem so careless—almost accidental, really. You're so *at ease* in the world, Alex. And I think, because you make it look so easy, that people think they can emulate you—can seize life by the throat as you do. But it requires skill to skirt the risks you run. And my brother never had that talent. He was not . . . watchful enough." She paused. "But I am."

He made a soft noise, of skepticism or scorn.

"I am," she said more sharply. "I am not my brother. And I knew my brother as well as you did, mind you. When I say you charmed him, that does not mean you were somehow to *blame*." By befriending Richard,

Alex had only done what her parents had hoped for. They had wanted Richard to learn to see the world from a particular vantage point: how to make the sort of assumptions, and to demand the sort of entitlements, and to formulate the sort of expectations, that any gentleman of the upper class did. How to gamble, how to drink, how to cut a stylish path through the Continent—why else had her parents sent Richard to Rugby?

Alas for her parents, Richard had fixed on the one aristocrat's son who'd learned his lessons outside the canon.

She cleared her throat. "You cared for Richard deeply—that I never doubted. And he knew you far better than I. Certainly he knew you well enough to understand the difference between style and substance, and also the relation between the two." She folded her hand over the ring. "He must have known your mettle. He knew what he was trying to emulate. And if he didn't . . . then that was his failing, not yours."

"Perhaps," he said.

"No," she replied instantly. "Since you have asked me the question, you will do me the favor of believing my reply. As his sister, I am best equipped to judge this question. And had you escorted him directly to that casino, it still would have had no bearing on the fact that some drunken barbarian shoved a knife into his chest. Yes?"

Her voice had grown very firm. He sat up a little,

doing her the favor of showing her that he was looking directly into her eyes. "Yes, Gwen," he said. "I heard you."

"But do you *believe* me?" When he did not immediately reply, she let go of the ring and reached out for his hand, grabbing it harder than ever would have come to her by habit or whim. "Do not offend me," she said, "by implying that I would long to touch a man who bore any blame in my brother's murder."

She felt his fingers move at that pronouncement, a small, indecipherable ripple. But his regard remained as neutral, as coolly speculative as his voice. "Perhaps you do see me clearly," he said. "And from what you've said about my effect, wanting to touch me seems very unwise. Better, I think, to stay away."

"Yes," she said. "For most. But not for me. And by your own admission, if you believed me incapable, you would not have invited me to come with you on this journey."

He gave her a lingering look, from eyes to lips to shoulders and breasts. "I begin to regret it," he said, almost beneath his breath.

Her hand moved of its own accord to her stomach. Such pain those words lashed into her. Only a quarter hour ago, he'd made her feel so replete. But now, all at once, she felt battered by him. Drained.

On a sigh, he turned back to the bottle. "Go to bed, Gwen," he said over his shoulder. "I'm done with company for the night."

Chapter Eleven

Alex woke slowly and with difficulty, fighting with an undertow of sleep that wanted to drag him back under and keep him there. His eyes opened briefly and the light fell like a weight upon his lids, pushing them closed again. He lay still for a long moment, listening to the roughness of his breathing, as though he indeed had just been through a fight. His mind wanted to remind him of something. Ah, yes. Last night, he'd shown Richard's sister far more about pleasure than was his right. Somewhere in the afterlife, a dead man was cursing his name.

Even this small amount of thinking felt difficult. *Exercise*, he thought groggily. He would feel more alert once he'd done his calisthenics. The burn in his muscles would force him awake. He could pay his penance to Richard in sweat.

He sat up slowly, a groan escaping him. Every bone in his body creaked, unhappy to rediscover the way of it. His head did not hurt, though.

He swung his legs off the bed, then paused. Why

should his head hurt? This misery could not be the effect of the liquor. He'd had only a few glasses of cognac, over the course of seven hours.

It struck that something else was amiss: the train was not moving.

He leaned over and pulled back the curtain. The station placard outside bore a single word: *Nice.*

His hand dropped like a stone.

Jesus Christ. No wonder he felt as though someone had bashed his skull with a mallet. He'd slept for—he quickly calculated it—nine hours straight.

He stared in disbelief at the platform. It *was* Nice, wasn't it? The sign wasn't a sham?

Yes. He recognized the station, the distinctive scrolling archways that led toward the concourse proper.

He sat slowly on the foot of the bed, staring out. On the platform, a handful of men were shifting luggage. A woman stalked past, elbows pumping angrily, a parasol swinging from the ribbon at her wrist. The man at her heels made a quick sidestep to save his thigh, then uttered some protest that made the woman look back, her mouth a perfect O.

She came to a stop. So did he. He clasped his hands to his heart. Quite suddenly she laughed. The anger melted from her spine. He held out his elbow, and she took it, proceeding onward at his side.

It looked warm out there. The woman's blue silk skirts gleamed. Lemony light bounced down on the green iron benches, called into blazing richness the crimson petals of the rosebushes beside the track. A bright day, sunny and alive.

His own lifting mood gave him pause. He had no right to feel cheerful. Had Richard been alive, the man would have been demanding Alex's blood for last night's betrayal. A pretty thing to do—indulging one's own appetites with the sister of the man one had directed to his death. He had fallen asleep furious with himself.

That anger now seemed very distant.

His hand paused, shoved halfway through his hair. In fact, the very reflex to castigate himself—to revile his own weakness with regard to Gwen—felt limp and tired, like an overused muscle that no longer held any power.

He did not feel guilty at all.

A banging came at the door. Bit aggressive for a porter hoping for a tip. He rose on a curiously light sensation, opened the door and discovered his Achilles' heel. Gwen stood with her arms crossed under her breasts, freshly dressed in a tweed walking outfit. On her head perched the most ridiculous hat he'd ever seen—some long-brimmed affair that featured an assortment of garden creatures, miniature birds and bees and butterflies, held aloft by rose stems made of gutta-percha.

He reached out to give the bird a chuck to the chin. Gwen stepped backward, and the bumblebee bobbed a cheerful nod.

He smiled as another buoying sensation washed

through him. It felt as though the sleep was knitting into his muscles now. He began to feel quite . . . alert. "Come in," he said.

Her manner was stiff as she ran a pointed eye down his bare chest. "The porter said he could not rouse you. But I'd assumed that you would be dressed by now. No matter. I'll be outside."

"Wait," he said as she turned away.

She paused. "What?"

He opened his mouth. But what was there to say? Strange thing: until last night, he'd had no idea that Richard's death still weighed so heavily on his conscience.

It was not within her power to absolve him, of course.

Yet he felt absolved. Jesus Christ. He felt weightless.

He stepped back. "Nothing," he said. "Only— modesty seems a bit disingenuous, now that I've had my hand on your—"

"I have no desire to watch you dress," she said sharply.

"Does the word offend you?"

She glared at him silently. Her color was rising.

"Or do you not know the words?" That was far more likely. "There are several to choose from," he said helpfully. "For all that you're determined to be wicked, I expect you'd favor the ladylike 'quim.' For the male apparatus, 'cock' is the term generally favored, although you may use 'manhood,' if you're feeling vaporish."

"Do we require soap?" she asked icily. "Apparently you haven't washed your mouth yet this morning."

He laughed. "What a prudish mood you're in. Is this my punishment for failing to shag you?" Properly, he deserved a bloody award for restraint. A hotter sight than her writhing on his bed beneath his touch, he'd never see in his life.

Unless he reconsidered his policy on shagging her. Then he might see other things, too.

Her face was now a very interesting shade of pink. Bordered on purple, really. "I don't know that word either," she said. "So I can't answer you."

"Oh, if your blush is anything to go by, I expect you've drawn the right conclusion. Come now, step inside. Unless you've changed your mind in the night, and fear for your virtue?"

She made an irritated noise, then shoved past him into the room, stalking—or attempting to, for the size of the room would not allow for drama—to the window. There she turned, giving him her very best glare. "You're entirely obnoxious," she said.

He offered a smile in reply. Had he any artistic talent, he would have sketched her like this, silhouetted against the window behind her, framed by the green velvet curtains caught up at either side by gold tasseled sashes. *Angry Young Miss En Determined Route to Ruin* would be the public title, and the private, *A Damned Nuisance I Could Have Avoided by Turning Back at Gibraltar.*

Except that the first title seemed flavorless, and the second . . . dishonest. He certainly could have avoided her by turning back for South America. But to what profit? She was amusing. She evinced surprising bravery, tossing over her little world and throwing off every restriction she'd ever known. And she was right: this Richard business was a poor excuse to trammel her. The Maudsleys had done their best by Gwen; had designed a path for her that many women would have been happy to walk. But Gwen herself had not proved content with it. The intentions of the dead should not have a hold on the living.

A new title, then: *The Unexpectedly Interesting Former Debutante.*

Ah, well. It seemed that he lacked a talent for titling, too. Happily, the scene would make a lovely painting no matter what one called it. The sunlight dancing through the window played over her hair, picking out, from amidst the predominant auburn, strands of gold and cinnamon and a shade (he would wager a year's profits on it) that could only be true crimson. Her hair seemed like a minor miracle, in fact—a national treasure far more inspiring than the Elgin Marbles or groaning, crumbling palaces. He had touched it last night simply for the tactile pleasure.

"Ginger is such an unjust name for the shade," he said.

She blinked. "I *beg* your pardon?"

"Although you do have bite," he said. "And you bite quite nicely, too. You take direction well. Did you enjoy that?"

Surprise parted her lips. That rouge the other day had been overkill; her mouth required no aid. It was her second chief beauty, long and full, tinted a natural pink. He enjoyed watching her eat radishes with it. Did she realize that in the bluish tint of gaslight, the color of that vegetable exactly matched her hair? And complemented her lips besides.

"You are flirting with me," she said slowly.

He considered it. Was he? "Yes," he said. "I am." The realization was strangely satisfying. He was flirting with Gwen Maudsley as he might have with any woman who had caught his fancy, whose brother had not been his closest friend, who did not retreat from the world behind a screen of hypocritical and simpering formalities. He'd never had a taste for girlishness.

A strange expression crossed her face. He did not know how to interpret it. That was intriguing, too. Until so recently, he'd fancied her more transparent than glass. "Does it bother you?" he asked. If it did, he supposed these half-formed ambitions would need crushing.

She rolled her eyes. He'd never seen her do that before. "No, it does not *bother* me," she said. "But you really must make up your mind, Alex. You are becoming more fickle than a debutante."

He felt his jaw drop. And then, out of nowhere, he began to laugh. Good God. She was right.

She inspected him narrowly. He wanted to say . . . hell, he didn't know what, but something in her expression made him laugh harder; he had the fleeting insight that he had probably looked at her in just this way when he'd encountered her on the stairs, the day of her would-be wedding. The idea somehow heightened the hilarity, and now he was breathless for air; this was the work of sleep deprivation, of course, except he'd just slept longer than he had in four years' time, so that didn't explain it. He struggled for a breath, trying to reclaim his composure, to say something that would address the sneer creeping over her lovely mouth.

She did not give him a chance. With a disgusted snort, she pulled her skirts tight and swept past him. At the door, she turned back, magnificently straight-spined. "Get dressed, you loon."

The door slammed behind her.

The drive toward Côte Bleue wound along the edge of the coast. On one side lay the aquamarine sea, glittering fiercely beneath a sky of brilliant blue; on the right, up the rolling hills, stretched groves of olive trees and palms. The climate and vegetation invited a very particular sort of landscape, Gwen thought, and she was not disappointed when the carriage turned down the graveled drive into Mr. Barrington's property and deposited them at the front steps of Côte Bleue.

The house was two modest stories of mellow pink stone, and vines of purple bougainvillea twined down its face, like strands of a woman's hair. Its green shutters were thrown open to the warm air and to the view of the terraced garden, tiers of lush vegetation that flowed down toward the cliffs overlooking the sea. Behind the house, on the wild hill above, blossom-spangled orange trees seemed to sag beneath the weight of their ripe, hanging fruit.

Alex exited the carriage first. He'd provided surprisingly agreeable company during the drive, making charming observations about the various towns they had passed, cracking jokes that she'd had to work not to laugh at. Indeed, the temptation to laugh had become its own form of hurt, cutting her just as deeply as his courteous façade. For all she knew, this was some sort of twisted game he'd devised to amuse himself: how many times could he tempt her into throwing herself at him? If that was the case, she would not cooperate. Men had humiliated her before, to be certain, but she had never and *would* never aid their efforts. She would *not* laugh at his jokes.

All during the long drive down the coast, then, she raged at herself. The loss was not great; there was no call for her to ache, so. But it took effort, sustained and pointed effort, to think of him just as she'd thought of those other men. To each of his comments, she made herself smile and reply with perfect courtesy. (The art of discouragement through flirtation was rather like badminton, she thought. So long as the birdie was kept afloat—a compliment offered in return for each one that was served—no points would be scored on either side.) If this *was* a game, she meant to win. Her earlier delusions about him, her stupid fancies, would not cripple her. She would be spitted and fried before she begged for his attentions again.

Alex lifted her out of the coach now into the warm, sunlit air. A melody of scents played over her—roses baking in the sun, the salted sea air, the sweetness of honeysuckle, the fresh bite of citrus. Beneath these lay the faintest note of spice. She took a deep breath and tasted its sharpness, then glanced up the hill again, knowing now what to look for. Pepper trees hid amongst the oranges. At dusk, their smell would strengthen, overwhelming the flowers' sweetness.

The inevitable effect caught her fancy. The gardens must create a shifting symphony of scents, dependent on the hour of the day. She did not spot any night-blooming jasmine, the presence of which would have made the advent of evening all the more noticeable. It was not a pretty plant, she supposed. Could one design a landscape organized by smell instead of sight but make it visually pleasing all the same?

The challenge was turning in her mind when Mr. Barrington bounded down the drive to greet them. In Paris he had looked a hair shy of bohemian; now, in a white linen suit with a straw boater crushed beneath his arm, his cheeks ruddy and his hair tossed by the wind, he looked more in the way of a yachtsman returned from a day at the races.

She wondered if Alex realized how much he had in common with this man. Both of them looked comfortable no matter where they popped up. It was not, perhaps, a trait to merit one's trust.

Mr. Barrington seized her hand and carried it very

dramatically to his mouth. "Your majesty!" he said. To Alex, he offered a cordial nod. "You're the last to arrive; I'd begun to fear you lost."

"But we came straightaway," Gwen said with a frown.

"Perhaps the others departed before the invitations were issued," Alex murmured.

Barrington laughed, as if this were a very funny joke. "Come," he said, and turned on his heel to lead them into the house.

The front lobby of the villa was spacious and cool, a fountain splashing in the light cast by a domed glass cupola two floors above. Tile mosaics bordered the pink stone floors, which were uncarpeted save for silk runners that formed a narrow path down the hall through which they walked toward their rooms. On the walls hung Renaissance paintings from the Italian school, and bright murals that Barrington said had been painted by local artists—tableaus of Nice's famous Battle of Flowers, its Mardi Gras revels, and sunset seen from the Promenade des Anglais.

Barrington drew them to a stop at the very end of the corridor, by a set of wooden doors carved in a rough, rustic style. "Drinks at five o'clock in the garden," he said. "Dinner at seven; we keep very early hours, to allow guests to pop over to Monte Carlo and catch one last round of cards before bed. Carriage leaves promptly at nine o'clock; usually we keep another for the casinos in Nice—open all night, you know—but we had a broken axle last night, so it's Monte Carlo for the time being or bust, as they say;

which perhaps is how it always should be, don't you think? If one's going to gamble, might as well do it in style. Now." He took a breath. "I expect you'll want a bit of rest before joining the fun. Although I must say, Miss Goodrick, you look fresh as a daisy, positively ripe for the plucking."

It had seemed a lovely compliment, until he'd reached the bit about ripeness. "Thank you," Gwen said hesitantly.

"Alas that harvest season has concluded," Alex said pleasantly.

Barrington chuckled. "So it has, so it has. Well, we're out on the terrace right now, so do feel free to wander out if you feel up to it. The Rizzardis—you don't know them, by any chance, do you? Giuseppe and Francesca? No? Well, they popped up yesterday, so I've put them in the room next to yours; they are great fans of Bizet, and over the moon at the prospect of a worthy delivery from Miss Goodrick. Oh—hold on there a moment." Still clinging to the door handle, he leaned around the corner. "Moakes! Come back here, you rascal."

A small, silver-haired man of advanced years stepped around the corner, a tray of champagne in hand. "Take one, do," Barrington urged them. "Lafittes and Margaux, of course; I drink nothing but. Might as well start the holiday in style. Here, I'll also lift a glass."

Gwen slid a glance to Alex, who was studying Barrington as though the man's face held the key to some riddle. Perhaps it did, at that: at odd intervals, the corners of Barrington's mouth kicked up. It was the smile of a child struggling to keep some wonderful secret.

"Cheers," said Alex. He took a drink, his lips smiling but his eyes deadly intent on their host.

Mr. Barrington seemed oblivious to the regard. He turned his boyish smile on Gwen. "I must confess," he said in a low voice. "I noticed something alarming upon your arrival."

"Oh?" Heart beating faster, she wondered if she'd already betrayed herself, somehow. Or perhaps he'd stumbled across a photograph of her. She could imagine that the London newspapers might have run one after the recent debacle.

"Your parasol, my dear." He eyed her, a salacious angle slanting his lips. "I do believe you've forgotten it again."

Gwen laughed. "Oh, I hardly require one now." She hooked her arm through Alex's. "I have brought a much bigger stick, you see."

Alex choked on his drink. Barrington, brow lifting, gave him a respectful nod, although the cause for it seemed obscure. "I will take your word on it," he said to her and slid the bar free, opening the suite doors. "Here then: your home for the next few days— or, indeed, so long as you wish to remain. We do not believe that old adage about guests; the longer you stay, the merrier."

He took his leave with a bow. As predicted, he had allotted them a single suite. The sitting room was quite large, done up in taupe and ivory, filled with light from the broad French doors that opened onto a balcony with an ocean view.

"Strange man," Gwen murmured.

Alex paused by the doors to look out toward the sea. "Why do you say that?" he asked.

She frowned at his back. "You don't think he's odd?"

"Certainly. But I'd like to hear your perception of him."

She thought about it a moment. "There is his accent," she said slowly. "He works very hard to sound like a public school boy. But he learned the accent too late; it doesn't fit comfortably with his vowels."

"Which doesn't condemn him, of course."

"Of course not! Goodness, for my sake, I should hope not. I suppose, beyond that, it's simply a feeling he inspires. No real cause for it."

"But intuition should never be dismissed," he said. He walked onward through the next door, and she followed. A minuscule dressing room opened onto a bedroom with wallpaper of pale peach and gold. The single window in the far corner looked onto a man-made lake at the side of the house. A transparent mesh mosquito net framed the bed. Sleeping was clearly meant to be an afterthought here; all the attention had been given to the sitting room, which was much larger.

Or perhaps not. Gwen paused in the doorway, looking at that bed. It would have been large enough for Henry VIII and half of his wives, to boot. It dominated the room completely.

Alex walked onward, apparently oblivious to how terribly awkward it was going to be to spend the night here. Perhaps he would be a gentleman—absurd thought, but since he'd done the tediously gentlemanly thing last night, the pattern might well continue—and he would offer to take the floor. Otherwise, she knew what would transpire: she would lie with her back to him, her agitated breath making the netting stir and tremble, too afraid to sleep lest her hands betray her and climb across his chest, as they had been longing to do even in the coach, while her dignity and pride had spat curses at him and her brain had marshaled words of cool, pleasant civility.

What sort of talent was it that led a woman to unerringly fix on men who did not want her in return?

Surely there *was* another kind of man out there?

"Lily. These are lovely flowers," Alex announced.

She looked up. He was poised by a vase of roses that sat in the corner opposite the window. "Those aren't lilies," she said dryly.

"Very funny, *Lily*." His intent stare gave her a start. So, even in the rooms they would play these roles?

"I always aim to amuse you," she said lightly.

"Then come have a closer look." His smile now teased. "You're some sort of expert on flowers, aren't you? A budding botanist, I hear."

Her temper strained. Not surprising; its restraints had endured a great deal of friction today. "I told you I am not particularly attached to flowers. I am not a *gardener*."

"Nevertheless," he said, and then paused significantly. His long fingers parted the petals to reveal a patch of the flocked velvet wall. "Come have a look."

It penetrated that he was not interested in the flowers at all. She glanced around in alarm, wondering if somebody was hiding behind the curtains to prevent their free communication.

He gave her a subtle shake of the head. "Come here," he said more softly.

Slowly she walked forward. He slid his hand around the back of her neck, fingers closing in a firm grip as he brushed his lips across hers.

She went still. Last night, she'd tossed for hours, powerless to turn her mind from the memory of that shattering pleasure he'd given her. Now, the faintest pressure of his mouth raised an echo of that wonder. A hot, delicious weakness trembled through her.

Anger chased it. Good Lord. The man was *addled*. He could not make up his mind, and he was going to make *her* addled in the process. Maybe that was his aim! Having received no success this morning, he was going to tease her to desperation, manipulate her into debasing herself again—

His mouth slid across her cheek to her ear. "Spy holes," he murmured, his hand idly brushing the line of her waist. "Lean down to sniff the roses. Take a look."

Spy holes? Great ghosts! What sort of business partner did Lord Weston encourage these days?

Alex began to nuzzle her neck. A pleasurable chill

lifted the hairs at her nape. She shrugged his mouth away with one shoulder. He caught her shoulder and squeezed. "Someone might be watching," he said into her ear. His hot breath made her shiver again. "Hurry up and take a look." His tongue flicked along her lobe. "Or give them an excuse for your dallying here."

She cleared her throat. "Let me have a look at these flowers!" she said brightly.

He winced and stepped back. All right, her delivery needed work. She would have to spend a few minutes mustering the Barbary Queen before she dared set foot outside their rooms.

She bent over, making a show of fingering one petal, meanwhile fighting the urge to reach up and touch her ear where he had licked it. He made her knees weak with one stroke of his tongue. This was not a magic any cautious woman would encourage.

His tanned hand slid over hers. "This one," he said, lifting a finger to indicate a rose nearby. "Beautiful," he said, and then stroked his finger back down hers, delicate as a man admiring the brushwork on a piece of priceless china. The contrast of his tanned skin against hers, the gentleness of his touch and the strength of his hand, riveted her. She almost missed the way his knuckles touched the wall before he removed his hand to his side. "The shade is striking. Dye, do you think?"

Had he not indicated the spot on the wall, she would never have noticed the spy hole. It was minute, pricked cleverly at the tip of one velvet floret.

Assuming, of course, that it was a spy hole, and

not simply the shoddy workmanship of an underpaid assistant.

She straightened. "The roses are Gloire de Dijon, Alex. A lovely but not uncommon breed. I do not think dye was required."

"Oh? I really must expand my knowledge of such things." He was walking along the wall now, his fingertips lightly dragging across the wallpaper as he appeared to idly inspect the furnishings. A framed watercolor of the Venetian canals caught his interest; he paused before it, staring hard. "Remarkable taste Barrington has," he murmured. "Have you ever been to Venice?" He glanced at her. "Stayed at the Piazza once. What a view it offered."

She looked from the painting toward the bed. A very direct view, indeed. If people were spying on them, so much for hoping that he would sleep on the floor.

He walked to the far wall, then stopped before the mirror atop the toilette, brushing down his suit jacket, running his fingers through his hair. It struck her that watching him primp was almost comical; he did not wear spectacles in public, but in all other ways, he seemed to possess very little vanity.

Perhaps he skipped the specs for the same reason she did. She always felt vulnerable when she wore them in public. They stripped her of one of her greatest weapons: her ability to ignore what she did not wish to see.

The idea was curious. What might Alex wish to ignore?

His family.

Any cause to change his itinerant lifestyle.

She cleared her throat. "Have a clear view of yourself, then?"

He turned back toward her, smiling wryly in acknowledgment of the double meaning. "Yes," he said. "I do wonder if this room is comfortable enough to suit you? I know you prefer something a bit more... ornate. We could always take a room in Cannes."

Two rooms, even. How very tempting. "Let me take one more look around," she said, and walked back into the dressing room.

A moment later, he joined her. The room was very small; when he walked inside, the enforced proximity set her nerves to firing. She stood very still, enduring the malfunctioning of these million small cells, which leapt and shivered at the prospect of some accidental contact with him.

It took him less than a minute's scrutiny to conclude that it was not similarly sabotaged. In the course of this silent survey, some slight adjustment brought his thigh into her skirts. She would not pretend to fidget, would not conspire to heighten this intimacy. It was not even intimacy: his leg was only touching the fabric of her gown.

And yet... she could guess now what lay beneath his clothes. He was a tall man, built on lean lines, and she had seen him without his shirt; she knew beyond doubt that his broad shoulders were not merely a trick of his bone structure. Throat to chest to arms to thighs to calves, his body was strapped with muscle. Clearly he disciplined it as firmly as he did his business concerns, not to mention the affection he allowed himself for those who loved him.

And there was the problem, of course. Any other man—a man of more human dimensions—would have taken her last night. Alex *had* wanted her. She was sure of it. But while his refusal might have resembled, by mere mechanical coincidence, the actions of a gentleman, that coincidence should not and *would* not make him more attractive to her. She was not so much an idiot that she would now begin, after all her sad history, to *romanticize* rejection as proof of some admirable quality in a man.

"All right," he said, and she realized she'd been holding her breath. "We can speak freely." He looked down at her at the precise moment that she looked up, away from his body to his face.

His eyes narrowed slightly. That was the only sign of his sudden realization that they stood so close. His mind had been elsewhere. Now it was only on her.

A wistful thought slipped free. *If only he—*

No. She slammed shut the window through which the beginning of this wish had strayed.

She drew a breath that felt, and sounded, unsteady. "So..."

His hands lifted very slowly. His thumb touched her upper arm. It traced the bare skin, drawing a circle, light but for the slight scrape of his nail. The other moved to her hair, plucking out one hairpin, and then another. A lock of her hair tumbled past her temple. He caught it up, drawing it through his fingers, from root to tip.

The breath left her on one long, sibilant rush. "There are no spy holes," she whispered. "Not here."

"We'll have to put on a good act outside. And practice makes perfect." His warm fingers cupped her elbows, forming a light vise that he tested, his grip tightening slightly. "Shall we practice?"

She swallowed and stepped back. Her shoulder blades hit a shelf. "Not like this."

He followed her. "Not like what?"

"Like . . . like you mean it," she mumbled. She felt a blush start up her throat.

"But I do mean it," he said with a faint smile. "That was never in doubt, Gwen."

She glanced away from his expression, fighting the urge to take hope from that statement. She was *done* with wrestling flattery from his obscurities. She looked away from his face, to his throat; unlike his eyes, it did not have the ability to look back, to study her so closely that she felt flustered and infuriated and manipulated but also peculiarly exposed. "I suppose animal lust is not extraordinary."

"Certainly not," he said. As his head bent, his hair brushed her chin. With his lips pressed to her throat, he breathed deeply, as if the scent of her was enough to lure him, to turn his voice to a low, rough pitch as he said, "But animal lust is also very easily contained. This, on the other hand . . ." The tip of his tongue touched her. Her eyes closed of their own volition.

"I think we might call it resonance," he murmured.

"Resonance." She meant to sound scathing, but the word was too breathy, and it tipped up at the end like a question.

"Every object vibrates at a particular and specific frequency." He dragged his mouth up to her jaw, and she felt, briefly, the edge of his teeth. Into her ear he said, "Place two of a kind side by side, and the first, if vibrating, will force the other to vibrate alongside it. I slept last night, the whole night, for the first time in six months. Did you?"

She fought for composure. It was true that when he was near, she felt attuned to him in every cell. But what was he implying? That their natures were the same? If he'd believed that, why would he have refused her? Why would he have any care for her virtue?

She averted her face. "I could not sleep for hours," she said to the wall. "I am done being toyed with, Alex. You made yourself quite clear last night. I am Richard's little sister to you. And while you play the rebel very well, you certainly sounded most conventional when refusing me." She manufactured a short laugh. "Indeed, I've no idea why I'm surprised. You may criticize our rude, fat MPs all you like, but it was their work that opened the trade routes to your ships, wasn't it? Why, even your rebellion suits our government. I'm sure you pay a fortune in taxes. You're far more boring than you realize."

He surprised her by laughing low in his throat, the warmth coasting over the skin of her temple. "A very neat set down," he said. "Do try not to flash your intelligence at Barrington. He won't expect it of the Barbary Queen."

She twisted away from him and made a face. "So we do mean to stay here, then?"

"We can always visit from Cannes." His light touch at her waist made her startle. "Shh," he said. "Just getting you comfortably into the role. Can't have you flinching when I touch you in public." After a pause, he said, "The blush is beautiful, though. I would regret to see you lose that."

She stared very hard at a hook set into the wall. *Focus.* "But what would be the point of staying so far away? Your aim is to gather information. It's most easily done here."

He traced a circle on her hip. This time, to her pride, she successfully denied any outward response to the touch, although inside, oh—low in her belly, in her fluttering chest, in the places he had taken and soothed last night—she was dissolving.

He spoke. "I don't appreciate being spied on. That's the point."

She choked on a surprised laugh—and then, when he lifted a brow, she said simply, "The irony, Alex."

After a moment, he smiled as well. "Touché. I suppose hypocrisy is the name of this game as well."

"Then I should be good at it." She paused. His hand still covered her hip, but when she focused all her attention on the task, instead of simply allowing her baser senses free reign, she could find it amusing, in an ironic sort of way. "You should be good at it yourself," she said. "No need to touch me now; I'm done with flinching and gasping."

His hand tightened on her hip. "Gwen—"

"*Lily*," she corrected. "We'll stay. We didn't come all this way for nothing. And if at night they don't see . . . well, what they expect to see, then we'll simply have to pretend that we've quarreled. Yes? So we will act very coldly toward one another today." In that regard, the spy holes were a blessing: she now had an excuse to curl as far away from him as possible. Perhaps even to lie on top of her traitorous hands, which would be sure, otherwise, to stray toward him.

His touch fell away. "I don't think that's wise," he said. "Barrington might see it as an opportunity to make his address to you."

"I can handle flirtation," she said. "I'm no green girl. Not *all* men are well behaved in a ballroom."

"All right," he said at length. "But only provided this is the last unpleasant surprise we discover. If he proves dangerous—"

"I know," she said in bored tones. "In your brotherly way, you will insist we leave at once."

She had the satisfaction of seeing his face go dark before she swept back into the enemy territory of the bedroom.

By the time they had bathed (Gwen requested the tub to be placed in the dressing room) and finished changing out of their traveling clothes, the sun had begun to set and the temperature to drop. Gwen plucked out a pashmina shawl in a beautiful ruby red to wear over her low-necked evening gown to dinner. Alex, in turn, donned full coat tails, and the sight gave her a moment's mute astonishment. She had not seen him so formally dressed in years. He never attended the parties that called for it—not in her circles, at least.

The look suited him. His jacket was cut to a more form-fitting silhouette than was fashionable in England at present, and it emphasized the sweep of his broad shoulders into his narrow waist, the long, muscled length of his legs.

"We are going to quarrel," she reminded him. And herself.

He smiled at her, those gorgeous eyes of his dancing. "I'll warn you," he said. "I never lose a quarrel."

"Ah, but you've never quarreled with me," she parried. "Recall that with a mere smile, I have driven men to turn tail and run. Imagine what I can do if I put my mind to a scowl."

He flashed her a brief look of evident surprise, then laughed and offered his arm. It occurred to her, a moment later, why he was startled: it was the first time she had ever made a lighthearted joke about her jiltings. She searched herself and found not a lick of wounded hurt to power the remark.

Heart light, she processed downstairs on his arm, and then, per their respective roles tonight, broke away from him to walk ahead into the drawing room.

Inside, a motley crew sat around a low table—six gentlemen crouched over hands of cards, bottles of open liquor at their elbows, bowler hats discarded by their feet. Draped on and around these men were four very young women, three of whom reposed in various states that even at a music hall could be termed as "undress."

The last lady, a raven-haired beauty who looked to be in her late thirties, was lounging on a nearby sofa, her heeled boots propped atop the arm, her red-and-white striped skirts frothing at her knees. Her posture left no doubt that she was fully dressed—right down to the scarlet garters holding up her stockings.

Despite her casual posture, she radiated an air of watchful repose, even authority; and this aura was bolstered by the glances sent her way by the younger women as Gwen paused on the carpet. She sat up, giving Gwen a leisurely inspection that slid up her lavender silk skirt, paused momentarily at her wide belt, and lingered again at the amethyst pendant holding in place the drape of Gwen's shawl.

By the time their eyes met, the woman's mouth had slipped sideways into a smile that seemed distinctly unfriendly.

"One of yours?" said a man at the table. "Darling, come here." He patted his knee.

"No, not one of mine," said the lady. "I've told you, Alessandro, if Veronique doesn't arrive on time, I'll play your flute for you."

Alex's arrival was announced by the broad hand

fitting into the small of Gwen's back—not to guide her onward, for he applied no pressure, but perhaps simply because he wished to ensure that she stayed upright. "What's this?" he asked lightly.

His touch recalled her to her purpose. She was not shocked by the sight of garters. Indeed, she wore them herself. "I don't know," she said with a bright smile. "But this gentleman has brought a flute, and a flautist is coming to play it for him, so it seems that the company will be musical all around."

The comment won a weird silence. The dark-haired woman fixed an amazed gaze upon her. Alex made a curious noise, deep in his throat.

She had the sudden feeling that she should be blushing. And then, all at once, she *was* blushing. She tried to paste a saucy smile over it, but the effect apparently looked miserably awkward, for one of the men sat forward, elbows on knees, to inquire with a frown: "I think you're Miss Goodrick and Mr. de Grey, no?"

"Indeed we are," Alex said flatly.

The man tweaked his ginger mustache, smoothing it to a fine, sharp tip. "Pardon me, sir. Dinner crowd gathering in the east wing." His glance shifted to Gwen, and he gave a lopsided grin. "Do come back afterward, if you like—always room for more at the game."

Gwen grew cognizant, abruptly, that the ratio of ladies to men left something to be desired.

"Will do," Alex said, and ushered Gwen back into the hallway, where he said in an undertone, "A *flautist*?"

"I know," she said miserably. "I don't know what I

was thinking. A code word of some sort, I'm sure of it. I doubt that man even *had* a flute with him."

He drew a strange, strangled breath through his nose. "Darling, perhaps you'd best keep your mouth shut tonight."

His tone was teasing, rueful, and she almost asked him to explain what she'd missed. And then she saw Barrington step out of the hallway five feet ahead of them. The opportunity was too perfect to resist. "Keep my mouth shut?" she repeated, injecting wounded anger into her voice. "How dare you, Alex. Perhaps I can find someone else here who might admire it better."

Predictable as clockwork, Barrington spoke. "Ah, mademoiselle, monsieur!" Giving an oily smile to Alex, he added, "Miss Goodrick, I wonder if I might have the honor of escorting you into dinner?"

Chapter Twelve

⚜

The party grew drunk, and then drunker. Gwen sat four seats away from Alex, at Barrington's elbow near the head of the table. At first, Alex monitored her only to make certain that she was not letting Barrington refill her glass. He was meant to be playing the irritated lover, so he supposed occasional dark looks were permitted. He manufactured a glare to lend his glances authenticity.

But by the time the fifth course was served, his dark looks no longer required effort. Indeed, he had dismissed the pretty Italian countess to his right and was probably doing a very good imitation of an obsessed, glowering fanatic. Was Gwen so good an actress, or was her displeasure with him genuine? She looked to be leaning into Barrington's touches now, and Alex would have been hard-pressed to distinguish her current smiles from those she had given him on the banks of the Seine, the morning after the adventure at Le Chat Noir.

When dinner was concluded and the party transferred outside for a moonlit boating expedition, he pulled Gwen off Barrington's arm and into the corner with a very showy sulk.

"Do you know what you're doing?" he breathed into her ear.

"Of course," she whispered back, fixing her brow into a thunderous scowl. "I have asked him about all his acquaintances in London. He claims to know almost nobody; says he prefers the society on the Continent."

"Dear God," he muttered, "you are *not* meant to be doing the interrogating. Just—go keep him busy on the lake. I'm going to have a look around the house."

She drew back very suddenly. "Of course," she said, coldly and loudly. "I am only a toy to you, no? A very pretty wind-up doll."

He stared at her, undecided on how to reply. She really was a bit too convincing. Richard had certainly had a flair for drama, which he and Alex had employed to good measure when seeking entertainment during their university days, but he'd never suspected it of Gwen. "Of course not," he said slowly.

Her frown deepened. "Don't be stupid," she said, and he heard the double meaning in it. *Don't apologize to me right now.*

He sketched her a cold bow. "I wish you a good evening, then. I do not think I will join your little boating party."

"You will not be missed," she said, and turned on her heel, stalking away.

He went directly to their rooms, sitting by the window until he saw the procession of guests wind out through the garden. Gwen walked arm in arm with Barrington. She tripped, and he pulled her closer as he helped her gain her balance.

Alex drew away from the window.

It was only a charade.

And yet . . . Gwen was out to live wildly; he himself had rebuffed her last night; perhaps she grew curious—

Only a charade, God damn it. He took a deep breath and left the room.

The house was laid out in the shape of a shallow C, the lobby and grand staircase at the middle of the house, with its high domed skylight, scoring the building in half. From the little discussion he'd initiated at dinner, he'd managed to solicit the location of every one of the female guests' bedrooms. That omitted the entire lower half of the C in which his and Gwen's rooms were located, and a good deal of the upper as well. He thought it likely that all the bedrooms were in the west, which left the bottom floor of the east, as he'd determined earlier, devoted to public rooms: morning room, drawing room, dining room, gallery.

Upstairs to the east was where he needed to go.

He walked toward the moonlit lobby on silent feet, wanting to check on the party in the less reputable drawing room. The merriment had grown muted; after two minutes' wait, he counted only three male voices inside. The women he was less concerned

about; it seemed that they had been hired to entertain whichever guests found themselves without easy
company this evening—and the guards as well, in the
meantime.

The lobby and the main staircase were too brightly
illuminated, so he retreated back in the direction he
had come, until he found a door covered in baize and
studded with upholstery nails. He could not disapprove of the spread of all English customs. This one
had proved useful to him more than once, when seeking subtler ways through a house. At this hour, with
the remains of the feast still littering the dining room,
and the guests outside, the servants would be more
intent on shifting plates to the scullery than spying on
matters abovestairs.

He stepped into the servants' passage and climbed
the stairs silently, then took a right, moving, in darkness, toward the other side of the house. Only once
did a noise come from the distance, causing him to
freeze. Belatedly he realized the grinding sound came
from a dumbwaiter. Someone was sending china down
from the dining room.

He let himself out into the main hallway of the east
wing. Yes, this part of the house was clearly not meant
for public consumption: the floors were covered not in
silk runners but in a far cheaper but harder-wearing
tapestry, and the walls were bare. The latter sank his
spirits. If Barrington did not spend much time here,
there might be nothing of interest on the property.

Or perhaps Barrington had the same philosophy

as Alex, and lived and traveled lightly, carrying only those items deemed essential—in which case Alex very much hoped that one of these doors opened onto a bedroom or a study.

The doors were locked, which did not stop him. He withdrew from his pocket two of Gwen's hairpins, and made quick work of the first tumbler. In his time, he'd reluctantly been forced to employ an industrial spy or two; sometimes there was no other way to discover what had happened to a shipment that had gone missing overnight, or a contract suddenly lost just before the documents could be notarized. And a few of these men had spared him an hour's lesson, here and there. He'd never master the art of breaking glass without a sound, but there were few door locks that could faze him.

The first room was a small library, with no desk or chest of drawers to pique his interest. Nevertheless, he did a dutiful scan of the bookshelves. For a man who preferred his springs in France, Barrington appeared an ardent admirer of his home country. He had over a hundred books on the history of England, its natural habitats and geological history, its flora and fauna.

Alex plucked out one of the books. *A Natural History of English Sediment*. Christ. Could there have been anything more boring?

On the other hand, Gwen would probably deem this far more interesting than his trade journals. He ran an eye again over the volumes on flora and fauna.

He sincerely hoped Barrington stuck to seductive flirtations. If he mentioned anything to do with parkland, Gwen would probably jump on the topic like a kitten on catnip, and the Barbary Queen would make a very odd admirer of landscape architects.

Although he supposed that if anyone could pull off such a Barbary Queen, Gwen could.

The thought was so startling that he proved clumsy in refitting the book into its slot.

The book safely stowed, he stood looking at it. She was a chameleon, wasn't she? He had always suspected she had potential in her. Had been tempted, even, to tease it out of her, once or twice. Had denied himself the urge because she was Richard's sister, and her path had been set.

But now her path had changed. And still he hesitated, fickle as a cowardly little debutante, as she'd put it.

No, he thought wryly. She'd never called him cowardly.

He reminded himself of what he'd been thinking so intently last night, as he'd watched her stir so sweetly beneath his touch. Humans were not technologies. They did not prove amenable to radical adjustments. Their essential traits always reclaimed them, and hers would pull her back to the narrow path, no matter how much she might come to genuinely revile its constraints. Better, then—honorable—to act on his understanding; to do nothing to prevent her from reclaiming the life she would inevitably be drawn back to.

The logic was sound, of course.

It was also fueled by fear. Old fear. A very specific one.

And, God *damn* it—if, after all this time, he was going to let *fear* dictate his actions, then he might as well trade in his lungs right now, and his legs to boot. He might as well be wheeled back to England to suffocate quietly in some cloistered little village rectory. Had he listened to fear, that would have been his life.

And so, too, if he had accepted others' visions of him.

He had always known that others were wrong about him, but Gwen had only just discovered that others were wrong about her. *That* was the only difference between them. And yet he'd dismissed her revelation, forcing her to remain within the mold she wished so much to break. And why? Only because it was easier for *him* that way. Otherwise, were he to take her at her word and behave accordingly, he would have no choice but to confront certain things he had hidden from himself.

What a bloody, self-righteous, *blind* coward he'd been, last night.

Well, he knew how to rectify that quick enough.

He walked out and tried the next door. This room looked more promising at first glance—a study of some sort, with framed prints on the walls, more of these bloody naturalist's diagrams, a dozen of them stacked on the desk. The large picture window had a breathtaking view of the ocean, and the moonlight filtering through the window lit the desktop quite clearly. He flipped through the documents. They meant nothing to him. Next to them were notes on— God above, various sorts of vegetation indigenous to Suffolk.

He recalled again the way that Barrington had drawn her closer when she'd stumbled. A sinking feeling was in his stomach. Wouldn't it be rich with irony if he had inadvertently driven her into the arms of a man who would actually sit down across from her and nod enthusiastically when she started talking of her goddamned gardens? Instead, of course, of making some mocking, juvenile remark about pressing flowers into a scrapbook—

A noise in the hallway made him freeze. He looked quickly around the room, but there were very few places to hide. A handsome wooden screen seemed the best option, not because it provided real cover—it was too finely filigreed to conceal his body entirely—but because it was positioned in the shadows, away from the window, near the door. Opening the door, walking in, a person would have to turn around and peer hard into the darkness until their eyes adjusted before they could distinguish a man standing in the shadows.

He stepped behind it just as the door opened with a soft click. "—been locked," said Barrington. "How curious. Ah, no matter. Come in, do."

"Oh, you were telling the truth," came Gwen's low voice. Alex pressed himself farther against the wall to still the impulse to leap around and ask her what the hell she thought she was doing, breaking away from the larger group to enter a disused area of the house with this man. Moreover, her consonants had a slight slur to them. Had she drunk more wine at dinner than he'd noticed?

Barrington put his hand at her waist—far too familiar for a host with a young lady, although just about right for a man with a music hall singer—and guided her to stand in front of the window. In the cold light, her profile was as pale and smooth as marble, her expression lit with clarity. "Oh," she said softly. "The waves breaking—it's very beautiful."

Something ugly stirred in Alex's gut. She did not look as if she was pretending enjoyment. The view truly enraptured her.

Barrington stepped up behind her. He delicately fingered a stray wisp of her hair. "I am surrounded by beauty," he murmured. "But nothing so compelling as the woman here before me, right now."

Alex was going to rip his arm off. *Step away from him. Gwen. What the hell are you doing?*

She turned toward him, in the process dislodging his hands from her waist and hair—by design, Alex wanted to think, but God damn it, he could not be sure. She gave Barrington a mysterious little smile, perfectly designed to madden a man with its indecipherable promise, and then brushed past him, walking around the room, trailing a casual hand across the furnishings. At the desk, she came to a stop. "Drawings!"

she said. "Are you an artist?" She spread out the pages casually.

Barrington followed her and caught up her hand, lifting it to his mouth. "Alas, no. I've lacked proper inspiration until now."

She gave a light, tinkling laugh. "I find that difficult to believe," she said as she walked onward, letting her hand remain in his as long as possible, until her arm was fully outstretched. Barrington trailed after her rather than release it. She was examining the walls, now—a series of masks hung in a row on the back wall.

If she kept strolling the perimeter, she was going to lead Barrington straight to him.

Turn around, Alex willed her. *Leave.*

But Barrington was growing bolder now, his hand skating down her rib cage, his head bowing to place a kiss upon the top of her head. It occurred to Alex that her casual stroll was actually not so casual: she was making a circle back toward the door, and had he not been hiding there, her facsimile of interest in the furnishings would have been a very clever route of escape.

But the screen was too damned lovely to ignore.

He saw the moment she spied it. Her mouth opened to make a comment.

And then her eyes met his and flew wide with realization.

He held his breath. He had no idea how his discovery could be smoothed over by talk. An unpleasant conversation followed by eviction never harmed any guest, but the fact that Barrington had armed guards strolling his property did put a different light on matters, greatly diminishing Alex's hope that they would be turned out with a simple round of scathing words.

He would have to immobilize the man. The prospect would not have bothered him if they'd met in a *salle d'armes*, or if he'd had proof that Barrington had harmed Gerard. But right now, all he knew was that he disliked the man. And he'd never been particularly interested in punishing people for failing to charm him. He'd left that role to the bullies of the world.

Gwen interrupted his silent deliberations by making a choice of her own. She turned away from him, spinning on the ball of her foot and launching herself directly into Barrington.

For a split second of disbelief, Alex thought she meant to attack the man. Perhaps Barrington had a similar idea; taken off guard, he grunted and staggered a pace backward. But he caught the idea before Alex did—and caught something else, besides. Hauling Gwen up by her arse, he smashed his face into hers.

Well, Alex thought. Well. This was . . . clever of her. A clever distraction.

Her arms twining around his shoulders, she forced Barrington around, putting his back to the door.

Also just to distract him.

Alex was beginning to see this scene through a peculiar red haze.

Gwen loosed a moan, a sound that really did not belong in the hearing of any other man that Alex had or ever would meet, and then clawed her fingers into Barrington's hair, yanking his head down toward her breasts.

Barrington obliged quite happily.

Her eyes found Alex's over the man's shoulders. *Go*, she mouthed. *Go now!*

He stared back at her. The little *idiot*. Did she really think that he was going to slip out of this room and let Barrington have what she had offered to *him* but he'd been too much of a goddamned unforgivably thick-headed cowardly idiot to take?

Jesus Christ, what had *ailed* him? This was what he had planned by refusing her, wasn't it? For her one day to be in some asinine Englishman's arms, with him apart, elsewhere, claimless, no one to blame for it but himself?

She widened her eyes dramatically. Lifted her hand and pointed emphatically toward the door. And then rotated her hand and made a come-hither crook of her finger.

What the hell did that mean?

Barrington lifted his head. She gave a breathy gasp and pushed his head back down. Now her leg started to wrap around Barrington's calf.

The meaning of the gesture suddenly penetrated. God above, he was a fool. He slipped out from behind the screen and opened the door, sliding silently into the corridor and pulling the door noiselessly shut behind him. And then he lifted his fist and banged. Once, twice, thrice. No more. Not waiting for an answer, he threw the door open so loudly that it cracked against the jamb.

"You little trollop," he spat.

Gwen slapped her hands over her mouth and leapt away from Barrington—but rather than springing toward Alex as he'd envisioned, she instead raced to stand behind the desk.

"Oh!" she cried. "Oh, Mr. de Grey—please, it was—not at all what you think!"

"It was exactly what you think," Barrington said. He yanked down his suit jacket. "What do you mean, poking about up here?"

Alex fixed him with a grim stare. He had no idea what Gwen thought she was achieving by loitering across the room from him. Did she want to witness bloodshed? He felt unusually willing to deliver it. "I will ask you," he said icily, "the same question. Did I not make it clear that Miss Goodrick is off limits to your attentions?"

Barrington worked up a smirk. "The lady does not seem to agree. Perhaps we should consult *her* in this matter."

"Oh!" Gwen put her hands behind her back and looked at her toes. "Oh," she said softly. She looked up to Alex, eyes woeful, almost pleading. "I'm so sorry, Mr. de Grey. But it is such a *hard* decision. On the one side, you've been everything good to me. On the other, Mr. Barrington . . ." She trailed off and sighed, as if his

magnificence were too large to be put into words. "I
begin to understand," she said hesitantly, "why ladies
used to insist that knights joust for their attention. If
only one victor were left standing... it would be so
much easier to decide, wouldn't it?"

For a brief moment, Alex actually felt in sympathy with Barrington: the man's sneer was fading into
a puzzled frown. "Miss Goodrick," Barrington said,
"I would joust any number of men for you, were we
knights."

"But I don't think you'd win against *Alex*," she said
pointedly, and gave Alex a sudden urgent look.

Oh, Christ. He understood where she was going
with this. He hoped she had a good reason for it. He
sighed and cracked his knuckles to loosen them. Fists
were not his forte, of course, but the week in Paris
had sharpened him up after the laziness of the sea
journey.

Barrington reached into his jacket, outright scowling now. "All right, enough," he said, and as he withdrew his hand, metal glinted in the light. Alex went
very still. "I must say, I'm disappointed," the man
continued to Gwen. "I'd hoped you were merely a talented trollop along for the ride." He lifted the gun,
then turned it on Alex. "Time for some truths," he
said evenly. "I waited for you to approach me, but now
I begin to think you never intended to do so. Which
leads me to ask: what the hell are you doing in my
house? Weston wises up, discovers shit where his liver
should be? That's a fine specimen of manhood."

Alex distantly registered Gwen's gasp. A cold calm descended, just as it did in the training salon. His thoughts felt clear and sharp. "I have no idea what you mean," he said flatly. Guns were tricky beasts. A kick could disarm the man or it could cause the gun to discharge. And Gwen had no cover to take.

Barrington gave a sharp laugh. His grip on the gun did not waver. "You think me a fool? I thought I recognized you that first night. Something familiar about the eyes. But it took a bit of inquiring to confirm it. The ruthless Mr. Ramsey. Curious choice of an emissary—I never heard Weston speak highly of you." His eyes narrowed suddenly. "But if it's dirty work he's designing, I can understand the choice."

Alex sensed some movement from Gwen. *Stay still*, he willed her. He could not risk looking to her to telegraph the message. He did not want to lead Barrington's attention back to her. "I'm no emissary of my brother," he said. *Christ.* How pathetic that he'd not remembered this truth before bringing Gwen along. He'd risked her, here, thinking himself in aid of his brother, when his brother was—*what*? The victim of a swindle? Common blackmail? What the hell was going on here? How had Barrington convinced him to part with the lands?

"Then explain yourself," said Barrington. "Or shall I ask the *lady* to explain?"

Thoughts of Gerry evaporated. "She knows nothing." He watched Barrington intently. The man was nervous. The corners of his mouth were twitching.

Earlier, Alex had mistaken that tic for a very irritating smile. "And I discuss nothing with a gun trained on me."

"Forgive my approach," the other man said dryly. "Your deception does not inspire politesse. Although why I bother, I don't know. Indeed, why *do* I bother? Weston is a gutless sack. If he hired you to play the man in his stead—well, I am sorry for you. Would that you had stuck to your own game; I can't afford distractions right now."

Instinct was everything. Alex could sense, in the minute shading of the man's voice, the slightest shift in his posture, that he had made a decision, and it boded no good for anyone. "All right," he said quietly, intention coiling through him. One single kick—

"You're an ass," Gwen burst out, and smashed a pot onto Barrington's head.

Alex sprang. Barrington staggered a pace and backhanded Gwen.

She fell into the desk, and some low, animalistic, unfamiliar noise ripped from Alex's throat as he collided with Barrington and took them both to the ground. He seized the man's wrist and pinned it, evading a knee to his balls on the way. Barrington's limbs thrashed like an eel's, but he had no practice in sparring. His grip around the pistol was white-knuckled. If Alex slammed his hand into the floor, if the gun fired, guards would come running. He placed his right knee on the man's testicles, his left knee on the man's left arm, and his left hand—*yes, by God, you son of a bitch*—on the man's throat, squeezing, squeezing, until Barrington's eyes rolled back in his head and his body went slack.

Take the gun. Relatch the safety. Gwen, by the desk. Face warm. No visible cuts.

Lashes fluttered.

Alex took a long, shuddering breath. Hand shaking, he cupped her cheek. Jesus God he had come here for goddamned *Gerry's* sake and she'd ended up crumpled on the floor. *He* was going to put a gun to his brother's head. "Gwen," he repeated, not recognizing his voice; hoarse, fit only for a thread of sound.

Her eyes came fully open. They rolled immediately to the left. Toward Barrington.

"Forget him." He helped her into a sitting position. "Look toward the ocean," he said.

"I'm fine," she whispered.

"The view is lovely," he said, and whipped free the cords that tied the curtains away from the window pane.

She cleared her throat. "Alex, the documents—"

"Is the moon full?" he asked. Efficiently he tied Barrington's wrists together. "I think we were due for a full moon tonight."

She did not reply. He watched his hands looping the rope over Barrington's ankles. No blood spilled, but it put him in mind of butchery all the same. He would have hog-tied and gutted this man gladly, whatever Gerry had done to invite this. The kosher style—strung from the heels to slowly bleed out.

His hands began to shake again.

"Yes, it's a full moon. Are you all right?"

It took a moment for these words to penetrate. "Brilliant," he said.

"Only that it seems an odd time for small talk, you know."

He fitted the second cord between the man's teeth, coiling it around Barrington's skull twice, then round his neck once, before running it behind his back, drawing the loops of wrist and ankles tight. Barrington wasn't going anywhere until someone came and found him. If he struggled, he would choke himself.

Let him struggle. Alex dragged him behind the screen for added concealment.

He turned back on a deep breath, preparing to pick Gwen up—his arms already focused on the feel of her, the reassurance of having her completely within his purview. Then he would be able to think again. This rage was so visceral that it numbed one. It lifted the hairs on his neck.

But Gwen was already on her feet, industriously stuffing her reticule with documents. Her quick glance upward ascertained that he was through with Barrington. She held up the reticule.

"These are maps," she said. "This might explain it."

He stared at her. "I'm going to carry you out of here," he said.

She tipped her head, and then, as if only now remembering, touched her cheek where Barrington had hit her. "It's only my face," she said. "I can walk."

"I'm going to carry you," he repeated.

"But these maps, Alex—"

"Fuck the maps," he said.

Her eyes widened. She studied him a moment, and then stuck the reticule under her arm. "All right," she said, and stepped toward him. "I suppose I do feel a bit faint."

They were halfway down the stairs when Gwen felt Alex's grip tighten. She lifted her head and spied a guard approaching them. Beneath the shadow cast by the brim of his bowler hat, the leer on his lips bespoke his misapprehension of Alex's embrace.

"Put me down," she whispered after the guard had passed them. He had turned in the direction of Barrington's private wing.

"Just lie *back*," Alex said, and his tone was so unaccustomedly harsh that she recoiled. And was pinned, by one large and bullying hand, against his chest, where this hand kept her firmly.

"But if he finds Barrington—"

"We'll go directly to the stables," he said under his breath. "Tell the lad to take us to Monte Carlo."

He carried her through the lobby as if she weighed nothing. The butler opened the door with no remark, clearly accustomed to odd goings-on. Down the short flight of stairs. Now gravel crunched beneath Alex's footsteps as he walked the path around the house. The moon hung overhead in a star-studded sky so black that it looked depthless.

She closed her eyes. From the distance came the dull crash of the tide against the cliffs and the babble of guests somewhere nearer by. The sun had taken its warmth with it; the deep breath she took held a bite more familiar to her in autumn, and the scent of the pepper trees, and Alex: starch from his shirt-sleeves, the tang of his sweat. He was a warm, solid presence, the strength in him undeniable. She had the sense of great struggles being waged inside him, but it seemed clear that questions were not going to unlock his tongue. All he wanted from her was to lie still in his grip.

Through her free-floating thoughts, this last observation refused to pass. It stopped squarely at the forefront of her brain. He was gripping her so tightly that she could hardly move. This was what he wanted.

Amazement made her jerk. His hand tightened briefly, as if in warning.

She caught her breath. She felt as though some soundless, enclosing bubble had burst abruptly, baring her senses to a new and altered and far more vibrant scene. His embrace was fierce, unyielding, but also comfortable—*more* than comfortable. His arms were strong and adept and he wanted them around her.

Heavens, she must be the shallowest woman in the world. She should find no joy in this moment. As adventures went, tonight was an awful and violent entertainment. If the guard found Barrington before they managed to leave the grounds . . .

"All right," he said quietly, and set her on her feet. "The Monte Carlo party is running late, it seems. Our good fortune." Taking her hand, he led her around the corner.

A handful of guests in their evening finery stood under the portico, waiting to board Barrington's carriage. Francesca Rizzardi spotted them immediately. "To the casino?" she called.

"Where else?" Alex sounded suddenly mischievous, playful, eager for a night of good fun.

"Then you've arrived just in time!" Signora Rizzardi laughed. "But we'll have to crush in like sardines!"

"Oh, I've no objection to it." Alex flashed the lady a suggestive smile. "Unless . . ." He turned to Gwen, his mouth quirked, his brow lifted.

She forced her own lips into a smile. "Darling," she said, and laid a hand on his arm. "So long as I'm crushed into *you*, I can think of no better way to travel."

It came out credibly, probably because it wasn't a lie.

Alex kept his eyes on the house until the carriage turned onto the coast road, which sloped downward past an embankment that blocked his view. He was watching for signs of alarm—as if alarm would make itself so visible. Hell. What did he imagine? An explosion of lights? The sudden howling of dogs? Barrington was not so well equipped. He traveled well-guarded but clearly he had little experience of hostile negotiations. Only a fool invited into his house a man whom he knew to be deceiving him.

Barrington was not the only fool here.

Alex took a long breath. This urge to violence was new to him. It made his muscles jump at odd intervals. He knew how to inflict pain, but until now he'd not understood the possible pleasure in it.

So *casually* he'd decided to include Gwen in this idiocy. Accepting the invitation to Côte Bleue had seemed harmless. Such an *economical* way to put Gerard's matter to rest. In his own mind, profit and cost had been the key considerations. And for Gwen? It would be a lark, a bit of fun, an escapade: such had been the terms in which he'd justified how she might profit by it. *Profit.* Always profit. Profit and entertainment; money and fun. Such bloodless words—bloodless, and boundless, too. Let the fun never end. May the profits never cease. Money knows no language. Let the world be your oyster. *Go, go, go. Run.* It had hurt to run as a boy but it never hurt now; he tested himself regularly.

He could have gotten her killed. Gwen's blood on his hands.

Try to run from that.

Gwen stirred at his side. Her hand settled on his arm, the lightest touch, recalling him to his role. He turned a bland smile onto the company. As the signora had predicted, they had piled in as closely and carelessly as children into a tree house, and about as cheerfully, besides. On the opposite bench, Francesca Rizzardi perched on her husband's lap, gasping and exclaiming in Italian as every bump in the road threatened to unseat her. Between bumps, she was reading aloud from a newspaper her husband held open for her, some chronicle of doings about Monte Carlo: Lord This had left on the green cloth a total of fifteen thousand dollars, but vowed to have it back within the week; Sir That had suffered similar losses, then made an excellent run at *trente et quarante*, and now sailed onward to Lazlo forty thousand in the black.

Beside the Rizzardis, Madame D'Argent, a dark-eyed and suspiciously youthful widow, cuddled the wall with a secret smile. Perhaps she knew these news items were nonsense—tales that the casino paid its mouthpieces to publish.

A half hour's journey lay before them on smooth, new roads. They might well arrive at the casino before Barrington's men discovered their master. Then the task would be to discover a clever place to hide until morning, when the trains would start running again.

He hadn't a cent on him and he doubted Gwen did, either. Their letters of credit, made out in their true names, were hidden in their room. And one did not carry coins at a house party without raising eyebrows.

Fleeing in the night like hares from hounds. Her face would be bruising, soon. *The only place I'd have a use for you is in bed.* He was a fool.

Gwen gave a very convincing giggle—a reply to some joke that Alex had missed. *Don't laugh*, he wanted to tell her. She had thrown her right leg atop his left knee upon boarding. She played her role beautifully, and he did not want her next to him. He wanted her as far away from him as possible. The opposite side of the earth. *Be safe.* Why the hell had she come with him? She had not one lick of sense in her head.

Into Alex's right side pressed the soft gut of a Spanish gentleman—de Cruz was his name. Shifting on the bench, Alex felt a telltale bulge in the inside pocket of the man's jacket. "Look there," he said, putting his finger to the window by de Cruz's face. "Glorious moon."

De Cruz looked, surrendering a twenty-franc coin for the privilege.

"It is so amusing," Signora Rizzardi was opining, "to see the truth of the casino, as compared to those dreadful little notices that the churchmen post at Nice." She had an elegant bone structure that lent her hazel eyes a faint slant; she put this slant to work in the teasing look she cast Alex. He kissed his fingertips in reply. Mechanical gesture. She fluttered her lashes. "Have you ever read those notices, Mr. de Grey? No? Oh, they are awful; I cannot bear to describe them!"

"Please do," Gwen said. Her tone was bright; nobody else would notice the rigidly erect posture of her spine, the tension in her shoulders. She had worn a backboard for six years. Whenever she felt uncertain, small or threatened or afraid, her posture was impossibly, painfully perfect. These things he knew about her—things which Gwen did not even suspect he

knew—were innumerable. For a man that had understood her so little, Richard had loved her fiercely and
talked of her often. And Alex had encouraged him—
subtly, continuously. Over the years, what hadn't he
wanted to know?

"No, no, Miss Goodrick! And I recommend you do
not look for them. Oh . . . very well. They are lists of
recent suicides, men supposedly broken at Monte Carlo's tables, but you mustn't believe half of the names.
These priests make up the tales to scare people."

"They do?" Gwen pressed her fingertips to her lips
with the appropriate show of shock. *She is learning not
to gape*: so Richard had said. *Such are the lessons a lady
must learn in lieu of Latin. Her governess warns her she will
swallow flies by accident.*

Why had he collected these pieces of information?
For years, he had collected them; he had tried again and
again to force the fragments safely into a picture, the
pastel debutante, the standard drawing-room watercolor. But he had never managed to fit them together.
And so he had carried them as so many souvenirs—as
warnings, as reminders, of how easy it would be, if
he did not take care, to fall into the comfortable, easy
catatonia inhabited by unimaginative men. And then at
some point the souvenirs had shifted in his hands and
come to show him the life he might have had, had he
been the sort of man she required. But he'd not been
able to be that man; he had not wanted to become that
sort of man; and this was the certainty that had pulled
him back aboard ship—the mantra to which he had lis-

tened, as he had watched Southampton retreat, again, for another six months, another season, another year.

"Perhaps they are lies," the Spaniard said to Francesca Rizzardi. "But I think there must be some truth to these lists, as well."

"Indeed? But no," the signora said. "How would such indigents gain entrance to Monte Carlo without the card of admission?"

Gwen sat next to him right now, a warm, breathing presence, her bravery unflagging, as obvious and evident as the smile she wore. And it was a strange and almost unconquerable need in him, like the need to draw air into his lungs, to pull her closer. To hold her still. But he was always the one to leave, because there seemed to be no other choice. To stay would be to lose himself.

His mind turned again to the coast, the receding shoreline. Had she been harmed tonight, no distance ever would have taken him far enough away to find himself again.

"Perhaps they are not indigents to start," said de Cruz. "Play-fever is real, you know. I have seen it. It can empty the deepest of pockets."

"Poor souls," Gwen murmured.

"A weak mind will break beneath any pressure," the signora retorted. "I cannot spare sympathy for those who sabotage themselves."

"True, true," the Spaniard said. "But I truly believe they are not in their own control. Men in the grips of the fever will gladly risk what they can ill afford to lose."

Of course, Alex thought. They risked what they could not lose because they thought that they would profit by that risk.

When she had fallen tonight something in him had broken—the frame in which he'd kept the pieces of her, perhaps. She had long since shattered the picture he'd tried to build from them.

No profit was worth the risk of losing her again.

Chapter Thirteen

Gwen had heard a great deal about Monte Carlo's famous gardens—the long emerald lawns dotted with peacocks, the fountains and footpaths to benches poised at scenic vistas over the ocean. She half expected that she and Alex would flee through them as soon as the carriage came to a stop, but instead he took her hand and led her up the broad white staircase into the casino proper, allowing her only a brief impression of flowering mimosa and the whispering of palm leaves stirred by the cool night air.

In the lobby, a grand marble affair supported by Grecian pillars and run round by a balcony full of merrymakers, they paused to check their hats and gloves. A number of people milled in the lobby, speaking in hushed tones; underneath their voices ran the murmur of distant music. Monte Carlo. She felt dazed. Why were they lingering here? Above, at either end of the balcony, were great murals of the sunrise over a white-walled town—Monaco, she would guess.

After Alex handed over his hat, he drew her a step

apart from the others, reaching up to cup her face as though to caress her. When he leaned near, he murmured, "Have you any money?"

Alarm jolted through her. "No," she whispered. He hadn't any, either?

He nodded. "Stay near to me, then. I'll play for ten minutes. The winnings should take us as far as Nice for the night."

He led her across the lobby, to the small bureau where they wrote their names and nationalities in a great, velvet-covered ledger and received in return cards of admission permitting them entrance into the next suite of rooms.

Card in hand, Alex made no pretense of waiting for the other guests. "Come," he said to her, and they set out at a rapid pace past the doors to the Reading Room and the famous Concert Hall, where, by the sound of it, a Mozart symphony was underway. Liveried men bowed and opened a set of double doors to the next anteroom, a polished corridor overhung by a dark blue ceiling that boasted a carved pattern of interlocking gold stars. The hush inside was marked; the few visitors who sat on the gilt benches sipped tea and read newspapers. How odd: Monte Carlo felt rather like a library.

On any other occasion, it might have stuck her as acutely unjust that she had no opportunity to explore this notorious place; that she was rushing past its main attractions with nary a glance backward. But all she wished now was to be gone. Barrington might be on the road this very moment. They had no money.

No money! All her life, she'd had money in hand and the comforting knowledge of what that money could secure: smiles, service, swift exits. She felt painfully vulnerable without any.

They passed through yet another gilded ante-room, even quieter than the first, before the double doors finally opened into the gaming salons. Here the silence was total, as if all the players at the long tables were holding their breath at once. Men and women hunkered into armchairs of crimson velvet, scowling down at their cards. She followed Alex across the Oriental carpet, past a boy of no more than twenty, who bit his knuckle and followed the roll of the roulette ball, round and round. Amidst all this fierce, wordless concentration, its bump and clatter seemed to make an outsized roar, grating along her nerves.

At the end of the hall, Alex drew up. In this section, each table boasted a delicately engraved silver bowl. He meant to play *trente et quarante*, then. Gwen had heard of the game; Elma favored it because it had a better return than roulette.

She went on tiptoe to speak into Alex's ear. "Do you have any coin to gamble with?"

"Only what I stole from the Spaniard."

Stole! She saw proof of her reaction in the slight smile that crossed his face. On a deep breath, she said, "And are you very good at gambling?"

"Luck is always useful," he murmured—and then surprised the breath out of her by lifting her hand to his mouth. His lips briefly pressed her gloved knuckles, a pressure as hot as a brand. For a moment, all her sharp anxiety seemed to tip into something hotter and far more pleasurable.

With a wink, he released her and turned toward a free chair at one of the tables. Clutching her hand to her chest, she retreated to a vacant bench set by the wall.

As she settled down, the croupier at Alex's table intoned, "*Messieurs, faites le jeu.*" Alex produced a coin. She sat up, straining with no luck to make out the denomination.

Whatever it was, Alex did not hesitate to place it as a bet—although perhaps he should, if their finances were such that he needed to gamble to pay their way out of Monte Carlo.

Perhaps they could charm somebody into giving them a ride to Nice?

She glanced nervously toward the door, then back to the game. The others at Alex's table—two young, well-fed gentlemen; a roughened old man who, with his white beard and ruddy cheeks and stern demeanor, might have made a convincing sea captain; and a petite woman dressed in widow's weeds, with a large jet pendant at her throat—proved more cautious in their judgment of luck and the board. The woman changed her bet twice before snatching her hands back into her lap, where Gwen suspected they continued to fidget amongst themselves.

She wished Alex would look at her. What were they to do if Barrington appeared? The dim lighting from the chandeliers rebounded off the green baize tables, creating a sallow glow that played unflatteringly on the gamblers' faces. She had never before seen Alex look pale.

"*Le jeu est fait; rien ne va plus*," said the croupier. *The betting is finished; no more bets.* With an elegant fillip of his hand, he began to deal the cards.

She leaned forward and bit her lip. And from the corner of her eye, she saw a bowler hat.

She turned on a soundless gasp. One of the liveried attendants had approached the man and stopped his advance, gesturing toward the hat. A sign in the lobby had proclaimed very clearly that hats were not allowed inside the *Salle de Jeu*.

The man looked contemptuous. With a curse sharp and loud enough to penetrate the low, constant rumble of the roulette boards, he took off his hat and tossed it at the attendant's feet.

The attendant took a step back, chin tilting in offense. Another employee approached, speaking in tones too quiet to hear as he picked up the hat and returned it to the man.

Alex was intent on the cards. She did not know whether she should rise to her feet to warn him, or go down on her knees to avoid notice. She did not recognize the man, but it seemed unwise, in this case, to hope for the best. His attitude and dress made him too likely to be one of Barrington's men. Alex's back was to the entry, though, so the man could not have noticed him, yet. There was a chance they could escape undetected—

The man looked directly into her eyes. He shook off the attendant's arm and pointed at her.

"Red wins," announced the croupier. He began to push money toward Alex, who pocketed the coins and notes.

She rose to her feet. "Alex," she said.

The terror in her voice won his instant attention. He came to his feet and made a shallow bow to the table, then caught her arm and turned her toward the entry. "Where?" he said calmly.

The evenness of his voice settled her somewhat. It was only one man, and they were in public now. "To the right. By the roulette tables, in the bowler hat. Oh, dear," she added, for the man *and* the attendants now began to walk toward them, moving with silent purpose down one of the aisles formed by the long baize tables.

Alex dropped her arm. "Cross the room and walk along the left wall," he murmured. "Wait for me by the entrance. Do *not* leave the *Salle* without me."

"But—"

"*Go.*"

She picked up her skirts and made a sharp turn, hurrying past rows of oblivious players, beneath a line of chandeliers that muted the colors in the Oriental carpet beneath her slippers. This light played such strange tricks; for a moment, the room appeared to her somehow unreal, like one of those old, painted daguerreotypes, somebody else's memory, nothing to do with her, oh, if only that had been the case and they had already been gone from here. *Faster*, she thought, but when she glanced over her shoulder, she stumbled to a stop: Alex was having a *conversation* with the group. Hands in pockets, weight on one foot, he looked quite at his leisure.

The man in the bowler hat raised his voice. "—*lying*, I tell you—"

The attendants caught him by the elbows. Alex shook his head, threw her a brief glance, then nodded toward the exit before strolling onward himself.

She started forward again, agonizingly aware of the number of tables remaining to be passed before she reached the exit—five, and then four, and then three—and also of Alex's progress, so unbelievably unhurried, on the opposite side of the room. The brief commotion, notable only because of the otherwise total silence, had attracted a few stares.

Two tables.

Another muffled curse pierced the tomblike silence of the room. More players laid down their cards.

One table.

She reached the entrance just as Alex did. He put his arm around her waist as the doors opened for them. "Head down," he said softly as they exited the gaming salon.

Ahead of them, at a distance enviably closer to the main exit, a couple strolled arm in arm. As the next pair of doors opened for them, Gwen released a breath: she did not see Barrington or his men anywhere down the long stretch before them. "Have we enough to get to Nice?"

"Yes."

By some silent, mutual decision, they picked up their pace. They had almost made it back to the lobby when a voice cried out, "Ramsey!"

The shout seemed to ring off the marble floors. Gwen looked up and saw Barrington standing at attention beside a very startled Signora Rizzardi.

"Music," Alex said decisively. He knocked open the doors to the concert hall with an elbow and yanked her after him.

The interior was dark, the great chandelier put out; she could make out nothing at first but rows upon rows of red velvet chairs, and then the backs of heads, all turned toward the spotlit stage where a huge orchestra was playing, seventy men at the least. Alex's grip slid to her hand, tightening; she followed him blindly along the back of the theater as her vision clarified. The walls were covered in paintings of Greek deities, the ceiling ornately carved and gilded, and so far above them that she felt very small, suddenly—almost childish. She had a fleeting feeling, based perhaps on dim memory, that she was sliding about in the shadows while the adults, her parents, glittering people, threw a party to which she'd not been invited.

They reached the very end of the back row. "Here," Alex whispered, and she heard the faint snick of a latch, and then the door was opening into fresh air, and he was pulling her outside, into a small courtyard that appended the main entrance.

Not until their feet touched the grass again did she

breathe freely. And then, all at once, she wanted to run. To dance? Oh, something wild and rollicking! An escape in Monte Carlo! She turned to him to say something—maybe only to laugh—and he was already smiling at her and behind him she saw the man creeping up, the man from the stairway in Barrington's house, and the glint of metal in his hand.

Instinct was all. She threw herself forward into Alex, knocking him out of the path of the descending pistol butt. He stumbled back, and the guard missed her; he had not gauged for her height. "Bitch!" he snapped at her and swung back his hand.

Alex hit him. She had never seen a man take a hit before. She had never gone to watch boxing. It was not appropriate for debutantes. She had not known the sound it made, the sickening crunch, the spray of blood it occasioned.

The man dropped to the ground.

"Bloody *Christ*," Alex said, shaking out his hand, and for a confused moment she thought he was complaining of the pain, until he took her by the shoulder and turned her roughly toward him. "Stop *doing* that," he said, and she shook her head. She had no idea what he meant.

He made a sound low in his throat, and from the way he let go of her, she interpreted it as disgust. "Come," he growled. "Let's find a cab."

Barrington's search made it inadvisable to stay at the best hotels, the second-rate hotels, the thoroughly average hotels, and also, to Gwen's regret, any hotels that had proper names. Stepping down from the carriage at Nice, she dogged Alex through a tangle of streets that led off the main stretch, past a diminishing number of stationers' stores with books on roulette in the windows, into an area where French flags no longer waved gaily from windows but hung in tattered strips from rusting poles. At a corner, they paused so he could shake awake a street urchin and ask, in rapid French, where a bed might be found. The boy looked as if he wouldn't answer, but he grew friendlier once he had his Napoleon. "Madame Gauthier," he said, and roused himself, on the promise of another coin, to show them the way.

Gwen was braced for very shabby appointments, and Madame Gauthier's unkempt appearance—she answered the door in a stained wrapper, with a shawl wrapped round her hair—did not invest greater confidence. But after retrieving a pitcher of water from one low shelf, the woman led them through a pleasant courtyard, whitewashed, with cactus growing at the edges, and then presented them with a room that was bare but clean: a bed large enough for two; a chamber pot; a washstand; a pitcher and glass. The plaster walls were cracked, but they were as white as marble.

When the door closed behind their hostess, Gwen sank onto the bed. "Do you think we're safe now?"

Alex slid the bolt home, locking them inside, then leaned back against the door and fixed her with a cold, steady regard. "For the time being," he said.

She blinked. Far from the reassuring tone she'd expected, he spoke very sharply. And he was looking at her as though he were sizing her up for execution—his eyes narrowed and blazing, his jaw so rigid that it made an almost perfect square. "Are you . . . angry?" she asked in bewilderment.

"Am I angry," he repeated softly. The corner of his mouth tipped. It was a smile she never wished to see again. "What do you think, Gwen?"

"I can't think of a single reason—"

"A *single* reason?" He paused for an audible breath. "Setting aside your stupid heroics on the lawn—you went into that room with him. With Barrington." Each word was distinct, a chip of ice. "You walked off, alone, with a man whom you knew I did not trust."

Astonishment briefly paralyzed her. And then she shot up on a laugh of disbelief. "You think this was all *my* fault?" Of *all* the things they had to talk about—"I thought to have information from him. To ask a few questions—"

"To have *information*?" He pushed himself straight, and if anything, he looked angrier. "I told you that *I* would do the goddamned investigating!"

"Only—only to see his private rooms," she said quickly. "To map out the house. And had *you* not been skulking about, I would have been safely in bed right now, having told you where to find his study! You see?"

He stared at her.

And in fact, she wasn't quite right. Barrington had clearly known of Alex's identity. "Well, he knew who you were," she said weakly. "We didn't realize that. So something was bound to happen. But, still—it wasn't *my* fault."

"Bound to happen. Yes. Bound to happen to *me*." He took a hard breath. "And tell me, what do you think would have happened to *you*? Had I not so fortuitously been 'skulking about,' do you think he would have let you leave?"

"Yes! He's a—" All right, clearly he wasn't a gentleman. "He didn't know that I was part of the deception," she said.

He didn't seem to have heard her. "But perhaps I have it wrong," he said. He spoke now with terrible pleasantness. "Was it a seduction you planned? Having given up on me, you turned your sights on him—"

"Don't be an idiot," she said sharply. "I will tell you what would have happened. I would never have kissed him had I not seen you hiding there. And if he had kissed me, I would have refused him!"

He laughed. It was not a pleasant sound. It raised the hairs on her nape. "Refused him."

"Yes!"

"Simply walked away."

"Yes, that's what I mean!"

"Could you, then?" He took her hand and pulled her up to him. "Demonstrate for me," he hissed in her ear. He snapped her around so expertly that despite her unpreparedness, or perhaps because of it, the result was like a move in a dance: she pivoted fluidly and gracefully, her back coming up against the full length of his body.

He had positioned them before the small mirror over the washstand. In the reflection, he looked—different, somehow. And so did she, her cheeks flushed and her chest rising so rapidly. Like photographs of themselves, clichéd types: the rogue with the black reputation; the heiress ripe for plunder.

She straightened her spine; she did not require his support. He pulled her right back against his chest.

"Walk away, then." His voice was low and rough. "Go ahead, Gwen. Try to break free."

She shoved at his arm. It was immovable. "I would have kicked him," she said.

"So try it."

"I have no desire to kick you!"

"Do you imagine that you could?" Abruptly his regard in the mirror seemed neutral and detached—studying her with the idle curiosity of a stranger. "Have you never heard of my little hobby? I was sure my sisters would have mentioned that I go about kicking men for fun. Smash their jaws, on occasion. Men much larger and stronger than you have learned it firsthand." His face darkened. His words took on a smooth, venomous lilt. "It's a very economical way to fight. Barrington would have learned so tonight had you not felt the need to *interfere*."

She swallowed. Alex had dispatched Barrington with the speed and ease of a lion taking down some aged, limping gazelle. She might have been terrified by it had anyone else performed that cool dispatch. But Alex had done it. And she knew him.

He was wrong, though, if he thought he could have taken Barrington without her help. A smashed jaw was one thing, but a gun could kill. This anger was unfair—and out of character, besides. Alex could be cruel, but he was never unfairly so.

"He had a gun," she said.

His indrawn breath audibly shook. "Yes," he said.

She looked into his face in the mirror, met his eyes, and something in her—her stomach, her heart, God knew what—something turned over.

He'd been frightened for her.

God above. Alex had been frightened.

She'd been clutching his forearm, braced against it. Her grip softened now. She tentatively stroked her hand down to his wrist, then back again. "It's all right," she whispered. "Alex, I'm fine."

His arm dropped. He stepped away from her. "I am amazed you have lived this long," he said in a dead voice. "You have no value for yourself, do you? No value apart from the number assigned to you by your parents' wealth." He made a scornful noise. "Miss Three Million Pounds, to be squandered on whichever man deigns to give her attention this month."

A breath escaped her. He knew so well exactly how to wound her. "I should slap you for that," she said faintly.

"But you won't, of course." He shrugged out of his jacket and tossed it onto the floor. For a moment he looked at it, then he turned back to her, leaning against the wall, tall and elegant in his shirtsleeves.

"You won't because you recognize that it's true. Poor Gwen. Life would be so much easier for you if all that ailed you was common stupidity."

"Stop it," she said. "This is unfair of you, Alex. I was only trying to help—"

"Oh, that's smashing," he said. He slid his hands into his pockets, looking down his nose at her, his smile taunting. "Trying to *help*—out of the goodness of your heart, I suppose? Yes, that must be it; what other reason could there be to risk yourself so carelessly? *I thought to have information from him.*" It was an unkind imitation of her voice; he made her sound like a whining child. "And what cause for your great bravery, Gwen? Love of the Ramsey lands? But what care have you for some no-name estate? Not even entailed, you noted. Was it a concern for Lord Weston's name, then? A chemist's daughter would appreciate the importance, no doubt."

The boor. "I have told you my opinion of sarcasm," she said hoarsely.

"No matter," he said. "It's a trick question, anyway. I've already told you the answer: you have no notion of your own worth. And so you trade on other people's idea of what matters."

She stepped back from him. "You are a boor!"

He laughed. "Your curses are pathetic. Call me a bastard. That would serve."

"Very well, you *bastard*, if we're talking of worth, what about your own opinion of yourself? Why are *you* here? A man pulled a gun on you, very well might have *killed* you, and for what? For your *brother's* sake?" Her own laughter scraped her throat. "Lord Weston does nothing but complain and disown you. If he sold the lands, let *him* deal with your sisters. Or let *them* buy back the land, if they love it so! Why must *you* solve the problem for them?"

His face went blank. An indecipherable emotion passed over his face. Slowly he sat onto the bed.

"Oh, Alex." All the fight went out of her. Everything—fear and adrenaline and anger—seemed to coalesce and transform into a great rush of agonized tenderness that made her knees fold, leaving her sitting, trembling, on the bed beside him. Wanting to touch him. Not daring. "I do not mean it, of course. You help Gerry and the twins because you love them. Exactly as you should."

The moment the words were out, she felt a curious chill—as though some strand of ice in her gut had been delicately plucked, sounding a premonitory note whose vibrations spread through her whole flesh.

She could not *love* Alex. She had known him too long. She knew all his faults. She even knew what he would say next—some dismissive, cynical remark that would shame her for introducing the idea that love might provide any motivation for him whatsoever.

Instead, he stared fixedly at the blank white wall and said, "I never wanted any of this."

She hesitated. "Yes, I know."

"I should have turned back for Lima at Gibraltar."

"Probably."

"England has never given me any reason to stay."

At that, she snorted. "You love your family. You *do*. Just because your brother *may* have made a mistake . . ."

He fixed her with a long, strange look, during which time his chest rose and fell on a deep breath—once, twice, like a man gearing himself up for a long, breathless dive.

"Let me explain something to you," he said.

Slowly she nodded.

He angled his body toward hers slightly, as though preparing to tell her a secret. Instead, in a calm voice, he said, "You speak of love, Gwen, as if it's something that should hold a person down."

Her lips parted on an unvoiced syllable. *Yes*, she wanted to say. *Love should hold you. It should bind you.*

But she did not speak, because with a sinking feeling, she suddenly divined the direction of his thoughts.

And, indeed: "I suppose that's what love properly is," he continued with a rueful half smile. "But you must understand—sometimes it feels indistinguishable from cowardice."

Here he lost her. "It takes bravery to love," she said. "I see no cowardice in being beholden to a person."

"Yes, well, perhaps you wouldn't," he said softly. "Here's a tale. Part of it you know. I had terrible asthma as a boy."

"Yes," she said slowly. She knew it through Richard, and of course his sisters, who forever feared that the childhood ailment had wrought some lasting weakness in him. Gwen had never understood such worries: Alex was the most vigorous man she knew.

"Terrible fucking disease," he said bluntly. "I would wish it on no one. What can you count on, if not your own breath? And there were no identifiable causes for it. I never knew when it would strike—one moment I would be well, the next, flat on my back on the floor. Then there was only one question: where was the medicine? Sometimes it was in my pocket, and sometimes, it even did the trick. But sometimes it was fifty yards away—or, worse yet, only a few inches past my reach—the nitre paper and matches on the table above me, and me staring up, unable to do so much as lift my hand or call out, my only hope that some-one . . . a maid . . . *someone* would come by."

He took a deep breath. "I remember—" He exhaled, and she did, too, through a throat that felt tight. "I remember those waits," he said quietly. "Every one of them. Suffocating, helpless as an infant. I was not calm, Gwen. I never mastered that art. I was terrified. I always knew that this would be the time when no one came."

She blinked, and flinched as she felt a tear fall free. She reached up to shove her hair out of her face, but really to wipe the tear. If he saw it, he would not appreciate it.

"I had no choice but to depend on others," he said.

"I know." Her voice betrayed her. It sounded full of gravel.

He glanced at her, light blue eyes penetrating. "The memories do not upset me. Perhaps I should have said that beforehand. I am sharing them by way of explaining something to you. After a few frightening episodes, my parents set someone to follow me about. Room to room, house to lawn, lawn to house. A bloody ear pressing to the door of the water closet. No woods for me; the pollen was suspect. No dogs, no horses; dander might trigger an episode. Other boys of my age played rough; I was kept to the company of my sisters, and of Gerard, when his self-respect could permit him to play with a cripple."

"Alex," she breathed.

"That is only the word he used," he said evenly. "I did not agree with it, of course. But all this care did not prevent the attacks. And so the doctors began to speculate that the asthma was a product of nerves. Off I was sent to Heverley End. Nobody else around. My parents hoped that solitude and a strict schedule would heal me. I was taken for daily walks. Fed and lectured and taught. Cleaned and put to bed. I was ten, eleven, during that time. Like a beast tethered at the end of a chain. But at least I felt safe. There was no chance that an episode would find me alone on the floor, inches from the medicine. All that ailed me was my own loathing. I was *glad*, for a time, to be a tame little pet.

"That didn't last long, of course. I was growing. My lungs began to catch up to my limbs. I grew bolder and decided I wanted to go to school. I begged and argued and pleaded and demanded to go. They refused. Out of love, no doubt. I threw fits. I ran away. They caught me and locked me inside my rooms to keep me safe. Out of love, you understand. They fitted up Heverley End like a prison, with locks that kept one inside. And even then—even *then*—I knew that their decisions, and the restrictions they placed upon me, seemed necessary to them. Because they loved me. They were keeping me alive, they thought. And I have never resented them or wished them ill for it. But it took some very spectacular threats to finally win the right to go to Eton. And I still find it very difficult—so difficult, Gwen—to think of love and concern without thinking, first, of how very many ways one might suffocate."

She sat very still as he let silence fall. His words were heartfelt. They sounded a death knell in her heart.

God above. Her bad taste in men was endless.

Finally, she managed a smile. "But how good you are to your family, despite it. The twins adore you. You've never denied them anything, Alex."

"It's easier not to deny them," he said with blunt precision. "They ask only small things because they are afraid, I think, to ask for more. Which speaks well of their perception but not so well of me. And perhaps it also speaks ill of me that I humor them because I am afraid that if I did not deliver on their requests—holidays, and gifts, and the occasional appearance at their dinners—they might grow angry enough to demand the larger things. My company. A presence in their children's lives. Commitment."

He spelled a vision that exactly matched her fantasies. "Would that be so awful?" she whispered. "Do you not . . . lose something by holding yourself so apart? Will you not come to regret it, ever?"

"Ah." He gave the barest ghost of a smile. "And there is the question I have never allowed myself to ask. I tell myself I want nothing more than what I have. But"—his smile sharpened into something distinctly unpleasant—"it comes to me now that this is *exactly* the philosophy I railed against as a boy. I accused them of entombing me to keep me from the tomb. Trapping me in that sad little house on the coast because it was safer than the risk of sending me to school, of letting me actually *live*."

He looked directly at her. "Avoiding a risk because it might cost," he said. His eyes searched hers, intent. "It's a sad calculation to make for love's sake, isn't it? It means putting love in service to fear. *That* is what I always objected to. And yet here I am, doing the same. I think it's high time I stopped."

Slowly, she nodded. "And this . . . is why you're helping Gerard?"

He laughed, a short, startled sound, and then tipped his head, studying her with those beautiful eyes of his. "I wasn't speaking of Gerard," he said. "Far from it."

She frowned. And then a frisson went through her, and she slowly sat back from him. If he was no longer discussing Gerard . . .

"At any rate," he said, "it's a hard habit to break. I developed a policy, once my lungs righted themselves.

You will have noticed it, throughout the years: I vowed not to depend on anyone. To take great pains, in fact, to avoid any situation in which that might be required of me. Richard . . ." He smiled a little, a painful smile. "Richard was an exception. And it did not encourage me to try again."

"Yes," she said. "I know."

"You do more than know," he said gently. "You do the same."

The comment startled her. She tried out a puzzled smile. And then, because his regard remained on her, unblinking, she said, "No, Alex. You're wrong. I've depended on so many people in my life. Goodness—I thought to wed, twice! I have never turned away from anyone."

"Of course you do. You're doing so right now. You're lying even to yourself." Lightly, so lightly, he pressed his knuckles to the space between her breasts. "Who are you in the dark, Gwen?"

That touch, so light it was barely a breath of sensation, seemed to pierce her like an anchor. She stared at him, this wicked man, traveler of the world, her brother's hero and her brother's downfall—and her own downfall, so she'd hoped. "I don't understand what you mean," she said, although the strange lick of fear that moved through her betrayed it for a lie.

"Gwendolyn Elizabeth Maudsley," he said softly, rolling the syllables in his low, smooth voice. "She is your secret, I think. She is the person you keep hidden from the world. I wonder, do you even know her yourself? Not when you walked to the altar, but in the night—some night when you're all alone—will you look into the mirror with honesty?"

Her heartbeat was quickening. He was right. A month ago, this question would have made no sense, because she would not have let it make sense. And certainly she would not have been able to answer it as she did now:

"Yes," she said.

A smile touched the edge of his mouth. "And who will you see?" he murmured. "Would Elma know her? Would Belinda? Would Richard have done?"

No. They would not. But . . .

You would know her, she thought. *You, Alex.*

The revelation flashed through her, bright and hot and transformative as fire. Perhaps he saw its effect, for his knuckles skated up to brush her collarbone, light as a feather, warm as a breath. His eyes followed the motion, an arrested expression on his face, which her fevered brain interpreted as tenderness, awe, the look of a man who felt amazed by the privilege to touch her.

Alone in the dark, she realized, she became the woman she was with Alex.

I trust only you and the dark always to look at me so honestly.

The idea unfurled through her like a slow, sweet poison, collapsing her thoughts and better intentions, dissolving her nerves and fear and longing into a hot, formless appetite for the whole hot press of his body against hers, atop hers. Into hers.

"There's nothing in you to be ashamed of," he murmured. "Never let the world tell you otherwise. *Never* let it trap you into hiding again. That would grieve me, Gwen . . . inexpressibly."

She caught his hand in her own. His pulse hammered beneath her thumb, news that gladdened her in a fierce, elemental way. He was not unmoved. He was not unmoved in the slightest. "Alex," she said.

"Gwendolyn Elizabeth Maudsley," he said, and kissed her.

Chapter Fourteen

It was the slowest, sweetest kiss. It carried her back toward the mattress like a warm wind, and the mattress caught her, soft as a cloud, as he came over her. She twined her hands in his hair and shut her eyes, and he lowered himself against her so his chest brushed hers. His mouth charted every inch of her lips, leisurely and thoroughly, before his tongue gently pressed for entrance. She opened her mouth and he deepened the kiss, his broad palm sliding up her waist, her ribs, the side of her breast, her throat, until it cupped her cheek, large and warm, a gentle reminder that he was here, all of him, as his mouth alone made love to her.

In the darkness behind her eyes, the world contracted to this: the sheets that crackled with starch as she restlessly stirred; the light scrape of his teeth, the quest of his lips and tongue; the brush of his chest against hers. She groped blindly up his back, feeling across the muscled expanse, the sharpness of one shoulder blade, the path of his spine, which swept her hand into the small of his back, the perfect place to press him closer to her. His body came fully against hers, and with a start she remembered the rest of him, so much taller and broader and harder, pressed against her now, over and around her. Her breasts ached; she shifted restlessly against him, and his hands slid down to her sides, over and over, steady and soothing until his knuckles brushed the sides of her breasts, a touch light enough to be accidental, but not soothing at all.

Her eyes opened just in time to catch the flutter and lift of his own long lashes. They stared at each other. The silence seemed too full to break. His eyes were the shade of high alpine lakes, the color of water in spaces close to the sky; so close that she could see the flecks of gold scattered through them, secrets that so few people would ever know.

Her impulse was to shove off his jacket. To strip away his shirt. Her brain bade her press herself against him, to act quickly before he changed his mind again.

Her instincts held her still. She did not move. Some defiant impulse made her turn her face away. If he wanted her, he would have to prove it.

He smoothed his hand over her hair, pushing it away from her face, and kissed her jaw. His mouth moved down her throat, and he licked her once, where her throat joined her collarbone. A shuddering breath escaped her. She wanted to move. Her fingers curled into her palm.

His hands slid around her waist. He pulled her up and she set her face into the darkness of his throat, breathing him, her fists at her sides as his clever hands unlaced her gown.

The corset gave his fingers brief pause. "My God," he said. "What is this?"

A giggle escaped her, scratchy and startled. "The Pretty Housemaid."

He gave her a look through his lashes, extreme skepticism, his brow quirked. But when it came off so quickly, he leaned into her ear and growled, "Always wear that corset," and then he was lifting away her chemise.

She was naked. Utterly bare. She felt the blush move across her skin; the air seemed painfully cool in comparison, brushing like another touch across her breasts. He went still, briefly, and then she felt the hot rush of his exhalation across her shoulder.

"Gwen," he said. The softest thread of sound. "You are . . ."

When he did not go on, the possibilities began to penetrate her daze. She was—naked, yes, but what else? Too round? Too full? Too long in the waist? "I'm what?" she whispered.

His hands moved slowly over her waist, one finger tracing a slow line to her navel, up her abdomen, to her collarbone. "You're the palette from some pre-Raphaelite's dream," he murmured. "Cream and strawberry and scarlet. You are . . . beyond my imagination. It's a wonder you can be touched at all."

She stared at him. His words were so far removed from her worries that for a moment, they did not seem to address her concerns in the least. And the next moment, as they turned in her brain, they seemed to reassemble her expectations entirely. Round, full, long-waisted, what matter?

His lips dipped to her skin now, tracing the same path that his finger had made, slowly wending upward. As his mouth reached hers again, he cupped her skull in one broad palm and laid her back onto the bed, kissing her as he lowered her onto the pillows. She had accused him—as a show for Barrington's guests, but with a ferocity that had felt, suddenly, all too genuine—of treating her like a wind-up doll. His hand at her head brought the comment back to mind. She crossed her arms over her breasts and immediately he drew them apart, placing them gently but firmly at either side of her torso.

For some reason, his decisiveness made her breathless. She tested it by looking away.

One long finger touched her jaw, nudging her face back toward his.

He met her eyes and smiled just a little: a knowing smile. A shock went through her, hot and delicious. He understood exactly the game she was playing.

He held her eyes as he lowered his head. And then, as his mouth closed on her nipple, her own lashes fluttered shut. With his free hand, he brushed a delicate path down her side, his thumb finding the crease between legs and torso, tracing it lightly, over and over, as the languid pleasure in her began to sharpen and solidify. His fingers slipped lower, drawing intentions on her inner thigh, turning to scratch lightly down the length of her leg. Her control broke; with no conscious design, she bent her knee, rubbing the sole of her foot against his clothed calf.

His mouth let go of her nipple with a wet, sucking sound. "Gwen," he said, his voice soft and rough.

Her foot froze. Traitorous foot. She kept her eyes closed, struggling to control the ragged pattern of her breathing. For some reason, it felt very important not to admit that she had moved of her own volition. Not yet. She wanted him to work for her attention.

His tongue flicked delicately over her nipple. She shuddered despite herself. He bit down very lightly, and her entire torso arched of its own volition toward his mouth.

His hand moved beneath her back, gathering her toward him as he suckled her. His free hand delved between her thighs, finding the hot, wet place between her legs and rubbing gently. Yes. *Yes*, this was what she had wanted. She opened her eyes. He was poised over her, the bulk of his weight supported by his arms, the rise of his biceps clearly delineated by the thin lawn of his white shirt. *Take it off*, she wanted to say.

He glanced up and met her eyes. "Open your legs," he murmured.

A hot blush washed over her. She swallowed. She would have pretended not to hear him, but the pressure of his hand abruptly increased, causing her whole body to contract on a startled wave of pleasure. Her head fell back, and a soft noise filled her ears.

Oh, good Lord! The noise had come from her.

"Gwen," he said, and there was a note of laughter in the word that disarmed her as nothing else could have. She looked back to him and he took her hand, lifting it to his mouth, planting a kiss in her palm before placing her fingers against his cheek.

The feel of his hot, rough skin fractured her control. She had no idea why she'd delayed, what her aim had been; everything she wanted was here, being offered to her with his smiles and body and the intent, burning focus of his eyes. She pushed herself up, groping for the buttons of his waistcoat, unclipping the suspenders, stripping away his shirt—freeing his chest of all encumbrances.

She rose on her knees to press her breasts to his bare chest—a full-bodied, electric shock; he made a noise deep in his throat, and she felt the vibration register through her flesh. She burrowed closer yet so their thighs touched; she put her arms around him and drew him close, closer, her grip so tight that it awoke a reflexive panic deep within her; one did not hold anybody so tight unless one feared he might try to get away. But, "Shh," Alex was saying into her ear, "shh," and now he was kissing his way down her body, his mouth hot against her belly, tracing a path downward. Without warning, he ran his tongue along her seam, and the breath hissed out of her; he tipped her back and she sank as limply as a deflating balloon.

His hands gripped her thighs firmly as he laid her bare. His mouth settled between her legs, and she almost could not—bear—the feeling of his tongue; it made her aware, too aware, of that part of her, her quim as he called it. He slowly licked her, delicately charting the outlines of parts of her that she did not even know or understand. The spot that had given her such pleasure the night before throbbed now, and he tongued it, again and again, until strange little noises slipped out of her, pleading noises; she would have thrashed had his hands not held her down so firmly. Again and again he abraded her, and then he released her thigh to press his thumb firmly against the spot as his tongue moved lower, pushed into her.

The pleasure did not creep up, this time; it crashed onto and through her so forcefully that a split second of fear accompanied it. As she gasped and seized, his fingers replaced his mouth. They pushed slowly and steadily into her, a slight, burning pressure that made her cry out and buck harder. She barely felt his kisses to her thigh; and then his mouth was working its way back up her body again; he was gathering her to him tightly, pulling her against his body as she calmed.

Shame and grudges and complicated designs and anxiety seemed like the languages of a foreign land now; the long, liquid, loose feeling in her had burned away everything but the most elemental and important knowledge. She curled her leg up over his and felt the solid jut of his erection; she rocked against it, and he gasped. *Yes.* She could make him cry out, too. She reached between them for his trousers; his hands brushed hers, but if he meant to stop her, she gave him no chance. She rolled on top of him and shoved his arms away, laying them out at his sides as he had done to hers. She met his eyes.

"Be still," she whispered.

He was breathing hard, and a sheen of sweat showed on his forehead. But as he met her eyes, the barest whisper of a smile moved his lips. "*Oui, mademoiselle.*"

She unfastened his trousers and bared him completely. His hips were lean, his musculature cut as though by a blade. He looked like one of those Greek statues in the British Museum that she had always made such a show of ignoring—only he was hotter, and larger, and his eyes were watching her. She reached out to touch the line that started at his hip bone, a faint groove where the muscles of his upper and lower body met, and he made a faint sound, between a gasp and a hiss. She watched her finger trace the line toward his manhood. *Oh, really, Gwen.* Toward his *cock*, which was straight and large and far thicker than she had expected, and also . . . well, she supposed she had thought it would look like white marble. Her hand paused.

His breathing paused.

She cupped her hand around it and closed her fingers.

Soft, she thought with wonder. Soft but so hard, beneath. She bent to kiss it.

A hoarse oath came from him. He caught her beneath the arms and pulled her up. "Later," he said breathlessly when she started to ask where she'd erred. A hard kiss silenced her. He rolled her onto her back and came on top of her. *Oh*, she thought, a silent and formless revelation that glittered through her like fireworks. He felt right atop her. He felt like he was hers. He was kissing her now with intention, with an enthusiasm so fierce and focused that it carried an edge of desperation, and this, too, seemed like a miracle—that her touch seemed as necessary to him as his did to her.

His hunger was contagious. It kindled hers again as well. She wrapped her arms around him and lifted her legs. Desire built low in her belly, a pressure that wanted puncturing, release. He broke away to reach down her body again, to touch her quim, but the pleasure he'd given her that way now seemed like a delay. She took his hand and brought it to her mouth, looking into his eyes as she kissed his palm as he'd done to hers. Then she lifted her hips against him, angling so his cock brushed against the place he'd wanted to touch.

He turned his hand in hers, lifting hers to his lips and taking her index finger into his mouth. Below, the head of his cock found her entrance. As he sucked her finger into his mouth, he gave a slow, smooth push below. The force of his exhalation washed down her hand, her forearm.

He pushed again, harder this time, and she caught her breath. The premonition of pain was suddenly upon her.

The sound made him go still. He took a deep breath. Then another.

She pulled her hand free of his mouth. If he was struggling with notions of honor, she had no tolerance for it. She *was* wicked. She grabbed his arse, so smooth and hard, and dug in her nails as she lifted her hips again.

His hand speared through her hair and tightened. "Be *still*," he said through his teeth.

"Don't stop," she whispered.

"God save you if you think I would," he said hoarsely. "Just a... moment."

She waited, breathing hard. A shudder moved through him. And then he pushed again

She bit her lip. No, this *definitely* would not be comfortable.

"Gwen," he murmured. He kissed her, harshly, his fingers tightening in her hair to a shade short of painful, and pushed again.

She inhaled in startlement.

He was inside her.

It did not hurt so much after all.

His lips molded hers as he settled into a slow, rocking movement. She kissed him back, too astonished to do much more, too rattled by this bizarre sensation, his tongue inside her mouth and his, yes, his cock inside her down below. The soreness was subsiding. It felt very queer; her fingers twitched atop his back like startled birds as new sensations registered, the slide of his abdomen across hers, the jab of his hip bones into her stomach. This was more complicated than what had come before; it was very athletic, for him. She had no idea what to do. Was she meant to move? Would he mind if she simply lay here?

He slid his hand up her arm, and her startled attention flew to him. "Gwen," he said softly, and ran a rough thumb over her mouth, pushing inside. She sucked it obediently, and then watched, wide-eyed, when he put it down between them. When he touched the space where they joined, she gasped and felt herself contract.

Inside her, he pulsed.

Her mouth went dry. She swallowed with an effort and tightened her legs around his hips. She wanted to lick him, devour him, wrap herself so closely around him that no inch of his skin was spared. But she had no idea of how to do it. "I don't . . . what should I do?"

His finger probed gently, stroking, causing her to gasp again. "There is no way to do this wrong," he murmured, his voice like banked coals, dark and hot. "Everything about you is right."

The words struck her dumb. So simple, they were. But such a statement . . .

She seized his hair and pulled his mouth down to hers, and he began to move again. This time, it was different. This time, she tried not to hear her doubts, and his mouth and his hands did not permit her to dwell on them. His palm at the small of her back guided her so she was moving with him, and she found a way to rub against him that stroked the pleasure higher, so suddenly they were both moaning as they moved, together, as if they were in one skin, the sweat between them no barrier; she licked a bead off his chin and he sucked her earlobe as his thrusts quickened.

The final pleasure took her gradually this time, stealing up in bits and pieces; she imagined herself as a well, being filled to the brim—a drop here, a bucketful there, slowly, pleasure mounting so slowly—and then, all at once, *too much*, overflowing, pure bliss. She clung to him as she trembled, then felt him move hard into her, again and again, until his own climax took him with a groan.

He pulled her on top of him as he rolled to his back, keeping her joined to him, as close as their skins would allow.

She lay listening to the diminishment of their breathing, as beneath her cheek, his heartbeat began to slow.

Gradually the silence began to assume overtones. Someone needed to say something. The thought made her tense. She could think of nothing to say. *Love me, Alex, and I will never cling too tightly to you*: it was the only thing she might say that was remotely close to honest. But it was still a lie.

In the end, it was he who filled the silence. He smoothed the hair away from her eyes, and then combed his fingers through her hair, an idle, contemplative gesture. "The Christmas you were eighteen," he said. "Just before your debut. You and Richard spent the holidays at Caroline's. I was about to make my first trip to Argentina. Richard spilled my plan to do that trek through the Andes. Do you remember?"

"Yes," she said absently. His eyelashes distracted her. They were long enough to grace a woman's face. His eyes were purely beautiful. "The twins were furious."

"Mm. They asked if you had any advice for their mad, suicidal brother. Do you recall what you said?"

She reached out, very tentatively, to touch his lashes. He did not flinch. He watched her, unblinking, as she ran the lightest finger across them. *This is trust*, she thought. "I said that I could have no opinion on such matters, as I was afraid of heights and knew nothing of mountains. And you made some irritating reply, of course—*That is why ladies don't climb mountains*, or some such masculine nonsense."

The lines bracketing his mouth creased in a smile. "Actually, your answer was slightly different. You never said you feared heights. You said, 'I would be afraid to take some misstep and fall off.'"

"Oh." She put her thumb to his brow now, tracing the rough arch, simply for the sheer pleasure of witnessing her entitlement. She could touch him as she liked.

His voice lowered. "And I said, 'That is why *you* don't climb mountains, Gwen.' But now I wonder. You aren't afraid of heights."

"No," she said. "Not particularly."

"Only missteps."

She paused midstroke. Did he mean to imply this had been a misstep? "I *was* afraid," she said carefully. "For a very long time. But no longer."

"So was I," he said, and lifted her chin and kissed her.

The next morning, she woke twined around him, her face tucked into his shoulder, her leg between his, her arms wrapped around his torso. The hour was early; the ghostly glow of dawn barely lit the room. Alex was sleeping soundlessly, one arm thrown over his head, the other wrapped around her waist.

Disbelief moved through her, sweet as a strain of music. Her eyes fluttered shut, and she fell back asleep wondering how much she dared to dream.

When her eyes opened again, she found him sitting cross-legged beside her, fully dressed, his head bent over the maps she'd purloined from Barrington's desk. His expression looked dark in thought.

Trepidation roused her to full alertness. "Alex," she whispered, and he lifted his chin to meet her eyes, and smiled.

That smile was like the sunrise for her. She smiled back at him. Stubble darkened his angular jaw, and his brown hair was rumpled. She tentatively reached up to brush a stray lock from his forehead. Fully a wicked woman now, with license to do such shocking and unspeakable things as to lie around with a man not one's husband, and handle his overlong hair with a tenderness too spiced by desire to be anything bordering on virtue.

"Good morning," he said. He leaned forward to kiss her ear. His tongue curled around her lobe as he withdrew, sending a shiver through her. "Coffee?" he asked, and waved toward a small clay pot on the nearby table. "Madame Gauthier just delivered it."

"No," she said, and pushed herself up into a sitting position. The maps niggled at her.

He followed her look. "These seemed to alarm you last night. I can't make heads or tails of them."

"Oh?" She picked them up. She had not given them a long look the night before, but as she flipped through them now, her suspicions clarified. "They're survey maps."

"Yes," he said. "I gathered that much. But why did you find them significant?"

She cleared her throat and selected two particular sheets. "This," she said, lying the sheets out side by side.

He moved closer, his shoulder brushing hers. "Explain to me what I'm looking at. A map of some kind. Topographical?"

The proximity, the casual way he reached out to stroke the back of her neck, made her dizzy. She willed herself to focus. The map consisted of shaded lines and polymorphous shapes, colored variously to signify different qualities of land. "Yes," she said, "it's the typical surveyor's map, the sort drawn up when assessing the value of a property, or proposing to alter it. They come in very useful when designing a parkland. You've got various pieces of information here: elevation, soil composition, water tables . . ." She pulled a desperate face. "*Drainage* and so on. Above all, drainage! After the first redesign of the gardens at Heaton Dale, the pond started draining into the Grecian folly. Put quite a damper on the classical feel. Athens as swampland."

He laughed. "But there's something amiss with these maps?"

"Not with the maps per se," she said. "Only . . ." She spread out the maps in pairs, keeping aside the widowed seventh. "Do you see?"

He considered them row by row. "Only three properties here, with copies of each."

"Yes. The same topography," she said. "The same surveyor, as well—you see the name at the bottom, one Mr. Hopkins. But you see how certain of the shadings are different?"

His eyes narrowed. "Very good catch," he said softly.

She smiled. "The swampland gave me a powerful motive to learn to read these things. Certainly I no longer trusted the contractors so blindly! At any rate, one of these is false. Only I don't know the key for the shadings, so I can't guess which element has been falsified."

An unpleasant smile twisted his lips. "I can," he said. "Soil composition, you say? Would that comprise information on mineral deposits?"

"Of course," she said. "Oh. You think—"

"I think land without significant mineral assets would sell more cheaply." He paused. "Heverley End, for instance, sits on some very rich copper and tin deposits. One would think that Gerry would know that, but then, perhaps that's why he's so damned stubborn in his refusal to discuss the sale. If he were given altered survey data that obscured the mineral wealth . . . and he *believed* it . . . then the price of the estate would drop significantly." His smile faded. "Still doesn't explain why he sold it in the first place, of course."

"Well." She hesitated. "Heaven knows men do strange things. None of us are perfect."

"Oh, Gerry offers ample evidence of imperfection. But not in matters like this." He lifted her hair away from her neck, idly toying with a strand as he gazed past her toward some invisible thought. "Death before dishonorable profit," he said lightly.

There was some curious emphasis in his tone, which all at once she divined. *Gerry* would not stoop to profit. That was *Alex's* role.

"Oh, dear," she said sardonically. "However will you play the black sheep now that Lord Weston is in on the game?"

He flashed her an impish grin and rose off the bed. "My point exactly. But let's put aside such philosophical debates until we're safely out of Nice. Barrington will be expecting us to head east for Marseilles, so I propose we go instead to Lake Como."

"Oh! Elma, of course." She was on her feet the next second. Twinges registered in various delicious and very useful spots throughout her body, bringing a blush to her face. "Only give me ten minutes," she said, "and I'll be ready to leave."

It was her fault, of course, that forty-five minutes later, as they lingered at the edge of the train station in wait for the southbound train, she stood wound around Alex like a vine. He had only offered his elbow; it was she who had threaded both her arms around it and hugged it to her like a rare treasure.

And this was the pose in which she was discovered.

"Why—Miss Maudlsey! Is that you?"

The greeting fell over Gwen like the shadow of an axe. She looked down the platform into the rapidly fading smile of Lady Milton. Her sister, Lady Fanshawe,

the way in which they passed out, and woke up. Had this pattern been pointed out to him, no doubt he would have noted that these women were invariably awakened by the hands or lips of some sickeningly humble but aggressively competent prince—and that the awakening itself was a sanitized metaphor for the good rogering the prince had probably delivered. Indeed, which he *did* deliver, in the less treacly versions that circulated in old French manuscripts.

But after this morning, Alex would never be able to view such tales so cynically. This morning, he had watched Gwen Maudsley wake from sleep, and there had, indeed, been something magical about it. He'd sat beside her, his thoughts strangely quiescent, and watched consciousness steal over her, spreading first as a faint blush across her pale cheeks, and then in the twitch of her lashes, and the soft sigh that stirred her dark red hair. She came to life like a character from a place far sweeter and less cruel than anywhere he'd ever traveled. The half-conscious brush of her knuckles over her mouth had reddened her lips. When she'd shifted, the scent of her had perfumed the air around him.

He might have mocked himself if he hadn't been tired of always mocking at what others took seriously. It was easier to mock, of course, but other people refrained, and not always because they lacked the imagination or sense of humor required to mock. Sometimes they refrained because they dared to long for something that was not easily grasped, something that might slip away if one did not pay it the proper respect—prayerful respect, the sort that moved one to remove one's hat by the side of a grave, or to bow one's head to soldiers marching off to war, even while damning the fat MPs that sent them to die. Life was not all for mockery. Nor was laughter. But it was harder to spot the prayerful moments when they called for laughter instead of tears. Tears spelled an end.

Laughter could spell a beginning.

He had watched her wake, and he'd thought to himself that he had no idea what sort of beginning he might offer her. But he'd seen, in her face, which he'd touched lightly with one hand as she'd rolled toward him, that he had certainly reached an end when he'd met her again in London.

On the platform, when the sneering crone and her assistant harpy had popped up to peck at them, he'd thought he had found the answer. What a sleeping princess required was a heroic rescue.

Apparently that was incorrect.

"Are you *mad*?" she demanded. They were on the Milan-bound train. He was growing rather sick of trains. By the looks of her, so was she. She turned a tight circle in the compartment and then kicked the door, exhaling through flattened lips as she turned on him. "Really, Alex, have you lost your mind? Two days ago, you would not . . . and now we are supposedly married!"

He fell back onto the mattress, bracketing his eyes with a hand. He had already exceeded his weekly quota for the care and soothing of enraged womanhood. "It seems likely," he said. "Madness, I mean. You will have to blame yourself for it."

"What possessed you? Did I give you any impression that I would expect you to stand for me? Do you not think I heard you last night? Your speech about suffocating? Do you think I would ask this of you?"

He sighed. She made him sound like a martyr, which seemed highly unfair. He loathed martyrs. His mother had been a martyr, an endless slave to the whims of his lungs. *I used to love London in the season . . . of course, Alex cannot take the air there, and so we keep in the country year round. Perhaps when the twins come out . . .*

"Sit up! You cannot mean to go to sleep! Tell me why on earth you would have made that preposterous claim, and explain to me what we are going to do about it!"

Aside from the obvious fact that he'd shagged her silly last night, and was waiting with the barest thread of patience for another opportunity? Yes, aside from that small detail, the *why* was simple enough. "You would not have been running about, sans chaperone, had I not suggested the adventure." True. "Any harm that befalls you as a result is therefore my responsibility to defray." Also true. "There was no other alternative to what I did." Even now, he could not think of one.

"You might have said *nothing*. Did you think of that? I told you—ruin was my aim!"

He smiled despite himself. Her hiss was audible, sharp as a snake's.

"You do not believe me?" she demanded. "Last

night you seemed to take me at my word. Last night, we did as we pleased without worrying about others' opinions. Today you come out the moralist. Surely I'm owed a reason for it?"

He sighed. "Gwen, last night and this morning are two separate matters. I would not have mentioned last night, but you may bet every pence of your three million that Lady Milton has headed directly to the telegraph office."

"So? What of it?"

"So, you may say that you won't mind infamy, but I reserve the right to doubt." One's essential traits had a way of reclaiming a person. "You're a pleaser, Gwen." Her instincts would pull her back to the narrow path, no matter how much she might come to genuinely revile its constraints. And even if he was wrong—he would not be responsible for putting her to the test.

A savage pain in his foot made him spring upright.

She was holding a chamber pot over his toes.

"Did that please you, Alex?" she asked with a very sweet smile. "Shall I please you again?"

He swung his legs to safer ground. "Had it been anyone else—*anyone* but that woman—I might have tried . . . I don't know, to purchase their discretion. But . . ." Bloody hell. He trailed off as astonishment overtook him. Running a hand over his face, he admitted it to himself: he was *lying*. He was damned cheerful about this turn of events.

He eyed her with new intent. Gwen Ramsey. Queen

of the Barbary Coast. He'd take her there for a holiday.
Make her sing. She'd enjoy making the lie a reality.

Perhaps now was not the best time to introduce
this idea, or admit his own sudden good cheer. She
looked furious. He cleared his throat. "As I said.
Anyone else. But Lady Milton?" He shrugged. "She
ardently admired her son's profile. And I was person-
ally responsible for changing it."

Her shoulders sagged. "Yes," she said, and returned
the chamber pot to the floor. "Richard told me how
you interceded for him in that fight. But that is beside
the point, Alex. What are we to *do* now?"

He laughed softly. The sound was odd, a bit—all
right, he could say it; the sound was a bit hysterical.
And he felt odd: boneless, supremely light, thoroughly
enervated—as if some great weight had lifted off him.
A beginning, indeed. "We find a chaplain," he said.

"What?" Her brown eyes widened. "You can't be
serious."

"Perfectly," he said.

"But—" She sank down on the chair opposite. "But
Alex," she said softly. "What if we don't suit?"

He sat up at that. How in the hell could she doubt
they'd suit? Had she not been there last night? The
past weeks? "You've known me over half your life,"
he said dryly. "Do you expect any surprises? If so,
I assure you, all my skeletons live well outside the
closet, creating tales that regularly terrorize the
Ramsey clan. Handy, that." She looked pale as parch-
ment, truly and deeply horrified. A laugh rose in him,

rusty; it seemed to catch on something in his chest as it passed onward. "All right, cheer up. If we don't suit, we'll find a lawyer. Three cheers for the Marriage Reform Bill. Gerry voted against it, of course."

He lay back again, repositioning his hand over his eyes. So. Not a true marriage, of course, but something convenient. Why not? She was already part of his circle. She belonged in that same arena as did his sisters and nieces.

The idea made him wince. All right, not *precisely* the same. But obligations already tied them together. He'd simply continue to honor those obligations.

"*Divorce?*" Now *her* voice sounded full of rust and nails.

"Less exciting to you than ruin, is it?" He spoke in a bored drawl. "I suppose it's true, divorcées are a dime a dozen, these days. Fashionable, almost."

"Fashionable—" The word ended on a choking noise. "Oh, *please* do sit up! You've gotten me into this mess; you can't mean to nod off while I think how to fix it!"

He lifted the edge of his palm to look at her.

She had her arms wrapped around herself again. And a *tear* slipping down her cheek.

He swung up and came off the bed. "Christ, Gwen—what's this? You must have known there was a risk that someone would spot us when you agreed to this charade with Barrington."

"Of *course* I did!" she cried. Her arms tightened around herself; she must be bruising her own ribs. "But I thought I was *choosing* the risk! Instead you have made the decision for me, a decision I've never thought about—did not plan for—did *you* plan for this?" She looked up at him, mouth agape, face lit by some emotion he could not parse. "Did you?" she asked softly. "Alex, did you think the outcome might be marriage?"

He cupped her elbows, as bony and delicate as a bird's wings. She was shaking. The violence of her reaction made no sense. "I never planned for it," he said slowly. "But if you were ready to be ruined, I fail to see why this turn of events should seem so much greater in magnitude."

Her face bowed. Silently she shook her head.

He frowned down at her.

Oh, what the hell.

"Gwen," he said. "I never had any intention to marry. I never had any intention to show you around Paris. I never had the slightest intention of shagging you—but I can swear by God and everything holy that I had dreamed of it for years."

Perhaps her breath caught. He could not be sure. Certainly, he reflected, it was not the most romantic sentiment one could speak to a woman. But at least her shaking ceased.

This was a good enough result to merit greater investment. "For years," he said. His fingers tightened of their own volition. "And not just because you are lovely, truly lovely, beautiful in a way that is only partly an effect of your looks. The way you see the world is beautiful. And you make others see its beauty through your eyes. And you have made me *exceedingly* irritated by wasting yourself on tossers. I have cursed you repeatedly for selling yourself so cheaply. And I have never placed a bid because I never believed you were for sale, and I did not know that I was capable of offering what you deserved. So"—he drew a great breath—"if it's the divorce that troubles you, we can shelve that part."

No reaction.

"That is, marry. For good." Was he really proposing this? Dear God, his sisters would throw a party that would last until the new year. "For real," he clarified. Christ, he sounded like a five-year-old. Next he'd be adding, *For keeps! No take-backs!*

A sigh escaped her, almost soundless.

He had no idea how to interpret it. His own thoughts felt a bit muzzy, but he supposed he was making sense. Wasn't he?

Then why was she not replying?

"My bases are New York and Buenos Aires," he said, feeling more and more the idiot, "but if you prefer to stay in London, I can move the operations here. Indeed, at this rate, with the Peruvian business—well, that's no matter. Perhaps biannual trips would serve us. We can choose a house in town. Wherever you like—Grosvenor Square, if you prefer. If you must," he added under his breath, because he could really only go *so* far.

She flashed him a dark look and pulled out of his grip. Giving him her back, she went to stare out the window.

"Do you love me?" she asked.

Her voice sounded very small. And he wondered, suddenly, what sort of divide it created between them, that he knew pieces of her that she had never shared with him—facts and stories and moments and memories to which she had no idea he was privy. He had collected them for so long, denying to himself that this acquisition was anything more than casual amusement, when in fact it was zealous, and jealous besides; disowning as accidental the fact that he never forgot a single remark she made, or that others made about her, and that he approved of these other people, or disdained them, according to their treatment of her. Such a lopsided intimacy existed between him and her. Inevitably, it created a chasm whose depth neither of them could know until they tried to chart it. Would this chasm prove impossible to bridge?

"Yes," he said quietly. "I do love you, Gwen." How had she never realized that? Even Richard had known it.

He was watching her posture as she turned to face him. She stood so painfully erect. He was waiting for her shoulders to relax.

They never did relax, even as she lifted her face to him and smiled, a smile so unearthly radiant that he had a brief, uncanny fear: he was in a dream; none of this was real; he was dreaming, and she was not really saying, "Then yes, Alex. I will marry you."

Chapter Fifteen

For the rest of Gwen's life, memories of the masked ball would be vague and indistinct, washed out by the immense, blazing light in which they were made. At the moment, however, the illumination lent an overpowering precision to the scene. One thousand French lamps had been lit within the Cornelyses' house in Grosvenor Square. The flames reflected crazily off the scarlet and gilt molding of the Chinese décor, the best jewels of some six hundred guests, the sequins affixed to their shiny, expressionless masks. Combined with the tumult of hundreds of conversations, three overcompetitive orchestras scattered across two floors, and the ring of crystal and steel-toed shoes, the effect rippled through one's senses like champagne. Gwen had gone in search of the water closet and had lost her way back to the ballroom twice.

Or perhaps, Gwen thought, her brain was malfunctioning. All of these last twelve days seemed to her to have passed in a sort of intoxicated haze. From Milan, she had wired Elma to come quickly—an edict obeyed even more quickly than Gwen had hoped; she'd spent only one more breathless night with Alex before Elma had appeared, anxious to know the cause of this early recall, and a bit put out, besides (although Gwen did not dare ask how Elma had been occupying herself that made her early return so much to be regretted).

Once revealed, their cause for recalling her had achieved the impossible: Elma had been rendered temporarily mute. And then, as astonishment had ebbed, she'd thrown herself into crisis mode. "Shall we bother with bribing an Italian priest? Oh, bosh, simply another mouth to tape shut. No, let us go to where we know our friends, and figure it all out there," she'd decided. "We book tickets for London directly. Mr. Ramsey, go, go, go!"

It had occurred to Gwen that there was no point in bothering to make the marriage match Lady Milton's dates. "What do we care?" she'd asked Alex, when Elma had finally turned her back long enough to give them an opportunity for private conference. "Will it matter, in Buenos Aires and New York, if people in London say we were traveling alone together before we wed?"

"It will matter in London," he'd said. "And one day, it might matter to you."

He would not listen to her arguments to the contrary. Indeed, he'd proved surprisingly amenable to all of Elma's moralizing and marshaling, and his sisters' besides. They had been waiting at St. Pancras, four days later—alerted by Elma's wire that a "terrible tangle" caused by "two idiotic lovebirds" required their best efforts at reconciliation.

Gwen had predicted to Alex that at least one of his sisters would fall down from shock upon learning of the marriage plans. In reply, he'd merely smiled and said they might surprise her.

And indeed, upon hearing the news shortly after retrieving them from the station, Belinda had done no more than lift her brow and nod, while Caroline, with a cry, had thrown herself across the carriage to embrace Gwen and Alex in turn. "Well done," she'd said to Alex, winking as she pulled away.

The trick was this: stirred by Lady Milton's industrious hand, the news of the marriage had spread far and wide. A flurry of cards was appearing at the Beechams, all from acquaintances dying to learn the story. They needed a very influential person, then, to facilitate the procuring of the special license, perhaps even to twist an arm in fudging the date of issue; otherwise, news of its belated usage would become the season's next scandal. "And Gwen has already provided two," Elma said, "for everybody is saying now that she must have bribed Pennington into crying off so she could have Mr. Ramsey instead."

While Alex's connections spanned the government, he'd never had cause to befriend anybody connected to the church. And so the matter of the special license came down to Gerard.

The twins, together with Alex, broke the news to their brother as Gwen waited outside with Elma. In the hallway, all that could be heard of the moment of revelation was a clatter and a great thump.

"Oh dear," Gwen murmured.

Elma patted her hand. "He will be your brother-in-law," she said.

For a moment, Gwen could not tell if this was a caution against further criticism, or a caution against the marriage itself. And then came another crash. Elma's hand closed firmly over hers. "One can see why Mr. Ramsey prefers to travel abroad," she said, her smile pleasant, her voice steely.

Silence fell. And then a voice lifted—Lord Weston's. Gwen strained to hear, but she could not make out the words.

A sharp female reply. That would be Belinda.

The door slammed. The twins came into the hallway, Belinda stalking, Caroline slumping. Even the feather in Caro's hat was wilting. But her smile was bright when she said, "Only give them a moment. He is very glad to see you join the family, Gwen."

"As well he should be," Elma said coldly. "But I daresay he has an odd manner for expressing his joy."

The twins exchanged a look. "Oh, it isn't you," Caroline said. "Only . . ."

"Only he is upset with Alex," Belinda said flatly. "Alex never does take the straight path when a spiral or zigzag will do."

"He is yelling at *Alex*?" Gwen could not imagine anyone daring to do so.

"Oh, indeed," Belinda said. "And Alex is no doubt sitting back and smiling, and thereby taunting him onward."

"I am the last straw?" Gwen asked politely.

Lord Weston stuttered to a stop. Alex turned in the chair. "Ah, Gwen," he said pleasantly. He came to his feet, crossing to catch up her hands and draw them, one by one, to his mouth. "Martyr," he accused beneath his breath. "I thought you chucked your virtues some time ago. Save yourself and run."

She laughed despite her nerves and might have replied, had Lord Weston not stalked up and sketched a very stiff bow. "Miss Maudsley," he said. "Welcome to the family. My apologies for the truly *unforgivable* circumstances of this match. I pray you pardon him. I pray you pardon all of us for supporting such a rascal."

Such was the fervor of his tone that she felt offended for Alex's sake. "Forgive me if I take a very different view," she said flatly. "I have always found your brother to be thoroughly admirable in every way." Alex's snort, she ignored. "I cannot understand why you judge him so harshly, *particularly* when—"

"Why? You cannot understand why?" The earl's eyes bulged. "Dragging you off to Paris—landing you in such a situation—why, I pity you if you cannot imagine the why of it! I fear you will be in for an unpleasant surprise before your honeymoon even concludes." Here he paused, turning a dull red. Perhaps he suddenly recalled the circumstances in which Lady Milton had discovered Gwen and his brother, and divined that the honeymoon would not hold as many surprises as it properly should. More gruffly he continued, "It has always been thus with him. I would have expected you to know this! Certainly you know how he chose to make his . . . living." He nearly sneered the word. "And of course, there is the small matter of your brother—"

She cut him off, in a tone far colder than she had ever used with anyone. "It was by my own desire that we contracted to marry. I must conclude, then, that you either mistake me for a fool because I wish to marry him, or you mean to twit me now by speaking so outrageously although you don't mean a word of it. Yes, he makes a *living*—a very fine one. Indeed, you will forgive me if my personal experience of men with inherited privileges leads me to believe that a man who works for greatness is far more trustworthy than one who is handed it at birth."

Lord Weston opened his mouth to reply, but Alex spoke first. "Oh," he said softly from behind her. "Do be careful with him, Gwen. He's a bit more fragile than he looks. And not all these titled sorts are rotters."

The earl's glare transferred over her shoulder.

She crossed her arms. An apology was called for.

Lord Weston's lips remained sealed.

"I do not think the earl so fragile as *that*," she said grimly. Perhaps his siblings' cosseting was all that ailed him. "By my calculation, sir, you owe Alex your thanks."

"My . . . thanks." He spoke as though the words were some foreign language, meaningless syllables on the tongue.

"Yes. He has done you a great favor. You were conned

by a criminal. Alex has brought you the proof to see this man jailed, and your land returned to you."

Lord Weston's eyes were nearly the same shade as Alex's, but did not have nearly the same effect. When they opened wide and his lips parted in surprise, he looked like a glassy-eyed fish, appalled to find himself on the butcher's slab.

"Mm," said Alex, taking her arm and shoving his free hand into his pocket. "Hadn't gotten around to telling him that bit, Gwen."

"Oh." She felt her cheeks warm. "Dreadfully sorry."

"No harm done," Alex said. "What say, Gerry? Proof of Barrington's unlawful ways in exchange for one small favor in the form of a quiet marriage license."

Lord Weston assented, of course. But, so Gwen noted, he did not bother to thank his brother for saving him from the hands of a conman. Family, it seemed, was not always the idyll she had imagined.

Four days it took to procure the license, once Lord Weston turned his mind to it. As she stood now at the edge of the Cornelyses' ballroom, safely anonymous behind her mask, with less than twelve hours until the appointed time of her marriage, she wondered again what she was doing here. She felt distant, curiously apart from the scene. She and Alex had come on the twins' insistence, for no newlyweds, if not bound for their honeymoon, would hide from the London season. People might expect odd behavior of Alex, but not of Gwen. And so they would go, Alex had told her.

But why? Why were they bothering with these people?

The mask probably did not help her sense of detachment. She lifted it away as she searched the crowd for the Ramseys. Stares began to find her immediately. A balcony ran along one side of the ballroom, and an entire group of women craned over the rail to peer at her. These looks were not wholly malicious, but they were curious, prying; it would take only one misstep, in the days to come, to sway public opinion against her. Then what seemed, right now, like a romantic spectacle would become a sordid scandal of the kind that deserved condemnation, cold cuts, turned shoulders.

A month ago, she might have crumpled beneath the weight of such censure. Now it felt no more than annoying.

She did not want to live amongst these people.

Why were they here?

By noon tomorrow, she would be married to Alex Ramsey.

She spotted him, finally. He had removed his own mask and was walking straight toward her, but he had not spotted her yet. The sight of his profile as he looked over the crowd, his hawkish nose, the firm straightness of his body, filled her with something hot and covetous.

I want this.

Oh, yes, she did. She had never wished for anything more in her life than to be married to him—to make his laughter, his wit, his slyness, his ferocity, his protectiveness, his encouragement, his courage and determination, hers by right and by law.

But she did not believe for a moment that he loved her.

Oh, he told her so. His sisters told her so. Elma claimed she had known it all along, had seen it in how he'd looked at her when she'd not been paying attention. Balderdash. She wanted to believe it—she would even pretend to believe it tomorrow. But she knew him too well. She knew his secret: for all his wandering, his independence and his unorthodox ways, he took his responsibilities very seriously. He even borrowed others' responsibilities, making them his own simply because he thought this sort of service was owed to those whom he loved. From the moment Lady Milton had spotted them together, there had been no question that he would offer for her. He had promised Richard to look after her. Marriage was the only option the situation had offered.

His eyes fixed on her. His expression changed. He sent her a smile so slow and tender that her lungs squeezed.

Maybe he loved her.

He started across the floor toward her. She held still, watching him approach. It was *possible* he loved her. He did not require her money. He'd had her virginity with no promises made or asked for.

He did not stop at a polite distance. He came directly into her, his hands closing on her waist. She resisted the urge to look up toward the balcony. Everyone thought them married, and these touches were permissible among married couples. That did not change the effect it would have: in a minute, if he did not release her, they'd make a spectacle so powerful that the balcony would probably collapse beneath the weight of the crowd craning over.

She put her hand over his. He offered her his trademark rogue's smile. She understood now exactly what that smile signified. It was a personal promise of long, sweaty nights and no quarter given.

Her grip tightened over his by no conscious volition. If he loved her . . . then what couldn't she do? What couldn't the world show to her? What wasn't possible?

"I am bored out of my skull," he said. "Do you think we've put sufficient time into this purgatory?"

"We promised we would not leave until the twins did," she reminded him.

His head tipped slightly. A new gleam entered his eye. "Would not leave the house," he said.

Beneath her palm, his skin was hot, his fingers strong. The possibility in his suggestive smile made her pulse quicken. "Alex, we can't . . ."

"Come," he said, turning her toward the door. In her ear, he breathed, "Be a little wicked, Miss Maudsley."

Here, indeed, was wickedness: she realized, as she followed him out of the ballroom and down the hall, that she had been dreaming of this while she'd wandered, lost, through the house. She knew exactly where they should go. She stepped ahead to lead him and he followed close on her heels, not speaking, nudging her when she paused, nipping at her ear and muddying her doubts when the curious glance of some masked passerby made her courage falter.

She stopped by the baize door, now standing shut, through which she had spied the open linen closet. Turning back to Alex on a great breath, she said, "I think this might work. Just inside, there's a—"

He took her under the arms and put his mouth to hers as he backed her through the door. Some distant, rational part of her listened for the thump that spelled the door's closure; the rest of her wits were already scattered beneath the driving pressure of his kiss. They had not kissed with this intent since Milan. There had been no opportunity. In the days since, she had started to wonder if the wildness and freedom she'd felt in his arms had been the product of an over-fevered imagination, the wishful thinking of a woman afraid of slipping back into deadly, dulling comforts.

But she had not imagined it. His lips on hers made every part of her come alive. She pressed herself into him for more of it, then let him push her back against the wall, breathing encouragements into his mouth, urging him on to greater ferocity. Her nails caught in his shirt, beneath his shoulder blades, digging into the density of his muscle, daring it to try to resist her. His mouth slipped down her neck, teeth scraping, testing; he bit the place where her throat joined her shoulders, as if to hold her in place, when she wanted to be nowhere else.

She tasted his chin, his jaw, the skin which had been rough with stubble in Milan, now so smooth from the wick of a sharp-edged blade. His palm covered her breast, lifting it clear of her corset as he sucked the skin at the base of her throat, just inside the lacy neckline of the silver tissue gown she wore. She hoped he marked her. She wished he could make her somehow indelibly his; that they were still children so they could cut their fingers and mingle their blood and know this meant something. She longed for some transformation more lasting than that wrought by the law and his name, some visceral change he might effect in her so that anyone on the street with one glance would know she was his.

The fabric of her gown was so thin that she could feel the chafing of his thumb, now, the slight, sweet abrasion of his nail across her nipple, as though she were naked, and he, too. Flesh to flesh, pressing into each other, every doubt in her melting. *I want this.* God above, she wanted to be his.

His mouth closed over her nipple through the fabric, sucking strongly. It pulled a hot, sweet current from low in her belly; she ran her hands up and down his broad back, restless, impatient, ready to jump from her skin if he did not take her now. This was mad, insane. A servant could come along at any moment.

The thought cleared her brain a little. She had no desire to kowtow to convention any longer, but decency was a noble concept all the same.

She groped blindly along the wall behind her. The door was there somewhere, she knew it. Her fingers closed on nothing. "Wait," she panted.

"No," he said, and bit down lightly on her nipple, startling a low, hot sound from her throat.

"Someone—Alex, someone could come. We should... stop."

He lifted her by her bottom, pinning her between his body and the wall. "Yes," he agreed in her ear. "Someone could come."

A hot, dark thrill ran through her. She understood, all at once, that games had a place in this matter, too. But . . . a strand of fear intruded, constricting her ardor. "Alex—" She wasn't ready for such things. Not yet. "Please," she whispered.

He hesitated only a fraction of a moment before drawing her a pace down the dark, narrow passage. She heard the click of a latch, and the smell of the linen closet flooded the space: starch and lemon and lavender. His hand at her waist guided her inside; he pulled the door shut and total darkness enfolded them.

His lips touched her ear. His voice was soft and so, so low. "You're right," he murmured. His hand smoothed over her bottom, tickled the tops of her thighs. "This is much better. Anything might happen in such darkness."

The shiver that passed through her, the current of want that powered it, dried her throat to dust. She turned blindly for his mouth, and he ran his tongue along her lower lip. His hands slid slowly, slowly, down her arms. Encircling her wrists, he pulled them behind her, his silent squeeze an order: she would leave them there.

His mouth returned to hers now, his kiss slow and deliberate and thorough as she stood still, all the pleasure points in her body pulsing ever stronger, the imagined restriction of her arms somehow feeding this desire: standing in the dark, blind, willingly trusting him. "What do you want?" he whispered.

"You," she said.

Without warning, his finger brushed lightly between her legs, making her jump and whimper. He stroked again more firmly, rubbing almost contemplatively at the juncture of her thighs. "What do you want for yourself?"

She frowned. "*You*."

He laughed, a low, sexual sound. Between her legs, his light, teasing strokes were not enough; the skirt, while thin, impeded his touch. She strained toward him, and he said against her mouth, "Shh. In a moment."

He pressed harder now, reminding her body of how empty it was, of the ways he could solve that, the ways he could satisfy her. But she did not want to wait anymore. Even as his hand rubbed and goaded her and the hunger built, that strange panic began to seep back into her thoughts. *Take me, Alex.* Was it so easy for him to wait? Did he not burn the same way she did?

She reached down and laid a palm on his erection, and when he took a sharp breath, no doubt to chide her for her insurrection, she said to him, "Shh," and cupped him more firmly. She *wanted* this. She *needed* this. His hands curved around her bottom, clenching and squeezing her, lifting her against him, against her own hand. She went on her tiptoes to help him, to help them both. "Have me," she whispered as she rubbed against him. *Have me.* Her fingers learned the catch on his trousers and flipped it open.

His cock sprang into her hand, hard and full and ready. He was drawing up her skirts now, pulling them up in great handfuls. Their mouths met and their tongues tangled as his palm met her stocking and smoothed up past her garter, finding the bare flesh of her thigh beneath her thin silk drawers. His other hand he lifted to his mouth; she heard a wet sound, and then he placed his finger to her quim, to the throbbing spot that leapt at his touch and made her swallow another garbled moan. For a moment, as he rubbed her and she writhed, the only sound was of their fevered breathing and the whispering shush of her gown.

She pushed against him, one final demand. His hand slipped back to her thigh, lifting her leg and placing her knee over his hip bone. The head of his cock, startlingly hot, brushed her entrance. "Yes," she breathed. "Now."

He slid his hand beneath her drawers and cupped her bare bottom in one large hand, while the other he laid across her back, his hand cradling her head. And then, very slowly, he pushed inside.

Twelve days. He was larger than she'd remembered.

She could feel her body's brief resistance before she remembered how to take him, so broad and blunt, demanding nothing but submission. Very gradually he pushed into her, so gradually, as though every infinitesimal fraction required its own moment of decision, of request and consent. He shifted in the darkness— using the shelves to brace himself, she realized, while he used his own bone and muscle to support her. And then he pushed once more and seated himself completely inside her.

Her head fell back into his palm. She felt pinned, held down, immobilized as he thrust into her steadily, aggressively, filling her without hesitation, his face a darker shadow over hers in the darkness. If the closet had been smaller, if he could have held her even more closely in his grip, she would only have welcomed it. *Make me yours*, she thought as she gripped him to her. *Never let me go.*

Her climax came over her quickly, and as fiercely as the emotions in her breast. She clenched around him and he gave a soft, low moan in reply, and then pushed into her harder, and harder yet, and set up a steady, pounding rhythm that made her own satisfaction extend, spreading out in ripples and quivers, ebbing from her like a sweet dream as he sucked in his breath and came.

Afterward, his lips turned into her neck and he spoke very quietly. "Not purgatory after all," he said. "Not with you here. Idiotic of me to think otherwise, even for a moment."

And deep inside her, that small, cold kernel of doubt began to melt. Against his forehead, she smiled.

They returned to the ballroom separately, Gwen going first. Her mission, so they had agreed, was to find the twins and pull rank: as the bride-to-be, she was certainly entitled to demand an early night's sleep.

She paused on the edge of the floor, mask now atop her head in a strategic decision—to disguise, or account for, the disorder of her hair. The crush seemed to have grown even thicker, and the air now held the distinct tang of sweat and alcohol. The Cornelyses must be overjoyed; no host could declare his party a success until the air began to grow foul.

"So the bastard finally saw it through."

So absorbed was she in scouring the crowd that the familiar voice barely registered on her at first.

And then she stiffened and glanced sidelong.

Trent stood beside her. He wore a mask, but she could not mistake him. He had a small birthmark at the corner of his mouth, very distinctive, the shape of the African continent.

The last time they had spoken, she had been engaged to him, still. After the note he'd sent breaking it off, she had not wished to hear his voice again, much less give him the honor of hearing hers.

She looked behind her for Alex, but if he had come back already, he had entered through the far doors. He could not be far off, though; they were meant to find each other again as soon as possible. *He* had suggested this. He did not wish to be parted from her: that was the only conclusion she could draw from his suggestion.

She smiled. She would pretend as though she hadn't heard Trent's remark, whatever on earth he'd meant by it.

But he had the bad taste to speak again. "I would pay good money to be with Pennington when he hears this news," he said.

Now no doubt remained that he was speaking to her. She bit her lip very hard.

He laughed suddenly. "Why, you have no idea, do you?" he asked. "You should see your face right now. What did you think—that I broke it off of my own free will?"

She would not give him the satisfaction. She would *not*.

"You always were a bit thick." Incredulity flooded his voice. "But affection aside, you knew how badly I needed your money. I can't believe you never wondered."

She whirled on him. "Sir, I do not know why you are addressing me, but you will cease to do so *at once*."

His brows lifted high, clearing the edge of his black domino. "Of course. Do accept my felicitations on your marriage, madam." Sweeping her a low bow, he turned on his heel, checkered cape swirling, and walked off.

She stared after him.

He was lying, of course.

But to what end?

A hand touched her arm. She gasped and whirled. Only Alex. *Alex*. He was smiling at her, but a frown quickly overshadowed the smile. "What is it?" he asked, glancing past her, searching the crowd. In vain, of course. Everybody was masked. Not everyone knew a man well enough to pick him out by a small birthmark. Perhaps only fiancées and wives could do so. Those who had laid a claim, a personal claim, of their own volition, and had cause to learn such small things.

Three million pounds. Alex's hair was rumpled—from her fingers, as only she knew; from her kisses, from the moans she had breathed into his hair just now.

She had wondered—had raged—had asked herself again and again what could have driven a bankrupt man away from three million pounds. Had asked herself what was wrong with her.

Nothing. That had been her answer, in the end.

Everything about you is right.

"What is it?" He searched her eyes, his own so light, such a light and clear blue, that one could almost convince oneself they were transparent, truly the windows into his brain and heart and soul. His hand was gripping her arm; she did not know when he had taken hold of her. "Gwen, *what is it?*"

She could not believe this of him. She cleared her throat. She meant to speak strongly, to indicate with her tone how absurd she found Trent's claim.

Instead, what came out was a whisper. "Was it you?"

At the top of the room, the orchestra was sawing into some wild melody, a reel, a schottische, something that made the crowd squeal, sparking a sudden rush into the dance, crushing bystanders back toward the walls, elbows and heels jostling and knocking her like so much flotsam into Alex's chest. She took a step back, stamping on someone's hem, eliciting a squeal that she ignored.

He did not answer her. He was staring at her with a look she could not decipher. He was so good at impassivity when it suited him.

She squared her shoulders. "Alex." He lifted his hand as if to touch her cheek. "Are you the reason they jilted me?"

His hand paused, a hair's breadth from her face.

He did not need to answer. The muscle in his jaw replied for him. He was clenching his teeth to bite something back. So much for fearlessness in the face of unpleasant truths.

So much for impassivity, too. At least she had that much satisfaction.

She turned on her heel. He caught her elbow and pulled her back. "Not Pennington," he said. "I have no idea what happened with Pennington. There was nothing in his history, nothing in his relationships that would account for it—"

"In his history?" She gaped at him. "Alex, did you— did you set *spies* on my fiancés? As if . . . as if they were your business competitors?"

His hand fell away. "I made a promise to your brother," he said flatly. "I did what I could to honor it."

Disbelieving laughter scraped out of her throat. "Oh yes, so I see. You spied on these men—"

"*I* did nothing," he said tersely. "I hired private investigators. Pennington turned out to be unobjectionable. *Seemed* to be, at any rate. Trent did not. So I intervened."

"Intervened." She shook her head slowly. "Intervened. You mean that rather than coming to *me*, sharing with *me* this mysterious knowledge of his . . . his *objectionable nature*—objectionable in *your* view, at least—"

"Syphilis," he said curtly. "If your view differs, you are standing in a very peculiar place."

"I don't care what it was!" Although, God above, that did explain his sickly appearance, and perhaps his indiscretion, too. She would spare a prayer for him tonight. "You did not come to me. You did not tell me!"

"I couldn't—" He cursed. "I couldn't be sure that you would . . ."

"Would believe you? Would show good sense? Would *value* myself enough to avoid sacrificing my health for a title?" She scoffed. "God above, you must think me the *stupidest* woman on the planet."

"No." His voice was flat now. "But could you blame me if I did?" So unapologetically he spoke. "Your choices in men do not recommend your intellect."

Temper whipped through her. "Yes, so I see. How

very stupid I must be. How else have I ended up engaged to marry *you*? A manipulative bully who sabotaged my wedding so you—so you could . . . *what*? How did *you* stand to gain from this? Or is it so obvious? I say, Alex—have *you* been having financial difficulties?" She heard the ugliness creeping into her voice, but she had no interest in dispelling it. Dear God—only minutes ago, she had been begging him to take her. To *have* her. This man who thought her too stupid to decide for herself what and whom she wanted! "You needn't make the greatest sacrifice," she said. "I am glad to offer my brother's dear friend a loan. Marriage is not required."

He looked now as cold and disinterested as though he were disputing with a stranger. "I assure you, Gwen, I do not require your aid. Unlike some, I plan very carefully before I enter rash ventures."

"Yes, so you do," she agreed. "And tell me, what does your careful planning entail? Threats? Blackmail? What did you use to drive Trent off?"

"He did not wish certain news to be made public," he said evenly. "So I did him the favor of keeping it private."

"Blackmail," she whispered. She put her hand to her mouth to trap a laugh, but it came out anyway— wild, a little unbalanced. "Do you know what I felt— what I thought—how I doubted myself afterward! And none of it had anything to do with me! All that time . . . and then, when it happened *again*—I was so *sure* with Pennington—"

"Gwen." He seized her by the shoulders, and for a shocked moment she thought he would shake her. But his fingers merely pressed her upper arms, each finger asserting itself distinctly, as if he was trying to imprint the pattern in her flesh. "Gwen," he said, leaning in, perhaps so his quieter tone would carry amidst the revelry around them, "I swear on everything I hold dear—my sisters, my nieces, Richard, *you*—that I had nothing to do with the viscount."

She stared at him, wondering desperately if she could trust his word.

How amazing. Only minutes ago, she'd been wondering if he could love her.

How sad that she found him easier to credit on the matter of the viscount.

"I believe you," she said slowly. She tried to pull free, but his hands tightened once more. His expression was beginning to frighten her. He looked—grim, his mouth tense, his eyes hooded. As though he was folding in on himself, shuttering, shutting himself away.

"What does this change?" he asked. He spoke so flatly and rapidly that it took a moment to work out that he was asking her a question.

He was asking if the wedding was to be canceled.

She felt a pang of loss, a flash of panic, the sort of hot, deep spark that created firestorms. *Alex*, she thought. *Smile at me. Tell me you love me.*

On the heels of this thought, which her lips even opened to speak, came a lash of anger.

Again and again and again. How many times would she repeat her mistakes? *Lie to me. Tell me what I wish to hear. Sing me sweet lies.*

"Will you be at the altar tomorrow?" she asked. Her voice came out so coldly. It seemed to belong to some other woman, who never cried.

"Yes," he said. His eyes never left hers. "I do not break a promise."

Now, no talk of love. Now the talk turned to *responsibility*. "No," she said. "You never do break a promise, I suppose. But there is always a first time. I encourage you to consider the novelty."

"Gwen." He spoke slowly and emphatically. "This is God's own truth: I will leave the altar after you do."

"I suppose we'll find out." She pulled her mask back over her face and turned on her heel.

This time, he did not try to stop her from leaving.

Chapter Sixteen

As Alex waited the next morning in his brother's library, he almost hoped that Gwen did not show up. He hoped it for his own sake as much as hers, but not because he would make a poor husband to her. If she gave him the chance, he would love her more fiercely and constantly and creatively than any of the spineless bastards who had ever danced her across a sweaty ballroom or lifted their eyes to her on the street. And he did not hope it for his own sake because he had regrets about this path; he had seen himself too clearly now to imagine that freedom lay in flight, or to believe that any city across the world would ever awaken his exhilaration again without another pair of eyes, her eyes, through which to see it.

He hoped, then, as he waited and his sisters leaned over their husbands to chat with Lady Weston and various girl children gamboled on the floor and Gerard spoke in low, officious, threatening tones to the cowed minister, that she would not appear. If she appeared now, knowing what she did, knowing the one thing that Alex had thought to keep from her (because why should she know at this late date? She had not loved Trent; she would not have married him had she known; no harm had been done; the secret was old and expired and inert and harmless, like gunpowder left to rot on the ocean floor; also, he was a bloody high-handed idiot)—if she appeared now knowing that he had kept this from her, she came to marry a man who didn't deserve her. And he wanted her only if she knew her own worth and deemed him worthy of her all the same.

He was a twisted bastard, and if he had a shred of honor in him, he would tell her to tell him to go to hell. If he had a single instinct of self-preservation, he would do the same, because he did not think their union would flourish if she went into it in this fashion. He would love her with all the intensity in him—but he knew himself well enough to know his own faults. Impatient and judgmental and stubborn and often too quick to act: he would try never to crush her, never to overwhelm her or bend her to his will, but if she did not demand only the best from him, it would happen. It might happen. Possibly.

A good man would have found a way to pull her aside and tell her these things. To warn her.

To hell with good men. They made for very sympathetic characters when they lost, but he aimed to win.

The door opened. Elma and Henry Beecham walked in, Gwen between them. She was dressed in a simple white morning gown, the neckline shrouded by a fringed white pashmina; in her left hand was a bouquet of pink roses. She met his eyes and held them as the minister crossed to stand behind the makeshift pulpit—a podium Gerard had purloined from his club. The twins exclaimed and came to their feet, pulling up their assorted daughters; their husbands remained seated, looking a bit puzzled, as well they might, about why such ceremony was required in somebody's goddamned library. Alex was already standing at his station. He had been standing here for some time. He had not wanted to risk Gwen's early appearance and an empty altar to greet her.

"Cue bridal music," Caroline cried out gaily as Elma released Gwen. Henry Beecham, silver mustache twitching in what might equally have been a smile or a grimace, squared his shoulders and led Gwen the short steps to Alex's side.

He could not read the expression in her rich brown eyes. Or perhaps he was misreading it, for to his mind, she stared at him as belligerently as any opponent in the *salle d'armes*. He took her hand, and her fingers tapped across his, a decisive little Morse code whose meaning he would give an arm to decipher. Her plump mouth was a flat, determined line.

The minister began to speak.

Her look seemed more and more clearly like a challenge.

"Do you take this woman to be your lawfully wedded wife," the minister began. Terribly nasal drone, there. Like a hive of bees.

Her brow lifted as the minister fell silent. Alex had the faintest inkling of suspicion. "I do," he said slowly.

The minister nodded and turned to Gwen. "Do you take this man..."

She nodded along as the question was being asked of her. When the churchman concluded, she glanced away to survey the whole room before returning her gaze to Alex.

"What a novel question," she said.

The minister gave a visible start. "I beg your pardon?"

He was not mistaken. He knew what was coming. She was going to give him a taste of the panic she had experienced. A queer mix of feelings stirred in him— amusement and pride and love warring with regret and the inevitable disbelief. With an effort, he produced a droll tone. "She never has made it this far before," he told the minister.

"No, never," she said thoughtfully. Alex tried for a smile in reply, a silent message to her: *You see how well I understand you?*

But a moment's doubt sabotaged his attempt at lightness. She looked to be biting the inside of her cheek. That he did not understand. Did she need the pain to control a smile, or to steel her will? But no act of will was required. Did she not realize that? He would give her as much time as she needed to decide, here. He would even sweat for her, if she would enjoy it.

"Well, miss?" the minister prompted.

"Speak, Gwen," Elma said irritably. "This game is not amusing."

Gwen took a breath. "No," she said. "It is not amusing. None of it. I do *not* take this man to be my husband."

Well. Alex exhaled.

That was a bit more than indecision.

How comical to have hoped, even briefly, that she would settle for merely twitting him.

Not a coward, she looked him squarely in the eye. "I cannot marry you," she said.

He had not expected this. His disbelief was too large to manage, or marshal into words.

The stunned silence could not last, though. "*What?*" Elma cried.

Gwen looked toward the gathered company. "I do beg your pardon," she said, then paused to clear her throat. Her voice only trembled a little as she pushed onward. "I know this is a disappointment to everybody." She looked down to the bouquet, fumbling as she tried to remove the strap from her wrist. The gesture, after a moment, became a frantic sort of clawing.

As if in a dream, Alex watched himself reach out and slide the ribbon off her hand. *Freed*, he thought. *Remember this moment, Gwen. From here on out, you're fair game for the chase.*

She gave him a look of astonishment as he took the flowers. He no doubt looked equally astonished. He could not believe she'd done this. She was braver even than he'd imagined.

The thought clamped down on his next breath. In fact, he had *counted* on her being less brave than this.

Lovemaking was not without possible consequences, and—so he realized, all at once—he had assumed, God forgive him, that her fear of those consequences would hold her to him as much as the love that she did, she *must* feel for him.

But if she was so unafraid, what might she not do? She might well walk out of this room and never look back to him, no matter what had passed between them.

He looked down at the bouquet. His mind felt strangely sluggish. "Lovely roses." *Oh, brilliant remark.* "Gloire de Dijon, I think?" A thousand times he'd won the advantage in tricky negotiations by thinking on his feet, and now a remark on *flowers* was the best he could manage?

Her chest rose and fell on a deep breath. "Sir," she said. "I do hope you will survive this, the tarnish of your first jilting."

Smart girl. She would not be distracted by talk of roses.

"But you will understand," she continued, "at least I think you will, when I tell you that there can be no more sham marriages for me."

Sham marriages? His brain latched onto that phrase and demanded that it anger him. His senses were attuned to other, more important details. Her blanched face. Her shoulders, which kilted at an unnaturally straight angle.

His wits began to reassemble. She was jilting him by the skin of her teeth, here. It was costing her some great and terrible effort.

There was hope in that fact. More than hope. She would never come to him out of fear. She would only come to him in honesty. He almost wanted to take her hand and give her the encouragement she needed. To say, *It's all right; keep going. Give me hell. You're almost done.*

A thorn stabbed his palm: his hand was crushing the bouquet. He did not look down. "Bravo," he murmured to her. Her courage deserved his admiration. "Well done, Gwen. Fearless."

The remark visibly confused her. She took a step back from him. A tremor moved her mouth. "Was this always a joke to you, then?" she whispered. "Did you never mean any of it?"

"*No.*" He stepped forward, heedless of the company, to slide his palm around the back of her neck. "I meant every word." Distantly he heard Gerard's protest, his sisters' sharp rebuttal, Henry Beecham's harrumph. None of it mattered. Into Gwen's ear, he said, "You've just jilted me, darling. Wait at least five minutes before you goad me into proposing marriage again."

She recoiled so fast that it was a wonder her head did not strike the wall behind her. "You're mad," she said, wide-eyed.

"In love," he said.

"I highly doubt it."

He took a sharp breath. "Yes, I see that you do." Enough, now, with flippancy: he felt the last thing from flippant. "I will have to prove it to you, then."

"No." She shook her head once. "Do not bother.

I am sure you love me as much as you love Heverley End. But I told you, Alex, I am *done* with these shams."

Heverley End? What in God's name did that pathetic little estate have to do with anything? "And well you should be done with them," he said, the first strop of temper roughening his voice. "But if you count me in with the other two shams you have courted, then you're lying to yourself. I am not another Pennington. I need nothing from you but *you*. And I am not going to walk away."

Gwen's lips parted. She stared at him, her expression arrested; almost, it seemed, she started to speak. Every fiber in him tightened in anticipation.

And then another voice—Gerard's voice—thundered, "What the hell is going on here?"

She cast a glance over Alex's shoulder at the blustering ass, then snatched up her skirts. Her brown eyes flashed toward Alex; her chin lifted. "You do not need to walk away," she said. "*I* will." And turning on her heel, she bolted for the door.

Dumb surprise dulled his reflexes. After such bravery, she would flee like a coward?

A second too late, he lunged for her elbow—he would be *damned* if she would leave like this. But Elma and Caroline rose up in front of him, Caro catching hold of his hand, Elma's face flushed and furious. "What did you do!" Elma cried. "What did you—*oh*!" She whirled and ran after Gwen.

The door thumped shut as Caroline hung like a dead weight on his elbow. "Not now," she was saying into his ear. "Alex, *not now*. Heaven knows what ails her but she's in no state to hear you! Give her a minute—an hour, perhaps—"

An hour? He took a step backward. An hour to do *what*? What in God's name ailed her?

The question echoed in his brain and finally pulled him to a halt. He did not fully understand what had happened here. He'd had no opportunity to find out. How the hell could he fix it, then?

He turned on his brother, who was standing with arms crossed and brow furrowed, so comfortably and self-righteously aggrieved. "Can you never keep your mouth shut? Christ—five minutes, Gerard! Would that be so much to ask?"

"I quite agree," Belinda snapped.

Gerard went purple, choking on his own words as he waved wordlessly toward Alex for the benefit of the glaring company. "Can ... can ... can he not even manage to get *married* without driving off the goddamned bride? Do you know how hard I worked to get that license—not to mention this goddamned minister—"

"Sir," the minister gasped. "Your language is blasphemous!"

"Blasphemy, is it? What of him? What do you call what *he*—"

"Could you *both* desist from fighting for once?" This from Caroline, who set hands to hips and looked sternly between them. Alex's niece, Madeleine, clambered to her feet as well, mimicking her mother's pose with a fiercely jutting five-year-old lip.

This miniature imitation caught Gerard's attention and neatly deflated him. He muttered some expletive in tones too soft to corrupt young minds. Then, at normal volume, he added with disgust, "Thoroughly typical."

Alex looked at him. What a pathetically poor judgment of the situation. Typical would be brilliant. Typical would be much easier. It would mean a cool head and calm confidence. *I will fix this*: that was his typical resolve, the tried-and-tested approach. But he had no idea who had created this particular mess.

He turned away to stare at nothing. His role in the Trent debacle could not fully explain this. His handling of that episode had done him no credit, but it certainly did not, in any way, give Gwen cause to doubt his love—or to think him in any way similar to the two *shams* that had greeted her at more formal altars.

The door thudded again, this time on the exit of Henry Beecham.

The minister snatched up his Bible and, with a hunted look, ducked out after Beecham.

With every exit, that thud was sounding more and more significant. The sound of finality.

Which it was *not*.

Of course he could fix this problem. There was no need to panic. He turned back to the mumchance assembly. "I only need to know what the problem is," he said.

Belinda and Caro exchanged veiled looks.

He did not like that. "Say it to my face," he said, and his voice had a grim note in it that made him wonder whether his instincts had recognized something that his brain had not yet. In an *hour*, perhaps, he would not feel so calm at all.

"I believe that she told you," Belinda's husband said helpfully. "Doesn't think you love her."

Belinda shot her husband a glare.

Ah. But the man was right. At present, Alex's truths held no value or meaning to her. He would not know how to speak them persuasively until he cracked this riddle. It would take more than an hour to do that. *Why do you doubt me, Gwen?* What was the true cause?

Little Madeleine spoke. "Why did the bride run away, Mama?"

"Because she got scared," Caroline said, smoothing down her daughter's hair. "Uncle Alex is going to fix it by proving to her that she doesn't need to be scared anymore."

"Does Uncle Alex love her?"

"Of course he does," Gerry snapped.

Hearing this truth from Gerry's mouth brought a wave of foreboding over Alex. Christ, if *Gerry* could believe this but not *Gwen*—

"Well," Gerard continued gruffly. He took a seat at the desk, graceless as a sack of turnips. "I'll say no more, then. But it's a damned shame. Family could have used three million pounds."

"Oh, *Gerard*," Caroline sighed. Alex opened his mouth to deliver the truly cutting reply that his brother's asinine remark deserved—and a nudge of intuition stopped his tongue.

"Could we, then?" he asked mildly.

Gerard's eyes, meeting his, widened infinitesimally—then dropped. "Who couldn't?" he muttered.

Alex did not look away. A possibility, theretofore unthinkable, spun through him. He did not like unthinkable possibilities. He liked none of this. *You love me as much as you love Heverley End.* Is that what she thought she was to him? A problematic millstone around his neck? Some unwanted weight?

A glimmer of inspiration struck him. "I'll fix this," he said slowly.

At the Beechams', he discovered that Gwen had fled to Heaton Dale, and Elma had taken to bed. She called him up to her sitting room, where she subsided across a chaise longue, tipping her head to the cold compress held by a solicitous maid. "Do not chase after her," she advised. "You will waste the trip. She would not permit even me to accompany her. I have never seen her in such a state!"

He did not argue. "If she asks after me—"

Elma took charge of the compress and sat up. "She won't, Mr. Ramsey. I tell you, she has lost her wits. I reasoned with her all the way to the station. I might as well have been speaking to a lump of clay!"

He mustered a smile. "If she asks," he said, "tell her I have gone to Heverley End."

The compress thumped to the floor. "But why?" Elma frowned. "That's the opposite direction! Surely you can't mean to listen to me? You *must* go after her!"

He laughed. "And so I will," he said. But first he had to find Gwen what he had promised her: the proof she required.

Heverley End was a Jacobean cottage of Portland stone, weathered and pocked by the centuries of salt that had scoured its golden face. It sat atop a serpentine cliff veined with copper, and its mullioned windows overlooked the surf's retreat. In Alex's memory it was fearsome, a place better fit to abandonment and hauntings. In his more recent imaginings on the journey here, men with bowler hats had menaced the perimeter.

The truth was far less remarkable. The house was pretty in the setting sun. Quaint, even. And if Barrington had yet visited his new possession, he'd made no changes to the staff. The gatekeeper recognized Alex from boyhood, and the front door opened on another familiar face: the housekeeper, Mrs. Regis, still as spare and tall as a Maypole. He remembered her as a stiff and bloodless presence, always hovering a few paces from the doctors and nursemaids. Now, to his surprise, she insisted on crying briefly into her apron before leading him on a tour of the old terrain.

As he followed her, he grew conscious of a stupid disappointment. He would have taken pleasure from fighting his way into the house. It would have seemed fitting, for he'd certainly fought his way out of it, once upon a time.

"We have kept it up," Mrs. Regis assured him as she guided him down the creaking corridors. No electricity here yet; gaslight lent the scene the bluish tinge of history, things already receding, soon forgotten to the world. Emptiness pervaded the rooms: walls denuded of their paintings, rugs rolled away, furniture put to sleep beneath dust sheets. But Mrs. Regis spoke the truth: the oak floorboards squeaked beneath a layer of fresh wax.

On the second floor, outside his old bedroom, she stepped aside to permit him entrance and he thought that *here*, surely, was the moment when things would finally become difficult. He stepped in on a breath that wanted to falter in physical memory of his time here. They had removed the bookshelves and armoire. Stripped the bed of its mattress. But the view of the sea, of the whitewashed cliff and the pale blue waters stretching endlessly out beyond, was the same.

He walked to the window. The vista felt more intimate and familiar to him than his own reflection. His reflection was a fluke, a product of chance. In that endless vista he had looked to find his courage and his future as the sour smoke of burning nitre-paper had roiled endlessly up behind him. He had worked to discover himself.

For your own good, Alex.

He pressed his fingertips to the pane. He forced a long breath.

It came easily. Of course it did. Sometimes life was kind, and illness faded more gracefully even than the dead.

He blinked, and the view was not so portentous, after all. It was merely . . . pretty. Yes, he thought, if Gwen thought the Seine at sunrise lovely, she would find this view no less pleasing. This view: how curious that it had once meant so much to him, so much anger and desperation and possibility as well. It was only a small slice of the world, a pleasant slice, framed and made coherent by wood and glass and plaster, rude, dumb material that had no pull on him, no claim, no weight.

This house laid no weight on him. He pressed his hand now against the window frame. Of course it didn't. It was only a damned building.

He breathed again, even more deeply. How could she think she weighed on him? Even standing in this house, thinking of her, he felt light. As a boy, if he could have looked out this window and seen *her* instead of the sea, he still would have proved no less ambitious for himself.

Well . . . perhaps not. He felt himself smile—here, in this house, without effort. Boys were dim-witted about women. Even as a man, he'd been dim-witted for too long.

A groaning floorboard announced Mrs. Regis's approach. He turned, and the smile still lingering on his lips appeared to startle her. Her hands flew together at her waist, burrowing into her apron strings like two bony birds in search of cover.

He supposed his sudden appearance, his silent survey, might have looked a bit queer to her, particularly in light of the sale to Barrington. "And how is it with your new master?" he asked, seeking to put her at ease. "Have you met the gentleman yet?"

Her brow knitted. Myopically, she peered at him. "Sir? We've not seen the master for some months, now. But . . . that is to say——" She spoke more hastily, perhaps fearing that this remark would be taken as criticism. "He is in regular communication with Mr. Landry—that would be the steward, now, sir. A very good master, Lord Weston is; the rent rollback saved many a family in the village this spring."

Alex stared at her. "Lord Weston," he said slowly.

She blinked at him, a startled sparrow. "Aye, sir. Your . . . brother?"

"This spring?" He sounded like a parrot. No matter. Here it was: his intuition finding its aim.

Her sunken face took on a delicate pink hue. "Ah—perhaps more properly summer, sir. We count May as spring in these parts, you know."

So. The smile was back on his lips now. A month ago, long after news of the sale had circulated, Gerry had been rolling back rents on the property.

He laughed, and she flinched. Poor Mrs. Regis. No doubt the village would soon be whispering that the boy asthmatic, who had bedeviled the family with his reckless antics, now had grown into a full-fledged madman. "He never sold this place."

Mrs. Regis drew herself up, affronted by the idea.

"Certainly not! This property has been in your family for near to three hundred years, sir."

"True enough," Alex said. That hypocritical, two-faced bastard. "And so it shall remain."

Of all the things to be loathed in a London season—the hypocrisies and charades, the cruelties small and large, the shallow praise and shallower judgments—none was worse than this: the season had robbed Gwen of springs in the countryside. She had forgotten how beautiful Heaton Dale was in June, even with the pagodas, which made such a ridiculous mismatch with the surrounding cornfields.

She sat in a wicker chair on the back terrace, overlooking this land, the light shawl across her shoulders donned for a chill that the morning sun had long since burned away. *So take it off*, she thought. But she did not move.

She had moved very little in the last two days. It was as if making her way out of London had exhausted all her strength and now she could do nothing but sit very still, and look, and try not to think.

She looked, then, and tried to nourish herself on beauty. Heaton Dale sat on a slight rise—a hillock, really—to which her parents had added. Layer upon layer of sediment had been pressed into the earth, lifting the house farther toward the sky than nature had intended. From this lofty vantage point, the countryside rolled out in all directions, the grass walks that bordered the cornfields drawing a geometrical grid to guide the eye. The hedges bristled with shepherd's roses and blossoms of white hawthorne, and closer by, interspersing the remaining pagodas (she'd had two chopped up and carted away this morning, and the rest would fall to the axe tomorrow), limes and honeysuckle dotted the lawn. Nightingales and larks flitted from limb to limb, serenading the sky, the season, the sun.

Such a lovely view. Too lovely to be viewed and admired by nobody but her. Behind her, from inside, came a great racket amongst the staff. There were eighteen bedrooms to be aired—*eighteen*; she could not imagine what her parents had been thinking—and half as many drawing rooms. Also: two dining rooms, a billiards room, a smoking room, a morning room, two conservatories, a music room, quarters to house over sixty servants, and, of course, the nurseries. Very large nurseries, with great, glorious windows that let in light both in the morning and afternoon. Her parents had nursed grand plans for their children, of which marriage had only been the beginning.

Well, they had sent her away, and then they had died.

And then Richard had died.

Anger flickered, and with it stirred a horrifying urge to cry, still not quite vanquished. She took a sharp breath against it. She did not care what her parents' plans had been. If, somewhere above, they were upset with her for failing to honor their dreams, they must look to themselves for the reason. They had died. Everyone who loved her had died, but *she* had survived and done her best. She was done with being left and abandoned.

I love you, he said, and *I will prove it*, as if, by doing so, it would become his right to demand another chance from her. Oh, he was worse than Pennington and Trent by far. At least *they* had only wanted her money. He wanted far more than that. He was the last man any sane woman would trust; leaving was his art form. Yet he wanted to take her trust in his hands, to lure her into loving him, with her only reassurance his single, slim promise not to break faith and abandon her. And what did this promise come down to? Merely two words, two syllables, scripted by somebody else, and spoken countless times by a million cads or more: *I do.* How many men had said those two words while already plotting their peccadilloes and betrayals? Her parents had loved her truly, by blood as well as by heart, and Richard had, too; but that had not stopped *them* from leaving. How dare he think a simple promise more powerful than what had bound her family to her? How dare he ask her to imagine that he could deliver to her what her own family had failed to do? Nobody could promise to stay.

"Mistress," came a voice from behind her. One of her new footmen. It had taken under two days to assemble a staff; money did have its advantages. "Lady Anne rather wishes to see you. Are you at home?"

She turned in her seat. How curious that of all the people she might have imagined would call on her here—although Elma was fuming at her, and the

Ramsey twins were maintaining their distance, per her wishes—the first should be Lady Anne. Gwen could not imagine what might have prompted it. Heaton Dale was two hours outside the city by rail, no small effort for a girl whose social schedule was—so Anne assured her in regular notes—remarkably full.

She breathed deeply of the warm air. "Show her out here," she said, and turned back around.

So much land. She had no idea what she would do with all of this. She had worked and reworked it to please others, to suit the tastes of men who had never bothered to learn her own tastes, or even to come and view what she had wrought for them. In the end, the only transformation she had undertaken that would last was the transformation she had wrought on herself. Alex was *wrong*. She could change. She would no longer seek to please. She could be alone and content. Romantic love was not so thick as blood. This sense of mourning, in turns as vivid-bright as the lash of a razor, or as numbing and crushing as a boulder on the chest—it would dull. He would forget her. She would forget him. They were not family and nothing permanent bound them. People could change.

He should realize this. He had changed himself. He had made himself from a sickly boy into a strong, vibrant man. He had sacrificed in order to do it—cutting ties and avoiding connections lest he surrender some part of himself vital to the person he needed to become. And she, too, had sacrificed. To become this person she needed to be—a woman unafraid to build a garden to her own tastes; a woman confident in her right to honor her own desires—she had sacrificed him.

Only . . . the thoughts in her head did not feel as though they belonged to such a woman. They circled some dark pit she had looked into before, when loved ones had been lost to her.

He was alive, but she was mourning him as though he were dead.

She closed her eyes. She would not cry.

The sound of footsteps came from behind her, emerging from the house. Glad for the distraction, Gwen rose. "Lady Anne," she said. Her voice sounded like gravel.

"Gwen!" The girl looked radiant, glowing in her spangled day gown. She came forward to give Gwen a light kiss on the cheek. "What a magnificent house," she said. "And what a cunning garden!"

Gwen managed a smile. "It will be more cunning yet." She would redesign the garden now, in the evenings, when her thoughts would be most inclined to wander, to turn toward him, to wonder where he was, if he was already leaving her behind, letting her grow ever smaller in his view and memory, like the dark shadow of the coast in the wake of a ship.

She took a breath. The garden would be beautiful. She envisioned a rolling wooded parkland, near to natural, only a slight bit of landscaping. She would thread it through with wildflowers. She had never minded wildflowers; it was only the hothouse variety that bored her. And maybe, by the time she was done with this project, she would have planned out a use for some of these rooms, particularly that deserted nursery above. Maybe she *would* open an orphanage.

It was a bold idea, but she did not feel brave. She felt... battered. Already broken.

"Will you have something?" The question emerged stiltedly. "Tea, of course, but have you lunched yet?"

"Thank you, I did," said Lady Anne. "I promise, I am not so ill-bred as to appear uninvited *and* demand to be fed!"

The very fact that Lady Anne admitted the possibility that an earl's daughter might be ill-bred was enough to surprise Gwen into brief silence. Nobody had ever called Lady Anne beautiful—her nose was too prominent, her jaw wider than her temples—but she truly was glowing. "Do you have good news?" Gwen asked cautiously. Was a marriage in the works?

"I would not call it *good* news," Lady Anne said. "But news, yes. That is... I have come to do you a favor—one that I think you will gather I was very grateful for myself." She paused to draw breath, and her expression grew very serious. One slim, gloved hand settled atop Gwen's knuckles. *It's to do with Alex*, Gwen thought. But no, it couldn't be. What truck did Lady Anne have with him? Still, she felt her pulse bump and begin to speed as Lady Anne continued, "Brace yourself, dear." The girl's hand delivered a squeeze. "It concerns the Viscount Pennington."

Gwen's hopes deflated. "Oh? What of him?"

Her flat tone visibly surprised Lady Anne, who

then misinterpreted it entirely. "Is it still so sore a subject? I had hoped Mr. Ramsey—is he about, by the way? One hears such delicious rumors about him, I had hoped to see him in person, to beard the devil, as it were! Joking, dearest Gwen—oh, he isn't? Pity. What was I saying? Oh yes, I had hoped—but ah, well, I know how slow hopes are to heal."

"Very slow," Gwen murmured. Painfully slow, she feared.

"Yes," Lady Anne said soberly. "You did gather, I think—that is, you may have gathered that for a brief period, *before* of course the gentleman fixed his attentions on you, that I was rather . . . taken with him myself. Which is why I say with full confidence that it may comfort you to know why the viscount fled so ignominiously from the altar."

Gwen blinked. Alex had said he wasn't responsible, and she believed him. The cause therefore seemed thoroughly immaterial to her.

But Lady Anne was clearly waiting for some reaction. And perhaps it was a mark of her own addled state that she felt no curiosity. She cleared her throat. "Oh, dear," she said.

"Yes, it is just that shocking," Anne said righteously. "I am afraid, Gwen, that the viscount has found himself in an . . . indelicate situation . . . with a certain man, a very wealthy German from Baden-Baden, who blackmailed him and threatened to expose him to prosecution—if he should go through with marriage to *you*."

Gwen frowned. "I know no Germans," she said. "Why should this gentleman object to our marriage?"

"*That* is the shocking part! The German was seen entering your ceremony just before the vows were taken. But he did not appear in order to threaten the viscount. No—he appeared to prove his love!"

It took Gwen a moment to work through this. "Do you mean to say that the viscount . . ."

"He was romantically involved with this man," Anne hissed. "A foreigner. Yes. And now the German has cleared the viscount's debts, and together they are fled to the Continent, for fear that here, they will be prosecuted for unnatural behavior!"

"How . . . astounding," Gwen said. It was so far outside anything she had expected that she barely knew how to react. "I feel very—terrible—for the viscount, I think." And also—could it be?—the first bit envious. She had no idea of how to understand such love between men, but if Pennington would risk the whole world's wrath and his own freedom for it, the German could never doubt him now.

"As well you should, I think," said Lady Anne, surprising her again. "I told you, it was a foreigner who he took up with. Besides, he might have gone through with the marriage and used your wealth to mount his defense in court, should their affair be discovered. But he spared you the infamy, Gwen! So you see, his disinterest in you was not at all personal. He has no feelings of that sort for *any* woman."

Gwen's mouth twitched. She could not help it.

No wonder Lady Anne had come running to her. By spreading this story, she also salvaged her own wounded pride.

Her small smile appeared to unnerve Lady Anne, who collected her purse and rose. "Well," she said, and her tone was more in line with what Gwen remembered of her: starchy and a touch condescending. "I thought it would soothe you, at any rate. But I suppose you have no care now you are safely—if I may say a *bit* hastily—married." She glanced around again. "Although I *do* find it odd that Mr. Ramsey is not here." Her regard switched back to Gwen, speculative now.

Gwen came to her feet as well. "It was lovely of you to pay a call on me, and to be the first to share these tidings. I will give you even more exciting news to spread, if you like." Why not? Otherwise she would wait, breathless and nauseated by nerves, for the truth to slip out. She might as well let it slip now herself. "You see, Mr. Ramsey and I aren't actually married."

Anne blinked. And then her mouth fell open. "*What?*"

"It's true." She wanted to speak the words boldly, carelessly. But they felt leaden in her mouth, and they dropped her voice to a pitch better suited to gravesides. "Not married. We never were."

Anne's eyes unfocused. Her expression grew a little dreamy. No doubt she was beholding her own social celebrity the moment she dropped this truth like a bomb onto London. "Oh, Gwen," she sighed. "You're mad, do you know that?"

Gwen hesitated. This remark had not been issued in any of the appropriate veins—she heard no censure, astonishment, disbelief, or sympathy, only a chiding and indulgent note.

A suspicion seized her. What was Lady Anne staring at, somewhere behind her?

The suspicion grew into a cold certainty as Lady Anne's smile widened, and then fractured into a giggle. Her blue eyes returned to Gwen's, widening dramatically, as if to say, *You naughty girl, you! Telling me such lies!*

Hands slipped around Gwen's eyes. She went rigid. She would know him anywhere, simply by the feel of him. His skin made her skin come alive.

She thought desperately of her landscape. Of transformations. "He is not my husband," she said stonily.

"That's right," he said, very near to her ear. "Sometimes she likes to call me Mr. de Grey. Lovely little game, we play."

The sound of his voice raised a physical pain in her, a longing so acute that it made her throat clog. This was not fair—that she should feel this way when he was *here*, when he was *next* to her, when he was hers for the touching if only she would lift her hands.

His hands gentled slightly. She knew then that he felt the tears rising in her lashes.

"Perhaps," he said, "you might give us a minute, Lady Anne?"

"Oh yes," came the girl's breathless reply. "I'll just be on my way, then. Gwen, you're an awful tease. I will write you this very evening."

Gwen stood still for a very long moment, waiting for Alex to release her.

He slid his hands straight down her face, to her waist. The sunshine poured back over her, but it seemed now out of season. What she wanted were gray clouds to weep with her.

"Gwen." He pressed his cheek to hers and spoke in her ear as his arms closed around her torso. "Darling, this is the bottom of stupid, and perhaps halfway onward to abominable idiocy. Why are you crying?"

She stared very hard at the pagodas. "You know why." *I want you to leave*: that was what she should add. But she could not say it. Why couldn't she say it? He had called her fearless, but she was a coward. She was a coward with *him*. She had forgotten Trent and Pennington so easily! Their loss had stung less than the scandal attached. She had never loved them in the first place. It had been so easy to wait at the altar for a man she hadn't loved. Without love, one could not be crippled by loss.

But he was standing here with her. Where was the loss?

It never showed its face before it arrived. It would come. And there were reasons, solid reasons, to doubt him.

She ripped out of his grasp and took a step toward the terrace rail. "You above *all* people should know why I rebuff you," she said. One of the pagodas lay in fragments; the axmen had grown tired and stopped midwork. Had she the strength, she would chop the rest of them up herself. Yes, she would enjoy such violent activity. "Were you not the one who said I must recognize my own desires? Accept them without shame? But how does that fit with you, Alex? You did not respect me enough to let me make my own decision about Trent. You did not bother to consult my wishes. Do you think that spells the path to freedom for me?"

He sighed. "I was wrong," he said. "I should have shared the news about Trent. I do not argue that. My only excuse is idiocy. I was working very hard, then, to keep as far from you as possible."

Her hands closed over the railing, clenching tightly. "I don't believe that. You simply didn't want to waste your time on informing me. Your interest is fickle. Today you have found me interesting, but tomorrow—"

He caught her elbow. "Spare us," he said, and his voice had hardened. "Spare us both these tales. Your objections have nothing to do with the Trent affair, and you know it."

She held silent.

"Don't be a coward," he said. "Look me in the face."

She shrugged out of his grip and pivoted.

No wonder Lady Anne had blushed and shuffled like a child. He was dressed only in his shirtsleeves, a blinding white in the midday light, offering stark contrast to the tanned skin of his throat. A passing breeze ruffled his thick hair, played with the spare material of his sleeves, but he himself was motionless.

"No," she said. "It has nothing to do with Trent."

"Yes," he said. "I know. And here's something else it has nothing to do with."

He held out his hand.

She regarded the document warily. And then, looking to his face once more, she took it from him.

"This . . ." She frowned and turned over the document. The seal looked legitimate. Astonishment briefly slackened her grip. "This is the title to Heverley End."

"Yes," he said.

"But how—Barrington sold it to you?"

"He never owned it. Gerry didn't sell the place."

"But—" She covered her mouth with her hand. None of this made sense. Had he—surely he hadn't come only to show this to her? But shouldn't that be precisely her hope?

"Gerry was part of Barrington's scam." He pushed his hand through his hair, then sighed and took a seat. "Well, he was. *Was* being the operative word, here."

She sank into the chair across from him. She hardly trusted herself to stand. Some storm seemed to breaking inside her, silently, ferociously, scattering her wits and addling her emotions; she barely knew how she felt. "What on earth can you mean?" she asked faintly.

He rolled his eyes. "God knows it only makes sense to Gerry. The rumors about the sale were meant to lend Barrington credibility. He asked Gerry to refer potential clients to him—people looking to sell their estates—and in turn, Barrington passed on a percentage of the selling price. Gerry was using the profits to defray a rent rollback, help his tenants through a poor year's returns." Alex drummed his fingers atop the table for a moment. "Idiocy," he said in disgust. "My brother finally decides to dabble in commerce, and he does so in the name of noblesse oblige."

She choked on a laugh. She could not help it; he simply looked so put out. But how surreal this scene was becoming—sitting across from each other, speaking so civilly of *real estate*. At least her amazement had temporarily numbed her distress. "But then—Heverley End? Why is it deeded to *you*?"

"That was my price," Alex said. "Gerry deeded me Heverley End, and in return, I give him the grand honor of turning Barrington in to the authorities himself. Otherwise, I would have done it, and God knows I would have strung Gerry up by the heels, as well."

"No, you wouldn't have done," she said instantly.

He hesitated, regarding her curiously, a smile finally turning his lips. "No, probably not," he said. "But Gerry didn't know that."

By some silent accord, they both settled back in their chairs. Another warm wind swept the terrace. Alex tipped his face back to the sun and shut his eyes. The sight struck a dagger through her, unleashing a sense of terrible urgency: so long as the conversation remained on these other matters, he could stay. He could stay as long as he liked.

It would not last, though.

It would break her heart when it ended, and she could not bear the wait. "You would never be happy here," she blurted.

One eye opened. "No? Why not?"

"You hate the country," she said. "The city is where people with ambitions go. The country is dull. It's a boring cousin to the city."

The eye closed again. "God above, I am a pompous prick sometimes," he said. "Gwen, I made Gerard *deed* me Heverley End. Had you asked me a year ago, I would have named it, above all places in the world, as the *last* place I should wish to live. And now I own it. Think on that, a moment."

She hesitated, too afraid, briefly, to speak. "I don't follow," she finally whispered.

Now he looked at her, mouth quirking, becoming a wry slant. "It's the only property I own outright. Always thought about investing in land, but—well, to the point. I told you, the next time you decide to marry, you really need to pick a man with a roof of his own. One that doesn't leak. Heverley End doesn't."

The breath seemed to have leapt directly into her lungs; it was more a silent gasp than an inhalation, really. "Alex—"

"You might like it," he said. "I was not eager to return to it yesterday. I walked its halls half expecting to choke. And then—I began to imagine you there beside me. I wondered what you might see when you looked out its windows. And I discovered, in the process, that the place is rather pretty. More than pretty. My childhood prison is quite charming. And it would be no prison if you were there with me. It would be . . . a home."

"Heverley End," she said in disbelief. "You would . . . live there. Again."

"With you," he said. His light eyes never left her face. "Anywhere with you, Gwen. *That* is the freedom I was always seeking. Not to be beholden to any place but to a person—one person. *You*. And without you . . ." He smiled a little, a wry, almost lost smile. "What difference where I am? On a city street flooded with people, on a ship bound for a new port . . . without you, it won't matter. Might as well still be that boy suffocating alone in an echoing room, waiting for footsteps to come. Only now, I will be waiting for your footsteps. Only yours."

He watched her a long moment as she struggled with what she wanted to say, what she had to say.

But habit won out. What she said was, "You love me. You *do* love me." She sprang to her feet, but he remained sitting. He looked up at her, shading his hand to block the sun from his eyes.

"For God's sake, Gwen," he said gently. "What matter that I love you? That's not the bit that's always been missing."

Her lips parted. They wished to ask a question she could not bear to bring herself to ask. He was never less than honest. The answer, then, was bound to be wrong.

So she did not ask it as a question. "You won't leave me," she said.

He drew a long breath. "*There*," he said, quietly, fiercely. He came to his feet. "*That* is the answer to this riddle. The promises I can make, and the one I can't. Gwen." His hands closed on her wrists, tightening until she swallowed and found her courage and looked up at him. "I will never leave you willingly," he said. "Life is a risk, and so love is, as well. But I swear to God, you will not regret the gamble."

The light was so bright that it pricked tears into her eyes. Instead of squinting, she widened her eyes further so the sun blinded her. She saw him as a silhouette, a dark shape against the sky. So easily his face began to fade.

But she knew his features well enough to see him in the dark. And his hands were warm and alive and vital. The strength in him was tremendous. She could feel it, leashed in the tension of his grip.

"I love you," she whispered.

How horrifying, and how thrilling. It felt like a secret, a confession, a taunt: a dare to fate.

But he did not seem to think it remarkable or daring. "I know," he said, and his thumbs stroked her wrists, once. "We love each other. And look, darling: the world continues to turn."

She pulled out of his grip. He let her go, his fingers sliding softly over hers, a lover's caress. She stepped around him, to put the sun at her back, and he turned toward her, and his features clarified. He smiled, and some sharp, sweet pain caught her heart.

Since Richard's death, she had never been afraid to lose anyone. She had never entertained any suitor who might have inspired that fear.

I am so afraid to lose him.

And so—what? She must lose him now, at once, as quickly as possible?

What sort of logic was that?

She looked at him, his eyes so blue, his hair ruffling in the wind, so relaxed on his feet, hands in pockets, lounging as gentlemen were not meant to lounge, while beyond him in the garden lay one dismantled pagoda and two more awaiting the axe, and beyond them the cornfields in the sun, and the sky, and farther out yet, the sea. "I *love* you," she said.

"Yes," he said. "Say it again. Louder, if you please."

She laughed. She *could* say it aloud. She could let herself say it. She could scream it. He would not leave; lightning would not split the sky. The gamble was honest and earnest and it carried no punishment. Why—how could fate be cruel? Fate had brought *him* to her. Alex, the most unlikely suitor in all of England, loved her!

She jumped once, and then gave a wild laugh, feeling... mad—insane—who cared, indeed? "I *love* you," she said. What couldn't she do, now? Especially with this garden! "Alex—help me fetch an axe!" Turning on her heel, she raced for the house.

He caught her by the elbow, laughing, breathless, just inside the door. His eyes were sparkling. "An *axe*, Gwen?"

"For the—oh, never mind!" she cried. "Later!" And threw herself at him, her arms going around his neck, her mouth finding his. He turned her, backing her against the wall, running his hand up her wrist, capturing it against the wall, breaking away briefly to say something—a comment forever lost as he glanced beyond her, out the door, into the garden. His gaze abruptly narrowed.

"The pagodas," he said.

"An axe," she said.

"Definitely." He looked at her. "Later," he said, and then he kissed her again, and she planted her hands in his hair and pulled him down—down, down, down; she did not worry about the ground, their inevitable collision with the marble floor, or the servants, or tomorrow, or the next day, or ten years from now. He had her in his arms and he was kissing her, and *I want this*, she thought. *I want you*. And then, as his lips moved to her throat, *I need you*. And finally, at last, as his arms tightened around her and the sun spilled over them like a blessing:

I have you, Alex.

I have you.

True love
is timeless with historical romances from Pocket Books!

A Malory novel

Johanna Lindsey
No Choice But Seduction
He'd stop at nothing to make her love him.
But should she surrender to his bold charms?

Liz Carlyle
Tempted All Night
When deception meets desire, even the most
careful lady can be swayed by a scoundrel....

Julia London
Highland Scandal
Which is a London rakehell more likely to survive—
a hanging, or a handfasting to a spirited Highland lass?

Jane Feather
A Husband's Wicked Ways
When a spymaster proposes marriage as a cover,
a lovely young woman discovers the danger—and
delight—of risking everything for love.

Available wherever books are sold or at www.simonandschuster.com

Delve into a *passion* from the *past* with a *romance* from Pocket Books!

LIZ CARLYLE
Never Romance a Rake
Love is always a gamble....But never romance a rake!

JULIA LONDON
The Book of Scandal
Will royal gossip reignite her husband's passion for her?

KARIN TABKE
Master of Surrender
The Blood Sword Legacy
A mercenary knight is bound by a blood oath to reclaim his legacy—and the body of the one woman he desires.

KATHLEEN GIVENS
Rivals for the Crown
The fierce struggle for Scotland's throne leads two women to courageous new destinies...

Available wherever books are sold or at www.simonandschuster.com.

POCKET BOOKS
A Division of Simon & Schuster
A CBS COMPANY

POCKET STAR BOOKS
A Division of Simon & Schuster
A CBS COMPANY

19096